TALNIER

TALNIER

— Phantasm Book II —

CHRISTOPHER HALL
AKA MAXLEX

Podium

To David Mali,

a good friend who's fallen on some hard times.

Published in 2023 by Podium Publishing, ULC
www.podiumaudio.com

TALNIER

FAREWELLS

I'd arrived in Anchorbury with style, but my departure was more a flurry of logistical preparations. Not only did I have more luggage, but I was travelling with friends. This time I was travelling by boat, and my destination was expecting me. Cloridan had sent word to his friends, and they would be meeting us at the Talnier docks. This had all taken time to organize, which was fine since it gave my *other* companions a chance to join up.

"Felicia, Kyle, it's good to see you!" I'd naively expected that they would meet us in Talnier, but Cloridan had said something about "strength in numbers" and insisted they come down to Anchorbury and travel with us.

It had only been a few weeks, but it felt like months since I'd seen them. Some of that might have been due to certain changes.

"I see that there have been some developments between you two!" I teased, and was rewarded with Felicia's immediate blush.

"What? No, there's nothing . . ." she tried to deny, but Kyle was made of sterner stuff. He put his arm around her and met my gaze, pleased and embarrassed at the same time.

"Good for you," I said. "Good thing I've still got this spare room; we won't be leaving for a few days." I was referring to my old rental house. The workshop area was cluttered with our luggage—mostly mine—but the bedroom was still clear.

I introduced them to the gang. Levels and professions were exchanged. Both Felicia and Kyle had gotten to level four—Felicia had gotten her Healer class, and Kyle had become a Protector. I guess it was pretty obvious why he'd chosen that.

Cloridan and Kyle took a little while to size each other up. I waited for them each to sniff the other one's butt, but they never did.

"Adventurer family?" Cloridan eventually said, after they'd exchange a few meaningless pleasantries.

"Aye."

"There's been a few Warners around the place. Good people," Cloridan said, and that seemed to be enough.

Preparations made the time pass quickly. Gustave insisted on getting me lessons enough to unlock Craft (Smithing).

"I can't have you go out in the world as a senior member of the Anchorbury Ironworkers Guild without the skill," he said, somewhat pompously. "People will wonder what sort of crafters we're turning out."

"Even if I buy the skill, this isn't going to convince someone I'm a master smith," I pointed out.

He waved his hand dismissively. "I'm sure you'll think of something," he said. "This will just give you the basics."

I unlocked the Teach skill for both Elodie and Janie. Neither had the Skill points yet, but both of them were young enough to be due a point on their birthday.

"What do I even need Teach for?" Janie had asked.

"You've got an apprentice now," I said. "You need to be able to instruct them."

"Psssch," she snorted. "You already gave him all the skills he won't get from the profession, so what's the point of me having it? You just want me to come teach you Fire Magic when I've got the skill."

"That'd be nice," I said. "But really, it's up to you what you do with it. You won't be running around dungeons forever."

"Says you."

Cloridan got us crossbows. Well, I bought them, but Cloridan was the one who insisted we all get the Weapon Mastery: Triggered Weapons and found us the weapons and ammunition.

I was quite surprised, even though I'd seen guards in Anchorbury carrying them. Oakway's weapon market hadn't had any, and I'd started thinking they hadn't been developed yet.

"Yeah, they're not used much in dungeons," Cloridan explained. "Range is too close."

"Isn't there a dungeon in Talnier?" I asked.

"Sure, two of them—but they're not close to the walls. For a lot of people, getting to the dungeon is half the battle, and that's why we'll need these. That, and getting to the town in the first place."

"Is it really that dangerous getting there?" I asked. "We sent mail there, after all."

"Griffins don't often come down off the mountains," he admitted, "But if they do, you'll be glad you've got a distance weapon."

"Blind works pretty well against flyers," I pointed out.

"Yeah? What's the range?" he asked knowingly.

"About 25 meters," I admitted.

"You want to cast that on a griffin stooping on you?"

I thought about something the size of a horse, swooping down on me like a giant hawk, getting blinded at the last second. "No."

"Get the skill."

I was saving those skills for more magic, but he had a point. And it would be good to have access to a high damage weapon. In our world, crossbows were heavy, clumsy weapons, but even I could easily hold the weapon in one hand and cock it with the other. Once I got the skill, anyway.

Kyle also had Skill points free, but Felicia had spent all hers on the skills for Healer. So there were three of us with ranged capability, once we'd practiced for a bit.

A lot of people came to say goodbye, a lot more than I expected. Maybe it was because I was a local celebrity, their exotic generator of stories and gossip. My neighbors, people I'd bought stuff from in the market . . . a few householders that I'd had to smooth over after some of Cutter's exploits. A lot of them offered commiserations over the unfairness of my being kicked out—which I could offer right back, because living under Aubert Duvost might not be any kind of picnic.

Eventually, all the preparations were done, the goodbyes were all said, and all of us and our luggage were loaded on a boat headed upriver.

I'd expected our trip upriver to be a leisurely cruise, but I'd been deceived. While the ground downstream of Anchorbury was relatively flat, upstream led into hills, and that meant rapids and waterfalls.

Portage is a fancy word that means walking, which we had to do a number of times on the trip. There was one notable village along the way where they'd constructed a lock, but the rest of the time we had to take the path.

I'm pretty sure in our world, the boats would have been unloaded and then dragged on rollers up the hill, followed by the cargo. Then they'd be loaded up again and head upriver to the next waterfall. Here, though, they just picked up the boats. Superhuman strength comes in handy sometimes. Maybe some superhuman crafting as well—I'm pretty sure wooden boats in my world don't get carried by handles on the edge while fully loaded.

It had been explained to me that the Average/Good/Great/Excellent quality, when applied to ordinary goods, indicated a greatly increased resistance to damage, something that applied with walls, doors, and boats.

So the portage sections were quick interruptions to what was mostly a leisurely journey taking most of a day. I could contribute by keeping an eye on the sky, while spending most of my attention on Mana Sense. As we got closer to the border, I could see the increase in mana. More of it was wild, the smoky gears and cogs becoming wrapped in streams of mana that followed no pattern I could discern. Up ahead of us, I could see the wild mana rise up, like a storm cloud on the horizon.

We passed a number of standing stones on the way up. I'd noticed a few around Oakway, but they were much more numerous here.

> **[Identification]: – Mana Guidestone (Type III) – Quality: Great**

They did seem to be doing something to the mana. It wasn't clear to me *what*, since they tended to be surrounded by a haze of unshaped mana, but there always seemed to be a stream of mana flowing away from them, to the east.

I didn't want to show my ignorance by asking questions, but then I remembered that Felicia was here. The boat was big enough that a private conversation was easily arranged.

"Um, they . . . guide the mana . . ." she said. Unhelpfully.

"I got that," I said. "How? Why? Where's it going?"

"Well, it's a kind of magic, I guess? Theurgy, I think. If you don't have a dungeon around to suck up all the mana, you need to send it somewhere. All the streams are going to the capital, I should think."

"So the capital, just . . . sucks up the mana from the entire country?"

"Not all of it, just enough to keep the monsters down. There's a Guild of Theurgists, I'm not sure about the name. They haven't needed to come to Oakway for a generation. They manage the mana—I'm not sure if all of it goes to the King, but they distribute it like he wants."

"And what does he do with it?" I wondered.

"Important ruling stuff?" Felicia said.

"Huh."

We passed few miles in companionable silence before Felicia spoke up with a question of her own.

"So are you going to tell me about it?"

"About what?"

"About why you had to leave."

"I already told you in the letter," I protested.

"The details, yes, but something was missing." Felicia paused, considering. "Something like: why you let yourself get kicked out."

I gave her a look. "What was I supposed to do? He's the Count, now. He *could* have had me imprisoned."

"Like that would have held you for five seconds. I don't know," she said. "Something . . . unexpected. Like stealing the Dungeon core—I know that wouldn't have helped in this case, but something like that."

"I can't always come up with a black swan," I said sourly.

"You actually have a name for it?" she asked incredulously. "What kind of name is black swan?"

"Ahhh . . . what color are swans in this world?"

"White."

"Oh good, it's the same, then. In my world, people thought they were white for a very long time. Then they travelled to a faraway country—that happens to be the country where I lived—and found some black swans."

"I don't get it."

"Until that day, no one had ever thought a swan could be black. After that, it was just obvious that they could be. A black swan is an event that no one could predict, but afterwards seems obvious."

"Huh, and these events happen so often that you need a name for them?"

I laughed. "It's more that people spend a lot of time trying to predict them. If you can manage it, you can make a lot of money."

"You just said that they can't be predicted," she objected.

I shrugged. "Doesn't stop people trying."

"So, no black swan this time?"

"No," I said bitterly. "It's not like last time. I can't pull off something crazy and disappear. I'm using my real identity, and there were people there I care about. Elodie, the kids, and even the Guild."

"Most of them you're leaving behind, though," she argued.

"Better that than making them a target for Aubert. It hurts, but sometimes you have to take the loss."

"Ah," she said, and we were quiet for a while.

"You know what really stings?" I asked. "I actually felt sorry for him."

"Well, he lost his father, yes? It's only natural."

"I guess." Suddenly a thought struck me. "You know, now I've officially left, there's nothing stopping me from dropping by here again. It's only a two-hour run if I'm not carrying luggage."

"The guards at the gate wouldn't be able to stop you. Did you have some plan in mind?"

"Not yet," I said. "But this isn't over."

"Now, that sounds like you're planning something dangerously irresponsible." Felicia's voice was stern, but there was a twinkle in her eye.

"You'll help, though?"

"Of course," she said. "We're partners, after all."

TALNIER

In the beginning, there were Three. Three gods, three principles that governed.

Ix, the Creator, brought all things into being. Some say that She brought the others into existence, that she was the first, but the other two have never spoken of it.

Ashmor, the Destroyer, sought to destroy all of Ix's works. Ravening, unrestrained destruction that leaves not even ash behind.

Between those two principles, always acting to moderate their unending contest, was the principle of Balance.

—*Heresies of Kaval*

There were a few odd things about Talnier that struck me as we approached. I was no expert on medieval fortifications, so I'm sure there was a good reason for them. The most easily noticed strangeness was the towers. I could only see one as we approached, but I could see the tops of what looked like others farther around the walls.

The tower that I could see sat outside the walls, at twice their height and connected to them by another wall at a right angle. I wondered if the entrance to the tower was a tunnel going through that wall, as I couldn't see any other way in.

The walls themselves held the second odd thing, which was that instead of being topped by battlements, they were lined with stakes. Pointed up in the air, they looked too widely spaced to deter men climbing up the walls.

"It's to stop flyers," Kyle told me when I asked about them. "They don't like landing on spikes."

"Oh, right." I'd seen the same technique used to keep pigeons off building ledges. The size and spacing of those spikes, though, suggested something much larger than a pigeon. "Do you know why the towers are like that?"

"Maybe . . ." He thought for a moment. "Could it be to kill-box animal hordes?"

"I don't know what that means," I said.

"You've got it right," Cloridan interjected. "It's a larger version of an adventurer technique," he explained to me. "You block the animals' advance, pen the attacking animals in with walls on three sides, then pour in fire from the sides." He indicated the wall. "And behind," he said, pointing at the tower.

"It only works on dumb animals," Kyle said. "I guess they get a lot of them here."

"Humans would just pick off the towers; they're strong, but too exposed," I said, musing my way through the strategy.

"Exactly," Cloridan said.

"So can one of you explain why there aren't any gates?"

"Gates are a weakness," Cloridan said in an amused tone. "Your wall's much stronger when it doesn't have any gates."

"That—but, you need gates? What about traffic and trade?"

"Most of it comes via the river, and you can see the gates for that up ahead. There are some smaller gates for wagons, but they kept them small. One on each side of the river."

"I see," I said, and soon enough I did. First came the river gate, a short tunnel that enclosed the river as it went under the town wall. There was a . . . portcullis? Was that still an appropriate name when it went over a river instead of a road? Whatever the name, there was one of them at each end of the tunnel, and they raised them one at a time so we could enter.

Floating under the gate, I could see the metal above us gleaming, which suggested they'd made it out of silversteel. That should help with rust problems. Once through, we entered the town, except that we didn't.

Although the town wall extended across to the south side of the river, there was another wall on the north side, separating us from the main city. Contained within this narrow strip of land were the docks, and some low buildings that looked like warehouses.

"This town is really paranoid about their security," I said uneasily.

"A lot of really nasty stuff can come down a river that starts in the wildlands," Cloridan said. "This place keeps that stuff from flowing downriver."

"I thought that high-threat monsters couldn't live in low-mana areas."

"To an extent," Cloridan explained. "It doesn't kill them instantly. The main ones you have to worry about are the flyers, who move fast enough to get a long way before running into trouble, and the waterborne who can just float downstream even when they get sickly."

"Mana-sick beasts are the worst," Kyle added softly. "They feel it as a hunger, and they attack everything desperately."

"Speaking of," I said, "look there!" I pointed at the griffin that suddenly rose over the wall.

> **[Identification]: Tawny Griffin (Male) – Threat Level: 15 – Properties: Tamed**

"Tamed?" I exclaimed in surprise. Then I saw there was a guy riding it. They circled the town, gaining height, then flew off upriver.

"Yeah, the Royal Griffin Rider Corps have a base here," Cloridan told me. "This is one of the places they capture and train new flights."

"How do they keep their beasts alive?" I asked. "That griffin was Threat Fifteen!"

"Beats me," he said. "Whatever they do, it's limited. You only see griffins on the border or in the capital."

At that point, we arrived at the docks, and everyone became very busy. We were met at the docks by four men with a cart, who seemed to know Cloridan. He exchanged words and handshakes with them, while I let Intrigue give them a going over out of habit. From the sound of this place, it was a habit I should get into.

Intrigue told me . . . that they were probably honest and that they knew Cloridan, which was useful confirmation at least? Anyway, we loaded up our luggage and headed into the town proper. Felicia and Cutter rode on the wagon, Kyle took the lead, and I brought up the rear with Cloridan.

"Four guys, plus us," I murmured to Cloridan as we headed off. "Are you expecting that much trouble?"

"I would if we didn't have the four guys," he said. "The gangs in this town pick on new arrivals that don't know what they're doing. We look like we know what we're doing, *and* that we're not to be messed with. We won't have any trouble."

"I see. Are we going to have to hire guards the entire time we're here?" I asked.

"Nah, it's just that we're going through the docks and have readily transportable goods," he replied. "Once we're established, we shouldn't have any—any more than the *usual* amount of trouble."

"Comforting," I said, and then paused for a bit before asking: "I've been wondering, what's the real reason you came here with me? And don't give me those chivalrous lines you spouted last time."

"Chivalrous, hey? I like the sound of that."

"It's been a refreshing change, *not* having you talk like that all the time," I said. "So don't start again."

He laughed, "Ah well, don't think for a moment that I've given up. It's just that with Kyle and Felicia being part of the group, I'm worried he'd think I was hitting on his lady."

"Fine, but you still haven't answered the question."

"Well, I hate to admit it, but it's the same reason as the kid."

"Cutter?" I asked, surprised. What had Cutter wanted again?

"He can sense it about you," Cloridan explained. "That you're someone who will be going somewhere, that will do things. Helping you, we'll go with you."

"Are you sure it's not just my Charisma you're sensing?" I inquired uneasily. Was this a Worldwalker thing?

"Maybe. Or perhaps your Charisma is the *reason* you're destined for greatness?"

"What, you're sensing my destiny now?" I was really feeling uneasy now. For some reason, I was reminded of Milly, right at the start, and the intense way she insisted that the right thing to do was hide and move. I'd thought I'd been dumped on this world with nothing and no one to guide me, but was that really true?

"I don't know," he confessed. "It's just a feeling. But when you said you were going to my old haunts, I knew that I could help. That you *needed* me to help."

"That is really fucking scary," I said. "It sounds like you're throwing your life away in service to some sort of prophecy that you can't even express."

"It's not like that," he reassured me. "I'm still in it for the profits, and we can definitely make some coming here."

"We just have to make sure we keep them," I said. He laughed in agreement and started pointing out the sights.

Dominating the town was the Baron's tower, a structure that rose on the side of town furthest from the river. Taller than any of the guard towers, it was visible from pretty much anywhere in town.

"It actually dates back from before the Empire," Cloridan told me. "It's supposed to have belonged to a wizard back then, before the Empire expanded up here. The rest of the fortifications were constructed by the Empire."

He pointed up the road to some imposing buildings. "That's where the temples are, and the major guilds. We'll check those out once we've secured our property."

The four men led us off the main street, and into a fairly prosperous looking residential area.

"I gave Therrien your requirements; we'll see what he's managed to find," Cloridan said. We ended up stopping at a three-story house.

"It's a little big, don't you think?" I said.

He shrugged. "We'll need four bedrooms, to start with. Workrooms for you and Felicia . . . it adds up."

He had a point, and it was pretty small for three stories. Space was at a premium here, even more so than it had been in Anchorbury. Cloridan's friend Therrien was inside, along with a man who turned out to be the owner. He showed us around the place, as we Identified everything to check the quality. It wasn't as detailed as if we'd had Craft (Carpentry) or Craft (Stonemason), but it gave us an idea. A quick exchange of gold, and I was the new owner.

It might seem excessive to buy when the longest I'd stayed in a place up until now was two weeks, but real estate was so cheap compared to renting here. If you managed to sell it before moving on, it was actually free, as long as you had the cash to swing it. The finance industry was still in the Dark Ages here, I had half a mind to try setting something up. There was a problem with that, though. If I managed to collect a really meaningful store of wealth, I had no guarantee that a noble, the King, or a powerful wizard wouldn't swoop in and take it from me.

A problem for the future; right now, we needed to move in. Supernatural strength made it easy, although we still left the heavy bits for the menfolk. I let Felicia and Kyle have the room that was actually furnished with a bed. Cutter and Cloridan were fine sleeping on the floor until beds arrived. Not on the floor—they had what they called bedding, which was *like* a mattress, but was really just rags in a large sack.

For me, I recreated my IKEA futon in the room that I'd chosen. I'd brought some of my furniture, a writing desk and a dresser, but the dresses would stay in the trunks for now.

With everything unloaded, Cloridan saw the boys off with some friendly words and coin.

"Can we go exploring now?" Cutter asked. He meant himself, of course, but it was nice for him to include us. I looked at Cloridan.

"It should be safe enough," he said. "As long as you don't get lost and stay out of anything that looks like trouble." He sounded just like a dad.

"Fine, then, be back before sunset," I said, trying not to think about that making me the mom. He yelled his agreement as he went out the door.

"Until we get to know the place, we should probably stay in pairs," Cloridan cautioned. "No one's going to think it worth robbing a kid, but unaccompanied women are another matter. It should be fine, but let's make sure."

I saw a new resolve to never let Felicia go anywhere alone write itself on Kyle's face.

"Fine," I said. "We're going to need some food if we're going to cook something to eat tonight, so do you want to come with me, Cloridan?"

"I'd be honored, my lady," he said, bowing.

"I'll get the kitchen going?" Felicia said. "Get the fire started and such?"

"Sure," I said. "You can use this." I tossed her the Fire Gem. She looked at it and took a second to use Identify.

"I can't use a Fire Gem to start a stove! That's ludicrous!" she exclaimed.

"Why does everyone say that?" I said innocently. "Come on, Cloridan." I pointedly ignored his offered arm.

At the market, meat was cheap, as well as some fruits. Farmed products were quite expensive, but not prohibitively so. Gossip was free, as always. The latest rumor doing the rounds was a juicy one. Apparently, one of the Chosen was going to be arriving in town soon.

REGISTRATION

Little is known about the world before the coming of the Seven, and nothing is known for sure. There are no known written records or oral traditions that go back to before there were nine gods. One theory holds that the different races were created in the same event that created the Seven.

The two gods that remain from that time choose not to speak of it, and so the mortal races are left wondering. What was the reason for Ix's death? The only two witnesses are also, as far as we know, the only possible perpetrators.

—Heresies of Kaval

The next day, the first priority was registration with the Adventurers Guild. Kyle and Felicia were members in good standing, but Cloridan needed to renew his lapsed membership, and I had to register for the (*cough*) first time.

Actually, before that, I needed to see what my "reward" from Aubert was. The package had arrived at the last minute, almost as if the man had been having my preparations to leave watched. Past caring, I'd thrown it in with the rest of my luggage. Now, with most of my unpacking done, I stared at it on the breakfast table as if it were a snake.

"What do you think it is?" Felicia asked.

"No idea," I said, frowning. "He said he owed me for saving his life, so you'd think it would be something worthwhile, but he does hate me a lot."

"Probably something decent," Cloridan opined. "If he doesn't clear the debt, he'll feel like he still owes you, and won't be able to dismiss you like he wants."

"Seems to me that a reward should be presented, and not just sent in the post," I grumbled.

"Well, he does hate you a lot," Kyle said.

"Whatever," I said, and started opening my present. It was sealed in a box, so the process involved a lot of prying and cutting away wax. When it was done, the contents were revealed.

> **[Identification]: Codex of Flood and Flow – Quality: Good – Properties: Teach (Water Magic)**

"Fuuuuuucck," I said.

"That's actually a valuable reward," Cloridan said. "I know you've been looking for magical texts, so you know how hard they are to find."

"Aubert knows that as well," I said. "So I guess it *is* valuable, but it's a water magic text."

"It's support magic, yes. You still want it, though, don't you?"

"I suppose." I sulked. "What are the chances that this was the only magical text he had sitting around?"

"Almost none," Kyle said. "A noble house like his would have had a hundred years to gather up all the texts they could."

A library gathered over a hundred years? That gave me an idea, but I put it to one side for now.

"So he picked the one that was least useful," I said. "Ice, Fire or Earth would have combat applications—Air would have let me *fly* . . . small mercy he didn't find a Mental text."

"If he had given you one of those, you could have reported him for possession of one," Cloridan pointed out. "I doubt he would have opened himself up like that."

"Feels like wasting a Skill point on this," I complained. "But . . . I'm not likely to find books out here. I guess I'll start studying this afternoon."

"Right," Cloridan said. "The Guild. Shall we get going?"

"How about we go in separately," I replied. "I don't want any rumors starting about the two of us."

"I suppose I should take that as a request not to start any then," he joked, laughing as I glared at him. He made a mock bow as he took his leave.

"Did you want to talk about the Chosen coming?" Felicia asked. Cutter had gobbled breakfast and left already, so it was just those of us in the know remaining.

"Not much to talk about," I said. "I think I'll definitely try to contact them, compare notes. Paladin of Life, eh? I wonder if that means they've heard from . . . Duit, wasn't it?"

Felicia nodded. "Have you thought about contacting the churches to see if they know which god chose you?"

"I've avoided churches entirely," I said, scowling. "Eight out of the nine will want nothing to do with me, and the remaining one is responsible for kidnapping . . . or whatever-ing me."

"Was that book of the Chosen any help?" she asked.

"Not really. There were some warnings about not trusting the gods, about not introducing technology, that sort of thing. A lot of it was opinions on the politics of the time, which I guess is a hundred years out of date."

"What's technology, and why shouldn't you introduce it?"

"Technology is . . . better, more advanced versions of the tools you're using," I said. "All the weapons you guys use are only historical artifacts where I come from." I sighed. "And as for why not to introduce them . . . well. The thing about this world is that if I teach someone to make a better crossbow, then that knowledge gets entered into the System. As an improvement to an existing Craft skill, or a new skill entirely. At which point anyone in the world can make them."

"That's normal . . . Oh! It isn't in your world?"

"No," I said. "Normally the point of teaching your friends new technology is to give them an advantage. The way knowledge is distributed instantly . . . well it has some advantages."

"I see," Felicia said, still catching up. "In your world, if your country had better technology, you'd have an advantage against other countries."

"Yeah. That said, I don't think it's a reason *not* to introduce any technology. Just stuff that makes things better, unlike weapons."

"So are you going to do that, then?" Felicia asked excitedly. "That sounds like it could be fun!"

"Well, maybe," I said. "There are two problems with the idea. First of all, I wasn't a . . . a Crafter in my world. So my knowledge of technology is somewhat lacking.

"The other problem is that it's hard to know which advances are safe and which will lead to better weapons."

"Oh," she said, deflating somewhat. "So it's back to the enchanting?"

"And killing monsters," I said. "Why don't we head to the Guild?"

The Guild was, well, much like the first time I joined.

Just like a franchise, I thought. The procedure was the same. This time, on Cloridan's advice, I declined to name my [Profession], just saying, "support mage."

Yes, it was a little irritating to know that I could have just done that the first time. Although I was also hiding my level that time, so I guess it wouldn't have helped.

Joining up with Cloridan, we registered as a team. Felicia, giggling, had suggested the Black Swan Company for the name, and no one objected. Kyle and Felicia had managed to get Silver rank, so as a team we could apply for better jobs. Checking out the board, I saw that the majority of Bronze jobs were for hunting beasts in the forest, for skins or meat.

I asked Kyle about traps, and he told me that they did get used, but you had to keep a watch over them. A trapped beast made a lot of noise, which attracted other beasts. They would attack the trapped creature, ruining the skin, wrecking the trap, and eating the meat.

"If you're up for it, you can get a lot of kills that way," he said. "But you'll be fighting just about every monster that comes looking, and they'll all be trying to sneak up on you."

The Cult of Toriao apparently had a presence in the town—they were offering a few quests to either capture or record details about certain specific monsters found in the deep woods. Kyle didn't think much of these quests, either.

"Capture a monster?" he exclaimed. "That'd be a real pain to do. Felicia has Hunt, so we should be able to track down the monsters they're looking for, but . . ." He trailed off, shaking his head.

"It might be easier with Blind?" I suggested.

"Um, yeah, it might be," he said, reconsidering. "Cloridan, do you know these monsters?"

"Nope," Cloridan said. "I don't think they were around when I was up here. If people knew about them, the Temple of Knowledge wouldn't be funding quests to gather information about them."

Both of them made concerned noises at each other. Apparently going looking for an unknown monster was asking for trouble.

The jobs Kyle *did* like were for rare drops from monsters contained in the two dungeons. Here again, we were lacking information. We noted the details so we could look into how hard the items were to get, which dungeons they dropped in, and whether we could sell the items for more.

"Old trick that newbies still fall for," Cloridan said. "Put up a quest for something, then turn around and sell it for a profit. I mean that's what most of these jobs are, but generally, they'll be selling it after processing, or in a different town or something. But sometimes you can get away with just going next door and selling it for a profit."

We split up. Felicia and I headed to the Guild library to research monsters, while Cloridan and Kyle went to the Market to get prices.

"Who'd have thought adventuring would involve going through so many books?" I joked to Felicia.

She smiled. "We met in the Oakway Guild library, didn't we? It only makes sense to start an expedition by informing yourself."

"I guess so," I said, and put my head down. After we finished this, I had some more studying to do at home.

"Are we ready, then?" I asked the group. We had maps, we had supplies, we had a list of monsters. We had a plan.

Everyone nodded, so I cast Greater Invisibility on Cloridan and let him head out. Once he was out of sight, we followed along.

We weren't expecting any problems on the trip, but we all agreed it was better to be prepared. The trail was pretty well marked, so even those of us without Hunt should be able to follow it. Others should have gone before us on the trail, so the chance of encountering monsters was also quite low.

Nonetheless, we had Cloridan out scouting ahead of us. The journey to the dungeon was quite far, and we needed to hustle to get there and back within the day. None of us wanted to camp out in the forest at night. Invisible, Cloridan didn't have to worry about stealth, and could move quickly while still keeping an eye out.

You couldn't run properly in the forest; the ground was too uneven. Still, we moved as quickly as we could. It was about an hour later when I spotted Cloridan's outline and called it out to the others. He had stopped and was waiting for us.

"What's up?" I asked. He put his hand to his ear in response. Listening, we could hear shouts and snarls from up ahead.

"Combat?" I asked, and he nodded. "I guess we proceed cautiously and see if they need help?" He nodded again. I looked at the others, and they were up to speed. As a group, we moved cautiously forward.

The noise quickly increased as we approached, and we quickly came to within sight of the conflict.

Four adventurers were holding off a group of what had to be hawk-wolves.

[Identification]: Harrier-Wolf (Male) – Threat: 10 – Status: Injured

Right, because the System needed to distinguish between different *types* of hawk-wolves. They were easy for me to identify, as they were wolves with hawk heads, naturally. Much like a griffin, and like the griffins they were supposed to have escaped from one of the dungeons here—which had a chimera theme.

I wasn't looking forward to the rat-snakes.

Facing them was a ragtag group of individuals . . . no, really—they weren't even of the same race. There was one human, a fox-kin, a short and stocky individual that might well be a dwarf, and an even smaller girl. Unless she was a short nine year old, she must be a halfling.

This was pretty rare, in my oh-so-extensive experience. Latora was a human nation, which didn't mean that the other races were *excluded*, but they were much less common. Non-humans were overrepresented in the Adventuring profession—the Delvers back in Oakway were an example of that—but I'd learned since that they were an exception to the normal rule.

Regardless, this group didn't appear to be having much trouble with the hawk-wolves. Only five remained out of a pack of about eight, judging from the corpses on the ground. The adventurers were bleeding, but none of them were down.

Aside from our invisible scout, we weren't the stealthiest of woodland creatures. When we came into sight, it was with enough noise for both sides to notice us. Evidently taking us for reinforcements, the hawk-wolves started screeching and all broke off from the fight at the same time.

A few seconds later, it was just us adventurers in the clearing looking at each other nervously. The other party all eyed us warily, and showed no sign of putting up their weapons.

"Um, hi there!" I said. "We come in peace?"

OVERTURES

Each god and goddess has told their followers a story of what happened to Ix. Some of them have told more than one. Each story is colored by the personality and designs of the one who told it. Comparing as many stories as we have access to, one can hope to tease out the bare bones of a story we can hope is true.

It should be noted, however, that trying to outwit the gods is a fool's pastime. They are more capable than mere mortals—more capable than mortals can even understand. So if we have the truth, it is only because at least one god wanted us to have it.

The story, then, is this. Ix tired of the endless stalemate. She wanted a world that would grow, and she convinced, or tricked, the other gods to help her. We can assume that it takes the power of at least one god to end another. According to the story, it took three. Three gods joined their power to one end, to shatter Ix into seven pieces.

—Heresies of Kaval

Both groups eyed each other warily. "Uh . . . this isn't an ambush or anything," I said carefully. "We were just heading to the dungeon. If you want, we can just skirt around you guys and leave you to do your harvesting."

There was a brief pause, and then the human woman sheathed her sword and stepped forward. The others followed her example.

"Sorry about that," she said. "You can't be too careful out here." She looked us over. "Is that all of you? Three's a small party for the dungeon."

"We have a scout," I replied. "He's scouting." Her eyes narrowed at that. I shrugged. "Like you said, you can't be too careful."

"Hrmn," she said, but she didn't disagree. "I haven't seen you around?"

"We're new," I said. "Just got in two days ago. This is our first trip."

"I see." She considered for a moment more, then stepped forward and put out her hand. "I'm Cerise. The others are Oadi, Ildas, and Ralin." She indicated who was who as I stepped forward to join her. Oadi was the red-furred fox-kin, Ildas was the armored dwarf, and Ralin was the halfling.

"I'm Kandis," I said and introduced the others. "We registered as the Black Swan Company."

"Our party name is Outlanders, on account of us all being from elsewhere," she said.

"Is there a story there?" I asked, curious.

"Not much of one. It can be difficult here, joining a party, if you're not Latorran."

"Ah, I'm sorry to hear that," I said. "Anyway, do you want us to get out of your hair while you take care of the corpses?"

She looked at me for a second, considering. "Nah, we'll go with you to the dungeon—there's room for more than one party. And this won't take long." She gestured to Ralin, who pointed at one of the corpses.

"Nature's Harvest," she chanted, pointing at one of the wolves. It started twitching, and then contorting grotesquely. It looked as if it was turning itself inside out, and I had to look away for a second. When I looked again, the corpse had been replaced with a neatly folded skin, with cuts of meat tied up on top of it. All the bones, guts, and blood had disappeared.

"Druid magic," Cerise explained, as Ralin moved on to the other bodies. "It's convenient. All the other stuff goes into the soil." The other two adventurers started packing away the neatly packaged meat and furs.

"Right . . ." I said, my voice trailing off at the sight of another corpse brutalizing itself. "How did you want to arrange things for us travelling together? Coordinating scouts and such."

She shrugged. "There shouldn't be a need for scouting ahead," she said. "This pack should have scared all the other monsters off. Not that they'd attack such a large group."

Now it was my turn to consider. None of my Social skills were warning me about anything, so I decided a show of trust was in order.

"Cloridan, you can come out now," I called, making a point of not looking in his direction. I gave him a few seconds to figure out what was going on before cancelling the spell. No need to give away all our secrets.

The group all jumped at Cloridan's sudden appearance. I was pleased to note that Kyle and Felicia took it in stride.

"That's quite an impressive Stealth you've got there," Cerise said.

"I'm impressive in many ways," Cloridan boasted, giving her a wink. Apparently, he was far enough away from Felicia to return to his normal manner. Cerise snorted.

"Adventurers—always think they're such hot shit," she said. She didn't seem bothered by the attention, and I think it helped convince her that we were a normal party.

Soon we were on our way once again. The path was wide enough for us to travel two abreast, so each party travelled in single file next to each other. Cloridan was in the lead, which put him next to Oadi, who was the Outlander's ranger, and I was second, putting me next to Ildas. She was a Cleric, and I was able to identify her god from her holy symbol. It was the symbol for Rakaro, the God of Storms, which was about the limit of my knowledge.

Ildas was the closest I'd come to a Cleric since coming here, and I was a little nervous that she'd either welcome me as a sister or denounce me as another god's Champion, but she did neither. Instead, we just chatted.

From the sound of it, most of the others were doing the same thing. Well, Cloridan was chatting *up* Oadi, but the others were mostly sharing information about the town. You might think we would be more interested in the upcoming dungeon, but we'd all been researching and briefing each other yesterday about that until we were sick of it. Learning which store sold the best dried rations was much more engaging.

My own conversation was somewhat reduced, as Ildas had the hardest time matching our pace with her short legs. She managed, but she was running rather than jogging. From what I knew of dwarves, I suspected her increased Stamina burn wasn't going to bother her, though.

You might think Ralin was in an even worse spot, but she had her own solution. Her reduced weight, combined with comparable strength to bigger folk, meant she could sort of *skip* along, travelling about four of her paces with each small jump. It must still have counted as running, though, as I knew that the Stamina cost for repeated jumps added up quickly.

We reached the dungeon without further incident. It was quite picturesque—a small building overrun with vines, which seemed to consist of nothing more than the steps down. Ancient flagstones all around seemed to have prevented trees from taking over, and four broken columns stood in a square at the furthest extent of the paving.

The building was covered in intricate carvings of animals. Looking more closely, I realized that they were of the chimeras that this dungeon produced. Griffins, owlbears, hawk-wolves . . .

The other party had seen this before and paid no attention to it, walking straight up to the stairs. They stopped when they saw we were gawking at the decorations.

"Come on," Cerise said. "You'll be seeing the real things soon enough."

I flushed slightly, and we moved forward hurriedly. The stairs led down to a large room with three arched entryways. Cerise gestured for me to take the first pick. Each archway led a different way to the next level, meaning that three parties could run the dungeon without interacting except at the final boss chamber.

"Cloridan?" I asked, and he moved forward, examining the first archway.

"Found it!" he called. "It's been triggered."

Each route had a trap right at the entrance. The traps reset a little while after all three had been triggered or disabled. Cloridan moved on to the next entrance.

"This one's good," he said. He poked a dagger between two stones in the wall, and there was a twanging sound.

"Do you want him to take a look at the third corridor?" I asked. "You don't seem to have a trap specialist."

"It's fine," Cerise assured me. "We know where the traps are, for the upper level at least." She took a rock and threw it at the wall just behind the third archway. There was a *thwok* noise, and three darts hit the opposite wall.

"See you on the other side," she said. "Best hurry before they reset."

We took her advice, moving into the middle corridor. This dungeon had an abandoned ruins theme, so the walls consisted of stones that had once been finely cut and laid, but were now weathered and covered with moss. Rhis had informed me that such things were a purely aesthetic choice, having no effect on the durability of the walls.

Adventurers loved to bash down walls, Rhis had told me—it was one of his pet peeves. He'd made extensive use of dimensional manipulation in his dungeon just to prevent this. Except for a few special areas where he'd permitted it, all of the barriers were at least ten meters thick, even if they appeared to be much less. Stunts like that were the main reason that Oakway had grown so slowly.

I had no idea if this dungeon used similar tricks, but we hadn't heard of any benefit from wall smashing, so I wasn't inclined to try here. If only because I would never hear the end of it.

Somewhat detracting from the "ruin" theme were the lit torches attached to the walls. I think the idea was that the ruins had been taken over by the mad wizard making all the chimeras, and he needed to see where he was going.

We came to the first door, and Cloridan got to work disarming the trap and picking the lock. We carefully opened the door and peeked inside. This dungeon changed up its monsters each run, so we wanted to get an identification before entering.

The four cages in this room contained what looked like normal panthers, except for the fact that their fur glistened slickly. The bars were too close together to get a crossbow bolt through, but there was enough line of sight for an identification.

[Identification]: Milax Panther – Threat: 12 – Properties: Immune (Blunt Weapons), Acidic Slime

Ah, if Janie was here, we could have toasted them in the cages, I lamented to myself. But there were other ways to cheat. As we'd discussed, I started the fight by casting.

I cast Blind twice, and only then did Cloridan and Kyle enter. Triggered by their entrance—it was a magical trigger that couldn't be disabled—the cages slid into the floor, releasing the panthers. Two of them continued to snarl in confusion, while the two that were left leapt to the attack.

They were met by Kyle. His Protector profession gave him a free parry, so he was easily able to fend the two cats off with his shield, while still dealing damage. That left Cloridan to use his crossbow to pick off the two blinded ones. It would have been faster for him to join Kyle, but daggers weren't the best weapons against something that oozed acidic slime.

Felicia and I handled reloading. Not the most glamorous of roles, but it was faster for us to switch crossbows with Cloridan, rather than have him reload himself. He had to make a lot of shots. Kyle finished his opponents first and was able to put the finishing blow on the final blinded one.

Your party has killed a Milax Panther – your experience share is 180 XP.
Your party has killed a Milax Panther – your experience share is 180 XP.
Your party has killed a Milax Panther – your experience share is 180 XP.
Your party has killed a Milax Panther – your experience share is 180 XP.

"Are these worth anything?" I asked Felicia. She shook her head.

"They can be boiled down to valuable alchemical components, but we don't have the time," she said. "And we can't take them with us, since the acid will spoil whatever else is in the bag."

"Ick. How's your sword, Kyle?" I asked.

"It's fine," he said, carefully wiping it down with a rag. The rag smoked, but he was wearing gauntlets, so he'd probably be fine. "Silversteel isn't normally affected by acids."

"These crossbow bolts are mostly ruined," Cloridan said ruefully. "But I found our rewards." He held up four—

"Collars?" I asked skeptically, and then Felicia gasped.

[Identification]: Dragon-hide Collars – Quality: Great – Properties: Immunity (All typed)

"There's not much of it," Cloridan allowed, "and it's not like it makes the wearer immune. But still."

"Where does a dungeon get dragon-hide from?" Felicia asked incredulously.

"It just makes it, like everything else," I said.

"Most of the dragon-hide in the world is of dungeon-make," Cloridan agreed. "After all, who'd be crazy enough to kill a dragon just to skin it?"

CHIMERA

The death of Ix was not an ordered event, or in any way rational. Many have tried to make some sense of the result, but it defies easy analysis. A God of the Seas, but not of land? A Goddess of Nature and a Goddess of Life? The truth is that Creation encompassed all things, and each of Ix's successors inherited a part of each of her aspects. It was not Ix's powers that were split; it was her personality, and each successor chose a role that suited their unique personality.

According to the story, this same fundamental misunderstanding is why the God of Destruction participated in the event in the first place.

—Heresies of Kaval

The goal of the adventuring profession was to turn the struggle for life and death into a boring affair. Proper preparation, planning, and advanced identification of the monsters you would be fighting all added up to a one-sided slaughter of monsters.

At the same time, adventurers needed to push themselves in order to progress. 180 experience points for a Threat Twelve monster meant more than 500 fights to get to level five. A Threat of one level higher turned that into 300.

That tension, plus the nature of random chance, meant that eventually, a string of boring fights got . . . interesting.

The first sign, in retrospect, was the fourth chamber—an empty room. It looked as if something had happened here; the weathered stone walls were cracked and damaged. There were no traps, though, and no monsters. Cloridan didn't like it.

"I don't remember anything like this from before," he said. "And I don't recall anyone else mentioning an empty cracked room. Anyone else?"

No one had. We carefully inspected for traps and secret doors, but there was nothing. Eventually, we had no option but to try the other door. Cloridan opened it as usual and took a peek in.

"Nope!" he said quickly, and backed off. Our procedure for this situation was for everyone to retreat, but the dungeon had other ideas.

A stone slab slammed down, covering the exit to the cracked room. An angry screech came from the door ahead of us, and it was slammed open by the creature beyond.

[Identification]: Tenta-bull – Threat: 13 – Properties: Multiple Attacks

The creature had the body of a bull, but the head had been swapped with a crocodile, or something like it. Coming off of its shoulders were four . . . tentacles, I guess, but they looked more like snakes. Especially since they were tipped with reptilian heads. These tentacles were what it had opened the door with, and they now extended into the room, hissing menacingly as the main creature shouldered its way into the room. It was too wide for the door, but a few shoves made a much bigger entrance.

I quickly cast Improved Blind, but there was a problem. The crocodile head in the center was enveloped, but the snake heads on the tentacles were not.

"I can't blind it! The spell only targets the head!" I yelled. Kyle cursed and ran at the thing, heavy shield up in front of him. He blocked two heads with his shield, but two more sank their teeth into his side. Cloridan ran to join him.

"Kyle, fall back and block! Let Cloridan flank it!" I called, and cast Greater Invisibility on Cloridan. The chance of Kyle hitting Cloridan accidentally would be greatly reduced that way.

Felicia was moving closer, no doubt to heal Kyle, but it was at that moment that the rat-snakes arrived.

[Identification]: Rat-Snake – Threat: 5 – Properties: Immune (Poison)

They came crawling out of the cracks in the wall, dozens of them. Lots of little rat legs attached to a snake body. They also had the rat heads, which weren't *ideal*, but better gross than poisonous.

Much of the beast's noise was muted from its central head being muffled, but intense hisses from the snakes suggested that Cloridan had landed a hit. It tried to whirl to face him, but Kyle was keeping it busy.

Meanwhile, we had smaller problems of our own.

> **Your party has killed a Rat-Snake – your experience share is 25 XP.**
> **You have inflicted 103 damage!**
> **For killing a Rat-Snake, you have earned 25 XP.**
> **You have inflicted 107 damage!**
> **For killing a Rat-Snake, you have earned 25 XP.**

Without a word, Felicia and I blocked as many snakes as we could from reaching the front line. The rat-snakes had too low a Threat to actually hurt us, unless we stopped Dodging. I wasn't sure they could actually hurt Kyle through his armor, but they would make a nasty distraction if they got to him while he was still fighting the beast.

We stopped a lot, but a few got through. Felicia shouted a warning, so Kyle wasn't surprised. It still cost him a blow from the bull, but the tenta-bull was on its last legs. Cloridan had landed another backstab.

> **Your party has killed a Rat-Snake – your experience share is 25 XP.**
> **You have inflicted 105 damage!**
> **For killing a Rat-Snake, you have earned 25 XP.**
> **You have inflicted 107 damage!**
> **For killing a Rat-Snake, you have earned 25 XP.**
> **Your party has killed a Tenta-bull – your experience share is 325 XP.**

After that, it was just cleanup. Lots of squirming cleanup.

"Ugh. Thank the gods that's over," Felicia said as soon as the last one was dead. "Kyle, are you all right?" She went over to heal him.

Cloridan waved to attract my attention.

"Unless you've got something important to say, I think I should keep the spell up," I said to his invisible form. "My mana's limited and I don't want to waste the spell." He shrugged and pointed to the slab blocking the exit.

I looked over. "Shouldn't that have gone by now?" I said, going over to it. Using Mana Sense showed me that it was chock full of magic. That wasn't unusual in dungeons—most of the cages were magically endowed so that they could be opened when adventurers arrived. Such items tended to evaporate when you tried to take them, or when their purpose was ended.

This slab, though, was still here. It didn't budge when I tried to move it, but that wasn't a surprise.

"Kyle? Can you try to move this thing?"

He came over. "What's up?"

"Can you try to lift this? Cloridan will take that side," I said, pointing. They both gave it a go, but it seemed fixed in place, and a few tentative shoulder slams from Kyle suggested it wasn't going to break, either.

"If we had a heavy hammer or something . . ." he lamented. "Hang on." He went over to the cracked walls and with some effort levered out one of the stones. He then proceeded to smash the stone into the slab, to no effect.

"We're not meant to go back that way," I said.

"Well, we were going to continue forward anyway?" Felicia suggested.

"Yeah, but now we don't have a choice. The routes join up *before* the boss chamber, right?"

Kyle nodded. "That's what the guides said. They didn't say anything about *this,* though."

"Well, if the guides were right, there should be two more chambers before that." Cloridan waved at me and held up three fingers.

"Three?" I said, and started counting in my head. Cloridan shook his head and pointed at this room and the next, then held up one finger. "Oh . . . so these two rooms are actually one?" I asked, and he nodded.

"Did anyone find the treasure?" Felicia asked, and we all started looking around. Kyle was the first one to speak up.

"Found it—it's another collar!" he called out. He held up a metal collar.

[Identification]: Controller Collar (Beast) – Quality: Perfect – Properties: Control (Beast)

"Nice," I said. "Do they use those on the griffins?"

"Probably," he answered. "There are skills to control them, but not everyone has those."

"Can we use it on the beasts we find in here?" I wondered.

"I'm . . . not sure," he said, frowning. "I think it won't work for us until we leave the dungeon, or maybe the dungeon can take control again . . . I don't know."

"Should we harvest the meat?" Felicia asked. "I don't think it's especially valued, but . . ."

"No?" I said, looking at Kyle and Cloridan.

Kyle nodded and Cloridan shrugged. "We don't have unlimited carrying capacity, and there's no way we can carry all of that."

The rest of the group agreed, so we moved on to the next chamber.

"Uh, oh," Kyle said, peeking in. "I don't like the looks of this."

We all took turns taking a look in. Again, the room seemed empty, but there were some holes in the upper halves of the walls. *Big* holes.

"Another ambush?"

"A pretty obvious one . . ." I muttered.

"Would Cloridan trigger it?" Kyle wondered. "Actually, if we were all invisible, could we just walk through?"

"Risky to test," I pointed out. "It could close off the exit again, and trap him inside."

We all pondered for a moment.

"How about this?" I said. "I'll send in some illusions, and if they trigger it, we can fight them in the doorway."

"What if the door closes? We'd be trapped between two magical doors," Felicia said.

"We'd be safe, though . . . and it would have to open them eventually," I said. While being stuck in a room didn't appeal, we had plenty of food, and we weren't going to run out of water.

In the end, that's what we went with, although we placed a few large stones under where the slab would fall in the hopes of stopping it. Then I sent in our crash test dummy.

[Phantasmal Entity].

My old adversary Reynard, looking as dangerous as ever, stepped forward into the room. Nothing happened immediately to the illusion, and I had him move over to the exit, thinking that was the most likely action to trigger the trap. Sure enough, as he touched the door, a rustling noise sounded from within the holes. Feline looking heads poked out—big ones. Four of them in all, they looked around and then scuttled out of their hiding holes to attack with a roar!

[Identification]: Tiger Beetle – Threat: 13 – Properties: Armored

As the name suggested, they were giant beetles—about three meters long, with vivid orange and black stripes across their carapaces. Crossbow bolts from Cloridan and myself hit them but didn't seem to do much other than attract their attention.

Kyle met the charge of the first one just short of the door. We wanted to get fighters flanking it while it was pinned. I could see two of the beetles going after Reynard. He could take a hit or two, I was sure, but it looked like curtains for the poor guy.

Kyle and Cloridan both landed blows, but I could tell the armor was causing them trouble. My own strike just skittered off its armor. In return, it shoved open its wing cases at me. I wasn't expecting it, and the hard blow knocked me to the ground.

The bug slashed ineffectively at Kyle with its front legs, but the monster behind it wasn't going to be denied a turn. It placed its two front legs on its brother and *pushed* with its remaining four. To our surprise and dismay, Kyle was forced back further into the room, until the first beetle was free of the doorway.

"Shit!" Kyle shouted, and tried to push back, but the damage was done. The first beetle just had to turn its body to make more room for Beetle Two. Cloridan should have been in the way, but I could see now that he'd been knocked down like me. Beetle Two could now enter the room unopposed, and headed for me!

Fuckfuckfuck, I thought as I tried to scramble to my feet again and get back behind Kyle, where it was safe.

You have taken 51 damage!

A claw swipe almost sent me flying. At the same time, I felt (though much less intensely) my illusion of Reynard end. Two more bugs would be coming through at any time now!

I was on my feet. I needed to cast a spell, and quickly.

[Improved Blind].

It was the one that came to mind. The bug twitched violently and spread its wing cases again, but I was in front of it now. I did have to fend off some swipes of its claws, but that was a lot easier when it couldn't see.

I, on the other hand, could see Cloridan's invisible form, as he *leapt* onto the back of my attacker. This was partly to get out of the way of Bug Number Three as it charged into the room, right through where he would have been. Invisible or not, he would have been trampled.

Still, jumping on the back of my attacker and plunging his blades into its back were certainly appreciated on my part. He even managed to avoid the armor, as the wing cases were still extended. I'm sure it screamed in pain, but we couldn't hear it.

Bugs Three and Four were now in the room, but only Three had an opponent, having joined Bug One in attacking Kyle. He was being forced back by their strength, but he was holding his own. It was only a matter of time before Bug Four came for me, so it was time for another—

[Improved Blind].

> **Your party has killed a Tiger Beetle – your experience share is 325 XP.**
> **Your party has killed a Tiger Beetle – your experience share is 325 XP.**

Both Cloridan and Kyle managed to finish one at the same time. It had looked a little shaky for a bit there, but it seemed to me the tide had turned. Kyle was able to hold off Bug Three, for long enough that Cloridan could kill the blinded Bug Four. They finished off Bug Three together.

And with that, it was over. I grinned at Felicia who had emerged from behind Kyle.

"Heal, please!"

WATER MAGIC

It is barely credible that Ashmor was deceived or mistaken about what would happen to Ix. Despite his reputation, he is a god, with intelligence and apprehension beyond human comprehension, let alone human limits. However, the killing of a god was something new in the world. It is just possible that two other gods could convince him that it would leave him with one less peer, and a host of lesser gods that could be overpowered or destroyed in turn.

Ix, on the other hand, managed to find a result much closer than what she is said to have wanted. Seven successors to keep the ravening forces of Destruction in check. Outnumbered seven to one, Destruction could surely be defeated and Ix's creations left to exist in peace.

But there was one fly in this ointment.

—*Heresies of Kaval*

Two more rooms, and we had reached the boss area antechamber. The fights had been nothing to speak of. Hiding behind Kyle's defense, while invisible Cloridan cut them up from behind, was a workable tactic most of the time.

I'd joined in professing ignorance with the others as to why the "kangapas" were bipedal. Not so much to hide my origins as to put the traumatic memory behind me. Whoever had thought of putting the front half of a panther on a kangaroo was truly an enemy of humanity.

It did make me wonder: if this world had 'roos, was there an Australia-equivalent continent somewhere about? Really, I should have wondered that about the other animals as well, but I thought of 'roos as part of Australia. Seeing one (well, half of one) here was jarring.

"Are we the first here?" Felicia asked, looking at the three doors that led back to the entrance. Two of them were still firmly closed.

"Seems so," I said, eying the much larger double doors on the opposite wall. I put down my burden. We'd decided to take the tiger beetles' wing cases with us—they were just too strong and light to not be worth something. Unfortunately, they were awkward as hell to carry. Tying them all up together had left me with a single load that I could carry—and I got stuck with it because the stronger party members needed their hands free.

"First come, first served?" I said. "Is that the etiquette here?"

"Pretty much," Kyle replied, and Cloridan nodded as well. "Everybody ready?" Kyle asked as he moved to the door. I grabbed my bundle of insect chitin and moved up behind him with Felicia. Cloridan was also in position, so I gave the go-ahead.

Unlatching the doors, Kyle pushed on them with his shield. A cold wind blew out. Behind the doors was a short passageway that opened up into a larger, much more brightly lit area. That was all I could see at this point—we weren't going to get a look at our opponent right away.

As we moved forward, the open area became more clear. We were looking at an arena, but with snow instead of sand, and what looked like viewing stands all around. The cold wasn't too bad, but it was definitely noticeable. Coming right up to the entrance, though, we still couldn't see the monster.

Asking Kyle to stop, I gestured for Cloridan to go forward. He dashed forward for about ten meters and then quickly looked around. I couldn't make out his facial expression, but he pointed upwards.

"It's above us," I informed the others.

"Probably planning on jumping down on our backline," Kyle said. "Can you get up there?" he called out.

Cloridan nodded. "Yes," I said.

"Then give us the count of ten before attacking. We'll come out as you're attacking." Cloridan nodded and disappeared from view.

It might have been nice to let Cloridan do all the fighting, but he didn't do as well without Kyle to attract the monsters' attention. He could get one stab in, but after that, they were aware and could defend against him. It took someone else stabbing them in the face to make them neglect their back long enough for another backstab.

As our count expired, we ran forward, Felicia and I going first, Kyle right behind us, running sideways with his shield between us and whatever was coming.

As we came out, we heard a massive, terrifying roar from above. *That should be Cloridan's attack landing*, I thought. It wasn't all good news, though.

Bear's Mighty Roar: Strength reduction (-2) applied.

All of a sudden, I felt my armor weighing me down. Fortunately, I'd already dropped my insect armor, but even so, I stumbled. Felicia, on the other hand, collapsed.

"Felicia!" I cried, trying to pull her up and failing. We were still in what Kyle had judged the "jump zone," and we had to get out of it. With my reduced strength, it was all I could do to drag her a few meters further. That was enough, because when I heard the massive thud of the monster landing, it was behind us. I took a quick look behind.

[Identification]: Hard-Shell Polar Bear – Threat: 15 – Properties: Roar, Armored

Oh, that's big . . . It towered over Kyle, who was standing right in front of it with his shield raised. As its name implied, its front was covered in large plates of shell, and one huge shell dome covered its back. Still roaring, it took two swipes at Kyle with its claws. He got his shield in front, but he was forced back towards us, and I could see blood on the bear's claws.

How's Cloridan going to backstab that? I wondered, but even as I did, I saw his invisible form slip in under the dome and slash at the bear's legs. I couldn't see how effective it was, but it seemed to feel it. It twisted around, looking for the threat and opening itself to Kyle's counterstrike. He struck, but his blow was weakened by the debuff and bounced off a shell.

Right, debuffs. That was my job, so I cast Improved Blind, then turned my attention to Felicia. She was actually conscious but was unable to lift herself off the ground. I guess the roar had reduced her to zero Strength.

"Let's get you a bit further from the fight," I said. At least the snow was easier to drag her across than sand would have been.

"Sorry I'm so useless," she muttered.

"You and me both," I said, looking back over my shoulder. The fight was ongoing, both sides fighting at less than their best. It was a bit of a stalemate with only minor damage on both sides. The bear had hunkered down and now seemed invulnerable to anything the Strength-reduced boys could throw at him.

"That Roar can't last forever, right?" I wondered aloud, and it proved to be so. With the bear unable to renew it through Improved Blind, it was only another minute or so before I felt my Strength return.

"Feeling better?" I asked Felicia as she got up.

"Much," she said, grimly. Walking together, we cautiously approached the fight.

"Any idea how this is going to end?" I asked Kyle. He and Cloridan were on opposite sides of the hunkered-down bear. From time to time, the bear would raise his shell and lash out randomly. The guys had given up trying to penetrate the shell.

"Well," Kyle said, "the head's there." He pointed at where a small part of the blindness bubble extended through the shell.

"So?"

"You've got that Water Ball spell, right?"

I gave him a look. The logic behind my first choice of water spells was sound, but I hadn't liked where it led me. There had been useful water spells that I could have purchased with the fifteen points that I got from Extra Spells. Water Breathing, for example. But I couldn't *practice* Water Magic with that spell unless I spent the day underwater. Most spells required a source of water, so I'd purchased Water Stream. That left five points to do something with the water, so I'd gotten Water Ball.

> **5 points: Water Ball: Gathers existing water into a ball, which you can move slowly. Duration: 2 minutes (10 mana).**

Oh, and notice how it cost twice as much mana as its level? That was normal for Water Magic.

"What of it?"

"Well, it's got to breathe, right?" Kyle asked with a grin.

I considered it. "There's no way I'm going to drown it with Water Ball," I said. "It'll just move its head."

"That's enough," Kyle assured me. "If we can get around its shell, we can kill it."

So we tried it. I cast Water Stream and Water Ball. How much water a spell created or controlled was based on the effect level, so the two spells matched amounts nicely. I rolled the water up to the shell and then under it. It was still water, only loosely held in the shape of the ball, so it was easy to get it through the small gap at the bottom of the shell.

It took a moment to react, but then the bear surged to its feet.

"Should have called it Water Board," I said. I couldn't quite get the tone right when trying to imitate the System.

The boys had been waiting for this and pounced. Blinded, presumably choking, the bear put up much less resistance. It tried to hunker down again, but that just meant I pushed the water in again. I would have thought it would try to flee, but running didn't seem to be something dungeon monsters did. The snake-rats had fought to the last as well.

> **Your party has killed a Hard-Shell Polar Bear – your experience share is 450 XP.**
> **For clearing the first level of the Forbidden Laboratory, you have earned a reward.**

"No first-time clear bonus?" I asked, disappointed.

Cloridan waved at me. I cancelled the spell—this was as far as we were planning to go. "Sorry, that's my fault," he said. "I've been here before."

"Same boss?" I asked.

"No, it was some kind of tiger-monkey."

"Of course." I looked around and quickly spotted where the chest had appeared. I moved over to it. "They never trap these, right?"

"Right," Cloridan confirmed. "Though if you see one without a reward notification, it's *definitely* a trap."

"Good to know," I said and opened the definitely-not-trapped chest. Inside were about twenty small bottles. "Oh!" I exclaimed, "Potions, like they said . . . I think. They're not labelled."

"I'd forgotten about that," Cloridan said, coming over. "They're labelled, all right, just not with words." He pointed and I could see that there was a complex design on each bottle, different for each one. "We'll need to consult the label chart at the Guild, find out what we got."

"It's random?"

"Yep. Could be anything, from a Smoker to a top-quality Alchemical Healing." We loaded up his backpack with the hopefully valuable bottles.

Meanwhile, Felicia was extracting the mana crystal from the bear.

"Do we want anything from this?" she asked. "I don't remember any quests for it."

"I don't either," I said. "Do you think the armor plates are worth anything?"

"They're tough, but they seem much heavier than our beetle casings," she said, considering. "And there's some weird slime involved as well."

"The back does look more like a snail than a turtle," I said. "That doesn't bode well for the meat." Bear-turtle meat *might* have been awesome, but I wasn't feeling so positive about bear-snail.

"I think you're right," Felicia reported. "It's rubbery in a way that meat shouldn't be. And that slime is coming out of it."

"We'll take it off your hands if you don't want it," a voice said from the entrance. Everyone looked over towards it.

"I can't believe newbies beat us to the boss," Cerise continued. "We must be losing our touch."

DECISIONS

There are a few surviving records of the War of the Gods, though no civilizations from that era still survive. It was a time of great turmoil. Civilizations rose quickly, buoyed by the direct support of one or more gods, clashed against another supported by different gods, and fell, usually at the instigation of yet another god.

The problem was that the gods could rarely come to an agreement on anything. Confrontations between gods were common during this era but normally ended in stalemates. When they formed alliances with one another, progress could be made, but these alliances never lasted for long.

The powers of the gods were so overwhelming in both magnitude and scope that nothing was beyond their whim—when it was not opposed. Races were destroyed, and may have been created. Cultures could be developed in days, and then erased even more easily.

Things only stabilized when the gods finally agreed to cease large-scale interference in mortal affairs. The mortal races were not a party to the agreement or informed of its terms. It seems to allow for some interventions, but exactly what the new rules are can only be inferred.

—Heresies of Kaval

I wasn't aware that it was a race," I said cautiously. Cerise wasn't approaching, so this still seemed like a friendly interaction. The rest of her crew was just behind her, but they weren't holding weapons or anything.

"Best way to win one," she returned, grinning. "It's first-come, first-fought for the boss; of course it's a race."

"Right." I looked back at our fresh-slain corpse. "You've got a use for that? How are you going to carry it?" I looked over at her group. For a party that must have harvested seven rooms of monsters and that pack of hawk-wolves, their packs were nowhere near as full as they should have been.

"I've got a storage ring," Cerise said. Her grin turned smug. "We'll have to make some room for it, but it's nothing we can't handle." She pointed at her feet and a large bundle of tightly tied furs appeared with a shimmer in front of her.

"You lucky . . ." I trailed off before I could give offense. "Bastard," however it got translated, might not go down well with strangers. "Where did you get that?"

"From my mentor, when he retired," she said. "It's one of the better random prizes on level five."

That meant . . . a Threat Thirty monster, if I remembered how the levels went. I whistled. "Your mentor must have been quite the fighter."

"That he was," she agreed. "So how's about I give you five gold to take that monster off your hands?"

"Oh, I couldn't let it go for less than fifty," I said, the words coming automatically out of my mouth. I was actually paying more attention to the fact that she made the offer. Since we were planning on leaving it, she could have gotten what she wanted just by letting us leave. Offering us money did seem like she was trying to make friends.

"Oh, come on, that's ridiculous!" she exclaimed. "You were just going to leave it there. No way I can go more than ten."

She was right, but Bargain was feeding me information now, based on her reaction. At least I hoped that's where it was getting it from. The possibility that skills could read minds to get the results that the effect totals called for couldn't be dismissed.

"That was before you offered us money," I informed her. "You know something about this corpse that makes it worth something."

She started to protest, but I quelled her with just a look. I wasn't finished. "It's valuable . . . but you're not sure it applies. Based on the risk it won't pan out, and the transportation hassle—I notice that you weren't planning on harvesting it here—I figure you're willing to go as high as 35 gold."

She tried to hide it, but I could see that I was dead on. I continued.

"But since we're just getting to know each other, how about we settle for 25? And you tell us what you're planning to do with it?"

Judging by her face, she went from surprise, regret, and finally resignation all in the space of a second.

"Phadan's mercy, lady, just how high *is* your Charisma?"

"That's confidential," I said. "Do we have a deal?"

"Fine, fine, I know when I'm beat," she said. "With chimeras that have a snail-type, you can generally boil them down to get an elixir base that works for a lot of potions."

I looked at the massive beast. "You're going to put the whole thing in a pot?"

"I'm not," she snorted. "But I know a guy who will." She handed me a small stack of coins.

"Pleasure doing business with you," I said.

"I'm sure it was," she said wryly, "I guess I just found out how a support class became the leader of this crew."

"Well, it's more of a democracy—" I stopped as I noticed the others all nodding. "What the—I've just been deferring to you two these last fights!" I said accusingly to Kyle.

"You take advice," Cloridan said. "And that's welcome. But you're definitely the leader."

Cerise laughed. "You guys seem like you might be going places. Are you continuing down?"

"About that . . ." I said. "Do you think the group that took the other track is doing all right?"

"What do you mean?" she asked.

"Well, they went through before we did, and they haven't shown up."

"They were probably just too weak to continue and turned back," she said, shrugging.

"Maybe. Did you guys run into a trap that blocked your way back?"

"You too?" She started looking thoughtful. "We thought that was just a fluke . . . do you think it's a new feature?"

"I do, but . . . it seems odd," I said. "I've seen a few dungeons now, and this doesn't mesh with what I've seen so far. Dungeons like to trap the unwary, but this seems unfair."

"There's probably a way to open the way back," Ildas, the dwarven Cleric, put in. "We didn't look for it, because we were headed on."

"So what I'm getting is, you want to go back and see if they need rescuing," Cerise said. "And—"

"And if all three entrances are cleared and someone goes to the second level, this level resets, right?"

"Right. That might have changed along with the new traps, though."

"It might," I agreed. "But it's a bit of a risk to take if someone's trapped in there, isn't it?"

"Fine," Cerise groaned. "We'll wait and give you a chance to play hero."

I cleared my throat. "As long as you're just going to be sitting around . . ."

"Oh come on, the rewards are going to be crap with eight people!"

I shrugged. "It's not about the reward? And the risk will be less as well."

She looked back at her party and sighed at what she saw. "Fine."

"Actually," Ildas spoke up again, "if the young lady is up to healing for the group, I'll stay here and ask any other parties that come through to wait."

"I should be fine," Felicia said. "I've got almost half my Faith left."

Your party has killed a Spider Jaguar – your experience share is 186 XP.
Your party has killed a Spider Jaguar – your experience share is 186 XP.
Your party has killed a Spider Jaguar – your experience share is 186 XP.
Your party has killed a Spider Jaguar – your experience share is 186 XP.
Your party has killed a Spider Jaguar – your experience share is 186 XP.
Your party has killed a Spider Jaguar – your experience share is 186 XP.

Many hands made light work of killing spider jaguars. These were not really insectile in appearance, looking like regular giant cats, only with eight legs and eyes. They scuttled around on the walls and ceiling, and they were agile enough that Cloridan couldn't hit them with his crossbow. Oadi could, though, and they became a lot less agile when Blinded. Ralin, the Druid, also had some luck dropping them with a stone to mud spell. Hard to cling to mud.

I made sure to chant when casting. I didn't want them to know all my secrets.

Your party has killed a Pteroshrew – your experience share is 186 XP.
Your party has killed a Pteroshrew – your experience share is 186 XP.
Your party has killed a Pteroshrew – your experience share is 186 XP.
Your party has killed a Pteroshrew – your experience share is 186 XP.
Your party has killed a Pteroshrew – your experience share is 186 XP.
Your party has killed a Pteroshrew – your experience share is 186 XP.
Your party has killed a Pteroshrew – your experience share is 186 XP.
Your party has killed a Pteroshrew – your experience share is 186 XP.

I wasn't sure why these annoying guys got the name they did—as far as I could tell, they were just really large bats. Both these monsters would have done a number on our one-man shield wall tactic, so I was glad to have the others along.

Two rooms were all we had to clear. In the third room, we found the body of a massive worm, half-buried, and two survivors from that fight.

[Identification]: Whaleworm Corpse – Quality: Good

I didn't think Cerise would be fitting *that* one in her store. Felicia was not distracted by the worm and ran forward to offer healing. Both adventurers were quite badly wounded and were clearly out of healing potions.

"Thank . . . you . . ." the human said. "Door blocked . . . Healer died . . . trapped."

"Just relax now," Felicia said, splitting her healing between the two of them. It took a few moments, but eventually she stopped, out of the Healer equivalent of mana. "That's all I can do for you for now. How do you feel?"

"I'm about halfway healed," the man informed her. That was enough for him to get up and shake his buddy, who had been unconscious but was now stirring. "Come on, Vasidi, we've been rescued."

Vasidi was a monkey type beast-kin, I was pretty sure. That often got shortened to "monkin" when people talked, but I wasn't sure if it was derogatory or not. He was wearing robes, so it looked like they were a mage/fighter/Healer party.

"Ah . . . my thanks to all of you," Vasidi said, taking in the crowd around him. "As you may have heard, my name is Vasidi, and this is Channing."

We started exchanging names, but I was pretty sure few of them would be remembered. I caught Cerise's eye and we moved aside to talk.

"They'll need escorting back, especially if they're carrying their party member," I said. "We'll take them, and you can get back to level two."

She was suspicious that I had an ulterior motive, but I knew that was what she wanted to do. "Sure, I guess you'll want your half of the harvest."

"How about you sell it, and then just give us our share in coin?" I suggested.

"You're far too trusting—unless you're that eager to not have to carry the load."

I laughed. "Actually, how about you look us up *before* you sell it, and I'll do the negotiating for you."

"Am I going to end up in debt over this?"

I clapped her on the arm. "Trust me."

We went our separate ways, and we led Vasidi and Channing back to the previous chamber. It was littered with winged cats.

> **[Identification]: Storking Puma Corpse – Quality: Mediocre**

Channing stumbled over to the side, where the body had been laid out.

"Fleurette," he said. "I thought we were going to join you soon."

He knelt down and carefully picked her up.

Vasidi joined us in silence as Channing paid his respects, but then he noticed that the door was open.

"Hey!" he said, "The slab's gone!"

We all looked over. "I guess now that the way is clear forward, it's not needed anymore?" I said.

Channing and Vasidi both looked pissed. "You mean we didn't have to fight that worm? We could have just waited?"

"Well, keep in mind that if you didn't, *we* would have had to fight it, so it did make rescuing you easier."

"I suppose. Again, thanks for rescuing us."

"You are welcome."

With the monsters cleared, the way up was easy enough, although Cloridan did have to disable one trap that had reset. It wasn't long before we were back in the forest.

PARTY

If neither Ix nor Ashmor got the results they wanted from Ix's death, what of the third participant? Fyskel, the God of Balance, is not highly respected among humanity. As one of the more numerous races, humanity often finds that "Balance" means tipping the scales against human progress and human interests. Not for nothing is he known as the Turncoat God.

If the world before was balanced between Ix and Ashmor, then the world after was still balanced, but in a much more complex manner. Alliances shift, treaties are broken, irreparable rifts are forged. And in the middle: Fyskel, playing both ends against the other.

It could well be argued that of the three participants in the Shattering, only one got what they wanted. Whether that was a coincidence or not is not for mortals to judge.

—*Heresies of Kaval*

I was at a party. My first one since coming here, unless you counted the Ball, which I did not. That was far too formal to be a party, even before the murders started. Hopefully, tonight would be murder-free, but I wasn't going to bet on it. Things were getting rowdy.

It had been Cerise's idea—probably something to do with the money burning a hole in her pocket. She had said that it was adventurer tradition to drink a toast for any departed companion, and had dragged us all to the tavern to do so. It was an adventurers' tavern, so there were plenty of people willing to be roped into a drinking session. *Another* drinking session, that is, as they were already drinking.

Cerise and Vasidi went around rounding up people that had known Fleurette, while we had the enviable job of trying to cheer up Channing. Mostly that meant listening to him tell stories of Fleurette.

He and Fleurette had been close, which seemed to explain why he was such a mess, while Vasidi was . . . broken up, but functional. As he told stories, I was struck by the parallels between the two of them and the couple in our group. I wasn't the only one, as I could see Kyle getting grimmer as Channing spoke. The possibility of being in the same position did not sit well with him.

Things cheered up as others arrived, to commiserate with Channing and to tell stories of their own. The toasts started getting made and the drinks started flowing.

I stayed in the background as much as I could. I'd never known her after all. But that just meant there were people who wanted to tell me about her, wanted to drink to her memory. I tried to keep that under control—I didn't know my limits in this world. Did three Strength mean three times the drinking?

That quickly proved not to be so. As the night progressed, it became clear that a high Strength did not mean a high drinking capacity. It seemed that my experience with Company parties was still serving in good stead. Of our team, Kyle was the first to drop out, getting led away by Felicia while he could still walk.

Cloridan was a true professional, drinking heavily and not showing it at all. He was off the clock, of course, and seemed to be making real progress with Oadi.

I decided that it was time for me to leave. Not a complete fool, I let Cloridan know I was leaving. He made as if to escort me, but I told him I was fine.

It's remarkably easy to leave a party unnoticed. Everyone's focused on who they're talking to, so all you have to do is make sure no one's talking to you, and you might as well be invisible. I looked around, just to be sure that there weren't any other antisocial types hanging around the edges, and then I cast Greater Invisibility.

People were going in and out of the tavern all the time, so it was easy to slip out behind someone. Soon I was standing in the street, breathing the nighttime air, and admiring the way the two moons lit up the place nicely.

I hadn't chosen to go invisible because I was afraid of being molested on my way home. Though that was a concern, and this should prevent any attempts, I had another reason.

I looked up. Cloridan had drilled into me that no one ever looked up, so above was the best place to hide. I'd been drinking in a tavern for hours, so it could well be assumed I'd be off my guard and not looking out carefully. It was a good time to relax, and not worry about little mistakes.

Like sitting a little too close to the edge of the roof while waiting for me to come out.

I thought about taking action. I could climb up there, Blind the guy. He'd probably fall. Maybe I could put a little Phantasmal ice under his feet, make him slip without ever realizing what had happened. It seemed a waste, though. He'd be replaced. Slipping away from him like this, he probably wouldn't even report it. As it stood, I knew they were watching me, but they didn't know I knew that, which put me ahead in the game.

Whatever. So Aubert was having me watched. If he thought that was going to help him . . . well, I guess I'd let him waste his money.

"So you didn't kill him?" Rhis asked.

"No." I leaned back on my deck chair. We'd learned that the featureless white void could be shaped into whatever you wanted. Right now, I was on a reasonable facsimile of Bondi Beach at night. It was less real than an illusion—the waves crashed and made a sound, but you couldn't walk over to them, let alone feel the sand under your feet. Still nice, though.

"I know you said you don't have to kill everyone," Rhis continued. "But you also said that sometimes you don't have a choice."

"Uh-huh," I said. He was getting better at this, I swear, but he was really finding the whole "not killing" thing a challenge. I'd be more concerned, but he still didn't have access to the real world.

"So I've been keeping track," Rhis said. Was that pride in his voice? I guess keeping track of things was new to him. "And the thing is, I'm pretty sure you haven't killed *anyone*!"

"Hmm, let me think," I said, humoring him. I pretended to search my memory. "Yep, I think you're right. Not a one." I looked over to see him radiating confusion. I sighed.

"Rhis, being forced to kill someone is a rare thing, even here. There's almost always something you can do instead. Back home, I went 24 years without killing anyone. The fact that I've kept my streak going for another month isn't that amazing."

Rhis didn't really get human timekeeping, but we'd been through days, months, and years enough times for him to be able to puzzle it out. I let him ponder it for a while, before bringing up the other reason I'd activated him. I'd wanted to tell him about tonight, about how humans reacted when they lost someone, but he didn't really get it.

"So, I also wanted to talk about the dungeon today," I said. I'd already recounted the basics.

"Phfft, chimeras," he snorted dismissively. "I suppose it counts as a theme, with the whole 'Forbidden Laboratory' thing, but it's just lazy, if you ask me."

"How so?" I asked, amused. I guess it shouldn't be surprising that he was so into dungeon design, but he was really a perfectionist and hadn't been at all complimentary about the dungeons I'd seen so far.

"There's just one type of chimera monster available," he informed me. "So all that guy did was make a number of rooms, summon a chimera in each room, and call it a day. The summons is random as to what features each monster has."

He started ranting about how it made it impossible to put in a decent ecosystem since every monster had different dietary requirements, so as soon as one got killed, you had to re-jigger the entire lot.

"Wait, how does that work with multiple monsters of the same type?" I interrupted.

"All part of a single summons," he said with a shrug. "You specify the Threat, and it can give you one big monster or several smaller monsters. Such a hack."

"What about that trap room, though?" I said. "It looked set up for smaller beasts; how will that work the next time they summon more?"

"Well, I suppose that they made the minimum of effort to move creatures to an appropriate locale," he sneered. "It's not much, but it's *something*."

"Uh-huh. Also, it didn't look like they had anything to eat? That made sense for the undead dungeon, but how does it work with living creatures?"

"Oh, any creature can be sustained with additional mana. It's wasteful, though, which is why you want to set up a proper ecosystem. This guy probably got lazy because he had so much mana to use. That reminds me of something . . ." Rhis trailed off, thinking. "Oh yes!" he said, "I was going to tell you before. I've been getting notifications about the additional mana."

"What, you've been awake when I'm not here?" I asked.

"Not exactly . . ." he said. "It's more like I get woken up briefly to get told that there's more mana available. I think that this location might meet the minimum requirements to activate the seed."

He looked really eager, but I wasn't keen on having him go back to killing people.

"Maybe the minimum requirements, but I don't think this is a good location," I hedged. "It's right next to two other dungeons."

"That's true. You wouldn't want your dungeon to be mana starved," he said thoughtfully. I smiled in agreement and let him go back to talking about lizard breeding.

I really need to figure out what I want to do with this dungeon seed.

"They're probably the Baron's men, not Aubert's," Cloridan said. We were having a late brunch, and Felicia was distributing hangover cures to us all. Everyone except Cutter, who hadn't been drinking last night. This world might not have had a minimum drinking age law, but that didn't mean I was going to let it happen.

"Why?" I asked.

"It's his town, and he's Lord Aubert's man," Cloridan explained. "It would be rude to send his own men, but he can just order the guy to keep an eye on you and tell him what you're doing."

"Huh. Does it make a difference?"

"Maybe." Cloridan drank his potion, grimaced, and then ate some bread to erase the taste. "It means they'll be locals, and we might be able to tell something from *who* they are."

"What do you mean?"

"If they're actually the Baron's men, that's one thing, but most nobles don't have troops that are good at sneaking around. He might have hired one of the gangs to do the actual surveillance. If we can identify the men, we can work out which of the gangs the Baron is dealing with."

"I can do that!" Cutter interjected. He was sulking from having missed both the dungeon expedition and the party afterwards, but the prospect of doing something exciting fired him up again.

"Don't be dumb," Cloridan shot back. "This isn't Anchorbury; kids aren't so common they get ignored. Plus, these guys have seen you with us, so if they see you, they'll know we're onto them."

"I could do it if I were invisible?" Cutter suggested.

"I can't extend the spell if you get too far away from me, remember?" I said. "And how do you plan on identifying them, anyway? Cloridan might recognize them, but there's no way you will."

"I, uh . . . could follow them back to their base?"

"And what about when the spell runs out?"

"You were talking before about an enchantment that did Invisibility?" he asked hopefully.

"It might come to that," I said, and shuddered. "But let's try every other avenue before I give an Invisibility amulet to a thirteen-year-old boy."

PLUMBING

It's obvious why this world is so underdeveloped. Five thousand years of history and they haven't managed to come out of the Dark Ages! This stupid Status thing takes away all the reasons for innovation and just makes people lazy. It's worse than Communism!

Every improvement is spread throughout the world in an instant. The results of your hard work, distributed to the world without your permission. Without the opportunity to profit from your invention, why would anybody invent anything?

—Todd Franklin, *Thoughts of the God-Chosen*

Why, Todd? Because they wanted to shit on a toilet, that's why! I looked up from my work and sighed. Right now, I was "helping" Kyle dig a trench from our house to a nearby gutter. I say "helping" because he didn't actually need any help. I could use a shovel with much more ease since I came here, but Kyle was a machine. He actually had Craft (Stone) as a skill as well, so our trench would be covered and lined with stone once we were done.

Craft was a weird skill. When you unlocked it, it started with one available type—for example, I had unlocked Craft (Iron) but had not yet purchased it. Every time the skill improved, it offered a choice of additional types of crafting. Kyle—because he'd planned to be a farmer before meeting Felicia—had Craft (Wood, Stone, Shingles). The really crazy part was that if you had the Skill points, you could drop a level in the skill and bring out a subtype into its own skill, like Craft Wood.

That skill now got all the experience from crafting wood, but the original skill now acted as a bonus when you used Craft Wood. So you could get much higher effective skill levels than you could with one skill alone. Exactly what skill subtypes were available at each level was different for each person, but it seemed that some crafts were more adjacent to others.

So Kyle didn't need help, but he did need direction. Connecting the inside of a house with the hole that served as a sewer wasn't something that they'd done, back where he was from. And I wasn't willing to just stand there and tell him what to do, so I was doing my best to aid with the unskilled part of the labor.

Talnier didn't have proper sewers. Well, it had *one* sewer. The main keep, where the Count lived, predated the rest of the settlement and was supposedly plumbed. There was a sewer tunnel running from it to the river, terminating in two small grated openings. Too small for a monster—or a human—to get through, obviously.

Water constantly flowed through the tunnel into the river, suggesting that the tower had its own spring, or there was some sort of enchantment constantly producing water to keep it clean. When the town was built, the nobles had refused to allow anyone else to connect to the tunnel, leading to more speculation that the tunnel also led to where the family kept their darkest secrets. I'd been making a lot of inquiries around town on sewer-related matters, and that was a favorite story of the townsfolk.

So instead of proper sewers, they'd dug narrow, deep trenches down the center of the two main streets, with a couple of branches leading out to other areas. They were mostly covered by stone slabs, but they couldn't be *entirely* covered, because then people wouldn't have anywhere to dump their waste.

In the nicer areas, like mine, small branch trenches were leading off so we didn't have to walk into the middle of the road to offload. These terminated in small pits surrounded by a low wall and capped with a wooden lid. It looked a bit like an old-fashioned well, but without the bucket.

One of those was what we were connecting to our trench. I'd wanted to lay pipe, but pipes here were made of copper, and quite expensive. Not that I couldn't afford it, but I was worried about someone digging it up. So a covered trench lined with cut stone would have to do. I had been talking with an Alchemist about getting something to seal it with—they had a whole lot of compounds that they didn't keep in stock, but could make on demand.

Kyle moved on to placing and mortaring the cut stone we had bought. My sad contribution to the digging was completed, so I went to work on the other components.

My plumbing solution wasn't going to be for the masses, but that was a problem for the future. The actual toilet was going to be a Phantasmal Object, stabilized by a Spell Storing enchantment. I'd shown one to a Potter but he didn't think he could make it. For now—for me—this would have to do.

I'd ordered three tanks from a local Tinker—one for hot water, one for cold, and a smaller one for the toilet. All three were going to be filled by enchantment.

The hot tank would be heated by an enchantment as well. I wanted to use my Fire Gem for something, but a warming enchantment was more controllable, and less likely to start a fire.

My first enchantment was for the toilet, using Spell Store to manually trigger Water Stream for a volume calibrated to the size of the tank. We'd have to trigger the enchantment to fill the tank, then pull the plunger to flush it.

I was going to do the same arrangement for the main water tank, but . . .

> **You have crafted a Water Fountain – Quality: Good. You have earned 125 XP.**
> **[Enchanting] Level 3 acquired through use.**
> **For gaining a skill level, you have been awarded 1 XP.**

It was kind of irritating to think that doing one more Enchantment back in Anchorbury would have given me this, but I would take it.

> **[Sense Liquid] rune purchased for 2 points.**
> **[NOT] rune purchased for 1 point.**
> **[Freeze] rune purchased for 2 points.**

I'd been waiting for the skill to go up, so I didn't need a lot of time to consider what to purchase. Now the next enchantment could be triggered whenever it didn't detect water. Back in Anchorbury, I would have had to include a mana storing circuit, but here there was enough mana to power the enchantment continuously.

> **You have crafted an Endless Water Fountain – Quality: Great. You have earned 320 XP.**

I got distracted by the notification—that wasn't a bad XP reward! It seemed to have gone up significantly with the improved quality level. I checked my logs, and my effect total had been 52 for that enchantment. Average was effect level twenty, and Good was thirty, so my best guess for the next stage was probably eighty? I should be able to reach that with another two skill levels.

I returned my attention to the actual enchantment, now pouring water into a small pot I'd prepared. Theoretically, this spell would keep producing water until the world was drowned, but at such a slow rate that eventually evaporation would outstrip production. Assuming it didn't fall into a puddle of its own making. It did make me wonder where it all came from.

Eh, magic, not my problem.

I'd spent a couple of hours on these two enchantments, so it was time for lunch, and then training. I popped my endless water generator into the pot and headed out.

"Are you ready?" Felicia asked. When I nodded, she came at me with her staff. The two of us were fairly well matched. Neither of us could beat the other's defense total by enough to get through the other's armor—as long as I didn't use my enchanted daggers, anyway.

So we could fight as hard as we liked, knowing that injury wasn't a real possibility. Kyle watched over us, calling out tips and encouragement. This wasn't as good as the real thing—you got more skill experience when you were stressed and afraid for your life. Successful blows still hurt, though, so going at each other hammer and tongs built up a certain amount of stress.

Even so, by end of a gruelling, exhausting session, I still hadn't improved.

"It gets harder after level three," Kyle said when I complained. "And harder still as you go on. Even so, you should be able to get level four in Dodge and Dagger before we go on another expedition."

"What about Felicia?" I asked. She already had fours in those.

"Probably not?" he hazarded. "It takes about a year of normal use to get a skill to five."

"That long?" I groaned. I wanted everything now, dammit!

"Maybe less, depending on danger, of course," he said, amused by my petulance. "I hear a lot of noble families put their kids through hell, just to get them decent skills quickly."

"Aubert sort of said something about that," I said thoughtfully. "Like, punishment for failing?"

"Like whipped until you can't stand for failing," Kyle said, his face losing its smile. "Then healed back up again for the next day—trains your Body Development."

"Je—Phadan's mercy!" I exclaimed, switching to one of the local swears at the last minute. I needed to practice that. "Do they all do that?"

"I don't know—it was just a story my parents told me," he said. "My family doesn't have the best opinion of nobles."

"That's an understatement," Felicia chimed in, getting up off the floor. She'd run out of Stamina before me—she may have had a higher skill, but her Strength was letting her down. "Are we done? It's Kandis's turn to cook."

I'd been worried we wouldn't get it done before the next dungeon trip, but by some miracle, here we were. We crowded around the door to the toilet, encased in the small room we'd walled off from the newly constructed bathroom. That had been a stretch for these guys—when you didn't have plumbing, you just set your bath up wherever it was convenient. Now we had a dedicated bathroom. Walling off the toilet was less controversial— as long as it was going to be inside, they wanted it as separated as possible from everything else.

The plumbing had been tested for the bath, but this was the real test. A leak here could have disastrous consequences. We were listening to the gurgle as the water tank filled for the first time.

"Well, here goes nothing," I said and pulled the string that opened the valve. Something I'd long taken for granted, but then thought I'd never see again, happened. The toilet flushed.

Felicia had lost the toss and soon came in from outside. "The water came out," she said. "I guess that means it's working?"

"Probably," I said. "We might get some leakage somewhere, and we'll have to see if it gets blocked at any point, but for now . . ." I started shooing them out of the room. "If you'll excuse me for a moment, I need to pee."

Name: Kandis Hammond	Profession: Phantasmal Artificer	
Level: 4		[Unspent Ability Points]: 5
Age: 24		[Unspent Skill Points]: 2
Abilities	[HP]: 360/360 [Stamina]: 480/480 [Mana]: 800/800	
[Strength]: 3 [Agility]: 3 [Finesse]: 4 [Soul]: 3 [Intelligence]: 5 [Charisma] : 10		[Unspent Development Points]: 0 [Unspent Spell Levels]: 0 [Unspent Rune Levels]: 0

Skills		
[Body Dev.]: 3 [Stamina Dev.]: 4 [Perception]: 3 [Identify]: 4 [Scribe]: 3 [Calculate]: 4 [Mana Sense]: 3 [Mana Dev.]: 4 (5) [Illusion Magic]: 4 (7) [Water Magic]: 2 [Creativity]: 2	[Disguise]: 2 [Deceive]: 2 (5) [Charm]: 3 (4) [Conversation]: 4 (6) [Intimidate]: 2 (3) [Intrigue]: 2 (3) [Persuasion]: 3 (4) [Dodge]: 4 [Jump]: 2 [Climb]: 2 [Run]: 3	[Memorize]: 3 [Teach]: 3 [Enchanting]: 3 [Adv. Math.]: 2 [Sing]: 2 [Stealth]: 3 [Research]: 2 [Cook]: 3 [WM: Dagger]: 4 (5) [WM: Triggered]: 2

Unlocked Skills

[WM: Axe] [Thrown] [Hunt] [Gather] [Craft (Smithing)] [Craft (Tinker)]

Traits

[Worldwalker]: Level prerequisites for professions are overridden. +1 bonus to all stats.

[Gift of Tongues]: All languages are understood.

[Female]: +1 bonus to Charisma.

[Silent Casting]: Allows you to cast spells without a chant.

[Subtle Casting]: Allows you to cast spells without gestures.

[Disease Resistance]: You are more resistant to diseases of all types (upgradeable).

Spells Known

[Static Image] [Light] [Unseen Sound] [Simple Invisibility] [Disguise] [Conceal Mana] [Greater Invisibility] [Improved Blind] [Dispel Image] [Phantasmal Object] [Phantom World] [Water Stream] [Water Ball] [Water Walk]

Runes Known

[Cool] [Heat] [Effect: Touch] [Constant Effect] [Sense (Temperature)] [Trigger] [Accept Energy] [Sharpness] [Target Self] [Generate (Fire)] [Target (Cone Projection)] [Undead Bane] [Gather Energy] [Sense (Touch)] [Spell Storing] [Sense Liquid] [NOT] [Freeze]

CHAMPION

"A little higher, right about . . . there," I said. Cutter sliced according to my instructions. He had Hunt, but my Sense Mana could tell where the mana stone was, making the process a lot quicker. Shortly thereafter, he successfully pulled out the stone.

"Just where you said, Miss Kandis!" He proudly showed me his prize.

"Good work," I said, "Now there's just five more to go." I looked around with some disgust at the grub-hog corpses. Cutter had killed them all, with a little help from Greater Invisibility. Cloridan and I had taken him for a trip in the forest, looking for monsters to train against. The XP wasn't great split three ways—even though Cloridan had stayed out of it, he apparently wasn't far enough away to not be counted as a team member. Felicia and Kyle were looking after the house.

Eventually, I'd be able to take Cutter out here by myself, but right now there was too high a chance of us getting lost. I pointed out the cores as he cut into the disgusting mutant pigs. I didn't think we were getting anything else out of these.

"All done!" I called out when he was finished. Cloridan popped out of the woods a few seconds later. He glanced over at the corpses and frowned.

"You're not taking the tusks?" he asked.

I carefully didn't look. I already knew that each corpse had four wicked looking six-inch tusks. "I don't remember them as an alchemical ingredient?"

He laughed. "They're made of ivory, Kandis; it's valuable without going into a potion."

"Oh, right," I said. With a shrug, Cutter went back to the first corpse.

"Actually, wait up, there's something I've been meaning to tell you two. As long as we're alone out here," I said to Cloridan.

"As far as I can tell," he said curiously. Cutter just shrugged and came over to stand next to Cloridan.

"OK, well," I said awkwardly. "This is hard to say, but . . . I'm not from this world. I'm a Worldwalker."

"You're a Champion?" Cloridan asked incredulously. Cutter punched him lightly in the side.

"I told you she was special!" he exclaimed.

"Yeah, kid, we all felt it," Cloridan dismissed. "Actually, I don't know why I'm surprised. You never expect to meet one, but we know they've been summoned, so it's not really a stretch."

"I'd thought that the toilet was going to be a bit of a giveaway," I said wryly.

"We do *know* about plumbing," Cloridan shot back. "It was common back in the Empire—that's why Anchorbury's got sewers in the first place. I figured at the time that it had survived a bit better wherever you grew up. So which god are you a Champion for?"

"I don't know," I admitted. Cloridan gave me a skeptical look. "No, really! I haven't been contacted by a god or anything like that. I just woke up on this world and have been trying to get by ever since."

"What's it like, being a Champion?" Cutter interjected. "Do you get special powers?"

"Not really," I said. "I can understand any language, and I don't get level restrictions for professions. I'm actually a Phantasmal Artificer even though I'm just level four."

Both of them got blank looks while they checked the System for what that was. After a moment, Cloridan whistled appreciatively.

"So that's where those Phantasms are coming from," he said. "Oh, and Enchanting, Teaching, both unlocked. You don't have a patron at all, you just learned it all from the Status!"

"Guilty as charged," I said.

"You really don't know which god picked you?" Cloridan asked. I just nodded. "Have you talked to any of the churches?"

"I've been more concerned with staying under—er, keeping quiet about my status. I'm worried that whichever church lays a claim on me will want me to work for them."

"I'm sure they'd like to," Cloridan mused. "But in the stories, it's generally the other way around. You'll probably see when the Paladin gets—oh, that's why you were telling us now."

"I was planning on telling you both, but that's put a time limit on me, yeah."

Cutter didn't understand, so Cloridan filled him in. "We were probably going to figure it out if Kandis started talking in strange languages to the other Champion."

"Oh, right . . . are you going to fight the other Champion? You'd win, I bet!" Cutter started punching the air at the thought.

"I don't know about . . . either of those things," I said. "From what I've read, it could go either way right?"

"True enough," Cloridan said. "Generally, you clash when your gods want different things, which is pretty common. But you haven't even found out who your god is . . . and it doesn't sound like you want to?"

"I don't see why I should do the bidding of the entity that kidnapped me," I said dourly. "Maybe they can make me an offer when they deign to show up, but right now they can pound sand."

"Right . . ." Cloridan said carefully, glancing up at the sky. "Well just remember that they *can* take offense. For mortals, it's generally safest to just do whatever they want."

"I thought they didn't intervene in mortal affairs anymore?" I said.

"They *don't*, but that doesn't mean they *can't*. No one knows the rules, but they seem to be different for Champions—I'd be really surprised if a god doesn't show up for you sooner or later. You really should check out a few churches, though; you might get some answers."

"Not all of them are represented here, are they?"

"You don't know?" He sighed. "In your position, you should always check what temples exist in the town you're going to stay in. This town has temples to Tondeni, Phadan, Naldyna, Toriao and Duit."

"Duit is the Life one, right? We can eliminate that one."

"Sure. You might want to watch out for the priests of Toriao and Tondeni."

"More than the others?"

"Well, Clerics of Tondeni can see through illusions." He laughed at my panicked look. "And Toriao is the God of Knowledge, so her Clerics have an Identify that works on people."

"That's nasty!" I said. "Do they all have powers like that?"

"Oh yeah, you can look them up in the Status if you like. For now, let's get these tusks in the bag and then head back. Do you remember the way back?"

"Hmm." I considered, "If we were to retrace our steps, we'd go in *that* direction." I pointed. "But I think the town is actually that way."

"Not bad," Cloridan said, adjusting my arm about twenty degrees. "Keep working on it." He went to help Cutter with the tusks, leaving me to keep watch on them.

Coming back into town, we found the streets strangely empty. Frowning, I backtracked to the gate guards.

"Is something going on?"

The guard scowled. "Word is the Paladin's arriving at the south gate, and we're stuck here."

"The south gate? Not the river?" Cloridan asked.

"That's what they said," the man said, shrugging. "Either way, I'm not getting to see it."

"Don't sweat it," Cloridan said. "I'm sure you'll meet a Champion sooner or later." Thankfully, he managed to keep his smirk hidden until we'd moved away.

"Cute," I said, glowering at him. "I hope you don't plan on using that joke on everyone from now on."

"Cute? I think that counts as an upgrade," he said, openly smirking now. "I shall treasure it. Shall we go and see what's going on?"

The south gate was actually on the other side of the river, another small—I think the term was "postern"—gate. Hardly anyone came through it. The wall that separated the river from the main city was actually open to the public—when there wasn't an alert on—and as we drew closer, we could see a crowd had gathered on the wall to look over to the other side. From the looks of it, the Paladin had not yet made their appearance.

Not wanting to be too close to the action, we decided to head up and spectate from the wall. Once there, we could see a larger crowd had gathered near the docks. There seemed to be some action on the other side of the riverbank.

"Are those horses?" I asked. They were a fairly rare sight in Talnier—they made a tempting meal for large flying carnivorous creatures. But it appeared there were people trying to load more than a dozen of them into boats.

"Looks like," Cloridan said. "Do you think that's the Paladin?" He pointed, and I could see a small figure in full plate-mail. The others seemed to be deferring to it, so I thought he might be right.

It looked as if the Paladin had come with a full entourage—too many to ferry across in one hit—so they were making several trips. The first lot was already across, forming a perimeter to keep the crowd back. The horses were going across now—they had three boats, but they could only hold two or three each, so there would be a few trips.

As we watched, the whole thing became more organized. Some town guards showed up—well, more town guards—and the crowd below was encouraged back into the main town area. The townsfolk streaming in started taking up positions along the main street, and it started to look as if they were going to hold an old-fashioned parade into the center of town.

Up here on the wall, we would have a pretty good view, so we staked out a position close to the road and waited.

It actually started with a fanfare.

"What the hell? Were they carrying horns all the way here?" I asked. It was rhetorical, but Cloridan answered me anyway.

"Horns for signaling are a must for any large-scale combat formation," he said quietly. As he spoke, the first of the marchers came into view. Most of the formation was on foot; the first two were in some sort of uniform and were the ones blowing the horns. Behind them were about ten people who looked much less uniform. They were all armed and armored differently, though they all had a white and gold tabard thrown over whatever they were wearing.

Then came six knights on horseback. At least I assumed that's what they were. Wearing identical mixed chain and plate, they wore the same tabards as the others. In the middle of those was the one who had to be the Paladin. She—I could clearly see her now—was riding a horse and wearing the shiny plate-mail that I'd seen before.

[Identification]: Armor of Life – Quality: Divine – Properties: [Restricted]

What the fuck? *Divine* quality?

"That's what you can get when you accept the help of your deity," Cloridan murmured in my ear, evidently having Identified the armor as well.

"Does 'divine' mean it was actually crafted by the gods?" I asked.

"No . . . not necessarily. It's just the step beyond 'Perfect.'"

So, two levels higher than my best equipment. "And she just gets it for free? Wait." My surprise had made me forget the real reason I was here. I composed my message and sent it with Unseen Sound.

"If you can understand this, I think you know what it means," I sent—in English. She jerked and stopped her horse, looking wildly about for whoever was talking.

Whoops. I hadn't meant to crash the parade. The soldiers behind her seemed fairly well trained, no one fell over or anything, but they milled around while the rest of my message continued.

"I can't hear you over the crowd, but if you can get away from your entourage, I'll meet you at the Fisted Fish at noon tomorrow. If you *can't*—well, I'll try again."

She nodded, either a gesture to me or just to herself, and started moving again. After a moment of confusion, the parade started moving on.

I sighed to myself and watched them go. I wasn't sure what I was starting, but it was something. As the marchers cleared out of the way, my attention was drawn to a tall man standing on the sidelines. A tall man that I recognized. Just as I was about to back off out of sight, Tom Parkes looked up and met my eyes. He smiled and gave a little bow, and then moved off, following after the procession.

Oh, fuck.

ÍSÍDRE

"Do you think she'll show?" Kyle asked. Cloridan rolled his eyes.

"How many times you gonna ask that?" he replied. The boys were normally better at conversation than just repeating the same exchange, but they were being thrown off by my invisible presence. They were here to occupy the remaining seats at the table, to make sure that no one came and tried to sit on me.

I could have taken part in the conversation, but when I had my Phantasmal Entity speak for me, they got confused and awkward, not knowing where to address their remarks. Actually . . .

"Since we've got some time," I had her say, "would you mind telling me about the Seduction skill? Does it give you notifications when someone is using it on you?"

"And why would you be—" Cloridan started in his bedroom voice, only to cut himself off, looking away from the doll, and over to where I wasn't. The doll just smiled innocently. "Did you wait until now to ask that question, so I'd feel awkward while talking about Seduction?"

"Absolutely not," the doll said. It looked nothing like me but was attractive enough, with tanned skin, green eyes, and brown hair. "It's a complete coincidence."

Cloridan snorted in disbelief, but he did answer the question. "Seduction is like Charm; it affects your own actions to influence people. Only it makes you . . . attractive, instead of liked."

"So it doesn't have the . . . pressure that Intimidate and Persuasion have, then?"

"Guys can feel plenty of pressure . . ." he muttered. "As for notifications, you don't get those from skill use, you get those from Social Contests.

Pretty much any skill can be used—given the right conditions—to win one of those."

"Not just Social skills?"

"If you initiate combat with the other participant, the Contest gets cancelled, but aside from that, whatever works. You can even stab someone else if that helps the situation."

"Wait . . . I thought that Social Contests were when you fought with Social skills, but it can be anything? What causes the System to recognize one, then?"

"What matters is the stake," Cloridan informed me. "Something that you both want, or some decision that gets made. You have to want it—or not want it—really strongly."

I made my doll display a confused look. He sighed and continued. "Take Seduction as an example, since you asked about it. If you meet a guy at a bar and he uses Seduction on you, and you take him home, you probably don't trigger a Social Contest."

The doll looked at him with narrowed eyes.

"*Unless,*" he continued, "you *really* didn't want to sleep with him before he started for some reason. Like you hated him, or you were at the bar to meet someone or something. Doesn't matter. In which case you'd start a Contest, and you'd get a losing notification at the moment you decided 'what the heck' and agreed to take him home."

"Wouldn't that change my mind, getting the notification?"

"Probably, but you'd have lost the interaction at that point, you wouldn't be able to do anything about it until the next day."

"Ew," I said. "That's pretty rapey."

He shrugged, "Well obviously the *decent* thing to do in that situation is to say, 'Sorry, I didn't realize you felt so strongly about it,' and waive the penalty."

"Not everyone does that, though, do they—"

"Sorry to interrupt," Kyle said, "but someone's come in."

I looked over and immediately saw the person he was talking about. People had been coming into the tavern all this time, of course, but given it wasn't actually raining, people in hooded cloaks were much rarer. *Just like every fantasy cliché,* I thought. *Classic for a reason.* It wasn't a *great* disguise, but she hardly needed one. Hardly anyone would know her face behind the helmet, and she hardly cared if people were suspicious of her.

Some of us needed to make more of an effort. I had my doll get up and move over to her table. I followed, carefully. It took a lot of concentration to move the doll realistically, even with the help of a skill.

"Greetings from Earth," I said quietly in English. I wasn't sure if she was from an English speaking part of the world, or even from Earth, but it didn't matter. Worldwalker meant that she would understand.

"You're—" She stopped herself and gestured for me to sit. I had the doll do so, standing close behind her. This was actually the trickiest bit, if you didn't count the actual conversation.

This would have been so much easier with Phantasmal Emissary, I complained to myself. Away from my table, I didn't have the boys to stand on either side of me and prevent passersby from colliding with me. I got the feeling, though, that this conversation would be too quiet for me to eavesdrop from there.

"You're really a Worldwalker?" she asked in . . . Spanish, I think. She was looking me up and down in disbelief. She let down her hood, revealing a pleasant looking face with tanned skin and brown eyes.

"Kandis Hammond, Sydney, Australia," I said. I knew what was bothering her, but I waited to see if she would bring it up.

"Isidre Tamayo, Puerto Barrios, Guatemala," she returned, and we both paused to think about that.

"Both from Earth, then? Did your world recently have Trump as President of the United States?" I asked.

She scowled. "That cabrón. He's gone; it is the old man now."

"Biden," I said.

She nodded. "Why is this a question?"

"We're both from Earth, but they might be different Earths," I said. She gave me a puzzled look. "Different—like this world and Earth are different, but less so."

"Ah, so we would have different presidents . . . I see. Sydney, Australia . . ." She gave me a considering look. "You are rich, then?"

I shrugged. "Probably by Guatemalan standards, yeah. Does that matter now?"

"Probably not," she admitted. "I came with nothing, as did you?"

"Yeah, not a stitch. Have you met any of the others?"

"No, although I did hear that the Champion of Storms is on this landmass."

We paused at this point to be served our drinks. I did order one—the doll could actually drink, and eat foods soft enough to be swallowed unchewed. Whatever it ate just stayed in the stomach until the spell was dismissed, so there was little point to it, other than to hide the fact that the doll was an illusion.

After the waitress had gone, the exchange resumed. "What god do you serve?" she asked.

"None," I said. She raised her eyebrows.

"If you're actually asking what god kidnapped me and supposedly made me their Champion, the answer is I don't know." I clarified. "But if they think I'm going to 'serve' them whenever they deign to show up, they've got another think coming."

My answer dismayed her. "I hadn't thought of it as a kidnapping," she said. "Here or back home, it is surely a great honor to be chosen by God."

"I can't say I agree," I replied. "Maybe they've got a deal in mind, or maybe they're just going to threaten me, but for now—I'm a free agent."

"I suppose . . . that is good news. From what I've heard, the gods oppose each other more often than not."

"Are you on a divine mission then?"

"No," she said, and blushed. "Putting it that way sounds embarrassing, but I have not been contacted by Duit, either."

"Then how . . ."

"She had spoken to his priests before I arrived. They were waiting for me when I came down from the mountains. They aren't sure when exactly, but they think he will speak to me when my strength has improved."

"I suppose that means your level. Are you level four?"

She visibly considered whether or not to tell me for a moment. "Yes. Are you?"

"Oh yes," I said easily.

She frowned. "That's difficult for me to believe," she said. Was that Charm preventing her from calling me a liar?

I knew why she doubted me. This body was realistic enough, but it was so very unremarkable.

You couldn't exactly tell someone's level or stats by looking at them, but there was . . . a certain *something* that you could detect from someone whose level was different from yours. This doll had none of that. She was physically attractive, but she had no Charisma, no level, not even skills. Charm could still inform me of what words to speak, but I couldn't let it control the doll's expression and manner directly.

Even under Disguise as a less attractive person, I'd turned heads because my Charisma had shone through. Now it was hidden. It did put me at a disadvantage, but there were compensations.

"I'm in disguise," I said. "The next time we meet, I probably won't look like this."

"Why—no, how?"

"Magic," I said. "As to why, I'm keeping a low profile—so I'd appreciate it if you kept my existence to yourself."

She nodded. "I thought that would be the case when you wanted to meet secretly—it makes sense if you've not accepted the protection of your god."

I grimaced at the way she said that, but I kept my doll's expression neutral. "So what brings you to Talnier?"

"Griffins," she said, her eyes shining. "I want to outfit as many of my company as possible and become flying cavalry."

"That sounds like it will take a lot of resources," I said uncertainly.

"Yes, but the Church is willing to support us. And I also have some backing from the King."

"Wow, you've been . . . busy."

"Not me . . . my communications have been handled by the Church. The suggestion actually came from the King in the first place."

"What suggestion?"

"The King would like to extend the borders of civilized lands north-wards from here. If my company can provide protection, he will send Theurges to drain the forest of mana and allow for human occupation."

"Wait," I said, confused. "You're only level four and you're going to do what the King can't?"

"I'm only level four for now," she said firmly. "I have no intention of staying so low. Nor will my company—they're inspired by the thought of following a Champion."

I frowned. Was this plan feasible? She did have significant funding, after all, and it didn't seem that she was short of volunteers. *Not my problem*, I decided.

"It's going to mean a lot of killing, though," I mused. "How does that square with serving the God of Life?"

"A common misunderstanding," she said, leaning forward. I saw what looked like Persuasion in her eyes, but of course, she was directing it at the wrong target. "You're mistaking Duit for Naldyna—Duit isn't about the endless struggle of Nature; she is about *our* lives."

"Humans?" I asked.

"Sentients," she corrected me. "She is about development, improvement, making *life* better. For everyone. Hold on." She held up her hand and looked over my shoulder. It might have looked suspicious if my puppet turned to look, but invisible me could turn around without issue.

Shit, of course he showed up. It was Tom, Mister Parkes, looking over at us. He paused, clearly seeing that he'd been noticed, and then sauntered over.

"Recruiting?" he said familiarly. Isidre looked at him coldly.

"If you want to sign up, they're doing interviews at the church," she said.

"I know," he said, pulling up a chair uninvited. "But I really wanted a chance to talk with you without all your minders."

"This is not that opportunity; this is a private conversation," Isidre told him. He grinned unconcernedly.

"Well, I figure that *not* informing the room of your identity is worth at least a few moments of your time."

Isidre frowned, clearly torn about what to do.

"Isidre," I said, my puppet leaning forward to put a hand on hers. "It's fine; we were pretty much finished anyway. I'll contact you again."

"Are you sure?" she asked, and I nodded.

"And who might you be, young lady?" Tom said.

"None of your business," I replied, and walked out the door. Hopefully, the boys would refrain from rushing out after me, as that might attract Tom's attention.

I guess I'm never using this disguise again.

INFORMANTS

I pushed the money across the table. Half as much as he'd asked.

"Are you kidding me?" The man across from us was small and wiry, but that really didn't mean anything in this world. His unwashed clothes and nervous demeanor were more of a tell, but I knew better than to judge him on that alone. You never really knew what someone was capable of until they tried something. Of course, that was just as true for me.

"Don't mistake me for a fool, just because I'm new around here," I said calmly. I was wearing my regular face. I'd needed an escort—a visible one—to come here, and my only disguise spell was still Disguise Self. Anyone who saw Cloridan here would be able to track him back to me.

Of course, this was a perfectly legitimate deal, so it didn't really matter who saw me make it. Cloridan's contacts had been five years out of date, but that didn't mean they were useless. The ones who were still around had known whom we'd need to talk to, to find out what we wanted to know.

"Listen, I don't need to be insulted like this," he tried, but the way his eyes kept looking at the gold was as good as a written statement to me. He tried blustering for more, but his Intimidate wasn't high enough. With my Charisma, I could just ignore his attempt, as this wasn't a Social Contest. This was a Bargain, and I already had the better end of the deal.

"Finished?" I asked. "Then take the money and start talking."

"Fine," he said and swept the money off the table. "Fucking adventurers," he said in a much softer voice. I chose not to call him on it. If he didn't want to advance by risking his life or taking up a trade, it wasn't my problem.

"Where to start . . ." he muttered. "Well, for one, the Fangs aren't ganking adventurers coming back anymore. They've moved on to a protection racket."

"What? How?" Cloridan asked. "How are they even showing their faces in town?"

Marlon—that was his name—spat on the floor. "They've got the Baron's backing; they can do whatever they want."

"I think I need some context here," I interjected.

"Your boyfriend didn't tell you?" Marlon asked sardonically. "Well, let me fill you in. Five years ago, before he cut and ran, the Fangs were a group that ambushed adventurers coming back from one of the dungeons."

"Not every group," Cloridan said, "Just the ones that came out half dead. They . . . didn't leave survivors."

"Nah, they were careful, and vicious. Took a long time before anyone realized what they were up to. Everyone thought the victims were lost in the dungeon. It wasn't until some . . . identifiable items showed up on the Market that they started to suspect."

"They had some sort of hideout, out there. Everyone searched, but we couldn't find it."

"Yeah, it was a whole thing. The Adventurers Guild got all worked up about it." Marlon gave Cloridan a careful look. "They never did find whoever was passing on information to the gang."

Cloridan scowled and started to say something, but I talked over him. "Moving on—how *did* it end?"

Marlon kept looking at Cloridan, but he didn't say anything; he just glared. "Well, the Baron sorted it. Exactly how, no one really knows, but my money is that he found the hideout."

"How?" I asked.

"Well, he didn't have to deal with a leaker, see," Marlon explained. "I'm not really sure *what* he did, but I reckon he hired some high-level mercenaries to search the woods and report back *only* to him."

"Just find them?"

"Aye. That was the hard part. Once he'd found them, all he had to do was threaten to give them to the adventurers. Maybe there was something more—money, or some leaders that needed killing. The Fangs don't talk about it."

"So he brought them into town, and had them serve as his . . . secret assassin squad?"

"The Guild would never have stood for this," Cloridan objected.

"What can they do? If they went after the Fangs, they'd be done for murder. Some did, and got kicked out for it. They complained up the line, but it never went anywhere. The Baron had solved the problem that they'd failed at, after all."

"That's pretty cold. Stopped the crime by hiring the criminals?"

"The murders stopped, at least. Now they just collect a tax."

"How's that work, then?" I asked. No one at the Guild had mentioned a tax specific to adventurers.

"It's not out in the open. What'll happen is that they'll give you a few trips to settle in, then if no one's clued you in, you'll have a little 'accident' out there."

"I get it . . . when you complain or talk about it at the Guild, that's when someone lets you know what's going on." I was starting to get pissed off. If this was condoned by the Baron—no, he was surely getting a cut from this.

"Yeah, there's a house on the south side—"

"Probably the one we tracked those watchers to," Cloridan said sourly.

Marlon looked at him. "I wanna say those guys are sloppy, letting themselves get followed home, but the truth is, they want people knowing where that house is."

"After all, we need to know where to deliver the cash," I chimed in.

"Yeah, they've still got their *real* hideout out in the woods." Marlon paused, gauging Cloridan's reaction to all this. Cloridan didn't give him anything to work with, shutting down his expression and draining his glass.

"So, anyway," Marlon continued. "The Fangs are the top gang around here these days. Aside from the tax, they keep themselves busy with the regular shit—drugs, muggings, and break-ins. They just keep it down to an 'acceptable' level."

"What about the other gangs?" Cloridan asked.

"Tauk's crew got hit pretty bad," Marlon answered. "When there's a fight and only one side gets arrested, it doesn't go well for you long-term. They're still around, but they keep their heads down."

"I noticed Al's people were still on the docks," Cloridan said.

"Yeah, Al saw what happened to Tauk and took steps. He made sure that any beef between them didn't leave any survivors for the guards to set free." Marlon's gaze drifted off for a moment, his face twisting as if recalling a particularly unpleasant memory.

"The Fangs retaliated, of course—it got pretty nasty for a while. Now they strictly leave each other alone."

Marlon continued educating us, passing on details about territories and known hangouts. I Memorized the details, but they didn't command my attention. Finally, Cloridan was satisfied and Marlon slipped away to spend his gold.

"Are you all right?" I asked Cloridan.

He sighed. "There's someone in the Fangs I wanted to kill five years ago—but I didn't even know who they were then. Now that they're openly in town . . . it's not like I'm in a position to take revenge, but it's resurfacing old memories."

"Shall we head back?"

"Yeah," he said. "This isn't a good place to get drunk."

Between the adventurers, the marketplace, and the criminals, I thought that I had a pretty good idea of how this town was run. I still hadn't tracked down where Talnier's Enchanter was operating from—shopkeepers around here were pretty tight-lipped about the source of their wares. There were still a few blind spots, though.

I wasn't too worried about the nobles. There were so few of them, and they tended to make waves. Five minutes after they stepped out of their tower, the marketplace was abuzz with rumors of what they were supposed to be up to. The griffin trainers were a more serious concern. They didn't interact much with the rest of the town. My impression was that they answered to the Baron, but they stayed out of the town—and of town business. Nevertheless, they were a significant force, should they choose to take action. It would be nice to know what would cause them to intervene.

There was still one place that I had yet to go to for information, though, and it happened to be in the middle of the largest blank spot remaining. It was time to get over my fears and take the plunge.

"Welcome, Seeker, to the Temple of Knowledge." The priest of Toriao would have been an unassuming and ordinary man, if you ignored his head tattoos. His bald head was half-covered by what looked like—but did not Identify as—runes.

"Uh, hello." There *was* a proper way to address priests, but my puppet of the day was a teenage looking boy named Ben. Whatever it takes to shift the profile, you know? I wanted an excuse to ask stupid questions, and there was nothing better for that than appearing to be young and somewhat stupid. I had him stammer his way through the introductions, while I observed the temple we were in.

The Temple of Knowledge was the second smallest temple in this town, but that wasn't because of a lack of wealth. All of the temples were well-built, rivalled only by the Baron's tower in the solidity of their construction. The Temples of Life and Death were larger because they were designed to hold congregations. The Temple of Nature had a large walled-in garden. *This* temple seemed to be mainly used to hold books.

Not that I was complaining. Once I got past the guards and the initial waiting room, the ambience was much more like a library than the church that I was expecting. A fairly sparsely stocked library by my standards, perhaps—there might have been a hundred books visible. I'd much rather talk to a librarian than a priest, and if this guy had some piercings to go with his tattoos, he'd have fit nicely in Kings Cross.

" . . . I would normally be addressed as Scholar Cantin, in recognition of my rank within the Church. Now, Ben, what brings you to this Temple?" the man finally asked.

"Well, uh, first off, is it true that you can identify people?"

"It is," Cantin said, smiling.

"What does mine say?"

"It says your name is Benjamin Bouchard, that your gender is male, that you are aged sixteen, and your profession is Swindler. Oh, and you're level three." He said this quickly and easily, and he repeated all the information I'd tried to put into the Phantasmal Entity. Thus far he hadn't acted as if he suspected Ben was an illusion, either, so unless he was a great actor, it looked as if this ruse was working.

I didn't have a particular need to fool this priest, but I did need to know if it was *possible*.

"Everyone's gotta make a living," I had Ben mutter, an offended look on his face.

"I'm not judging you; you wanted to know what it said," the priest said calmly.

"Do ya tell everyone what they want to know?"

"Would that we could," Scholar Cantin mused. "You have hit on the great challenge that besets our Order."

"Huh?"

"The Church exists to disseminate knowledge wherever it can," the priest started to explain. "But there are several impediments to that holy mission."

"Like what?" It probably wasn't in character for Ben to understand half those words, but Cantin didn't seem to have noticed.

"The established powers, of course. They don't want anyone climbing up the same ladders they did, so they do what they can to keep knowledge of them secret. In order for our sect to operate freely, we had to agree to keep some of those secrets."

He started pacing back and forth, getting into his topic. I'd somehow set him off on a tangent he clearly felt strongly about.

"Secrets like . . . what Wizards do with a Dungeon core?" I asked. I wasn't sure where this was going, but it was worth a try.

"Exactly!" he shouted. "Would you like me to tell you? Well, I can't." He scowled. "I don't know that secret, and if I did, I would be forbidden to share it."

"That's a shame . . ." I commiserated. "Still, I'm sure there's—"

"You know who does know?" he asked rhetorically. "The Duvost family!"

"Really? They're not wizards."

"No, but one of the last copies of the *Tome of Ascension* wound up in their library about thirty years ago. They just sat on it since then!"

What the hell? I thought to myself

"That's interesting," I said aloud.

WARDS

W ell, he didn't act that way at all towards me."

"You're fucking kidding me," I said. Felicia rolled her eyes.

"Honestly, Kandis, didn't you send me down there to talk to him for just that reason? You said you wanted to see if you'd been targeted by some secret message by your mystery patron, but now you don't believe me?"

"I don't *want* to believe you," I groaned. "You're sure he didn't rant at all about the secrets of the world?"

"I'm sure," she said firmly. "We had a very normal discussion about who the important people are in this town, and even when I brought up the topic, he just told me about the restrictions that they're under. It seems that *keeping* secrets is where they get most of their funding from."

"Fascinating," I said sourly. "Remind me to ask you about it when I'm not trying to figure out if God is telling me to rob Aubey."

"*A* god, *Lord* Duvost, and don't be crazy," Cloridan told me. "He's not a lordling anymore; he has guards, mercenaries, and who knows what else protecting him."

"He's not even going to be in Anchorbury right now, though." I pointed out.

"All those other things still are," he said patiently.

"So . . . you don't think this was a message from a God?"

"If it was, are you going to do what he says? You were pretty adamant before about not following any instructions."

"I guess." I sighed. "It's more like, I *want* to rob the guy, and this is telling me it's a good idea."

"Well, it's not. Invisibility won't get you past the wards."

"Wards?"

"Remember your next project? Enchanted alarms? There's no way that the House of Duvost hasn't sprung for them at some point. They probably do more than make a noise though."

"Does Invisibility not work on them?" I asked.

"Pretty sure it doesn't, or we'd hear a lot more about invisible thieves."

"So how do you get past wards?" I asked.

"You don't," he said. "They're basically like the magical traps in the dungeons—you generally can't disable them, so you have to hope that you can go around or survive them."

"There must be some way . . ." I cajoled.

"Maybe you could ask our resident Enchanter," he said wryly.

"Haha." I stuck out my tongue. "I don't have the runes I'd need to investigate, and the shopkeep at the Enchanter's Staff has been very standoffish."

I was starting to suspect the guy knew that I had Enchanting. He'd refused to let me examine his wares, which was a pain. He wasn't the only place that sold Enchanted goods, but he was the only one that seemed to have a lead on the mysterious Enchanter. Everyone else just sold the hand-me-downs from adventurers. They had some nice pieces, but nothing I hadn't already copied the runes of.

"I'm sure he'd be happier if you bought something," Cloridan suggested.

"Kyle *is* due an armor upgrade," I mused. "We all are, actually. I still haven't seen any enchanted robes, though."

"That's always nice," Cloridan agreed, "But you could always ask about getting some wards for here."

"Huh. Anything else obvious that I've forgotten?"

"Well, you could check if any of the books in the Temple are about runecraft."

"So I'm looking to get some wards for my home," I said. The Temple had not, unfortunately, had any rune books.

The shopkeeper looked at me suspiciously, which I was starting to think was his normal mode of thinking. At least where I was concerned.

"What sort of wards?"

"What sorts are available? What are you using for this place?" I asked. Suddenly I realized that his security wards were probably inscribed some-where on the inside of this room. Most likely over the door.

I thought he might have come to the same realization—at the same moment—because his face just froze. It would have been rude to turn around and look, so I didn't. We both just stood there awkwardly for a second, before he responded.

"That's a secret!" he exclaimed.

I raised an eyebrow. "Sure, then perhaps you can just go over what kind of protection is available."

I thought this was a reasonable request, but it seemed to agitate him further.

"Well, there's . . . or . . . with . . ." he stammered. I took a glance around the front of the room, just in case his protection runes were visible there. They weren't, so I slowly started turning around.

"You'd need to consult!" he blurted out. "With the Enchanter!"

"Sounds great; is he in the back?"

He laughed nervously. "No, he's . . . out of town. Come back in three days; I'll have word for you, whether he'll see you or not."

"As you wish," I said, and turned to go. As I turned away, I saw him wince, but my attention was elsewhere.

[Identification]: Sense (Person) Rune – Quality: Great

Gotcha.

There had been a dozen runes written over the door, but I'd only had time to Identify one as I'd left. I'd memorized the whole formation, but you can't use Identify on a memory, apparently. I could Research it, but only if I knew what it was first. I'd started at the center of the formation, which turned out to be Sense (Person), so I guess I'd gotten lucky.

While I was making my test amulet, the others were preparing for another dungeon expedition. After some discussion, we'd sent Kyle to pay our "insurance" to the Fangs. I didn't want to, and Cloridan *really* didn't want to, but we all knew it was better to seem compliant for now. None of us wanted to find out what having an "accident" entailed.

As I enchanted the amulet, I learned that Sense (Person) could be set to detect either a list of people or everyone except for that list. The people needed to be present (within the range of detection) when you enchanted the item.

Since it was a test, I put everyone present on the exception list. Kyle was absent, so when he came back, we could test it. I linked the detector to a simple Light spell so we could tell when it was triggered.

Before we left for the dungeon, I had determined that none of my illusion spells could stop the rune from detecting someone. I had high hopes for Conceal Mana, but it didn't work either.

The other thing I learned was that there was a mana field that defined the detection range.

"Is there a rune that does the opposite?" Felicia asked. We were brainstorming solutions as we moved through the forest. Like last time, Felicia, Kyle and I were moving in a group, while Cloridan scouted ahead.

"I don't think so," I replied, after searching through the available options. "Not based on the names, at least. The only one with Mana in the name is Sense Mana."

"How does that work?" Kyle asked, "If it has a mana field out, won't it detect itself?"

"I'm not sure," I mused. "Maybe it's different types of mana?" I was slowly coming around to the idea that there were different types.

"You mean like ice and fire mana?" Felicia asked, puzzled. "Would that work?"

"No, it's more like . . ." I quickly conjured a Phantasmal Object—a tennis ball—and passed it to Kyle. "Can you see the mana conduit to the ball?"

"No," Felicia said, blinking at the ball. I stared at her for a second before realizing my mistake.

"Right," I said and cancelled Conceal Mana. "*Now* can you see it?"

"Oh yes!" she exclaimed. "It's like a thin thread."

"Yeah, so I think this is like a pipe to carry mana to my spell," I said. "But, it's made of mana. I think it's a different type of mana from the stuff that's flowing through it."

"Because it acts differently," Felicia agreed. "It's more solid than regular mana."

"Yeah. Check this out," I said. The conduit was coming out of my left palm, and I made as if to grab it with my right. I didn't feel anything, but the conduit itself moved as if my hand was affecting it. I stretched the conduit to one side, and then . . .

"That was weird," Felicia said. "I didn't see what happened, but it's outside of your hand now."

"Try it," I suggested, and she too grasped at the strand. Once again it slipped out of her grasp.

"I don't *think* it's going through my hand," she said, "but I don't know what it is doing." She and I both. It was hard to look at something that didn't make sense as aggressively as that did. If I had to guess, I'd say that higher dimensions were involved, but that didn't really match with what I was seeing, unless . . . did Sense Mana extend sight into additional dimensions? That would be freaky.

"It's doing something strange," I agreed. "So anyway, getting back to the subject, I think this is one type of mana, the mana we absorb is another type, and the mana field is a third type."

"Is the mana your spells are made of a fourth type?" Felicia speculated.

"Maybe, but I'm inclined to think it's the first type. The conduits are made by the spell after all; it makes sense that it would only use one type."

We continued discussing the matter all the way to the dungeon. "Hold up," I said as we approached the entrance. "I want to check something."

I focused Sense Mana, and it was faint, but there, the same kind of field that I'd seen from my rune. Rather than a smooth wall as I had generated, it seemed to emanate from the walls of the entrance, only a few centimeters from the stones at the front, but quickly extending further as you went in. A few meters from daylight, the fields seemed to merge.

[Sense Mana] Level 4 acquired through use.
For gaining a skill level, you have been awarded 1 XP.

Yay. "It looks like the dungeon is aware of us almost as soon as we step inside," I said.

"I wonder if there's a different field for each door? Or does it all get controlled by the dungeon?"

"We can check, I guess." I looked around at the group, now assembled. "Everybody ready? Then let's get to it. Cloridan, you're on point."

ENCHANTER

How'd it go?" Cutter asked excitedly. It wasn't really fair to leave the kid cooped up looking after the house while we were gone, but I wasn't taking him into the dungeon with me. So far, he had been taking it with some grace.

"Urghh," I said with all the eloquence I could muster. The others trooped in behind me, equally tired as I slumped onto the nearest chair. "We got the level two boss . . . Cloridan made level five . . ."

"Congratulations, boss!" Cutter said, with only a hint of envy.

"I need new armor," Kyle groaned. "I was taking too many hits once we got to level two. A new shield as well."

"I need a bath," I said. "Are we going out to celebrate Cloridan's level later?" A chorus of groans was my reply, but it was still an hour until dark—we'd probably recover some after dinner. I limped off for a recuperating soak.

The second level had been a series of rooms, all with four corridors leading off them. Rather than a simple grid, the corridors had twisted and turned, some leading back to the room they came from, others leading to further rooms. None of the rooms had doors, and the monsters all *wandered*. They would spawn overnight and wander around according to some pattern determined by the dungeon, so they never interacted.

There was no place to rest, and some of the monsters hit hard enough to get past Kyle's defenses. It was pretty tough wandering around the twisty passages, but we eventually found the boss chamber. After fighting the vampire crab, we were glad to have an exit.

The rest of the team took their turn in the bath—magic meant the hot water was endless—and we gathered in the kitchen for some food.

"We're not going to party tonight," Cloridan said firmly. "We're sitting on a fortune of coin and reagents here; we can't just leave it and get drunk."

"Boo," I said. "That's not something I'd expect from you."

Cloridan shrugged. "Not getting robbed means many more drinking sessions in the future. Tomorrow we can get this stuff sold and either turn it into enchanted goods or deposit it with the Guild."

"Fine. I suppose you want to keep a watch as well." The Guild was, supposedly, a safer place to keep our funds than the safe box that had come with the house. It wasn't a bank, though; they actually charged a fee for storage. This world was in desperate need of some decent financial institutions. *I wonder how much capital I'll need . . .*

That, though, was a thought for another day. Not even tomorrow or the day after that. Someday, though. For now, I needed to focus on more immediate goals.

"How can it possibly be safe?" I asked the man nervously. He just shrugged nonchalantly.

"I'm riding it, too, aren't I? You're not going to fall off, and she's not going to fall out of the sky. It's safe, long as something don't come after us."

"And you know where we're going."

"'Course I do. I've been to the Enchanter's place a bunch of times, and it's not exactly hard to find—from the air, anyways."

"Fine." *This is fine.* Really I was just delaying things now. "How do I get on?"

"Just put your hand here, and your foot in the stirrup," he explained. "Then pull and push to get your other leg over."

Once I'd done this, he started fastening the straps. From what he'd said, if I'd had the Ride skill, I wouldn't have needed them, but I think I still would have insisted. Riding a horse doesn't do much to prepare for taking flight on a griffin. Having firmly secured me, he took his own seat in the front.

"Ready?" he said with a grin.

"I suppose," I said. It was just the two of us for this trip. The Enchanter wasn't to be crowded by petitioners, apparently. That meant I, and my fat purse of gold, were entirely in Gifford's hands for this trip. He did have a good reputation, though, and the Enchanter wasn't known for disappearing his clients.

With a leap that put my stomach in my boots, the griffin took to the air. I managed to refrain from screaming.

This wasn't so bad; it was a little like being on a plane—in really bad turbulence.

Like a plane, we had a defined flight path. Gifford took us up in a tight spiral, staying above the grounds of the griffin stables until we rose high above the city walls. Curious, I took a look with Sense Mana.

It looked like a slow-moving tornado. Slowly revolving, a pillar of stronger natural mana was directly over the stables. It wasn't much stronger, but I suspected this was why the griffins didn't suffer from the lower mana levels of the town. *Is this natural? Did they build the stables there because of the feature, or did they create it somehow?*

I glanced over to one of the larger buildings off the central square. The Scholars of the Sacred Breath—or the Theurgy Guild, as most people called them. They were a lot older than the other guilds, though, and were one of my remaining blind spots as to how this place worked. They were supposed to be responsible for the obelisks and monoliths I'd seen scattered about. Devices for shaping the natural mana of the world.

Were they also responsible for the giant sky clockwork machine? I didn't think so. It seemed too large and complex to be of human construction.

We flew on, leaving the town behind, headed for the mountains. We were now outside of Latorran territory, entering the forest claimed by the beast-kin Tribes. It was a fairly soft border from all accounts—the kin that didn't like civilization wouldn't come within fifty miles of it, and the ones that did were happy living under the King's rule. The high density of monsters in the area kept the two countries safely separated.

It wasn't long before Gifford shouted, pointing out the mountain that was our destination. A short while later, and I could make out a cottage, incongruously perched on a ledge halfway up a sheer cliff.

It looked ridiculous. The ledge itself was wide—over fifty meters in each direction, and Gifford had no difficulty in landing. He carefully avoided the white picket fence and carefully manicured garden that surrounded the house, touching down on a spot that had clearly been designated for landings.

Gifford slipped out of his saddle and started releasing me from mine. "Don't reckon you need directions. I'll wait here until you're done."

"Thanks," I said and moved slowly towards the cottage. It would have looked fine tucked into a forest clearing, but to see it here, apparently transplanted onto bare rock . . . *How did they even get any part of it up here?* I wondered. *The soil, the stone, the plants* . . . I shook my head. If I wanted to ask, the person with the answers was inside.

I strolled up to the gate and passed through it, carefully closing it behind me. As I walked up the short path to the front door, it opened, and a man looked out.

"Ah," he said. "You're the new girl who's got Arber's knickers in a twist."

I raised an eyebrow. If I'd been wearing a dress, I'd have curtsied, but my leather armor was far more appropriate for a ride on a griffin. The man in front of me was fairly tall, but thin and weathered looking. His blond hair had started to thin, and he had a nasty looking scar on the side of his nose.

"I guess?" I said. Arber must have been the shopkeeper's name.

"You're the Enchanter that showed up in Anchorbury, right?" he asked. "Heard of you, seen your work. Pretty crap."

"Thanks," I said flatly. "I'm just starting out."

He snorted. "Your stuff is worse than that." He looked me over closely. "And you're too young. There's no way the likes of you is level seven—and you've got a weird Ability set if you're level five."

"I'm not an actual Enchanter," I admitted. "I got the skill from . . . an unusual confluence of events."

He waited for more, but that was all I was going to be saying for now. His eyes narrowed, and I felt pressure from Persuasion in that glare. I matched it. We were . . . surprisingly evenly matched.

"I came here for a Bargain," I said. "Are we doing a Social Contest instead?"

A look of calculation flitted over his face, then he grimaced. "Bargain is fine. You'd better come in." He backed off and led me inside. The door opened into a sitting room—or perhaps negotiation room was its actual function. It seemed to take up about half of the cottage's interior. Two couches faced each other over a sturdy looking tea table.

"So what are you looking for?" he said, taking a seat on one of the couches.

"Ultimately, more knowledge about runes," I said. "Either information about how to properly use them that isn't listed in the Status, or access to more runes."

He smirked. "So you want to buy enchantments so you can copy the runes?"

"That's the worst-case scenario, yes. You could just sell me the runes."

"And why would I help set up a competitor?"

"Why are you selling enchanted gear in the first place?" I asked. "You've got a shop full in town. Selling just one a year is enough to fund this"—I gestured—"extravagant lifestyle."

He scowled. "That's none of your business."

"Maybe not." I shrugged. "But whatever the reason, I don't think you're worried about a little competition. I can't believe you care about how many enchantments you sell."

"By the same logic," he said, slowly chewing over his words, "I don't need any of the money you're likely to pay for my runes."

"But you need *something*," I said. "Or you wouldn't have asked me to come."

Oddly enough, it wasn't Bargain that was telling me this. We were pretty well matched on skills. It was the fact that we *were* bargaining. It wasn't Persuade or Intimidate that were clashing. Whatever we were negotiating, it was an exchange of equivalent value.

The man glared at me, but didn't disagree. He changed tack instead.

"I heard you had a falling out with the Count."

I controlled my irritation. Just how many hoops did I have to jump through before the man would deal with me?

"I was working for the previous Count," I said calmly. "His son never liked me and got rid of me as soon as he could."

"I heard he likes pretty ladies more than anything."

"Not ones that say no," I said shortly.

"Yes to the father but not to the son?" he said with a smirk. I gave him my best icy glare.

"My relationship with Count Duvost was strictly business, so I'll thank you not to insinuate anything." That was all I wanted to say, but I thought I sensed a bit of anti-noble sentiment there. Maybe a little more information would get me a little further. "It wasn't employment I would have chosen, but his Lordship was just as unwilling to take no for an answer."

He pondered on that for a bit. "Why'd you come here, then? Baron Marseau is Duvost's vassal—you haven't gotten out from under him."

"It's not like I'm expecting him to come after me," I said. "He wanted me gone because I remind him of some unpleasant facts. I came here because of the opportunities that exist here at the frontier. I plan on having as little interaction with the Baron as possible."

I was half surprised I didn't get a level in Deceive from that statement. "As possible" was doing a lot of heavy lifting, considering that I was being watched by the Baron's pet thieves.

"Have you—" he started, but I'd had enough.

"Look, are we going to do business or not?" I interrupted. "I've told you what I'm after, and these questions aren't getting us anywhere. My ride isn't going to wait forever, and I still don't know your name, let alone what you *actually* want."

He stared at me, his mouth working. Were the high-levelled not used to being addressed this way? He looked as if he was working through something, so I gave him a minute. Eventually, he sighed.

"Fine. I suppose there's nothing for it but to take a chance." He drew himself up and looked directly at me. "My name, since you asked, is Mandel Monteminer . . . and I need your help."

MANDEL

elp with what?" I asked.

"I can teach you runes if that's what you want," Mandel said, ignoring me. "I don't know every rune, but I've seen your work—there's a lot you're missing." He looked away for a moment, his expression sour. "May you have more luck with it than I've had."

"Has it not worked out for you?" I asked, waiting for him to get to the point.

"I'll try not to bore you with my story," he sneered. "It might be quicker to show you what I need. Can you go invisible?"

"I don't recall telling you I was an Illusionist," I said calmly.

"Oh, Arber found out as much as he could about you before you came here." He gave me a sly look. "You wouldn't *be* here if I didn't think you could help me."

So he needs an Illusionist's help? Interesting. I cast Greater Invisibility and he watched me fade from view.

"Ha! I suppose I'll have to take it on faith that you're following me," he said, and led me around to the back half of the cottage. To my surprise, the back half mostly consisted of a set of wide stairs going down into the living rock.

"Surprised?" he asked. "The cottage is just the entrance." We headed down the spacious and well-lit stairway, passing one landing and stopping at a pair of impressive stone doors. Mandel sighed and waved his arm irritably. Without a sound, the doors swung open.

"One moment," he said, holding up his hand. "*Marie,*" he called in a louder tone. After a moment, the figure of a woman appeared out of nowhere. She was richly attired, wearing a dress the equal of any I'd seen at the Autumn Ball. However, her hair was a mess, unravelling from the elaborate style that went with the clothes. And her eyes were empty. She looked at me—at what should have been empty space, and spoke.

"*Intruder,*" she spat.

"Marie, this is Kandis Hammond, she is authorized to be here," Mandel said calmly. At his words, the woman calmed herself and looked at him. "Do not let anyone know that she is here, whether verbally, or by reacting to her presence or actions. Do you understand?"

Marie looked at him, emotions flitting across her face. I think I saw shock, anger, confusion . . . finally her face went blank.

"Y-yes, I under . . . stand." She spoke as if she was just remembering how.

"Where are the other humans?" Mandel said.

"In the . . . Warrens," she replied haltingly.

"Good. Let me know if any of them leave the Warrens."

"I w-will." She faded out, apparently of her own accord. Mandel sighed again. "You have questions, I'm sure," he said, addressing the same patch of air that Marie had faced. "How much do you know of the secret lore of dungeons?"

[Unseen Sound]. Just for kicks, I made my voice appear on the other side of him. "Let's say nothing at all."

He nodded. "Let's walk," he said and led me further into what I guessed now was a dungeon. "Marie is—or perhaps was—my wife. She died."

"Is there a point to me being invisible if we're going to talk?"

"Oh!" He considered for a moment. "No, that was just a precaution to make sure the others didn't find out. We should have plenty of warning before they come out of the Warrens."

"Fine," I said, cancelling the spell and speaking with my own voice. He jumped to see me where he didn't expect, but said nothing about it.

"So she's a ghost?" I asked. I knew this world had them, but I had been under the impression that they were just another type of monster.

"No . . . not really," he answered unhelpfully. "She's . . . well. All working dungeons contain an intelligence that controls them."

"You . . . put her in that to save her life?"

"I didn't," he said, and paused. I realized at this point that I'd been too distracted to notice the familiar sound of iron on iron. It seemed to be coming from up ahead along the corridor.

"Marie was part of an adventuring party," he said. "I wasn't an adventurer myself, but I did go with them sometimes to help me get up to level five."

"So you're actually an Enchanter, then?" That was the level five profession that most people assumed I had. It had enchanting as a prerequisite, but got good skill bonuses and extra runes. If you learned enchanting early, it was something to aim for.

"Yes. I supported them with enchanted goods. I made a good living, and I was trying to get Marie to retire from risking her life, but . . ."

"She had the bug." I'd felt it myself. Maybe it was just monkey psychology—the urge to make quick gains by taking risks . . . but sometimes I thought it might be an effect of the System.

"Yes, the adventuring bug," he said sourly. "Anyway, one day Kari came back with . . . an orb. With Marie inside it."

We'd reached the first of the doors. There was one to the left and five along the right-hand side. Mandel gestured to the left.

"The Warrens," he said. Pointing to the right, he added, "The crafting cells."

As we came level with the doors, I could see that the crafting cells were occupied by monsters. The doors had large barred windows in them, so I could see through to the inside. Humanoid monsters of a type I was unfamiliar with . . .

[Identification]: Troll (Male) – Threat: 10 – Qualities: Regeneration, Skills – Status: Healthy
[Identification]: Gnoll (Male) – Threat: 10 – Qualities: Tracker, Skills – Status: Healthy
[Identification]: Goblin (Male) – Threat: 8 – Qualities: Skills – Status: Healthy

---

Right, those. They ignored us as we walked by, being completely absorbed in their tasks. I saw ironworking, goldsmithing, and woodcarving.

"This is where I get my items from," Mandel said. "The raw materials come from the dungeon mine."

"Can't the dungeon just make items for you?"

"She could, but such things have to be paid for. In addition, as the master of the dungeon, I get a share of all XP earned in here. So those monsters are working for my XP gain."

"Huh," I said. "Do all dungeons have masters?"

"To be a master, you have to live in the dungeon," he told me. "Few people want to, and fewer still want to risk getting killed by an adventurer."

"So you came out here, in the middle of nowhere, to plant Marie's Dungeon core and live with her? It didn't look like that was working out."

"It was fine for a while," Mandel said wistfully. "Kari's party helped us get out here, and we lived peacefully with our daughter for . . . it must have been about ten years. Then . . . well, you'll see."

He led me on through some more stone doors into an open area with a floor that sloped upwards away from the entrance. Empty cages lined the walls and the room was littered with low walls and pits.

"This was our main line of defense, back in the day," he said, and led me through the mess. At the far side of the room was a double stairway that led up to the upper level, a balcony that would have been great for ranged attacks on attackers from below. He gestured to doors on either side of the upper level.

"Over there is where I live, and on the other side is where my . . . jailers live when they're not cleaning out the Warrens. But this is where we are going." He pointed at a third door at the tops of the stairs. Beyond them was a round room with a familiar looking sight.

[Identification]: Dungeon Core (Level 3)

As before, the core was a round glowing orb on a simple pedestal. This time, though, it was encased in a cage of . . .

[Identification]: Unadium Shield – Quality: Great – Properties: Unavailable

There are a lot of weird metals in this world, I thought. "What does unadium do?" I asked aloud.

"It blocks most forms of mana," Mandel said. "It's the reason Marie acts the way she does . . . it only lets just enough through for her to function as the dungeon's controller."

"So this is to . . . cripple the dungeon?"

"Yes . . ." he said sadly. "I could remove it, but that's what my 'guests' are for. They keep a careful eye on the core."

"And this is all in aid of . . ."

"Let's go back upstairs," he said. "My guests will come out of the Warrens eventually, and they mustn't see you."

"Fine," I agreed. Once we were seated again on the couches in the cottage, he resumed his story.

"This is all to keep me producing at a rate high enough to keep Talnier supplied with enchantments. You were right earlier—when we were all living here together, I might have made one or two items a year to keep us supplied."

"So who's behind this?"

"Who else but the Baron?" Mandel said bitterly. "His troops conquered my dungeon five years ago, and now he has me working for his profits."

"Those guards," I said, suddenly realizing. "Are they Fangs?"

"I believe so," he said. "They haven't identified themselves as such, but they are, without a doubt, criminals and not trained soldiers. I've kept up with the town gossip through Arber . . . they are almost certainly members of his pet gang."

"Is this . . . the secret base that they have out here?" I asked.

"No. No, they've only ever had two or three thugs here at a time. I suspect they've stumbled across an old fortification from before the Empire's collapse. That or they've got a rogue Theurge working for them."

"Rogue?"

"Not a member of the Theurges Guild. The King's law says that everyone with the skill has to join . . . that's not a law that's easy to enforce, though."

This was getting off-topic. "Getting back to the matter at hand: what is it that you need from me?"

"Two things, which likely only an Illusionist can do," he told me. "I can free Marie from that cage, but they would just put her back in. I need time once she's freed, to have her delve deeper, make more defenses, and gain the strength to protect herself from the Baron."

"So you want me to make an Illusion showing the core is still there?"

"That's right. I've heard that illusions will project a false Identification message; is that correct?"

"It is," I said carefully. "But I don't think it will stand up to Sense Mana. Dungeon cores are pretty unique when you look at them with that sense."

"That's not a concern," he dismissed with a wave of his hand. "These are just thugs; they will only have Identify."

"How much time do you need?" I asked.

"Weeks at least," he said, getting somewhat despondent at the thought. "Building dungeon levels . . . it takes time."

"So we're talking an illusion maintained by enchantment," I mused.

"If you can't do that, I can teach you the runes required."

I nodded and started thinking about the situation. Mandel was taking a real risk here—if I wanted to get in with the Baron, I could take Mandel's payment and then turn around and sell him out. I wouldn't be doing that, though. Aside from the immorality of it, I didn't want anything to do with nobles, so an in with the Baron didn't appeal.

Actually, maybe it wasn't *such* a risk for him. Regardless of how this turned out, the Baron wasn't going to kill his golden goose. Unless a replacement Enchanter happened along . . . I shuddered. *OK, first priority is making sure that* that *doesn't happen.*

"What's the second thing?" I asked.

"Ah, that," Mandel said with some embarrassment. "Marseau took my daughter when he raided my dungeon. I need someone who can sneak into his fortress and free her."

"That's . . . a lot harder than making a permanent illusion," I said.

"I know, I know—but you can take as much time as you need," he said. "As much as I want her freed now, I won't be in a position to protect her until Marie is deep enough . . ."

"I told you that I didn't want to get involved with the nobility," I said, but some part of me was quietly pleased by the idea. I kept that part firmly off my face.

"As an Illusionist, you can surely infiltrate without getting identified." He looked at me pleadingly. "Please; she's my daughter, and I haven't seen her in five years."

"Do you even know she's alive?"

"Alive and well treated was part of the deal." He said it firmly, but some doubts showed on his face. "I do get to send messages, and Arber has been permitted to see her. He's an old friend, and I trust him . . ."

"Unless he thinks finding out that your daughter is dead will make you do something stupid."

"That is my fear," he agreed. "That, and . . . he has profited greatly from this arrangement. The Baron has had him continue our arrange-ment, in order that he is not seen to be connected to me. Before, Arber took half the proceeds. Now he takes only a quarter, but he sells so much more."

"Don't trust the shopkeeper, got it." I sighed. "Anything else I need to know?"

He glared at me. "I trust him more than I trust *you* . . . but I don't have much of a choice. Illusionists are rare out here on the frontier."

Was this his only escape scheme? It had been five years; he had prob-ably tried some others. Probably not in his interest to admit to having other options, especially if this one failed and I got caught.

"Fine," I said. "I make you a fake Dungeon core, you teach me all you know about runes, and I will *try* and find and free your daughter."

"That's—" he tried to interject.

"I'm *not* going to promise you something if I can't deliver," I said firmly. "You don't have any information on how she's kept, or even if she's still alive. I can get past men, but not wards."

"For wards, you need Shadow magic . . . or Theurgy," he said.

"Thanks for the tip," I said. "I'll look into that. Now, are those terms acceptable?"

I felt his Bargain struggle with mine. It seemed like a fair deal to me—was that because it was fair and we were evenly matched? Or was it because one of us had won?

"Very well," he said. "We have a deal."

LESSONS

"Wait, why isn't Marie able to do this?" I asked, voicing the thought that had just occurred to me. We were in Mandel's workshop, and he was showing me how to rig a double spell storing enchantment. "Aren't dungeons able to craft far better enchanted items than Enchanters? And come to think of it, why are you selling your enchantments, rather than dungeon-made items?"

Mandel snorted. "Dungeon-made items mean a dungeon—and there are ways of telling from what dungeon they came from. We didn't want to attract delvers when it was just the three of us . . ."

". . . and the Baron has the same concern," I finished for him.

"Right. As for your first question, dungeons can't make anything that's fake."

"Um . . . what do you mean?"

"Everything they make is labelled with what it is. Unlike your illusions, they can't create items that aren't clearly labelled with what they are."

"So if Marie made a fake core, Identify would label it with 'Fake Core,' made by Marie."

"Exactly. I imagine it's one of the overriding rules put in place when the gods were finished hashing out the rules for dungeons."

I returned my attention to the spell structure. I had sent Gifford back home with a letter and an agreement to pick me up again in three days. That meant I was probably going to miss our next dungeon expedition, but the runes and the education should be worth it.

The fake core and its unadium cage had separate Identify tags, so they needed to be separate spells. The cage had to be fake as well, or it would choke off mana to the enchantment. I wasn't sure if Phantasmal unadium would also block mana—I was avoiding the question by making something that *looked* like unadium and labelling it as such.

Phantasmal Object needed fifteen mana to cast, and we were casting *two* of them. Fortunately, the upkeep was low, so we would be able to rely on ambient mana to keep the spell up. To cast the spells, we were using the largest mana stone I'd worked with yet, a thirty-mana stone almost half a centimeter in diameter. Mandel didn't have a shortage.

"There, it's done," I said. Without further ceremony, I activated the enchantment and tossed the small disk into the air. The Phantasm formed around it, and I caught the result. With the disk *in* the Phantasm, you couldn't see it or deactivate it without destroying the object.

"Toraio's secrets, a *solid* illusion?" Mandel exclaimed. "But those are . . ." He trailed off and gave me a speculative look. "That will be much better for our purpose, yes. Thank you."

Did I give something away? He probably thinks I'm a level seven now.

Mandel left to install the fake, while I stayed in his quarters and got to work on his spell-books. Rune-books. Whatever. I had wanted to Memorize all the new runes and then Research them from memory later—it would be slower, but I could do most of it at home instead of here. I ran into a problem, though. It appeared that when it came to learning spells, Memorize had limits.

I was up to my seventh rune, Control Object, but when I tried to add it to my memory, it just didn't . . . take. Confused, I tried a few others, but my memory seemed to be full. I hadn't encountered any limits with regular memories, but perhaps spells were different? I had a limit of six . . . was that twice my skill level, or . . . checking my logs, my effect totals for Memorize were in the sixties. It could be that I needed ten points of effect for each spell . . . or it could be my limit was higher, but all the runes I'd previously Memorized counted.

The only way to tell was to Research one of the runes and see if I could Memorize another. That was going to take some time, though.

I probably wouldn't finish before Mandel came back . . . but he would expect me to be studying runes anyway . . .

I sighed in irritation and got started.

A few hours later, the door to the room opened. I had expected to see Mandel, but instead, a goblin was standing there. I tensed, but it wasn't carrying a weapon—it was carrying a tray of food. I watched it as it made its way around the other couch and placed it gently on the table. The whole time, I could see it glaring at me with hostility, but it didn't so much as step out of place. Once it had placed the tray, it turned around and walked out of the room.

That was creepy, I thought. *Are all my meals going to be served with a side of hatred?*

The meal itself was perfectly fine. Bread, meat, cheese, and greens. Had it been made directly by the dungeon, or had it been prepared by that angry goblin? I put the question aside and started eating while resuming my Research.

Eventually, I proved one theory right: I could hold up to six runes in my memory, and Researching a rune cleared it out of storage. I needed to think about what runes to learn, and how to learn them.

There were more runes here than I could learn in the three days that I'd allowed myself. Researching a rune directly was faster than doing it from memory, but I'd still run out of time. On the other hand, if I used Memorize, I'd be training both skills at once.

I decided to stick with the Memorize route. I could come back again after this. Either way, though, I should look at prioritizing which runes I got.

I was halfway through making a list when Mandel finally came back. He looked both pleased and apprehensive—which was a level of nuance I don't think I'd have been able to pick up on back home.

"Did everything go well?" I asked.

"I think so," he said pensively. "There's some improvement, but she hasn't come back to normal. It may take some time."

I made a sympathetic noise and returned to my studies.

Two days later, and I was having another go at Theurgy. Theurgy, Mandel had explained, was the original magic skill. Controlling mana directly to achieve effects, it could do anything that the nine magic skills could do— and a few other things they couldn't. I had a few questions, one of which I couldn't ask.

One, why was it called Theurgy and not Mana Control? I couldn't ask this question, because it *wasn't* called Theurgy, not really. That was just what the System had chosen to translate it as. If I focused, I could hear the mishmash of syllables that they actually spoke. "Mana Control" and "Theurgy" sounded pretty similar to my ear, but the System could tell the difference.

I guessed that Theurgy was an old-fashioned word for magic in my language and so that's what the System decided to use.

The next question was why didn't people use Theurgy and be masters of all the types of magic? The answer was that Theurgy was *hard*.

When you cast a spell, you had to get an effect total higher than the level of the spell. Mandel had mentioned this as part of his explanation and I managed to smile and nod as if I knew that. I had actually missed it because it was so freaking easy to do.

When I cast my first spell during my fifteen-minute career as an Illusionist, I'd had a plus two skill bonus and a Charisma of seven. Despite only having a skill level of one, I'd had a base effect total of 21. Casting a level fifteen spell was a breeze back then, and my effect total had gone to 28 the moment I upgraded to Phantasmal Artificer. Once I hit level two, there was no chance of me failing any spell that was available.

Doing the same spells with Theurgy would be *ten times harder*, according to Mandel. I'd need an effect level of fifty just to do a level five spell.

The main reason people used Theurgy today—and for "today," read the last thousand years—was to do things that spells couldn't. Like move mana around. On a large scale, with the aid of those big stones I'd seen, and on a small scale, to get around runic fields.

Neither of those applications was approved of by governments. Well, they approved of it when *they* did it. That's why there was a Theurgy Guild. It predated the Kingdom—predated the Empire before it, apparently, but both governments had made sure that its members worked for them.

Fortunately, anyone with Sense Mana could manage to learn Theurgy. Unlike the other magic skills, it could be unlocked by a successful skill roll.

"Just do what you would do for a spell, without using the skill," Mandel had said breezily.

It wasn't that easy. The simplest spell I knew was level five, and my base effect total was a big fat zero. Instead, I needed to *imagine* a level *one* spell, figure out what that would look like, then make it a reality by moving mana without a skill.

I'd decided on mimicking Water Magic. It seemed simpler, and since I wouldn't be using the skill, it didn't matter that my Water Magic was lower than my Illusion Magic. I had decided to call the spell I was working on the "tea-stirring spell" because that was all it would be good for. A finger of mana that could shove just the *tiniest* amount of water—or tea—around a mug.

Mandel watched with interest as I used Water Ball to lift a small amount of water out of the bowl I was using as my test arena. We'd been living in each other's pockets for the last two days as he kept me hidden from his jailers, and I was getting a little sick of the sight of him. Fortunately, Marie had been able to carve out additional rooms for me so I didn't have to sleep on his couch.

What I wanted was just a fraction of this ball. I studied the mana construct closely, trying to figure out what could go without destabilizing the whole thing. The type of mana would be important, too, I knew. It needed to interact with water and nothing else.

I let the spell go and focused on a new one. It was easy enough to not use a skill—the System seemed to know when I wanted it and when I didn't. It *was* really hard to move the mana without one, though. Every other time I'd done it, I'd let the skill do the heavy lifting—all the lifting, really. But I'd been there when I'd done it, and I could sort of understand the mental muscles I needed to flex.

Strands of mana coalesced in front of me. Something like a spoon formed . . . and then dissipated. I felt the magic drain out of me, but it was a tiny loss. Only a level one spell after all. I tried again—and failed.

Persistence was the key, if luck failed. I didn't think I was doing anything wrong, so I would just have to try again. And again.

On the sixth try, it took, and the spoon dipped into the water and started stirring it.

> **[Theurgy] Skill unlocked**
> **[Theurgy] Level 1 purchased**
> **For gaining a skill level, you have been awarded 1 XP.**

"Congratulations," Mandel said. "You're now a rogue Theurgist."

"Catchy as that sounds," I said, "I don't think I'll be switching professions anytime soon."

OPPORTUNITY

Well, that's what you get when you skive off to read books!" Felicia's words were harsh, but she had a smile on her face. I stuck my tongue out at her.

"I missed *one* delve. I can't believe you guys got so far ahead of me!" I said, pouting.

"Well, we didn't want to brag at the time, but with Kyle's new armor and Cloridan's level, we got part of the way through level three."

I groaned. That wasn't actually a surprise—I'd had one delve with the group since then and we'd cleared level three. Cloridan was pretty nasty at level five, so I wasn't surprised that he didn't really need my Greater Invisibility to do well. And now these two had joined him.

One little encounter with a flock of dog bats as we made our way out for another delve had put them over the edge.

"With only three of you, you would have been making one-third of the XP instead of a quarter," I groused. "And now I'm getting twenty percent less than you guys."

"That's fine," Kyle interjected with a grin. "We don't mind carrying you for a while."

I gave him a scowl. At least Cutter was still on level three, or I'd never hear the end of the teasing. The thing was, I didn't think I'd get level five with this trip. We were getting more and more XP as we delved deeper, but I *thought* I had still around 40,000 XP to go. The System didn't provide totals, but I had been keeping a rough track. Maybe if we did significant damage to the fourth dungeon level . . .

"Hold up," I said suddenly. "Cloridan's back."

His invisible form came out of the woods ahead of us, and he made the gesture for me to lift Greater Invisibility.

"Problems?" I asked, after doing so. Was it pessimistic of me to use a plural?

"Maybe," he said thoughtfully, "Or maybe an opportunity."

"Oh?"

Cloridan frowned, clearly torn about something. "There's an ambush set up ahead. The Fangs, I think."

"That's what they do . . . but I thought we were paid up."

"Yeah, I'm pretty sure it's not for us; they're facing the wrong way."

"Ah . . ." I realized what was going on. "The new guys."

"Yeah, the Justiciars. They should be heading back around this time."

We had arranged some coordination with this group. They were a low level—fours, with a three—group that was even newer in town than us. They were going to clear out the top levels of the dungeon we were going to, which would help us get to the deeper levels more quickly.

"So . . . aren't they paid up? We told them about the tax."

Cloridan shrugged. "You remember they weren't that keen on paying it? They're called the *Justiciars,* after all."

I felt a little sick. "So this is their warning?" I said. "Crossbow bolt out of nowhere, better pay up next time?"

"Probably," Cloridan said uneasily. "Unless they did something stupid like go to the Fangs and tell them where they could shove their tax."

"Did they?"

"I haven't heard," Cloridan said. "But you saw what they were like— they're not the type to just sit and wait for something to happen. If they're dumb enough to not pay, they're dumb enough to dare the gang to do something about it."

"So where does the opportunity come in?" I asked.

"Well, they're not expecting us," Cloridan said. "They've got a lookout, but . . ." he waggled his fingers.

"My spells are the product of my intellect and will—triumphing over the very nature of the universe," I said loftily. "Don't cheapen them with your obscene gestures. But . . . I get your point. We could spoil the ambush."

"It'd be starting something with the Fangs—maybe the Baron as well," Cloridan said. "Can't say I'm opposed to that, but it might be a bad idea."

"Maybe not . . ." I mused. "It seems to me that we could do this without getting caught, but that would mean that the Justiciars would take the blame. Are we fine with using them as patsies?"

I looked at the rest of the team.

Kyle spoke up first. "Seems to me that they've already started something. We'd just be helping them with dealing with it." Felicia nodded in agreement.

"All right, then," I said. "Why don't you tell us how they're set up."

The waiting was the worst bit. No, that was a lie. The waiting was the only bit we'd done so far. The killing—if it came to that—would be worse. The waiting hadn't been *part* of the plan, but it turned out to be an inevitable consequence. The annoying thing about ambushes was that you had to wait for the victim to show up.

The Fangs had split their forces, so we did, too. They were hunkered down on two rocky outcroppings about equally distant from the beaten path. I didn't think it was a *great* ambush site, as there was too much cover between the path and their positions to be a proper trap. That did give me some hope that they were only there to deliver a warning. This setup would be good for a single shot on an unaware target, and they were far away enough from the path that they should be able to get away while the targets ran for cover.

Hopefully, the second group was just for backup if things went wrong.

I was with Cloridan, shadowing one group, while Felicia and Kyle were on the other. The lookout was left to his own devices; he was far enough away that he shouldn't be a factor. We were all invisible. To get around the coordination issues, only Kyle and Cloridan would be fighting.

We'd been waiting long enough that I was about to go over to Kyle's spot to renew their spell, but our targets suddenly perked up. *Their* targets had arrived.

Cloridan was the first to act, moving silently up to one of the crossbowmen just as the Justiciars came into view. Rather than backstab the man, he reached out to the man's crossbow. With one quick move, Cloridan's darksteel dagger sliced through the steel string without resistance.

The man cursed as his crossbow suddenly broke, and there was a loud twang as the tension was released. That was enough to put the Justiciars on high alert.

"Who's there?" their leader called out, shield up, actively scanning for threats.

A crossbow, any weapon really, was a serious threat to an unsuspecting target. As long as you managed to hit the base target, you got the full effect of your skill added to the damage. That was how I managed to do *any* damage. Against a target that was expecting a hit, you lost effect points to their defense, even if you managed to hit them. If you had the precision damage trait, you could do even more.

That option was no longer available to these guys, so we wanted to see what they did. With their ambush spoiled, would they fade away or double down?

A sudden scream from the other side of the path told me the answer. Another Fang member had tried to take a shot, and Kyle was dealing with him. The two members standing here gaped stupidly across to where the sound was coming from, which gave Cloridan a chance to make another strike.

This time, he drove his dagger into the Fang with the working weapon. He didn't make a sound, though, because I'd already cast Blind on him. Instead, he staggered back, while his companion stared in disbelief.

Not used to being on the other end, are you? I thought as he just stared at his partner getting stabbed again. I had plenty of time to cast Blind again, and at that point, the combat was over. He actually turned and fled, only to smash into a tree. It didn't do any serious damage, but it kept him busy until Cloridan could finish up.

> **Your party has killed Russell Primeau – your experience share is 526 XP.**
> **Your party has killed Scoville Fortin – your experience share is 336 XP.**

That second notification wasn't for the guy here, who was still alive. Kyle must have finished off one of the others. There was a lot of noise coming from over there, and the Justiciars were starting to make their way towards it. They moved cautiously and kept their eyes looking in this direction, as that was where the original sound had come from.

Time for the next phase. I cancelled Greater Invisibility and cast Disguise.

"No need for alarm, citizens," I called out confidently. "This is a sanctioned law enforcement operation."

The Justiciars gaped as I stepped out into view. What they saw, of course, was not me but an imposing figure in the King's secret armed forces. True, I didn't know how the Kingdom's secret forces were dressed. But neither did these guys.

I'd gone for expensive looking. A tabard in red and gold—the King's colors—over darksteel chain and plate . . . arm bits. Pauldrons and vambraces? The face and bearing of a German expat who'd worked two floors up from me before. He was a good head taller than me, so I made sure to keep my distance from the Justiciars. I wasn't sure if my voice was going to be issuing from my fake mouth or my armored chest.

"You can be on your way—we don't have any need of you," I said. I smiled, but Intimidate was cranked up to full. *Just go and do what you want to do and get out*, I thought.

The group was made of sterner stuff, though. A couple of them blanched, but the leader stood his ground.

"Who are you?" he asked uncertainly.

Your party has killed Agramant Fortin – your experience share is 526 XP.

Brothers? I wondered. Aloud, I said firmly, "I'm not at liberty to say. You should report this encounter to your guild. If there's something you're authorized to know, you'll be informed." I let my smile drop.

Well, they knew when they were getting an official brush-off. They looked at each other, but they didn't seem to want to make an issue of whatever this was. Cloridan came out to join me, still invisible. That meant he'd finished securing the prisoner. I jerked my head in the direction of the lookout to indicate he should follow him. The Justiciars took the gesture as a command as well, which worked for me. They left.

Which left me holding the body. Er, prisoner. I headed back to where I'd left him. Cloridan had left him with his hands tied behind his back and leashed him to a tree with a single rope. He was pretty helpless since the Blind spell was still in effect.

My strength may not have been superhuman, but I was strong enough to drag the captive to his feet. I untied him from the tree and took him to find Felicia and Kyle.

They were where I expected. Having dealt with that side of the ambush, they were to stick close to the bodies so they didn't lose each other. They saw me coming, and once I saw they were all right, I lifted all the spells on us.

"Are you guys all right?" I asked unnecessarily. Kyle was the toughest of us, and Felicia was a Healer.

"We're fine," Felicia said. "They didn't seem to know what was happening."

I nodded, and we stood around awkwardly for a bit. I didn't know if this was Kyle's first time killing someone, and I didn't want to ask. Eventually, he spoke up on his own.

"Should I get the other body?" he said.

"Ah . . ." I considered. "That'd be best. Cloridan will want a good look at them."

"Will he recognize the ones who killed his friend?" Felicia wondered.

I shrugged. "I doubt it, but I want to give him the chance." Felicia nodded and Kyle went over to where the other body was. Rather than drag it, he rolled it up in its own cloak and slung it over his shoulder. I still got jealous of fighters every time I saw them use their strength.

Maybe next level, I'll put points in it, I thought. *It'd be dumb, but I really want to.*

"What are we going to do with the bodies?" Felicia asked.

"Not sure," I answered. "We could get rid of them without a trace if we took them to the dungeon, but . . ."

"We don't know if any other parties are in there at the moment," Kyle finished for me.

"Yeah. I'd say we should strip them of their gear, but it's almost all crap except for the crossbows, which are too distinctive," I said.

Kyle sighed. "Cloridan may have an idea? He's taking a while."

"It means the lookout isn't headed back to town," I said. "Cloridan will be tracking him back to their hideout, maybe."

"Will it be that easy? Cloridan said they tried hard to find it before."

I shrugged. "The Baron found it, so it can't be *impossible*."

There was nothing to do but wait, so we did. We kept an eye out for others in the forest, but it would be a while before anybody reacting to us got out here. Before they did, Cloridan made his way back to us.

"I found it," he said, as soon as I'd removed my spell. To our surprise, he'd taken a wound. Felicia jumped to healing it.

"The hideout?" I asked.

"Yeah," he said. As soon as Felicia was finished, he moved over to the corpses and gave them a good looking over. Eventually, he sighed and shook his head.

"I'll show you." He grabbed a corpse under each arm and started heading back the way he'd come from. "Bring the others."

UNDERGROUND

Carrying three corpses and one prisoner, we moved quickly through the forest, headed for higher ground. We weren't exactly carrying the prisoner, but he was still blinded and helpless. Felicia and I supported and led him along with us, while the boys carried the dead weight.

"It's underground," Cloridan informed us, apparently unbothered by the two corpses he was carrying. "There was a lookout, and it's pretty easily defended. When we get there, let me scout ahead and make sure they haven't noticed us."

"Right," I said. "Are we going to attack them?"

Cloridan couldn't shrug with a corpse under each arm, but I'm sure he wanted to. "I figured my spell was running out, so I didn't scout them out properly. I don't think there's many there, though."

So it's still my decision, then? I wondered. I didn't mind Cloridan taking the lead here—I wasn't that attached to the role in the first place, and Cloridan was the one with the most emotional investment at stake. Still, this was already going beyond what I'd envisaged for my plan. I hadn't considered we'd have to hide bodies, and as for the prisoner . . . he had been a contingency for if we hadn't managed to track the lookout, or if he'd gone back to town. Now, it was looking very much like he was surplus to requirements.

We reached a cliff face, and Cloridan asked me to cast Greater Invisibility again so he could scout ahead. He took one of the corpses with him, to my confusion, and disappeared into the low brush that grew up to the face of the cliff.

"Why one?" Kyle asked.

"I don't know," I replied. "Hey, do you feel anything weird about this place?"

"Kind of . . ." he said, trailing off as he tried to identify the feeling. I was trying the same.

"Is it . . . a sound?" Felicia asked uncertainly. "Like a deep rumbling?"

"I don't . . . maybe?" I said. Was that what I was feeling?

Cloridan returned shortly, sans corpse, and I lifted the spell.

"Seems fine," he said. "I think we'll be good until there's a shift change. Come on."

He grabbed the other body and led us up to the cliff, into a fold which became a crack in the rock face. Entering what looked like a natural flaw, we soon saw that it had been carved out past the entrance. Dimly lit with a light crystal, what might have started as a natural cave was now a defensible guard post. Now I could hear a sound, very soft and deep, coming from further in the mountain.

The room was empty now, but it looked as if it was outfitted to hide at least five men. Stairs going up the wall led to another natural looking crack that was letting natural light in. Cloridan pointed at it.

"Natural arrow slit, with a perfect view of the approach. It's a nice setup, but that's only the start. Come on."

He led us past a sturdy looking door, into another passageway. This was better lit than the guard post and seemed entirely artificial. The sound increased and became clearer.

Soon enough, the corridor opened up into a natural cave. It wasn't excessively large, perhaps ten meters across at its widest point and a bit longer. Its main feature was a chasm that went all the way across the width of the cavern. Only two meters wide, it would have blocked our progress if a bridge hadn't been built across it.

The rumbling sound was coming from the chasm, and now that it was clearer, I recognized what it was.

"An underground river?" I said, and Cloridan nodded.

"A perfect way to dispose of bodies," he said. "A lot of the victims were never found, but a few did wash up in the river north of Talnier. I reckon it connects, but not everyone makes it through."

He walked up and dropped his burden into the rift without ceremony. After a glance at me, Kyle did the same. Both of the bodies made a splashing sound, but it was down pretty deep. I took a look and the water was about five meters down and swiftly flowing. The bodies were already gone.

"What now?" Felicia asked nervously.

"Let's go back and have this conversation in the guard room," Cloridan suggested.

Seated around a table in the guard room, we all looked at the prisoner.

"Before I unblind him," I said, "we should talk about what we're going to do with him."

Nobody wanted to be the first to speak, but eventually, Cloridan did. "If we let him go, he's seen your spells, so it will be only a matter of time before the Baron comes looking for you."

"Yeah," I said heavily. "I know."

We didn't have the means or the will to keep him prisoner forever, so there was only one way this could end.

"So is there anything we still need to learn from him?" I asked.

Cloridan grimaced. "I've got one question that I want to ask, but I doubt he'll know the answer. We could ask about the people further in, but we won't get better answers than we could get on our own."

Was that it? I couldn't think of any alternatives, but this wasn't self-defense, this was murder.

"I—I should be the one to do it," I said. "I was the one who planned on taking a captive without thinking it through."

Kyle and Felicia looked equal parts relieved and sick. Cloridan, though, shook his head.

"Nah, you can keep your hands clean a little longer," he said.

"Cloridan—"

"No, listen. I'm the one with a grudge again these folks. They may not remember who killed Albra, but one of them did. Each one I kill has a chance of being the one. That doesn't mean I need to kill all of them, but if someone's got to do it, let it be someone who's got a grudge."

That didn't sound like healthy reasoning, but the relief I felt made it hard to argue against. No one else did, either, so after another awkward silence, Cloridan stood and pulled the prisoner up.

"Wait," I said. Thoughts whirled around my head, and I struggled to put them into a comprehensible form.

"A philosopher from my world once asked: 'How many does it take?'"

"For what?" Felicia asked.

I remembered the first bit on my own, but I needed Memorize for the rest. "To metamorphose wickedness into righteousness." Puzzled looks all around; philosophers never could say anything simply. Hopefully, it got translated reasonably well.

"Look. Aubert, the Baron, the King—they all sit on their thrones and dispense 'justice.' When they kill someone, it's an execution or part of a war. Because everyone agrees—those deaths are acceptable, are righteous. So how many people do you need to agree? A thousand? A hundred? Four?"

Now they were really confused. The logic was hard to argue with, but everyone felt there was a distinct difference between society and a small group. Ask them to put a number on it, though . . . This wasn't a philosophy class, however. Knives were out and lives were on the line.

"It's not about the number," I answered for them. "It's about the *reason.* When you take lives to protect others, to protect your society, it's different from taking them for your own selfish benefit.

"These people have been preying on adventurers for years. The Baron—the supposed authority—is *protecting* them. Justice hasn't failed, but the system that administers it is corrupt. What we're doing here is starting a new system. A new *state.*"

"Well, that sounds better than murder," Kyle said cautiously, "But it seems rather . . . grand?"

"Yeah," I said. "Even if he doesn't know about it, this is as much a challenge to the Baron as walking into his court and slapping him in the face. It's only the first step on a long road, but it leads towards rebellion."

"But we're not doing anything different than what . . . we were going to do, are we?" Felicia asked.

"No, this is just a different perspective," I said. "For me as well. I think I'm starting to see the bigger picture of my presence here."

Kyle nodded. "Well, the gods know that my parents would be proud to hear I'm going to be overthrowing the nobility."

With that, the mood around the table improved. I took the spell off the prisoner. He looked around wildly, but before he could say anything, Cloridan pulled him out of the room.

"This won't take long," he said.

I nodded, but he had already left the room. "You guys stay here and keep watch on the outside. I'm going to scout the rest of the base."

"Alone?" Felicia asked.

"Yeah, I'll be fine. I'm just getting jittery that we've been left alone for so long."

I passed Cloridan in the cavern and let him know what I was going to do. Then I cast Greater Invisibility and headed further in, ignoring the prisoner.

Past the bridge, the way was blocked by a newly constructed gate. Or it would have been if the gate was shut. Now that the noise of the river had died down, I could hear faint laughter and talk ahead.

Cloridan had stopped here, but I continued on down the corridor. This section looked constructed, as if they'd filled in the empty cave with walls, stone floors, and ceilings. I passed and quickly investigated two side corridors that led to a dozen small rooms. Barracks or cells, I couldn't tell which, as the doors had long crumbled into splinters.

Following the sound of voices, I moved deeper in. The construction changed to look as if it was carved out of the living rock, and the corridor opened up into a large octagonal chamber.

The whole place was lit up, and I could see there were balconies above, as well as a high domed ceiling. I kept following the voices, which led me to one of the entrances coming off the side. Each side of the octagon had its own exit, and as I approached the walls, I saw that they must have had mosaics on them once. The walls were scarred and there was the occasional colored fragment.

> **Your party has killed Nicolas Doyon – your experience share is 526 XP.**

I winced at the notification as I silently entered the room. The voices were clear now, and as I stood at the entrance of the room, I could see their owners. Six thuggish looking people, playing cards and drinking, without a care in the world. The room was large enough that there was room for the twelve bedrolls to be laid out. It looked as though this was the last of them.

I guess the other team was on duty, I thought. This was going to be distastefully easy. I quickly checked the other rooms out, but they all seemed to be stripped of valuables except for one room that seemed to be used for storage. I made my way back to the others with a heavy heart.

Do they have to die as well? I wondered to myself, knowing the answer. This was our first blow against the Baron, and the stronger it was, the better our future chances. To that end, it might be even better if exactly *how* they died was kept a mystery.

I made myself visible as I came out of the fortress.

"Listen, guys, I've got an idea . . ."

The gurgling screech echoed around the octagonal room. I'd found the stairs leading up to the balcony, and the acoustics worked quite well when

I cast Unseen Sound from up here. Six drunk ruffians raced out, looking for the cause. Most of them had their weapons out, though two of them seemed to have only found empty bottles.

They moved to the center of the room, looking around for a threat, but of course, there was nothing to see . . . yet.

[Phantasmal Entity].

Two hands, with green-black skin and long fingers that ended in claws, gripped the balcony balustrade. One of the group yelled and pointed. Then they all yelled as the rest of the creature came into view. It quickly jumped down to their level, its long, wrongly jointed legs absorbing the impact. As it turned to face them, they could see that its face had no eyes, just an elongated dome for a skull and a mouth with far too many teeth. Black ichor seemed to drip off of its skin.

If they'd Identified it, they would have seen something like:

> **[Identification]: Geiger Xenomorph (Illusion) – Threat: 30 – Properties: Endless Spawn**

Hopefully without the illusion tag. I don't think any of them bothered, though, because they all turned and ran as fast as they could. I had it scream some more to encourage them and then headed down the stairs to see the results. As it turned out, I didn't need to.

> **Your party has killed Peverell Compagnon – your experience share is 526 XP.**
> **Your party has killed Royce Lamoureux – your experience share is 336 XP.**
> **Your party has killed Tom Jung – your experience share is 526 XP.**
> **Your party has killed Senapus Chaussée – your experience share is 526 XP.**
> **Your party has killed Hugues Dupuis – your experience share is 336 XP.**
> **Your party has killed Jan Propst – your experience share is 526 XP.**

Walking at a normal pace, when I reached the natural cavern, I didn't see any Fang members—just the invisible forms of my team. I cancelled the invisibility to see Cloridan and Kyle on the bridge and Felicia further back.

"It went just like you thought," Kyle said wonderingly. "They just ran out screaming. I'm not sure they even noticed when I knocked them off the bridge."

"What did you *show* them?" Felicia asked wonderingly.

"Oh, Felicia," I said smugly. "My world holds such terrors, the likes of which you can scarcely dream."

т о ɱ

Getting back into town was a bit of a thing. The guards were *pretty* lax about checking people in or out, but I wasn't sure if I would be noted. The only people who left by this gate were adventurers, who didn't pay entry fees, so the guards had never taken any names when I'd gone through before. However, I had a distinct feeling that the Baron would be very interested in everyone who was out today, and my looks were somewhat memorable. So I slipped through invisible.

Evading my specific watchers had become second nature by now; I wasn't sure why they kept trying. I was pretty sure they'd be under the impression I was still in the house, so I headed there on my own, invisible, while the others reported to the Guild.

Sure enough, I saw my watchers where they always were. I shrugged and did the normal song and dance to get inside. Since they had eyes on the front of my house, I had an illusion of me appear when I opened the door, take a little look around, and then pop back inside.

I really should be taking better security precautions, I thought to myself as I greeted Cutter. I should come up with some better ones for the future. What would Jason Bourne do?

Sadly, I couldn't come up with any idea of how Jason Bourne would handle this situation, aside from punching people. As it happened, I did have the combat skills to be a super-spy, but the problem was, everyone else was even tougher.

So, after filling Cutter in on what was going on—he seemed delighted to hear that we'd started something with the Baron—I went shopping. Would Jason Bourne go shopping? He must have at some point, right?

I took my tails with me. If I saw anybody selling common household items that could be turned into explosives, I'd wait until I lost them before buying. Unfortunately, there was a notable lack. I could try the alchemical store, but those weren't really *common* household items . . .

"Why, Mistress Hammond, what a joy to finally run into you," a familiar voice said from behind me.

Shit.

I turned around, and let Charm have its head. "Why, Master Parkes, how kind of you to say so."

I'd done my best to avoid Tom Parkes since seeing him during the parade, but I'd had a sneaking suspicion that I'd only succeeded because he was letting me. I knew what the information brokers of this town were capable of; there was no way he didn't know where I lived. He actually *was* a professional agent, while I was just an amateur. Not a Jason Bourne, though. He was more of a James Bond type: tall, dark, and handsome . . .

Focus, Kandis.

Right. One good thing about having skills was that I hadn't actually missed any of the conversation while I got distracted. So far it had just been polite noises, the sort of chitchat that people pad out the conversation with until they're ready to bring up the real topic.

Maybe I could keep it confined to that . . . "It's been so nice to catch up with you, Master Parkes, but I do have shopping to get to . . ."

"Actually, since I have run into you, there was one matter I wanted to bring up."

I gave him a stern look, and his friendly smile added a little smirk. Just a small twist in the corner. *Fine.*

"I was wondering if you'd be my guest at the Baron's dinner tomorrow night."

"Tomorrow night? There's no way I could have something ready to wear by then!"

His smile got wider. "I'm sure that's not true. This is a much more informal gathering than the Autumn Ball—the dress you wore then, while exquisite, would probably be overdressing for this event."

I frowned. Then it was probably true that I could find something. What was I saying—I could Disguise up whatever dress I wanted in that time. That wasn't why I was frowning, though.

"And to what do I owe this . . . opportunity?" I asked cautiously.

"My desire for an entertaining conversation would be reason enough for me to ask you," he said. "You would not believe how dull these dinners can be when everyone is afraid to talk to you."

"From what I've heard of the Baron, he does not seem like the easily intimidated type."

"Indeed not," he said, looking at me appraisingly. "But he has a guest that night, an old friend from the border. I expect his attention to be monopolized, and the rest of the guests averse to conversation."

I sighed. "I noticed you said '*would* be reason enough.' Is there some other reason?"

"I might have some ulterior motives," he allowed, "but they are best not spoken of on the street, perhaps?"

Well, it wasn't as if he didn't already know where I lived.

"Fine," I said. "But I still have to finish shopping for tonight's meal. You can carry the bags." I handed what I'd bought so far to him. He laughed and took it with a small bow.

"I shall endeavor to be of service, milady."

I rolled my eyes and went back to shopping.

On our way back, I realized my mistake. Well, *one* of my mistakes, probably. I had a sneaking suspicion that I was going to regret letting Tom into my home, but I couldn't see just how it was going to bite me. What I realized on my way home was simple enough. People recognized Tom, probably because of his clothes. He wasn't dressed in the cut silk as he had been at the ball, but he was still in black. *All* black. Black wasn't so unusual a color, but he'd managed to make every bit of his outfit jet-black.

So people recognized him, and of course they knew *me*. This was where I lived, after all. So talk was already starting about us walking together.

Face it, Kandis, you are shit at blending in.

We got back to my house without any incident, just a few startled looks. The others were back from the Guild, and I wanted to hear about how that had gone, but this took priority. Felicia read the room sufficiently to get the others to give us some privacy in the kitchen—our default room for meetings.

"So, ulterior motives?" I said once we were sitting down.

"I've had a chance to speak with my master about you," he said without preamble. "I said before that he would be interested in meeting with you, but I can now extend a formal invitation."

"That's uh . . . an honor, but . . ."

"No need to say it," he interrupted. "My master's attention provokes concern in most people. He understands . . . that trust takes time to grow."

"Does he," I said without emotion. I really didn't know what to make of this.

"He does. To this end, I have been directed to spend as much time with you as possible, and to give you what assistance I can."

"You . . . he . . . do what?" I said eloquently.

"I do have other duties, so don't expect to see me too often," he assured me. "And of course, only with your permission. This feast is a chance for me to accompany you while still fulfilling my diplomatic obligations."

"What makes you—makes your master—think that me getting to know you will make me trust *him*?"

He shrugged. "It's a start. There isn't much he *can* do to gain your trust. The best he can do is hope that his servant's actions reflect favorably on his own self."

"And he's doing all this because?"

"Well, as I said, he finds you—"

"Cards on the table, Parkes. Let's see some honesty if you want me to trust you."

"A shame," he said, with a sly grin. "I had been quite enjoying the ambiguity. But yes, as you suspect, we are almost certain that you are one of the Champions of the Gods. We don't know which one, though."

Well, at least it was out there. "Neither do I," I said. "They haven't contacted me."

"Interesting. They've been doing that more of late."

I raised an eyebrow. "Of late? Wasn't the last lot more than 200 years ago? Is ancient history part of the Ebon Order's training?"

"Not normally," he agreed. "But when it looked like I would be dealing with Chosen, I got a crash course in the history. In the last round, three Champions had unidentified patrons—the year before, only one. Before that, it was the common practice for them to be summoned directly to their god's main temple.

"This round, we've only had word of the Champions of Naldyna, Rakaro, and of course Duit. It's possible that they might have been summoned outside the range of my master's information network, but . . ."

"Have you made this offer to Isidre as well?" I asked.

"Of course, but she is relying on her church for support. I managed to pass on the message, but I don't expect anything to come from it."

"What does your master *want* with Chosen anyway?"

"I think I said before . . . Chosen are harbingers of change. Those in power naturally seek them out, to get advance warning of what's coming, or to influence what changes take place. Plus . . . there's always the chance to earn a favor from a god."

That did sound reasonable, but I suspected that "influence" covered a lot of shady territory. Spin was not limited to my world, apparently.

"Fine. So the feast," I said, changing the subject. Honestly, now that I'd had time to think about it, it sounded like a good idea. I needed to get inside the Baron's tower, and this seemed like a perfect opportunity.

A real James Bond move, I thought. *Waltz right into the enemy lair with an invitation and a date on one arm.*

Being with Tom would actually provide me with some protection as well. If Baron Marseau had figured out I was outside of the city when his men were being hit, he was much less likely to snatch me if he thought I was working with Aghen Shadthe.

"Maybe it isn't the worst idea in the world," I admitted.

"High praise, indeed," Tom said, smiling. "Shall I take that to mean I shall pick you up at sixth bell?"

"Sure," I said. "Now shoo, I need to discuss this with my team."

He took his leave, with one last bow for me, and a nod to the rest of the group.

"Well, that's dealt with for now," I said. "How did you guys do?"

"Wait wait wait," Felicia said. "What was that about?"

"Oh, nothing much," I said nonchalantly. "I just have an invitation to dine with the Baron tomorrow night."

Cloridan raised an eyebrow. "I thought those rumors about you two back in Anchorbury were false."

"They were," I said, giving him a look. "This is purely professional; he's just passing on his master's interest in me, is all."

Felicia shivered. "I don't know how you can say that so casually. You do know who his master is, right?"

"I do," I said. "And I also know he's very far from here." *And unlikely to show up,* I added privately. I now had an idea of why the famous Ice Arcanist had spent the last however many years holed up in his Ice Mountain. It had to be a dungeon, and he would be losing XP every time he left it.

"That didn't look like strictly business," Kyle mused.

"Anyway," I said, blushing slightly. "How did it go with the Guild?"

"Well, we reported that we saw the mysterious fighter," Cloridan said. "They didn't say much—seemed more confused than anything."

"Well, confusion is the goal," I said. "Keep in contact with the Justiciars—we should try to secretly shadow them the next time they go out. They're probably going to be a target for the Fangs."

"That, I can do," Cloridan said.

"As for me," I said, "I have a feast to get ready for."

FEAST

The next day, an announcement was made at the Guild that all adventuring was to be halted, while the Baron conducted a search of the area. As reactions went, it seemed pretty mild. I wasn't sure what his trackers would be able to tell him. Felicia had done her best to conceal our tracks, and she had a pretty good Hunt, but specialized Rangers would no doubt be better.

The Guild didn't ask any follow-up questions; no one came knocking on our door. I was counting on the Fangs' informant in the Guild to take our—and the Justiciar's—story to the Baron. I figured he had to be *somewhat* worried about the King looking into his affairs. Worried enough to discount the possibility of an Illusionist in his domain playing shenanigans? Who could say?

So I was only a little nervous when Tom came to pick me up.

"A carriage?" I exclaimed. "It's only a five-minute walk!" It wasn't that big a town. Actually, it was kind of impressive that he'd managed to *find* a carriage.

"Appearances matter," he said suavely. "It wouldn't do to show up on foot. People might suspect we're commoners."

"I already know that I am," I said, "but I'm a little uncertain of your own status."

"Ah, well, I said that I appreciated ambiguity," he said. "It's an acquired taste from continued consumption. The nobility can't seem to make up their minds whether to despise me or fear me. You may find yourself in the same position if they find out who you are."

"All the more reason to make sure they don't," I said warningly.

"Rest assured, your secret is safe with my master," he said. "You know, Lady Tamayo should be attending tonight."

"Lady, is it?"

"The Paladin profession is regarded as counting as a knight, in terms of status at least," he explained. "As a mage, you could ask to be referred to as 'Magister,' but few do."

"Sounds pretentious," I said.

"Exactly right. That doesn't appear to bother the higher classes, though," he said wryly.

A few moments later, we arrived at the tower's entrance. Tom helped me alight with a grace I'd only seen in movies. Charm told me that I should gently lay my hand on his forearm as we progressed inside. More than that would suggest unseemly familiarity, less would indicate I was mad at him.

Inside, they did that whole announcement thing as we entered. I gave the man at the entrance my name and title. He looked surprised but called it out.

"Ladies and Gentlemen, Tomas Parkes, Envoy of the Dread Shadthe, and Kandis Hammond, Senior Master of the Anchorbury Ironworkers Guild."

Charm kept me from wincing when they called out Tom. He'd given that title to the guy with a straight face, and now the other guests were all staring at us.

It was a small group, less than a dozen people standing around in the antechamber to the feast hall. I already knew some of them. Isidre, of course, and the Adventurers Guild Master. I hadn't spoken to him, but he'd been pointed out to me. I'd exchanged a few words with the Mayor's wife, so the stout, middle-aged man she was standing near would be the Mayor.

There were five martial looking men. One was wearing Duit's insignia and colors, so I assumed him to be Isidre's companion. Two of the others were more richly dressed, so I assumed they were the Baron and his guest. And indeed, Tom led me over to one of them for introductions.

"Baron, may I present Master Hammond, from Anchorbury," he said.

The baron looked me over leisurely. "Master, is it?" he said.

"Senior Mistress was already taken," I said, curtsying.

He laughed. "I've met your Guild Master," he said with amusement. "He seemed a little too old to be cheating on his wife."

"My lord misunderstands," I deadpanned. "The woman you're talking about *is* the Senior Mistress. The Guild Master is married to money, his one true love."

This was an old joke back in the Guild, but it went down well here. The Baron and his guest laughed their asses off, making fun of a guy they barely knew. I started to suspect they'd already started drinking.

"Where'd you find this one, Envoy?" The Baron asked, clapping Tom on the shoulder. I noted that he didn't move under the blow. "She's pretty *and* funny!"

I noticed that the other noble was looking at me speculatively, and sizing up my companion. He seemed unruffled by the attention, though.

"I met her during the Autumn Ball, my lord," he said calmly. Simple words, but they had a disproportionate effect. The Baron's smile slipped, and his friend went a little pale.

"Ah, you were at that event . . . terrible what happened there," the Baron managed before turning away. "I believe it's time for the feast to begin!"

"You certainly know how to kill a conversation," I said in a low tone as we watched the Baron stride away.

"It's what I do," he said. "Master Shadthe says that we dress in black to serve as a constant reminder of mortality to the people we deal with."

I snorted as we followed the Baron and the rest of the guests into the hall. "If I said your master was a goth, what do you hear?"

"I don't think the word translates—what is a goth?"

"Never mind."

We were led to our seats, about as far away from the Baron as it was possible to get. It was a fairly intimate setup, from what I knew about feasts. The Guild dinners had been much bigger than this. Two long tables seated seven guests each, while the nobility sat at a small table at the head of the room.

"I didn't actually get any introductions back there, thanks to you," I said to Tom once we were seated. "Do you know who all these people are?"

"Of course," he said. "You've met the Baron; his wife is seated next to him. I believe her name is Valerie. They've only been married for a short time. His guest is Baron Baer. I understand they know each other from before Baron Marseau was raised to his title."

"He wasn't born a Baron?" I asked.

"No, when I was last in this area, about nine years ago, there was another family ruling here. The Baron distinguished himself during the beast wave that extinguished that line and was awarded the title."

"A real warrior, then," I mused.

"Indeed." His eyes lingered on the main table for a moment. "Baron Baer is unmarried, and showed some interest in you. You should be careful of him."

"You think so?" I said as if it wasn't a concern. I'd noticed the look, but I was already being careful.

He nodded and lowered his voice. "These border barons . . . they're used to operating without supervision from the courts, ruling their little fiefdoms as if they were kings. Marseau will be somewhat constrained by the presence of his wife, and your relationship with his liege. Neither of those applies to Baer."

"Thank you for the warning," I said carefully.

He nodded at the table opposite. "The man in the chainmail vest is Captain Guertin, in charge of the Baron's forces. His wife is sitting next to him. I think you know the Mayor and his wife. The others . . ." He trailed off, looking at the younger guests taking up that end of the table. They hadn't been in the antechamber, arriving separately, and only now taking their seats.

"I'm not sure who they are," he said. "The Baron doesn't have any children, so my guess would be fosterlings."

"What's a fosterling?" I asked. I had an idea, but I thought it would be best not to let a fantasy TV series be my guide to this place.

"A hostage, dressed up nicely," he said. "It's common to trade children to be raised in other houses. Officially, they are guests, and it's supposed to reduce tensions. Having a family member in the building is supposed to temper thoughts of violence."

"Does that work?"

"Somewhat," he said. "Some families just write off anyone they send. But in this case . . ."

"What's wrong?"

"Well, the point of fosterlings is to *exchange* children, and the Baron doesn't have any. I could see an exception being made once, but three times?"

"That is strange." I didn't say anything more—I didn't trust Tom that much—but I looked more closely at the teenagers opposite. The one in the middle, a girl of about fifteen, did look quite a lot like Marie. It looked as if the Baron was quite the progressive, to extend noble traditions to commoners.

Tom looked appraisingly at the teenagers for a few moments more, then continued his introductions.

"On our table, you have your own Guild Master at the far end. Next to him is the woman everyone's talking about, Chosen Tamayo and her . . . companion from the Church."

"Is that the minder you were complaining about?"

"She has *lots* of people whose job it is to prevent me from talking to her," he groused. "But that's one of them."

I gave him an unsympathetic look. He shrugged.

"And finally," he said, raising his voice so that the person next to me could hear, "we have the person sitting next to you. This is Captain Boivin, of the Griffin Riders. That's his wife on the other side of him, no doubt counting up every surreptitious look he gives you."

Captain Boivin laughed nervously. "That's very funny, your Envoyship." He turned to me. "I'm very pleased to meet you, my lady, and so is my wife Belda." Belda nodded agreement and sent a shy smile my way. I thought that I might have seen her in the marketplace—it was a small town.

"Oh please, sir, I'm not in the nobility," I said warmly. Charm silently informed me that Captain was the equivalent of a knight, and entitled to be addressed as sir. From the way the Captain had busted out "Envoyship," he either didn't have Charm or knew that Tom liked being called ridiculous things. Could go either way.

"Just Kandis is fine," I continued. "Master Hammond, if you absolutely have to be formal."

The couple proved to be very down-to-earth and we made small talk while the soup course was brought out. I let Charm handle it, because I had another task on my mind.

Unseen Sound was an awkward way to conduct a conversation, but it had its advantages. Rather than pass my voice along, the sound was part of the spell construction, so I didn't actually have to speak to communicate. It did make it awkward for back and forth, but it was perfect for this.

I focused on making the sound appear quite close to her ear and reduced the volume to a whisper.

"Nod your head if you are Edele Monteminer."

She jerked in surprise, and looked around. The young man beside her didn't immediately react, so I think I got the volume right. Needless to say, I wasn't looking directly at her, so her panicked survey didn't help her any. Calming herself, she nodded briskly.

Target acquired, I thought.

"I was sent by your father. I'll be in touch," I sent. I really didn't have much more to say for now. I now knew who and where she was, but there was a lot more I needed before coming up with an escape plan.

Speaking of which . . . with the soup course finished, I gestured for a servant.

"Excuse me," I said quietly. "Can you direct me to the bathroom?"

The servant not only led me to the bathroom but informed me on how the facilities were to be used. Thoughtful, but unnecessary—I thanked him anyway. This tower had—as I'd heard—advanced bathroom technology like running water and flushing toilets. And not just a bolted-on addition like mine; this was fully installed. I approved.

That wasn't the reason for my excursion, of course. I wanted to get a larger picture of the layout of the tower—and a chance to see what security enchantments they had. So far I hadn't seen any, which seemed odd.

Perhaps it was because the Baron was new? Mandel had told me that he hadn't made any such enchantments for the Baron. Getting them made pretty much put yourself at the mercy of the Enchanter, so having them done by the man you were coercing was an exceptionally poor idea.

Aubert's house had had decades, if not centuries, to find trusted Enchanters and have them secure their properties. This guy, not so much.

The other possibility was that the enchantments were turned off or moved when there were guests around. That could be necessary if your exception lists weren't flexible enough.

I returned to the feast, not much wiser. One thing did come to mind, though.

Baron Baer is going to be staying in the tower tonight. There's no way that they can leave the enchantments up . . .

İΠFİLŤRAŤİOΠ

It would have been nice to sneak around while the feast was still going, but too many things got in the way for that. I didn't want Tom to know what I was doing, for one. I didn't think he'd betray me to the Baron, but I was operating under the principle of the less he knew, the better.

I also needed to let the rest of the team know my plan. Running off with a half-baked scheme was . . . not something I was doing. Anymore. So it was quite late when I made my way back to the tower and started looking around. I was pleased to see that they'd left the main doors open. They were massive things, about four meters high, and they clearly only closed them during emergencies. The rest of the time, they relied on guards posted in front of them to keep the riffraff out.

These slowed me not at all, and I ghosted into the fortress without any issues. I kept an eye out for magical fields, but saw none.

Now that I had time to examine it, I could see that the architecture of the tower was a step above anything else I'd seen so far in the Kingdom. It was less cramped and claustrophobic than the fortifications I'd seen previously. It didn't manage to match the open spans and wide spaces of skyscrapers back home, but it came closer. Some of it had been clearly constructed with Earth Magic, which must have made things easier in the absence of reinforced concrete.

Most of the doors to rooms were locked—or actually just closed. I couldn't really risk discovery by having someone see a door get opened by me. But I could move through the place and get an idea of the layout easily enough. It seemed to be based around an inner core that could only be accessed from the third floor. There were stairs going around inside the outer wall that connected all the floors, but all the floors but one had featureless stone walling off the center of the tower.

As I wandered around the tower, I could hear the occasional bursts of laughter from below. The two barons had kept drinking after the other guests had gone, and were still catching up on old times.

The entrance to the inner keep was guarded, but the doors were open, so I passed right through. It was one of those really thick and strong doors that must have been too much trouble to keep closing and opening in high traffic areas. I'd seen a number of them so far, separating important spaces like the stairway, but I'd yet to see one of them closed.

At least until I headed down on the inner staircase. The two levels there were sealed off behind locked doors *and* guards. That was probably where the good stuff was, but there wasn't much I could do about it. I headed up again.

Coming up to the inner third floor, I noticed that one of the smaller doors coming off the corridor here was open. I paused. Hadn't that been closed before? And hadn't there been guards on that corridor?

Intrigued, I wandered over to take a look.

I heard some movement from within the room, but I was distracted by the fact that I'd found the guards. Both of them were lying dead on the floor just inside the room.

What the—? Where's the blood?

It might seem strange that the lack of blood was the first thing I noticed, but I'd cleaned off my armor enough times to know—killing was a bloody business. More than that, though, they didn't seem to have any wounds. Well, almost. One of them was lying face down, and he had a small entry wound, perhaps from a dagger, in the middle of his back.

I didn't want to touch the bodies, so I could probably solve this mystery faster by taking a look at the person who did it. I moved farther into the room, past the bookcases that were blocking my view. This was some kind of an office or study. The walls were lined with scrolls and ledgers, and there was a large desk that dominated the room.

Oh, and there was a guy dressed in dark, concealing clothing going through the ledgers. His outfit screamed "assassin." Well, maybe "burglar" as well, but given the dead bodies, I was going with assassin. The outfit looked familiar, and the pair of daggers at his belt looked very familiar. I couldn't see much of them but that didn't matter to Identify.

> **[Identification]: Grey Hand Athame (2) – Quality: Excellent – Properties: Darksteel, Poisoned**

My hand went to my identical—except for the poison—daggers at my belt. I really needed to get around to enchanting those so I could change the name.

These guys again? Are they working for the same Duke as last time?

The man seemed to be going through the ledgers. I couldn't see his face, but he didn't seem happy with what he was finding. I watched him for a bit, as he went through the books methodically.

After a while of this, I heard the sounds of laughter get louder. The assassin heard that as well, and quickly made for the door. I only just got out of his way in time, as he moved to the entrance and quietly closed the door. He stayed there listening as the sounds got louder.

It sounded as if the Baron was passing quite close to us, perhaps on his way back to his quarters. He didn't seem to notice the absence of his guards, which struck me as sloppy.

Then again, if I had that many soldiers, would I be able to keep track of where they all were when I was drunk?

I wondered if the assassin was here to kill the Baron, but he waited, poised for action, behind the door until the voices had passed. When they did, he silently pulled the door open. I realized at this point that he'd actually been lifting the latch and holding the door in place so that he could now open the door without so much as a click.

Avoiding making a noise might be why he left the door open behind him, which let me follow him. Instead of heading directly up—which was where I now assumed the Baron's quarters were—he moved to the outer layer and started heading upstairs.

It was interesting watching a professional sneak who didn't have the benefit of Greater Invisibility. He took a lot longer to get to his destination than I would have, as he had to spend a lot of time hiding, waiting for people to pass by. I shadowed him all the way to the top of the tower, where Baron Baer was waiting, looking out into the darkness.

The assassin coughed quietly, and Baer turned without haste.

"The guards will be back shortly, so we don't have much time," he said. "Are you done?"

"I don't think that the good Baron is going to be susceptible to bribery," the assassin replied. "He has a lot of unreported income, so it might be possible to blackmail him if we find out where it's coming from."

"Everyone knows about his 'arrangement' with the Fangs," Baer said indifferently.

"More income than those criminals could contribute," the assassin said, sneering. "He must be sitting on a considerable fortune in his vault."

"While it's good to know that my old friend is probably good for a loan, that wasn't the question I asked," Baer said. "The arrangement was that once I got you into the tower, I was free and clear from your master. So, are we done?"

"Of course, my lord, I do apologize for bothering you with my own problems." The assassin took a step forward and bowed, then took another easy step as he straightened. "My employer is entirely satisfied with your actions this night and considers you free from any debt or ties."

"Good," the Baron said, and strode forward. "Then I'll let you find your own way out."

The assassin quickly stepped out of the way and bowed again. "Of course, my lord . . ." Then, as soon as he was out of the Baron's direct line of sight, he lunged forward. The dagger in his hand plunged deeply into the small of the Baron's back.

It all happened too quickly to react—if I'd even had a mind to. The Baron convulsed, seemingly unable to call out or strike back. The assassin kept one hand on the dagger, but grabbed his victim with his other hand, supporting him and gently easing him to the ground.

"Of course," he said thoughtfully to the dying man in front of him. "There are other ways to place pressure on the man. If, say, the Baron's old friend and guest were to be murdered in his home, people might start to think that he's not quite as honorable as he should be."

It took a little while for Baer to die. It seemed that the poison killed over time, but given the paralyzing effect, that didn't matter too much. It was no wonder they didn't sell this stuff in the alchemy shops. The assassin held onto Baer tightly until the end—perhaps worried about the paralyzation wearing off? Once the man was finally dead, the assassin pulled out a scrap of cloth from a pocket and curled Baer's hand about it.

"One last service for my employer," he said softly. Then, he moved quickly to the edge of the tower and slipped over the battlements.

I stared for a moment at the spot where he left, but that wasn't going to get me anywhere. I moved over to where the dead man was. It was hard to make out in the torchlight, but I thought the scrap of cloth was colored with indigo and blue. Duvost's colors.

Could anyone be so dumb as to fall for this? I wondered. *Surely not.*

Perhaps it didn't matter, though. Recalling that the guards were coming back, I snatched the scrap and put it in my pocket where the spell would cover it. Then I got the hell out of Dodge. I couldn't go over the wall, but I could take the stairs and hopefully I'd be out of here before the hue and cry arose.

I passed four guards carrying hot drinks going up the stairway I was going down. Shortly after that, there was a lot of shouting from upstairs. I didn't let that stop me and kept hurrying out of the castle as fast as I could.

Greater Invisibility really was the *best* spell; I don't say that enough. The guards were debating whether they should close the main doors when I passed through them. A minute more would have been too late.

I was about halfway back home when a bell began to ring from the tower. It sounded ominous, and lights sprung up all along the town wall, but it didn't impede me more than anything else had so far. It wasn't long before I arrived back.

My team was actually outside, like a lot of people who were wondering what all the bells were about. I tapped Felicia on the arm as I slipped past her into our house.

"Kandis?" she exclaimed, then headed inside. When she saw me, she called out to the others, and they all came back inside. I was collapsed on a chair, physically fine, but mentally exhausted.

"Look," I said. "I don't care what they say, it wasn't my fault."

Felicia gave me a stern look. "Kandis, what did you do?"

"I didn't do anything!"

LOCKDOWN

hy'd you take it?" Felicia asked. I'd given a brief explanation last night, and then gotten some sleep. Now, after a more detailed description of last night's events, we had moved on to speculation and second-guessing.

"I guess I just didn't want that guy's—whoever his employer was—plans to succeed."

Felicia looked at the blue and indigo scrap of cloth. "You think they wanted the Duvosts to be blamed," she mused. "But is this really enough evidence for even suspicion?"

"That's the weird part," I said. "From what he said, they plan on blaming Baron Marseau."

"He would be the obvious suspect," Cloridan said. "Even if this had been found, they'd only have the Baron's word that it was found on the scene."

"So everyone would believe the Baron did it, while he knew the evidence was genuine . . . well, not planted by him at least."

"It's too convoluted," Cloridan objected. "They had an assassin in the tower; why not just take out the Baron?"

"They don't want him dead," I replied. "Initially the assassin said something about trying to bribe or blackmail him . . . I think they want him to do something . . . turn against Aubert maybe?"

"Where do you get that from?" Felicia asked.

"Well, if we assume these Grey Hands are employed by the same guy, we know he wants Aubert dead. And if they're trying to lay blame for the murder on him as well . . ."

"That might work . . ." Cloridan allowed. "If there were some other incidents and the employer—"

"I think he might be the Duke of Arryen?" I hazarded.

"Fine, if the Duke then supports Marseau against this murder charge . . . it *might* work."

"But," Kyle finally spoke up, "there's not anything pointing to Aubert anymore, so what's going to happen now?"

"I doubt that will disrupt the plan completely," I said. "It might delay things a bit. The thing is, we're probably not going to be aware of any further developments. Unless there's a noble gossip source I'm unfamiliar with?"

"Not really," Cloridan said. "News trickles down, but normally well after the fact."

"So I guess we'll have to see what happens next as we go on with the plan."

"We have a plan?" Felicia asked, surprised.

"Well, the bare bones of one," I said. "We have to get Edele out of there. Which means we need to know how to get to her, a way to get her out, and a place to hide her until we can get her to her family."

"A tall order," Cloridan said. "Maybe we should wait a bit before filling in the details?"

I shrugged. "Maybe."

It was true that this wasn't a good time to scout out the tower. The guards were on alert, and no one was allowed to leave the town. Leaving your *house* was discouraged by foot patrols of aggressively suspicious guardsmen.

Stuck inside, I figured it was a good time to finally enchant my daggers. I'd picked up a pair of runes from Mandel that were much better than a simple Sharpness. Empower (Finesse) and Empower (Agility). It was a shame that Mandel didn't have Empower (Strength) to complete the trio, but this would do.

I'd also be trying something a little more complex this time. Mandel had sneered at my simple circles of runes. Apparently, a real Enchanter wasn't satisfied with just shoving an effect onto an item. This time, I was going to do what Mandel suggested was the bare minimum and trigger the enchantment on being held by me—or the others. As long as they were there when I was doing the enchantment, I could add them directly into the configuration.

A more complex enchantment meant a higher mana cost, of course. I calculated that this configuration would require an ambient mana of twelve . . . units. (I'd forgotten to ask Mandel what units you measured mana in.) That would work for dungeons, but I wanted it to work outside, so I was going to have to add in a mana crystal and a Gather Energy rune. Which took the complexity up even further, but that was fine. The new configuration would gather energy when it wasn't in use, and then trigger when I held the daggers. At that point, it would start draining the crystal . . . depending on the mana levels where I was fighting, I figured there would be enough juice for about five minutes of fighting.

Once it was all planned out, I called everyone together to do the first Sense (Person) rune. They watched me work for a bit longer, but then they drifted away, I think. I wasn't really paying attention, as I had to concentrate on the work.

> **You have crafted a Dagger of Dexterity – Quality: Great. You have earned 280 XP.**

Nice. I cheated and charged it up manually to test it out. Plus one Agility felt pretty nice as I moved about, dodging imaginary blows. I gathered the others—it looked as though they were still trapped inside the house. I got something to eat while they all tried it out, then we went back in to start Dagger Two.

> **You have crafted a Dagger of Deftness – Quality: Great. You have earned 280 XP.**

Now, I was . . . still not dangerous. Oh, I could probably get a few blows in while invisible, but I couldn't do damage to match our front line on even unaware targets. The good thing was, these daggers would continue to give me the plus one even as I increased my abilities, so they would continue to be useful as I got more Ability points.

Declaring my work over for the day, I joined the crew to see how their day had been.

"Weird," Felicia summarized. "We mostly just stayed in all day."

"You're allowed out, but those patrols sure give you the stink eye," Kyle agreed.

"I'm not sure what they think they're accomplishing," I said. "I'm almost certain that assassin is halfway to Arryen by now."

We all agreed and commiserated on how stupid this was, but there wasn't anything to do about it, so we went to bed. In the morning, we received word that the Guild wanted to talk to me.

"Now, this isn't a trial," the Guild Master said.

"That's very reassuring," I lied. I was sitting in a comfortable stuffed armchair, across from three others filled with the Guild officials. As I spoke, a mirror silently appeared behind them, courtesy of Static Image. I wanted to see if there was something behind me triggering when I lied.

To say that my guard was up would be an understatement. I didn't know why I'd been asked to come here, but I couldn't think of any good reason. Good for me, that is. I'd wanted to come fully armed and armored, but made do with my dress with the concealed slits for my daggers.

"Is that why there's no lie-detecting enchantment here?" I asked. I let the mirror fade away. They hadn't asked me to surrender my weapons, and I wasn't sure if it was courtesy or sloppy procedures.

The Guild Master made a face and gestured to the youngest of my three interviewers. That person, a young man with blond hair, cleared his throat and spoke up.

"Yes, as this isn't an official Guild investigation, the normal procedures don't apply."

"Damn things are useless anyway," the Guild Master snorted. He was a large man, with red hair and a full beard. "Only keep them around to cover our asses with Central."

"So if this isn't a trial, and it isn't an official investigation," I said carefully. "What is it?"

The blond man looked at his boss, who showed no sign of speaking. Taking that as a sign, he continued, but he kept his head at an angle to keep the man in view.

"Baron Marseau has some questions, for and about you," he said. "As an adventurer, you fall under our jurisdiction so he consulted with us before taking any action." His eyes flicked over to his boss again. "It was . . . *agreed* that we should handle any questions that needed to be asked."

"Like I was going to let that snake get his hands on any more of our people," the Guild Master growled.

"So . . . this is the alternative to getting taken off the street by guards?"

"I'm sure it wouldn't come to that."

I let the silence drag out a bit, and then changed the subject. "I'm sorry; I know Master Koenig, of course, but I'm not sure about your name . . . Officer?"

"Ah, I'm sorry," the man said. "I'm Millard Rochon, Officer is kind of . . . unwieldy. Just call me Millard. And this is—"

"Nadine," said the Deputy Master, speaking up for the first time. "No need for titles for us either."

"Just Koenig is fine," the Guild Master confirmed. "Not like there's another one in town to be confused with me."

"Thank you," I said. "Now, can you tell me what this is all about, first? I've heard rumors . . ."

Koenig glowered again, but Nadine took over the conversation. "After the feast last night, Baron Baer was killed, along with five guards.

Five? That surprise helped me display some shock at the news. "But he was *at* the feast," I said. "I spoke to him . . ."

"Yes, yes, it's all very tragic," Koenig said dismissively. When I raised an eyebrow, he shrugged. "Nobles killing each other is pretty much business as normal for them. I understand you were involved in a recent assassination attempt in Anchorbury?"

"I helped foil one, if that's what you mean," I said with a bit of ice. *Involved?* I thought. *Is Aubey spreading rumors about me?*

"Sorry," he said apologetically. "What we've heard is all thirdhand. Can you give us some details about that event?"

I narrowed my eyes, but decided to accept the apology. "Two members of the Grey Hand were disguised as servants and attacked the Count and his son."

"How were they identified as Grey Hand?" Koenig asked.

"By their weapons, as far as I was concerned. I don't know if they had other identifying features."

"A few members have mentioned noticing you have a pair of Grey Hand athames."

"I took a pair as a trophy," I said.

"Can I see them?"

I took one of them out. "I recently enchanted these, so the name's been changed," I said. *I really should have done this sooner.*

He glanced over it. "Not bad," he said, and looked over at Millard. He got up and fetched a ruler from a nearby cabinet. They measured the length and width of the blade, and then gave it back to me.

"It's not poisoned," Koenig noted.

"It's designed for it, but I didn't loot any poison samples," I said, shrugging. "And you can't buy that stuff from an Alchemist."

"True," Koenig said. He got a serious look on his face. "The Baron was killed by a knife of the same size as that one—with poison."

"You're not suggesting . . ."

He shook his head. "Marseau may suspect you, but that dagger isn't evidence. Lots of daggers are that size, and plenty of criminals use poison. If we were to judge by the wound, we would look to the Grey Hand as the ones responsible."

"Criminals like the Fangs?" I asked, ignoring the part about the Grey Hand.

"Damn straight, which points right back to the Snake," he said with some relish.

"Marseau is a suspect?" I said, "Why would he kill his friend in his own house?"

"My own theory is that Baer stumbled onto one of Marseau's schemes and was going to expose him," Koenig said with some satisfaction. "Or was going to blackmail him, and Marseau didn't like the price."

"How does it work, if the Baron is accused?" I asked.

"Normally the Count would have to step in and settle matters," Koenig explained. "But—"

"But he's still getting confirmed at the capital and won't be back for weeks."

"Aye," Koenig said, somewhat surprised at my knowledge. "So either the King sends him back early, or he sends someone to take care of this. An Inquisitor."

SCAM

I'm not familiar with this kingdom's higher officials," I said carefully.
"What's having an Inquisitor in a town like?"

Koenig laughed. "Like a nightmare—for Marseau!"

Nadine was more measured. "As far as commoners go, there are good
ones and bad. They do speak for the king, though, so you should show
respect and give your full cooperation. For nobles . . ." She glanced over at
Koenig, who was still chuckling at the thought. "Nobles reliably find them
hard to work around. With as many schemes as the Baron is involved in,
he should find himself quite beset."

"Whoever it is, they *will* want to speak with you," Koenig said.
"They're entitled to give us orders, so don't think we can shield you from
them."

"Right," I said. "Do you think they'll be investigating the other odd
occurrence?"

"The 'sanctioned operation'?" Nadine asked. "Probably. Inquisitors
don't have defined tasks. They can look into whatever strikes their fancy."

"Which is why Marseau is going to be pissing into his boots!" Koenig
exclaimed, starting to laugh again.

Nadine shrugged. "Possibly," she said. "This is all speculation. We
already got a report from your team about those people, didn't we . . . I
don't think we have further questions there?" She looked over at her superior for confirmation.

"Nah," he said. "Probably just a new gang trying to carve a space. Luck
to them, but many have tried."

"You're wishing luck to bandits?" I asked.

"Eh, as long as they're robbing the robbers, more power to 'em," he stated. "Though . . . Nadine, what's the chance that they're Guild members?"

"Neither group recognized the man, so I'd say it's unlikely. We should probably make sure our own house is in order before the Inquisitor arrives, though."

"On another note," I said, before they could think of more questions to ask me, "how long are we going to be kept in the city?"

"No idea," Koenig grunted. "Stupid idea in the first place. We were trying to get him to lift it before, and now he's trying to lock down the whole town."

"What's he trying to accomplish?" I asked. "We've been speculating, and can't think of anything—surely the assassin has left by now."

"Exactly," Koenig growled. "You see it, we see it, maybe I'll get a five year old in to argue with the man next time."

"So that was how *that* went," I said to the gang afterwards.

"So are we just going to lie low until the Inquisitor comes?" Felicia asked.

"I'm thinking . . . no," I said thoughtfully. "I think that's what Marseau is hoping for."

"What do you mean?"

"I think this is a show of force, to make us keep our heads down. So we shouldn't do it; we should keep hitting him."

"Uh, killing Fang members in the city might not go down well . . ." Cloridan said.

"Yeah, no," I said. "We're not doing that. But this is an information game, so there's a lot we can do without killing anyone."

The others looked at me. "You've lost me," Cloridan said.

"Us," Felicia agreed.

"Good, that helps me think that he won't see this for what it is," I said. "Now listen . . ."

It took a bit of planning. Felicia and Kyle got to stay behind while the rest of them got busy filling in the details of the Fangs that Cutter had started picking up. We didn't need much, just the identities of a few of the leaders and some of their habits. Once the timing had been sorted out, picking up one of them had been the easiest thing in the world.

Sitting across from me at a secluded bar table, he looked as if he couldn't believe his luck. Even Disguised, I still had my Charisma.

"I can't believe you wanted to have a drink with me," he mumbled. This wasn't a bar the Fangs normally frequented. I'd told him I didn't feel safe going to "his" bar, but that wasn't the reason we were here. I touched the top button of my dress and his eyes latched onto it. Predictable, but it meant that he was focused on me when the spell took hold.

I hadn't cast Phantom World often; it was too situational. Most of the time, it took too much concentration to keep track of details, and it was too easily broken when something went wrong. I thought I'd be okay changing just a few details here, especially since he wouldn't be interacting with them.

At first, the only thing in the room that changed was that a table emptied out. It wasn't in my field of view, but the spell helped with that. It didn't exactly let me see through his eyes, but I knew what he was seeing. Combined with my memory of what was there, I was able to edit that table's patrons out while he focused on my cleavage.

Next, I kept my image there, giggling away, while I moved a bit to the side. I did want to have eyes on what he was looking at, as I introduced the third change.

This one he noticed. At first only his eyes moved, as he noticed a fellow gang member enter the pub. Then he frowned when he didn't recognize the guy he was with. A certain German friend of mine, dressed in a red and gold tunic. That was why I'd decided to go with Phantom World. I wasn't sure how the bar staff would react to an unknown person wearing the King's colors, and this way I didn't have to find out.

The two of them appeared to move over to the empty table and started an intense discussion.

"Lars, are you all right?" I had my image say. "You look distracted." I fiddled with my top button again since it was in character.

"Sorry, sweetie, got distracted for a second there."

I led him on for a bit, watching him as he split his attention between the conversation and me, before moving on to the main event. My German passed over a large sum of money to the other gang member. Well, it was in a bag, but I thought it was pretty clear that it was pretty heavy. Mr. Gang Member (we hadn't gotten all of their names; I only knew Lars's because he'd been chatting me up) smiled and shook hands with his generous friend, and then headed out.

Of course, he ceased existing as soon as the illusory door had closed behind him. Red-and-Gold was next, headed for the door.

"Lars, is there somewhere you'd rather be?" I asked. He clearly wanted to follow those two.

"Ah . . . look, I just remembered there's an errand I had to do," he said. "Can you wait here for me?"

"Sure, I'll wait . . . for a little while," I said flirtatiously. He smiled nervously and headed out the door.

It was futile, of course; he was chasing phantoms that no longer existed and had only ever existed in his own mind. I lifted Phantom World as soon as his back was turned and watched him go out into the night.

"Poor Lars," Cloridan commiserated. "He came so close to the heavens, but he never had a chance."

"I—wait, this world has a heaven that people go to when they die?" This was a diversion, but we had time. The alley we were hanging out in was currently empty, and the patrols kept to the main streets.

Cloridan shrugged. "I don't know about *dying*, but the gods are said to have wonderful realms they can take people to whenever they want."

"So . . . the heavens are a really nice vacation spot?"

"That's one way of putting it. I guess you can ask your god about it when they show up."

"I'll make a note. All right, so you know the plan?"

"Of course; ready when you say."

"Greater Invisibility," I said, casting out loud for once. He turned and headed for the Fangs' hideout.

Right now, that unnamed member that I'd impersonated was spending some quality time with . . . a lady of negotiable virtue. I hadn't been sure if the Fangs leadership knew where he spent his time, but it seemed that they didn't, because they had half the gang out looking for him.

That meant they had fewer people guarding the place, so there was a good chance that an invisible thief who could pick locks would be able to make off with their stuff. I'd been a little worried that they had magical backup, but Cloridan hadn't been concerned.

"These guys have new recruits wandering all over the place, and they're bottom-feeders besides," he'd said. "The only way they'd have enchantments is if Mandel made them for them, and he said not."

Even with that reassurance, I still felt nervous waiting for him. My anxiety didn't lift until I saw his outline making its way towards me.

"Easy in," he said smugly, hefting a heavy leather satchel. "Couldn't take everything, but there was a lot of gold once I'd unlocked a few doors."

"And you left the sign?"

"Of course." I'd spent a while coming up with something simple that would get the point across. This world didn't have Officeworks to print up some business cards for me. Two coins left in a prominent place. One copper, one gold. Unusual enough to be noticed, and hopefully for its meaning to be decoded. Red and Gold.

"Well, it's not going to bankrupt him, but I'm sure it will hurt, not getting this money," I said.

"Hurt?" Cloridan said, grinning. "I don't feel any pain at all."

"I have been hearing the most *interesting* rumors," Tom said, taking a seat at my table.

"Do tell," I said, somewhat torn between interest and annoyance. It seemed that patrols weren't any deterrence for him to come and bother me.

"It seems that the Fangs are doing everything they can to find a man wearing the King's colors."

"Oh?" I said. "As it happens, I saw such a man outside the walls."

"I know," he replied. "The Guild leaks like a sieve."

"Do you think he's really working for the King?"

"Hard to say," he said thoughtfully. "Probably not, but I wouldn't say it's impossible."

"If you've seen the Guild report, the Fangs probably have as well . . . should I expect a visit from them?"

"I shouldn't think so," he said consideringly. "It doesn't sound like you'd know anything more than was in the report, and they seem to be keeping a low profile in the better part of town."

"If you're not here to warn me about them, then why are you here?" I asked.

Tom favored me with an innocent smile. "Why indeed. As it happens, I was told that if unexplained things were happening in the vicinity of a Champion, I should assume that the Champion is responsible for those things."

I made a face. "This is profiling. I'm not even the only Champion in town; how come you're not blaming Isidre?"

"Well, for one, she's leaving tomorrow on her expedition."

"How come she gets to leave while the rest of us are stuck in town?"

"She won't be passing through the forest. She's engaged most of the available griffins to take them up to the mountains. They can't fly all the way to the nest, in case they trigger the griffins' territorial instincts. It should take them about a week to make the rest of the trip on foot."

"So they'll be gone for about a week, then?"

"If all goes well, they should be able to fly back," he agreed. "Otherwise they have a scheduled pickup in eighteen days. But if we could return to local events . . ."

"I don't trust you, Envoy Parkes," I said flatly. "So even if I was up to something, there's no way I'd tell you about it."

"Understood. I just thought I'd ask." He stood up and bowed. "Oh! I do have one warning."

"Go on," I said.

"You're probably aware of the possibility of an Inquisitor being sent. You might not know that if the King decides to send one, he typically dispatches by griffin rider."

"Huh. So he could arrive any day now."

"Exactly. So if you did have anything going on that you wanted to keep from his notice, I'd make sure it finishes up in the next few days."

"Thank you; that may or may not be useful advice," I said. He smiled and took his leave.

I thought about it some more and then called everyone in.

"Everyone, we need to bring the plan forward."

PLOTS

Felicia frowned thoughtfully. "I thought we were going to give the Baron more time to get invested in looking for . . . we really need a name for that guy."

"Uh, whatever; the original was called Jürgen, so let's go with that," I said. "Yeah, that was the plan, but I'm thinking we don't know what things will be like when—if—this Inquisitor shows up. So we get as much done now as we can."

"How much can we get done right now?" Kyle asked doubtfully.

"I'm not sure," I admitted. "The big thing we're missing right now is a way to get Edele to her father. The only way I know how to do that is to take a griffin, and I can't conceal an invisible girl on a griffin from its rider."

"So we need a rider that we can trust not to go to the Baron . . ." Cloridan said thoughtfully.

"Ideally two, since a griffin can only take one passenger. Maybe Isidre can help when she gets back? Or . . . is anyone interested in getting a griffin?"

"No one wants to give up delving," Cutter said scornfully.

"What?" I asked, confused.

"Everyone knows Monster Tamers can't go into dungeons," he explained.

"They *can*," Kyle clarified in response to my confused look. "They just can't take their monsters. If you take a monster back to its dungeon, it will just get taken back. And if you take a monster to a different dungeon . . ."

"It gets mad," Cutter said with relish. "The dungeon gets mad and sends out a whole lot of other monsters."

"Something like that," Kyle said. "There are a few situations where monsters can come out of the dungeon, and that's one of them. It's said that when two dungeons are close enough to find each other, they'll send monsters across to fight, and eventually one of them will kill the other."

"That's why no one wants to buy that control collar we found," I said. "On the plus side, we do still have that. No one has to become a Monster Tamer. We just need to get a griffin and put that on it."

"We can't hide a griffin in the house," Felicia pointed out with some amusement. "And we can't steal one from the Griffin Riders; they'd notice. And we'd still need to get a rider and passenger harness, and that's the sort of purchase that would be noticed."

"What about scouting out a route on foot?" Cloridan suggested.

"Assuming we can get past the Baron's forces searching out there already?" I said. "The thing about that is . . . she's been kept a prisoner for . . . five years? And she looked about fourteen or so. So she's probably still level two."

There were groans around the table at the thought of shepherding someone so fragile through the wilderness and up a mountain. I felt for them, even though I'd been level one not long ago.

"Let's table that for now," I said. "Right now, I figure we can see if Marseau's patrols are actually looking for Jürgen, and increase their engagement if we fake a few sightings where the patrols can see. Assuming they go for it, then I think they'll be distracted enough for us—for Cloridan and myself—to try an invisible break-in on the tower."

"But we can't take Edele yet," Felicia objected.

"No, but we can check for magic defenses . . . and maybe make off with some of his treasury."

Cloridan laughed. "You're really getting into this steal things while invisible thing, aren't you? Aren't you worried that he'll connect an invisible thief with the Illusionist he's keeping an eye on?"

"I'll have an alibi of his own watchers, naturally," I said. "And the point of this is to *not* have an invisible thief be blamed. We want the blame pointed to a very visible culprit."

I paused for a moment and then continued. "We probably won't be able to steal anything—I'm betting if there's magical protection, it will be there. But we can look, at least."

"There's only so many times you can come here to consult before Marseau gets suspicious," Mandel grumbled.

"It can't be helped. I needed to speak with you—and your lovely wife," I said, including Marie in the conversation. "Marie, you're looking much more . . . human, this time."

"Thank you," the projection of Marie said, smiling. "And thank you for getting rid of that cage they had on me—I can't tell you how horrible it was."

"You're very much welcome; I'm glad I could help. And in that vein . . . I've laid eyes on Edele—she seems healthy and is being treated well."

The reactions of the two couldn't have been more different. Marie let out a little squeak of excitement, while Mandel just let out a slow breath and seemed to slump a bit.

"I'm three-quarters relieved," he said.

"Because now *both* Arber and I have to be betraying you for her to be dead?" I said with some amusement.

"Yes," he sighed. "I can almost hope."

"Mandel!" Marie exclaimed. "This is good news, and I'm sure that Mistress Kandis isn't betraying us!"

I coughed. "Actually if you must use a title, I think I prefer Master—or just leave it off entirely."

"Quite," Mandel said. "Mistress has some unwholesome connotations outside of an immediate guild setting. And my apologies. This is good news. But you did not come here to bring it, I fear."

"Well, I did, partly," I admitted. "I've exchanged a few words with her, and while I haven't broached the idea, I think that if she cooperates, I can get her out of the *tower*. Out of the town is another matter."

"What do you need?"

"Can you make me a griffin? Or some other kind of flying monster that can take passengers?"

Mandel looked at Marie, who frowned in concentration. "I don't see griffin listed . . ." she said, confused.

"Oh . . . I think it counts as a chimera?"

She grimaced. "That makes it awkward. Unless you have an example in stock to copy, what you get from summoning a chimera is random. I'd get one eventually, but . . ."

"Right, it could take a while," I said. "What about other flying monsters?"

"Well . . . I can't do a dragon. I can do a wyvern, but I'm not sure of their carrying capacity at the Threat levels I can manage. There are giant birds, but I don't think the ones I can do can carry more than one."

"That's not sounding good," I said.

"Dungeons aren't really meant for flyers," she said apologetically. "There are other types that open up with levels and achievements, but I can't see them until I unlock them. Have you thought about how to control them?"

"I've got a control collar from the chimera dungeon," I said. "So I can only manage one beast. In theory, I can give her the item and have her make her own way . . ." Both Mandel and Marie gave me some uneasy looks. "Yeah, it's probably not the best idea."

"Well, I have to summon monsters anyway," Marie said. "I can start now and see if we get lucky."

"Not committed to your theme, then?" I asked idly. Marie gave me a puzzled look.

"Theme?" she asked. "I just try to get the best defenders."

"She's a monster, Mistress! A philistine and a vandal. We can't help her run roughshod over all the rules of decency and elegance."

"Where are you even getting those words?" I asked. I was back home, filling Rhis in on what I'd been doing.

Rhis paused and cocked his head. "From you, I guess? You're the only one who speaks English, after all."

"Right, well, it's not actually a crime to not want your dungeon to be a work of art. She just wanted to live out her life as a hermit. I don't think she even developed levels until this all started."

"Well, at least from the sound of it, she won't make things worse from summoning chimeras," he sneered. "I can't believe you asked her to do that! Chimeras! I even explained them to you!"

"Well, do you know a better way of transporting people by air?"

"Wyverns aren't . . . great for carrying people," he admitted. "Unless it's in their claws. I doubt you could get a saddle on one."

"How would you do it, then?"

He thought for a moment. "Carrying people around isn't really a dungeon thing. I suppose if I *had* to, I'd look at some sort of capsule pulled around by a bunch of smaller giant birds."

"That sounds really elegant, but it's not an option here."

"I suppose," he said with a sulky frown.

"Something wrong?" I asked.

"It sounds like you made the right decision, not planting the seed around here," he said sadly. "There are too many other dungeons; it could be dangerous for me. But I really do want to be active again."

"I'm sorry about that," I said. "I'm still looking, but it seems to be tricky to find a place that isn't already taken. I get the impression that most high-level mages carve out a space by force."

"Is that wrong?"

"Well, for one, I don't *have* the force needed to do that," I said wryly.

"That's all right," he said. "Guile is a perfectly elegant way of solving your problems. So let's return to them."

"Well, unless Marie gets lucky, we're reduced to waiting for the expedition to come back and begging a favor from Isidre."

Isidre had left on her expedition and wasn't expected back for a while. I'd made overtures to the Griffin Riders, but they were a close-knit bunch and ostentatiously loyal to the King. That, and the careful logging of all flights, made me think I wasn't going to get anywhere with them.

"How has your provoking of the Baron gone?"

"Well, he's pissed off." We'd managed enough sightings of Jürgen to get a warrant out for his arrest. We hadn't managed the great tower heist, though. Baron Marseau *did* have some magical protection, and he saved it for his vault. It looked as if he was the only one who could enter the room without an alarm going off.

I had tried Theurgy, and while I *could* move mana fields, my limit was moving them about one foot. Not very useful.

Vault excepted, I had managed to get a good idea of the layout of the tower, and gotten in most places. Oddly, it was easier to get around during the day. During the day, people would go about their business, opening doors and making noise. I didn't make noise, but any door I opened or closed *did*, so it was nice to have cover for the sound.

I'd managed to have a conversation with Edele, through a Phantasmal Entity, and convinced her that I was from her father and was going to get her out of here. I couldn't give her a plan yet, so I just asked her to stay ready for when I did.

The forest was still off-limits, and sneaking around the castle, I was witness to one shouting match between the Baron and Koenig. Koenig was ranting about the necessity of culling the dungeons, while the Baron kept insisting that the woods needed to stay empty for his patrols.

"So basically, everyone's tense and pissed off," I said to Rhis, after explaining all this.

"Does it all end in violence?" he asked enthusiastically.

"Hopefully not," I answered with a glare. "I thought we were past that."

"Other people killing each other is different?" he tried hopefully. "It didn't happen often before, but sometimes when they got a good reward, parties would turn on each other."

"I'm sure that was a sight," I said. "But no, I don't think it will. No one has anything to gain from starting—or finishing—something, so I think they'll just yell at each other until something breaks the pattern."

"Something?"

"Well from our point of view, if we can get a ride from Isidre, we can stop harassing the guy and extract Edele. Otherwise . . . if the King does send an Inquisitor, that will probably de-escalate things."

The next morning, a messenger arrived from the Guild. The Inquisitor had arrived, and he wanted to see me.

INQUISITOR

Nadine was my escort to the tower.

"We haven't heard much about this one," she said as we made our way there. "He's said to be of noble blood, but without a title—a second son or something like that."

"I see," I said. For all their reassurances earlier, the two guild officials were taking the Inquisitor very seriously. On their advice, I was dressed for a social occasion, rather than in my armor. I was wearing my trophy daggers openly, which somewhat spoiled the look.

"That can work either way," she continued. "They can buy into the superiority doctrine, in the hopes of someday getting a title, or they get burned by their treatment as a second-class noble and start to despise the class."

"Not as simple as Koenig made out," I observed.

"There are a few Inquisitors who were raised from common rank," she explained. "They tend to be more loyal to the King, so they're the ones that get sent when there are noble interests at stake. I'm not sure what to make of him sending a noble, and an unknown one at that."

"Maybe the King is testing this guy more than us," I speculated, as we arrived at the tower and had to maintain a dignified silence in front of the guards. They seemed to be expecting us and allowed us entry without a challenge.

"This is as far as I go," Nadine said, as we stopped near a door that I knew led to a sitting room. There was a nervous-looking guard standing in front of it. I nodded to her and followed the man inside.

I quickly noticed that they'd changed the furniture. Instead of comfortable chairs, there was a large desk at which the Inquisitor was seated, and a single chair for me to sit on. Two guards were in the room, standing still enough they probably counted as furniture.

"Sir, this is Senior Master Kandis Hammond," the guard said, saluting. "Ma'am, this is Inquisitor Dunnar."

Seated behind the desk, the man didn't look terribly imposing. He had a square looking face and black hair cut very short. Then he looked up at me.

Whoa. Those brown eyes packed a strong punch of Intimidate. I don't think the guard was a target, but he whimpered a little as he quickly left the room. To my surprise, Charm let me keep my composure, and I curtsied and took my seat.

"My brief on you has you at level four," he said, frowning. He didn't diminish his intimidating pressure one whit.

"I have a high Charisma," I said. "And my Social skills are perhaps a bit higher than what you're used to adventurers having."

He grimaced and looked back to his papers. "I'm sure you've been warned to give your full cooperation to this investigation."

"Of course, I intend to," I said. "Might I inquire what it is you are investigating?"

"You don't know?"

"I've heard rumors of course, but I don't like to rely on them," I explained. "And if I know what you're seeking, I can give better answers." That was an attempt at Persuasion, but it crashed against his own defense. I hadn't exactly worked out what defended against Social attacks, and from what I'd read, neither had anyone else. Certainly, your highest Social skill total had something to do with it, but there were other factors. The prevailing theory seemed to be that there were additional, hidden stats that acted as hit points and armor did for physical damage.

He seemed pleased by the fact that my Persuasion hadn't broken through. Pleased enough to give me what I wanted anyway.

"As you likely surmised, I'm investigating the death of Baron Baer."

"Is that all?" I asked idly. "I'm sure that the Guild officials have had many complaints about Baron Marseau's recent behavior."

"There's no mystery there," he said, with a smirk. "The Baron is simply making sure his business outside of the town is kept private."

"And that's not a concern to the King's investigator?"

"It literally happens outside the Kingdom, so no," he explained. "Nor are his . . . arrangements with organizations that he makes to keep order within his domain."

"Well, I already knew that," I said sourly. "But if that's your only concern, then I doubt I can help you more than the papers you've already read."

He frowned. No doubt he'd expected to browbeat me into contradicting the testimony already given. I wasn't sure that was entirely off the table, though.

"Let's talk about this fellow in red and gold you saw. Baron Marseau blames him for the murder."

"I only had the briefest interaction with him, the entirety of which should be in your notes," I said. "Has he been seen in town?"

His smile was my only answer. "You gave a description to the Guild, but you are an Illusionist, are you not?" That smarted a bit, but he probably had that information from Marseau, who had it from Aubey.

"I don't have the profession, but I do have the skill," I admitted.

"Then can you *show* me what this man looked like?"

That felt like a trap. Not wanting to show off my Phantasmal spells, and not wanting to change myself to match a wanted killer, I opted to cast Static Image and placed an A4 photo of Jürgen with a forest background on Dunnar's desk. Facing him, obviously.

He raised his eyebrows in surprise and tried to pick the image. His fingers went through it, of course.

"Impressive. Such detail from such a brief interaction?"

"A good memory is essential for Illusion Magic," I explained. I cast a similar Static Image of the dead Baron next to the first.

"A wonderful trick," he said. "I'm sure that the Baron would have liked to see the face of his nemesis, but I'm not inclined to share it."

"He can always ask for himself," I said.

"I don't believe that would be a good idea," he said. "It would only encourage his false belief in this fellow as the assassin."

"Oh?"

"You've encountered the Grey Hand, Mistress Hammond," he said. "Do you think they'd have any trouble at all escaping first the tower, and then the town?"

"No," I admitted. "They seemed quite skilled and probably have enchantments or alchemy. I don't think the walls would hold anyone with decent Climb, Jump, or Strength."

"This has all the hallmarks of a Grey Hand assassination," he told me. "The poison, the weapon, even the angle of the strike. Of course, determining that it's Grey Hand is only half the problem—no, only a third."

"You need to know who sent the Hand," I said. "What's the other third?"

"Getting Marseau to accept it and get him to give up this ridiculous obsession." He gave me a conspiratorial grin. Was this the effect of Charm? He wasn't exactly treating me as a suspect now.

"The new Count Duvost had some speculation about who was behind the Hand that came after him," I said carefully. "I wouldn't want to accuse any nobles myself, but could this have been ordered by the same employer?"

"Perhaps," he said. "But I'm actually hoping you can help me with the third part."

"The obsession? I'm not sure that—"

"I have a theory, you see," he said, talking over me. "That this . . . fellow is meant as a distraction for the good Baron, someone for him to obsess over catching while his real enemies go unhindered."

He looked at me, but I didn't say anything, so he continued.

"When you think about it, it seems quite absurd that there have been so many sightings of the man, but no one can catch him. He seems to be quite the slippery character."

"Perhaps the fault lies in the competence of those searching for him?" I tried.

"Or perhaps there's another explanation," he said. "When you have an Illusionist in town—whether or not they have the profession—you have to ask yourself, could they be responsible for any odd happenings in that town?"

"Are you accusing me—" I started, but he interrupted again.

"Oh no, nothing of the sort," he said lightly. Then his voice hardened. "I don't need to accuse you of anything. Gerald!"

The door opened and the nervous guard came in.

"Are they in custody?" Dunnar asked.

"Yes, sir, all three of them," the man said.

"Excellent," Dunnar said approvingly. "Mistress Kandis, I'm going to keep you restrained here in the tower for a time. We shall see if that causes the mysterious man in red to disappear."

"I thought you only cared about the murder," I asked nervously. The guard took out a manacle and attached one end to his wrist.

"Oh, I don't care about whatever . . . this is all about. If you even are the one that's responsible. I'm just removing a distraction. If the man is sighted in the next few days, you will be free to go, with my apologies. If he doesn't . . . well, if it goes on for long enough to be persuasive to the Baron, we'll have another chat, and see if there's anything that you know that will be worth me not handing you over to him."

He smiled, as the guard approached me very carefully and attached the manacle to my wrist. I didn't resist—there were more guards blocking the only door, so I doubted I could slip out even if I went invisible.

"Thank you for your cooperation," the Inquisitor said smugly. "I'll see you in a few days, one way or the other."

"Well at least we're comfortable," I said to Felicia. "I was afraid they were going to throw us in a dungeon or something."

Instead, they seemed to have thrown the four of us into a guest suite. Why a guest suite would be pre-fitted with locks, I didn't want to know, but this was near where Edele was being kept, so perhaps it was just a spare hostage suite. We'd had our weapons confiscated, but we weren't searched. It was all very polite so far.

"How can you be so calm about this?" Felicia asked. She was . . . not panicking, but not far from it.

"It should be fine. In a few days, we'll be cleared and will be free to go back home." I glanced around, but there weren't really any good options here. If I wrote something down, Kyle would have to be told it anyway.

"On an unrelated note, back where I'm from, it was a common practice to put arrested conspirators together and listen to them talk, see if they incriminate themselves."

That was not news that Kyle and Felicia wanted to hear, but they got the point quickly. Cloridan seemed unsurprised.

"So I should ask, how's the house? Did they have to smash their way in?"

"Nah," Cloridan said while Kyle gave Felicia a hug. "They showed up and were very polite, but very insistent that we came with them. Seeing as you were already at the tower, we reckoned that coming quietly was the best option."

"Did you get a chance to secure the knives?" I tried. Cloridan laughed.

"Yeah, they're safe enough, at least for a while."

"Well, Inquisitor Dunnar is going to be keeping us here until the fellow in red and gold appears again, thus demonstrating that we have nothing to do with him. So getting out of here will just be a matter of waiting."

The others made sounds of agreement, but I could tell from their faces that they knew what was really going on. The only way we were getting out of here was if I managed to escape—and have that escape not detected. Then I could whistle up another illusion of Jürgen and sneak back in again.

I gave my best impression of a reassuring smile, but I have to admit it felt brittle from this side.

"Don't worry, guys," I said. "This will be a breeze."

INTERLUDE

The mountain air was crisp and clear. Mist billowed from Isidre's mouth, and her breaths were deep and heavy with exertion, though her Stamina wasn't greatly depleted. This looked to be a successful mission.

Perhaps because of their dungeon origins, griffins didn't have a set mating season. The nesting grounds were always occupied by nesting mothers and fledgling grifflets. However, there *was* a season for capturing mounts, and that was autumn.

In winter, the griffins all huddled for shelter in their nesting grounds, surviving off their stockpiled food stores. In spring and summer, they hunted for food, but spent most of their time mating and lazing around. Autumn was when they got serious about gathering meat, with the males hunting nonstop and depositing it to freeze above the snow line.

Autumn was the season when the numbers of male griffins were at their lowest. Not that the females were any less of a threat, but if you bonded one of their offspring, they wouldn't attack you.

It had taken a few days of sneaking around, but with the aid of a pair of experienced Monster Tamers, they'd managed to net and bond about ten adults and twice that number of fledglings. Some were bonded with Tame, others were controlled by a dungeon treasure that dropped from a local dungeon. Now the last of the hunters were returning to the camp, and it looked as if they'd be able to start heading back tomorrow.

Isidre took one last look at the view when something caught her eye down at the tree line. Movement. A small party of what looked like beast-kin was making its way up from the forest below.

"Orson! Get ready to break camp!" she called back. There were a few hours of daylight left, and if there was trouble, she wanted them ready to leave. They didn't have enough mounts for them all to fly—most of the younger griffins were too young to carry a rider.

The party below was small, only six people. Too small to be a threat, assuming matching levels, but they were moving quickly up the slope. Four days ago, she and her troop had spent hours pushing through the snow, but this group was somehow running over the six-foot drifts. It wasn't the strangest thing she'd seen since coming here, but it was annoying.

Calling up a few men as backup, she waited for the group to approach. They *were* all beast-kin, of different races. All of them were female, and not dressed for the climate, either—though they had fur, so they probably didn't need to be.

"That's close enough!" she called out when they got close enough to talk to. They stopped, but one of them took a step forward.

"Good afternoon!" she said. "Do I have the honor of talking to Lady Tamayo?"

"What the—how do you know that?" she exclaimed.

The beast-kin smiled. Isidre knew enough about beast-kin to know that it was a polite smile, because she didn't show her teeth. "When you are on a mission from a god, you don't lack for information," she said. *In Spanish.*

"You—" Isidre started. "You're another one, another Chosen."

"Yes. My name is Kaito Washiyama, from the nation of Japan," she said, still in Spanish. She gave a little bow, then straightened. "I am on a mission of diplomacy; may I approach?"

"I suppose so," Isidre said, still processing what had occurred. She quickly glanced back at her men to make sure none of them had drawn a weapon.

"It's an amazing thing, isn't it? This ability to speak all languages?" Washiyama said, smiling warmly.

"It's not every language," she said. "We speak Spanish at home, but there are more than twenty Mayan languages still spoken. I only speak Mam, and I can't speak any of the others."

"Mam, you say?" Washiyama said, in that language. She thought for a moment. "You're right!" There's a language called Ainu, spoken by a few people in the north of my country. I can't speak that, and yet I can speak Swahili, English . . . most of the European tongues I can think of."

"I think it must be only languages that people who have been taken from Earth have spoken," Isidre said. "If no Ainu have been taken, then the language didn't come across."

"Aaahh . . . interesting," Washiyama said. She seemed to be lost in thought, pondering the implications, so Isidre decided to get the conversation back on track.

"A diplomatic mission, you said?" she asked in Latorran. *Should I have switched to Japanese?* she thought. It seemed polite to do so, but at the same time, she wanted her men to hear what was being said.

"Oh, yes!" Washiyama said, snapping back to reality. "You are about to make a serious mistake. The Beast Nation—"

"Wait, what's the Beast Nation?" Isidre interrupted. "I thought all the inhabitants of this forest were in separate Tribes."

Washiyama frowned, clearly irritated at being interrupted. She paused for a moment, then continued. "The Kingdom of Latora doesn't recognize the Nation. And it is true that there isn't much in the way of central authority or permanent institutions beyond that of the Tribes themselves. But the Tribal Council is the final authority on those matters it chooses to deliberate on within the bounds of its territory."

She spoke as if she were reciting from memory—which she probably was. She hadn't been here any longer than Isidre had, after all. She paused and gave Isidre a questioning look. She nodded for Washiyama to continue.

"The Beast Nation does not begrudge hunters the opportunity of coming to the mountains to tame beasts," she continued. "Nor do they feel the need to control their borders the way that Latora or Earth nations do. You were free to enter, and you are free to leave."

"But?"

"But. The silver griffin must stay here, Lady Tamayo."

Isidre flushed. She'd guessed this was coming, but it still made her feel like a thief. "I was meant to have Manchas," she blurted.

"Meant by whom? The griffins are part of nature, which is part of the domain of Naldyna. She does not mean for you to take him."

"I don't think Duit . . . acknowledges Naldyna's authority in this area," Isidre said carefully.

"Has Duit told you this?" Washiyama asked knowingly.

"No," Isidre admitted. "But . . . it was like I was led here, to see him." She shrugged to find the words, of how it felt when she first saw the pure white griffin among all the others.

"For what it's worth," Washiyama said wryly, "Naldyna *also* thinks that Duit meant for you to take the griffin. Not speaking to you is just his way of maintaining plausible deniability."

"But I've bonded to him!" Isidre protested.

"That just means that if you order him to stay with his parents, he will," Washiyama told her. "The bond will fade in time, or be supplanted by a new one. I'm told that if you don't take the grifflet, the Council will provide a fully trained adult griffin of the highest quality for you to bond with. It can be in Talnier in three days."

Isidre thought about it. It *would* be more convenient to have a full-grown mount. As far as she could tell, there was nothing special about Manchas aside from his coloring. On the other hand, the thought of leaving the grifflet behind, now that she'd bonded with him was . . . unacceptable.

"What if we do take him," she asked, flatly. Was this group sufficient to stop them?

"Free to enter, and free to leave," Washiyama reminded her. "We're not going to try and stop you. But we won't shield you from the consequences of your actions, either."

"What consequences?"

"I'm sure you've realized by now just how intelligent the griffins are," she said. "They know that the griffins you take get fed and cared for. They put up a fight because they're wild animals, but they *understand*."

Isidre's eyes narrowed. That . . . actually matched up with what she'd observed up here. The griffins, however much they'd fought against it, didn't seem upset by being captured. Like it was a game that they'd lost.

"The silver griffin is different," Washiyama warned. "He's needed here. When the males come back and find him gone, they will come after him."

"It's just a color," Isidre protested uneasily. "And it's not like they can track us through the air."

"They don't need to," Washiyama said softly. "They already know where the humans live."

Isidre was taken aback by the implication. "Is that a threat?" she asked incredulously. "You're going to send them after us?"

Washiyama shook her head. "Just a consequence." One of the other girls behind her spoke up.

"We don't control the griffins, but we understand them. They're animals, but they have a greater understanding of the wider world than you imagine. All their past attacks on human settlements have been for reasons. Reasons that your nation has chosen to ignore."

Isidre looked back at Orson, her second. He gave the delegation a dismissive look.

"As far as *I* know," Orson said, "all the attacks have been random. There's never been a case of griffins following hunters back to Talnier."

"You said you'd never heard of a white griffin before, either," Isidre pointed out. She was starting to have doubts.

"The decision is yours, ma'am," the man told her. "Listen to your heart—if Duit didn't trust you, she would have told you what to do."

Would I have listened, if she had? Isn't she a false idol? Isidre thought. She still hadn't squared her Catholic faith with this new reality. She pushed the thought aside; it wasn't helping her with this decision.

Focusing on her feelings, she realized that they hadn't changed. If anything, this intervention only confirmed that Manchas had a uniqueness that went beyond his color.

"We're leaving," she told Orson. "Double-mount everyone you can; any that can't fit will have to camp in the forest and make their way to the meeting point." She didn't look at her fellow Chosen. "The rest of us will head to Talnier—if there's a griffin attack coming, we can warn them and help defend the place."

Her second saluted and started yelling at the troops. She turned her back on the tribal delegation. "Sorry," she said. "But I'm taking him with me."

Fast as griffins were, Wood Walk was faster, if somewhat limited. The party stepped out of one of the many trees that surrounded the second dungeon claimed by the town of Talnier. Called the Temple of the Ogre God, it boasted a variety of mostly humanoid monsters, a few of which were intelligent enough to have skills.

"Do we really have to do this?" Kaito asked her friends. Ettalle the fox-kin Druid hugged her.

"I know you don't like it, darling, but this is Nation stuff."

Orino, the other Druid in the party, directed the milax panther she was controlling into the cave-like entrance to the dungeon.

"Um, it's orders from the Tribal Council, you see?" Fassi said, her long ears twitching nervously. "If they ignored us, we were told to send this message to remind them who *really* controls this forest."

"Still . . ." Kaito said. He looked at the entrance. "This sort of thing never ends well."

"It's done," Orino said. "They found it. They're coming."

Ettalle focused on a spell of her own. Grass and flowers sprung up around the party's feet. They only rose up to their knees, but they marked a prayer of concealment.

The first monster that came out of the cave didn't notice the group. A misshapen humanoid with blood on its mouth and claws, it cast around. It wasn't long before it found the trail. Humans had been travelling to raid this dungeon for a long time. There wasn't a road, but to the enhanced smell of the ogreling, there might as well have been. It growled and started shambling off in the direction of Talnier.

It wasn't alone. Monsters began making their way out. For the moment, it was the lesser creatures of the first level, but the others would emerge soon enough.

"It's started," Ettalle said with a mixture of sadness and satisfaction. "It won't stop now until it runs out of mana. They should start arriving the day after the hunters get back. Let's get going."

The party linked hands again and stepped into the tree once more, heading for the other dungeon.

BREAKOUT

So all I had to do was escape this place, take a quick jaunt about town, and then sneak back in again. All without being detected.

The first order of business was to see if we were actually being observed. We spent the rest of the day cooling our heels and closely inspecting the walls, floor, and ceiling, looking for a hole or a crack or a magical crystal. We found nothing. In that time, we were served food, at which point it became clear that they'd considered the possibility of someone invisible escaping. Two guards stood directly behind the servant, blocking the door with their bodies. We all affected not to notice.

When night came, we extinguished the lights all at once—enchanted light crystals, probably a hundred years old—to see if there were any cracks that led to lighted rooms. Either they were wise to that trick, or there just wasn't anything.

"It's not that surprising," Cloridan pointed out. "This isn't a specialized cell; it looks like a regular guest suite where they've added a lock to the door. And the guy said he just needs to keep you out of circulation to see if that makes the guy in red go away."

"I suppose," I said. Maybe I was being too paranoid. "Well, there's no time like the present for getting out of here."

"And how are you going to do that?"

I'd had time to think of a plan while we were stuck in here all day. So I pointed to the window, one of three that the suite possessed. Everyone looked. It was big enough to fit through, but there were two problems.

"I think the bars will be a bit of an impediment," Cloridan pointed out. "This place is Crafted too high for us to just tear them out."

"Plus, it will make too much noise," Kyle pointed out. "You can't make the wall invisible, can you?"

"No, but I think this will be just as good," I said and pulled out my old dagger from its hiding place.

"Were you carrying that *under* your dress?" Felicia asked, scandalized.

"I'm more interested in how she got it out," Cloridan mused. "Have you had a hole made in *all* of your dresses?"

"Focus, people," I said, including Kyle in that. He hadn't said anything, but he was blushing furiously. "This is darksteel; can you use it to cut the bars?"

"Ah, right," Cloridan said. He thought for a moment. "I think so? We won't know for sure until we try—but it will at least be quiet."

"What about the drop?" Felicia asked. "We're five stories high!"

"She might be able to walk off jumping down, but there's no way you're going to climb the wall back up again with your skills," Cloridan agreed.

I grimaced. Cloridan was responsible for training my non-magical skills, so he knew better than anyone how lacking they were.

"I thought of that as well," I said and cast Phantasmal Object. One cubic meter can make for a *lot* of rope. I didn't come close to using my allowance, but I thought this should be plenty of length. "I'll go down on this one and cast another for you to lower down when I come back. Putting strain on it will reduce its lifespan, so I only want to use each one once."

"I should be used to this by now," Cloridan said, picking up the rope and running it through his fingers. "But Illusionist isn't supposed to be a utility class."

"And the Rogue class isn't supposed to be for working metal, but here we are," I said brightly. "Better get cutting."

After some discussion, we decided to cut the bars out entirely. There was some concern that if they cut one end and bent it, it would come out of the masonry. We were going to have to fix the bars when we were done, unfortunately. I had a few ideas for that, but the worst case was that I replaced them with Phantasmal Object. That would give us a day to make a run for it before it was discovered . . . not ideal.

The cutting went smoothly, and it wasn't long before I was clambering out the window. To Cloridan's delight, and Felicia's shocked disapproval, I was wearing a Phantasmal costume.

"It's as real as it needs to be; it's not going to go away if you stare at it," I said to the pair of them.

Felicia sniffed, "He hardly needs to be concerned about that, when what you're wearing is as indecent as that." From Cloridan's grin—and Kyle's averted gaze—she probably had a point. What I'd conjured up was my version of a ninja suit: a one-piece coverall in very dark grey. To my mind, it wasn't very revealing—everything except for my eyes was covered, after all. But it was more close-fitting than my leather armor, and I guess it was stimulating some imaginations.

"Whatever," I said, shrugging. "I'm going to be invisible for the whole thing anyway."

I made one last check to make sure I'd gotten everything in place. I put a Phantasmal version of me in one of the beds, pretending to be sick if anyone burst in while I was gone. The second rope was ready, so all that remained was to lower myself out the window.

The streets of Talnier were much as I'd left them the day before: quiet and heavily patrolled. It was easy enough to fake another Jürgen sighting. Once I'd scouted out the location, he could scuttle around until he was seen, then climb up to a roof to escape. Once line of sight was cut off by the roofline, I could let him disappear.

I left the guards searching the area and headed home. There were a few things I wanted to pick up.

"Mmph!" Cutter said, or tried to when I woke him up from sleeping under the kitchen table.

"How's it going there, kid?" I asked, releasing him. I'd cancelled my invisibility and the room was being lit by a dim light spell near the floor.

"Miss Kandis! I knew you'd get out!" he exclaimed, "There's no way they could have held you!"

"Thanks for believing in me," I said. "But I've got to go back, so you haven't seen me, understand?"

"You got it! What's the plan?"

"Right now, I just came back to pick up some things and make sure you were all right."

"I've been fine," he said. "They never searched the place or nothin', and I've got money to eat from my share of adventuring."

"Good," I said and headed over to where the safe box was. The light, and Cutter, came with me. "We should be back in a day or two; try to stay off the streets as much as possible, and stay out of trouble."

"No problem," he assured me, as I opened the box and took out the Fire Gem. "What are you going to do with that?"

"Nothing," I said. "Because I never took it, it was never here, and neither was I. Got it?"

"Got it, boss!" he said enthusiastically.

"Now get some sleep, I'm out of here."

A blacksmith's *shop* tended to be quite well secured. They generally sold weapons and armor, and that stuff was valuable. The workshop area tended to be much less so. Oh, it was all kept behind a barred door, but it was also well supplied with windows. Like most windows in this town, they were fortified with bars, but I could *look* right through them.

It was easy enough for my invisible self to Phantasmal Entity a man inside to unbar the door. I didn't stay long; what I needed was just lying about the place. I left a gold coin to pay for my depredations, which should surely puzzle the man.

My illusory version of Tom bowed as I left and barred the door behind me before fading away. *Utility mage, eh?* I thought. *It does seem to be turning out that way.*

Headed back, I could hear guards shouting. At first, I thought they were still chasing my guy, but when I got to the street they were on, they were pointing at the sky.

There were lights up there. As I watched, they came closer and I could see that they were being held by Griffin Riders. They had an assortment of weapons and shields, all glowing golden. The guards seemed quite excited, and it sounded as if they thought they were going to be under attack. But the procession slowly circled the town and made its way down to where the Rider's Academy was, just like every other Griffin Rider I'd seen.

Flying at night, though? That seems dangerous.

I moved on. Kyle dropped the rope when I flashed a signal, so all I had to do was walk up the wall while he pulled me up.

"Did everything go well? Is Cutter all right?" Felicia asked once I'd clambered in.

"Yes and yes," I said. "He's fine, and the guards should report another sighting in the morning—assuming they don't get distracted by the late-night griffins."

"I want to ask about that, but we should probably seal up the window again," Cloridan said.

I looked over at the severed bars and sighed. "Yeah, we might not get a chance if they free us first thing. I'm going to hate myself if we have to cut them open again because the guards' report isn't believed or something."

I brought out the items I'd liberated from the blacksmiths. A crucible, tongs, some heavy gloves, and some scrap metal. After casting a Static Illusion over the outside of the window to keep the light from attracting attention, I started heating up one end of the bar with the Fire Gem.

"I thought you didn't get Craft (Metal) skill," Felicia said.

"I didn't, but I did watch a video on welding on YouTube," I said. This job wasn't going to be up to that guy's standards, or anybody's, but hopefully it would pass for a while.

When the end of the bar was orange, I used Phantasmal Object to put a . . . cast on the stump at the top of the window and had Kyle jam the bar in there. I'm not sure if "cast" was the right word in metalworking, but then I'm not sure I'd ever heard of this as a technique. The idea was to wrap the heat-softened metal in a cylinder, so when it was jammed up against its mate, they bonded instead of deforming. I had no idea if it was going to work.

"Oh, it popped," Kyle said. "But it seems to be stuck? And . . . I unlocked Craft(Metal)?"

"Keep holding it in position, until it cools," I advised. The heat from the metal was intense enough to do damage to the Phantasm, and it couldn't take much. "Once it's done, we'll do the other bar."

Once it had cooled, I could see . . . it actually had worked! Oh, it wouldn't fool anyone examining it. I could clearly see the line where the steel had been joined, and it didn't look as strong as it should be. But it held, and I didn't think anyone using this room would know to be suspicious.

Of course, there was a good centimeter of clearance at the bottom end between the two ends. Between my crude cutting tool and even cruder welding, the bar was now much shorter than the gap between the two stumps.

But this was what the rest of the equipment was for. Putting the gem and half the scrap metal in the crucible, I turned the heat up even further, melting the steel. Feeling the heat coming off the gem, I started to appreciate just how wasteful I'd been, using this to heat water.

Once again, Phantasmal Object came to my rescue. This time, it formed a mold around the gap, and I carefully poured the liquid metal in.

I hope this works.

It . . . did, mostly. The Phantasm didn't last long, but doing damage had apparently cooled the outside of the metal down to a solid. I wasn't sure that was how physics . . . normally worked, but I wasn't going to complain.

I quickly cast it again in case the metal melted again. This time, it lasted longer—I guess the heat was no longer so intense.

> **Competency displayed with [Craft(Metal)], Level 1 awarded.**
> **For gaining a skill level, you have been awarded 1 XP.**

I guess the System approves.

"Okay," I said, too tired to avoid using that word. "Let's get the other one done, and then we can get to bed."

"Um, Kandis?" Felicia said questioningly. "What are we going to do with the equipment in the morning?"

A T T A C K

ost of the evidence wasn't too hard to hide. The Fire Gem was small enough for me to take with me, the gloves could be burnt up in the fireplace, and the crucible was brittle enough to be smashed into bits. The tongs were the only difficult bit. In the end, we cut them up into more manageable pieces, to be smuggled out under our clothes.

Contrary to my expectations, though, we didn't get released. In fact, we didn't get breakfast. Pounding on the door didn't get the guards coming in to see us. We were just . . . left alone.

It wasn't until mid-morning that the door was unlocked. Unexpectedly, it was Koenig that entered.

"What are you doing here?" I asked the Guild Master.

"Looking after my Guild members," he said with a tight smile. "Get your things; we're getting out of here."

The guards didn't look happy about giving us our weapons back, but they didn't argue with Koenig. It wasn't long before we were moving through the tower. We passed a few guards, some of whom were injured, and all of them spared a glare or a scowl for Koenig.

"Why are they upset at *you*?" I asked. None of them spared a glance for me.

"There were some developments," he said. "Which you will have missed because you were locked up, *where you couldn't help!*" He shouted the last bit at a guard we were passing, who only looked more pissed off.

"Are you going to fill us in, or do you just want to shout at the guards?"

"Ha! I can do both!" he yelled, though this time not in a guard's face. Nevertheless, he slowed the pace a bit and started explaining.

"The *idiotic* search parties that the Baron sent out this morning ran into more than the usual run of random monsters. They were swarmed by ogrelings."

"Swarmed?" I asked. Ogrelings were from the first level of the dungeon we hadn't been to. I didn't think that they were established on the surface—from what I'd heard, it sounded as if beast-type chimera like the milax panthers were better adapted to the conditions and had outcompeted the ogrelings.

"Swarmed," he confirmed. "Too many to just be a pack of random spawn. We're looking at a dungeon outbreak."

"Shit," Kyle swore. We all looked at him, as he wasn't prone to swearing. "Sorry," he said, embarrassed. "But my parents told me a lot of stories about outbreaks."

"Shit is about right," Koenig agreed. "It's not as bad as some of the stories. We're behind a nice strong wall that's designed to take a monster swarm. Bit of a shame that all those soldiers were *outside the wall* when the outbreak got to us."

"That's why these guys are injured," I realized. "They've got light duties, while the uninjured ones are on the wall."

"Right. The Baron's Healers have exhausted themselves healing the survivors that came back. They don't have the Spirit left to spare for minor injuries."

"What about the Guild Healers, like me?" Felicia asked. "Should I be healing someone?"

"That's where we're going," Koenig reassured her, as we swept out of the tower and started walking towards the walls. We seemed to be headed towards the main barracks. "But Guild-affiliated adventurers aren't required to help the noble's forces when they get into trouble."

I'd only skimmed through the Guild regulations when I signed up a second time, but I had Memorize. "We have to help Royal forces," I said, recalling the words. "But if the nobles want help, they have to do it through jobs posted through—"

"The Guild!" Koenig finished for me. "Which means getting approval from me!"

"And you didn't give it?" I asked. That would explain the dirty looks.

"Ha! Like I would give them dirt, when they're holding some of my people—and keeping us from our livelihoods."

I felt a bit of a weird feeling when I realized Koenig was talking about *us*. We hadn't interacted much besides that interview, and it was nice, to think that he cared enough to take what must be fairly drastic actions for our well-being.

"Is delving really a concern with an outbreak happening?" Kyle asked incredulously. Koenig waved dismissively.

"It'll be fine," he said. "We're behind walls; this sort of thing happens on the frontier. We're down defenders, which isn't great, but it gives us *leverage*."

"But couldn't the Inquisitor order you to help?" I asked, puzzled. He was the one who had imprisoned us, after all.

"That's true, he could have," Koenig allowed. "But he has not! Said something about the matter being none of his concern."

"The Baron must be pissed," I realized. "Even more than before."

By this time, we'd reached the barracks, and Felicia was intercepted by someone in robes that she seemed to know, who babbled something about urgent need and dragged her farther into the structure. Kyle followed, leaving us with Koenig, who didn't look as if he planned to go inside.

"So Felicia can heal," I said. "Should the rest of us go on the walls to help defend?"

Koenig shrugged. "If you want," he said. "If you do, find Nadine to get clocked on. It's a gold piece per hour on the wall, plus anything you get from the monsters is yours to claim."

"And that's it? We're free to go?"

"Until the Inquisitor decides to imprison you again," Koenig said, suddenly more serious. "I don't know what that's about. It seems like you're safe while this emergency is on, but after that, you'd have to ask him. Not that I recommend doing that!" he added hastily.

"Right. Oh, I noticed some griffins coming in late at night; did you know anything about that?"

"You could see that from your room? Well, that was the Chosen of Duit coming back early from their hunt. They've been closeted with the Baron all morning. Gives him someone else to rant at!"

"Well, we'll go find Nadine, then," I said.

"She should be near the river gate!" he told us and waved us off.

"Are we really going to man the walls?" Cloridan asked.

"Absent anything else? We can take a look at least," I said. "Oh, first we need to head back to the house and get armor."

"Just wondering if now would be a good time to . . . ah . . . bring that plan forward," he said. "What with all the disruption."

I grimaced. "Still don't have a way to get her out of town. Maybe Isidre will be available later? And I still need 20,000 XP to get to level five."

I'd actually wondered if our daggers would be of any use on a high wall during a siege, but it was fine. There was a lot more close-in fighting at the top of the wall than I'd expected. Once we'd checked in with Nadine and stepped on the outer wall, I got a notification.

> **Entering Massed Combat: Outbreak Defense Wave 2**
> **Accumulated Experience: 22,350**
> **Experience awarded based on contribution at end of wave.**
> **Contribution: 0.000%**

"Whoa, that's new," I said. "Is that normal?"

"Yeah," Cloridan said absently, his eyes distracted with his own notice. "That's how the big battles work. You kill monsters, supply troops, or heal to increase your contribution, and you get a share of the reward at the end. I hear that each level in Leadership is worth a full percentage point."

"That's . . . probably not right," I said. "The math would get weird if there happened to be more than 100 ranks of Leadership in a battle."

"I guess," he said. "I'll leave the math to you."

"Wait," I said, struck by a sudden thought. "Most people don't have Calculate, right? Do they even know what the numbers mean?"

"They know bigger numbers are better," Cloridan said. "Do we need to know more?"

I shook my head. "I guess not." *Why even show them, then?*

We moved on to the killing. As might be inferred from our casual conversation, it wasn't exactly a frenetic maelstrom of combat up here. Instead of some *World War Z*-like tide of monsters coming over the wall, there were little knots of people, some of them looking over the wall, others engaged with a monster that had made it to the top.

We wandered over to take a look for ourselves. That was more like it. At the bottom of the wall, the monsters that couldn't, or hadn't, managed the climb were frantically trying to get up. The fact that some of them *could* was pretty impressive, but they were slow doing it.

"This isn't as . . . overwhelming as I'd expected," I confessed to Cloridan.

"Towns wouldn't exist if they couldn't manage to fend off the occasional outbreak," he said. "But wait until the third day of this before you judge how easy it is."

"Three days of this?" I asked.

"It varies; the dungeon will keep pumping out monsters until it runs out of mana." He scowled. "It's probably got a bit more than normal from not having to deal with delvers for the last few days."

"So if the total time is three days, how many waves is it going to be?"

"Waves?" he asked.

"Yeah, the notice said we were in wave two."

"I don't know about that," he said, puzzled. "Normally it's just one long fight. Maybe the first fight outside the walls was the first wave?"

"Huh," I eloquently replied. "I guess it's the XP that matters, not how it's divided. Maybe it helps a bit since we weren't in a position to contribute to the first wave. What about the monsters at the bottom?"

"Unless they look like breaching, they'll wait until the dungeon stops before using the oil. Let's head that way—they look a little thin over there."

We did as he suggested, and it wasn't long before we were waiting with two guards armed with long spears for an ogre to make it to us. They looked askance at our weapons.

"Are you even going to get a chance to use those?" one of them asked.

I shrugged. "We'll see. There are some other ways I can contribute. Improved Blind!" I cast, using words and gestures for once.

The ogre didn't like that. He brought up his hands to paw at his covered face . . . apparently forgetting that he was using them to haul himself up the wall. He fell with a mighty crash, crushing a few wolf-like creatures that were swarming below.

"That's not going to kill him," the guard sneered.

"Yeah, but he's not climbing up, is he?" As we watched, the ogre got up and started laying about all around him. "He seems mad," I said with amusement. A knot of fighting developed below, as the smaller creatures took exception to being flailed at and stomped on. The blind ogre seemed to have the upper hand until he walked into the wall and fell on his ass.

"Things seem under control here," I said and moved on.

"You're not going to get any kills that way," Cloridan said, amused.

"Is that what's important? I'll surely get credit for taking out the small fry, and it takes pressure off the wall. Let's blind a few more ogres and see what it does for my contribution percentage."

Saying the word with intent was enough to pop up the notification again.

> **Accumulated Experience: 23,560**
> **Experience awarded based on contribution at end of wave.**
> **Contribution: 0.004%**

Still a long way to go, I thought.

It took two hours for me to work my contribution up to 0.1%. Not all of that was sending ogres plummeting off of the wall; there were a few fights with smaller ogrelings that were much better at climbing, but much less dangerous. I could actually hold them off without wasting Skill points. In practice, that meant I could fight mine until Cloridan killed his opponents with brutal efficiency, and then finished mine off.

"Let's take a break," I said. "You were right about pacing yourself." Three days of this . . . It wasn't hard exactly, but it certainly wasn't fun.

"You still want to do this? We're not getting much gold, and all the corpses are at the bottom of the wall," Cloridan said.

"The XP is piling up," I replied. "After three days of this, there should be a decent amount to share out. If we can get our contribution percentage up more, we might see some gains. We should see if Nadine is putting together a roster, sign up for the less populated shifts."

He shrugged. We signed out with Nadine and found that she was putting together a roster. We signed up for some shifts and then went to find the rest of our crew. Felicia had left the hospital, so we headed back and found her at home.

Over a much needed meal, we caught ourselves up on what we'd been doing. Apparently, healing soldiers from the *first* wave counted as a contribution to the *second* wave—Kyle was the only one who didn't have points.

"Should be plenty of time to catch up," Cloridan said, unconcerned. "We signed up for night shifts since Kandis can light up the place."

Kyle replied, but I didn't pay attention to what he said. I was distracted by a fresh notification.

> **Outbreak Defense Wave 2 Completed**
> **Accumulated Experience: 45,730**
> **Contribution: 0.103%**
> **Awarded Experience: 47**
> **Enter Wave 3? [Y]/[N]**

THIRD WAVE

W hat the fuck?" I exclaimed. "I thought you said it was going to be all one fight?"

"It was! I mean, I did, because it always has been," Cloridan protested. "I've never heard of multiple waves in an outbreak!"

"I have," Kyle said grimly. "Something must have changed at the wall. Maybe they've broken through?"

Everyone looked at him in alarm, then rushed to start reequipping. Armor and weapon belts were hastily donned.

"Cloridan, get to the roof, see if you can see anything," I ordered. He wasn't finished with his jacket, but he took off with it half buckled. "I'm down to about half mana and Stamina," I said. The Stamina, at least, would come back quickly.

"A quarter, for me," Felicia said. "My Stamina is fine, though."

"I'm fresh," Kyle said.

"Let's get outside so we can hear what Cloridan sees . . . Cutter, you're with us."

"Yeah!" Cutter exclaimed, "No more guarding the house!"

"Are you sure?" Felicia asked. "The house might be more defensible than the streets."

"We're going to have to go somewhere to find out what's going on. It'll be safer if we're all in a group," I theorized.

"I don't see a breach," Cloridan called down from the roof. "The fighting seems more intense on the walls."

"Then that's where we'll go," I said.

* * *

There was a crowd gathered around Nadine at the river wall. She was apparently waiting for a certain number of folks before she started shouting.

"Yes! A third wave has started!" she called. "It's an outbreak from the Forbidden Laboratory!"

That started a murmur in the crowd, as just about everyone muttered, "Two outbreaks?"

"Yes, two," she answered. "We now think it was a deliberate action by . . . someone."

"The Tribes!" someone called out. "They've done it before!"

There were a few beast-kin in the crowd that started looking nervous.

"That's *possible*, but keep in mind that any beast-kin that knew this was coming wouldn't still be in the city. The Guild will be coming down hard on any cases of violence between Guild members."

There was some more muttering, but Nadine continued on.

"In any case, who did it is less important than getting through this. The guards are getting overwhelmed, so the reward for time on the wall has been tripled. If you want to change your rostered hours, come see me."

She got off the step she was standing on and was immediately mobbed. "One at a time!"

I looked at the others. "I don't really want to go up there until I get my mana back. Shall we keep the roster as it is?"

"Sounds good to me," Cloridan said. "Let's see if we can get a look and see how it is, though."

We headed up. The fighting was a lot more intense than before. The monsters weren't allied; they still fought each other when they ran into each other, but they were approaching from different directions, so the vast majority were hitting the wall before hitting a rival dungeon's monster. The bastion towers extending out from the walls tended to separate the two mobs.

"I think it will be all right," Cloridan said uncertainly. "The wall is still holding most of them back. It's just going to be a harder fight."

We watched for a little while, but they did seem to have it under control. We went back home.

The man danced on the battlefield. Faster and more graceful than any man of flesh had a right to be, he stayed just out of reach of the ogre's swings. Frustrated, the ogre bellowed and charged after him, trampling more than a few of the lesser ogrelings that happened to be in the way. The man remained untouchable, however, leading the ogre on a merry chase along the base of the wall.

Just when the ogre thought it had the man, he rounded the corner of the bastion tower and faded away. Screeching in anger, it looked around for its missing prey. No sign of the man was to be found, but there were other enemies suddenly in sight. It charged into the mass of beasts, howling its rage.

"That's another one," I said to anyone who happened to be listening. A few of the nearby soldiers cheered appreciatively. The big ones were sometimes able to damage the wall, and they were a pain to fight without magic. Redirecting them to fight the other monsters was pretty efficient, even if it took a level thirty Phantom World to do it.

I had a sneaking suspicion that killing monsters this way didn't actually add to the event's total XP, but I kept it to myself. It did add to my contribution percentage, which was edging up on two percent. A small number, but when you considered there had to be 500 people contributing to this siege, it was no small achievement.

"Still no sign of his lordship," I said to my neighbor, a somewhat older veteran soldier. He was carefully keeping an eye on two younger soldiers hacking apart some kind of octopus-cockroach combination but made no move to intervene.

"Probably won't, unless things really go to shit," he replied. "He gets enough contribution from his Leadership just sitting on his ass, there's no need for him to get dirty."

"Must be nice," I said noncommittally. He gave me a considering look.

"Angling for nobility yourself?" he asked. "You've got the looks to find a way in. I hear the Count's unmarried."

I snorted. "I wouldn't be on the wall if I was going that route."

"True. There have been plenty of adventuring types who manage to impress the King with one feat or another. The King's grandfather was an adventurer himself, they say."

"And the Baron was just a humble soldier, so you're in with a chance yourself."

He laughed. "I think I've left my swift rise through the ranks a little late."

"Maybe," I allowed, "but as for me, I'm just trying to make my own way with as little interaction with nobles as I can manage." Down below, I saw what was probably my next target—some sort of elephant-reptile hybrid. Still out of range.

"Still, I have to admit that Leadership is a hell of a skill," I said wistfully. "Free XP and all."

"Ah, well, it's not all take," the soldier said. "We're all plus three with our swords on this wall because of his lordship—that's saved a few lives, because he took the trouble to get a decent skill."

"Is that why you're all using swords?" I asked. "I'd been wondering whether spears or pole-arms would be better for manning a wall."

"You're one to talk, with those daggers," he snorted. "But yeah, that's the reason. There's not many who are so much better with the spear that the bonus doesn't make up the difference."

"Hmm. Shame he never learned the spear, then," I said, eyes on my target. He was coming into my range. I'd learned today that Phantom World had the longest range of all my spells, a little more than 200 meters. It wasn't something that came up much in a dungeon. I started redirecting the—

[Identification]: Iguanaphant – Threat: 25 – Properties: Armor, Ferocious Charge

---

—uggh . . . the iguanaphant over to the middle of the ogres. It was going to be a long day, and I had a difficult lunchtime meeting.

"Absolutely not," Isidre said firmly. We were talking in a bar again. Well, I was talking to her, and she was talking to an illusion, but that was surely close enough. Precautions like this were starting to feel like a pain, but I still felt safer doing it.

"Why not?" I asked.

"Aside from the fact it feels like you're asking me to commit a crime?"

"That's not remotely true. I'm just asking you to take someone to a destination in the mountains."

"And hide the fact from the Baron."

"Last, I checked, he wasn't the boss of you."

"He is the legitimate authority here, and he has expressly forbidden anyone leaving town . . ." She trailed off and sighed. "But even allowing for that, my riders are needed in town."

"Really?" I asked. "I haven't seen them doing anything about this outbreak. Or the regular Griffin Corps, for that matter. Why is that?"

"Griffins aren't great against monsters climbing a wall," she said. "And the walls are holding, so there's been no call for an emergency deployment."

"So what are you needed for?"

Isidre sighed again and took a long swig of her drink. "I may have put this town in danger," she said.

"I guess you haven't been on the wall," I said. "Don't worry; the wall looks like it going to hold, and as long as that's true, the town isn't in any real danger. Are you saying you're responsible for the outbreak?"

"No," Isidre said. "At least, I'm not sure if it's connected." She looked at her drink, then up at me again. "The Kingdom has done expeditions like ours many times," she said. "We had advice, guides. This was a pretty good time of year to go, but even when the males are around, it's still possible to capture a few and leave."

"Okay . . ." I said, wondering where this was going.

"The griffins are somewhat intelligent, we all knew that before, but even though they live in a big herd up in the mountains, they don't have the same family connections that humans do. They're monsters, after all. Everyone said that we could capture some griffins and take them home and that would be the end of it."

"Uh-huh, and are you saying that's not the case?" I was getting a little worried now.

"When we were up there, we ran into the Chosen of Naldyna. She's a Japanese girl, Kaito Washiyama. A *cat-kin* girl."

"Whoa, someone actually took a racial option?" The thought of being in a body radically different from mine made me shudder for a bit.

"Yeah, she told me . . . We found this special griffin, up there. All white—I called him Manchas. They told me that he was special, that the other griffins *would* come after him."

More than a little worried now. "You took him anyway," I said. She nodded.

"I've informed the Baron; he thinks the threat is unlikely, but he's preparing for it nonetheless. All of the griffins will be needed for aerial combat—the wall isn't going to stop them."

"No, it won't," I said. Talnier was as well prepared for griffin attacks as a town *could* be, at least without building a massive dome over the place. I'd have to ask what the history of massed griffin attacks was.

"So this is what we're here for?" I asked. "Life clashes with nature, and when they do, the two Chosen are right in the middle of it?"

"I don't know," Isidre replied. "Washiyama sounded like she'd heard directly from her goddess, but Duit hasn't said anything to me." She gave me a considering look. "It's three Chosen, though. Does that mean that your god has a stake in this?"

"If they do, they haven't told me about it." I scowled at the thought of getting marching orders from some god. "I've got enough on my plate already, so if they've got stuff for me to do, they can wait in line."

I thanked Isidre for the warning and left. So not only was the meeting a bust, there was a new problem on the way. Great. Still . . .

I felt bad for thinking it, but an attack on the town might be a useful opportunity for me. It was something that had been drilled into me during my time at the firm: *A disaster that we don't profit from is just a pointless waste.*

It was, I suspected, an attitude that would meet with approval from a lot of people in this world. Still, one thing that I had gotten out of that meeting was an idea. And since I didn't know when the griffins were going to show up, I guess I was in a hurry.

The temple of Naldyna was a fairly plain blocky building on the outside. Getting in meant going through not one but two sets of large ornate doors that were opened for me by the attending guards. Despite the well guarded entrance, the guards let me in without even a question. The apparent contradiction was answered when I went past the second set of doors to find that the high walls hid an inner courtyard that was teeming with life. Plant *and* animal life, I saw, as a deer jumped out of the bushes along my path.

"Is there a spawn point in here?" I asked incredulously, to no one in particular.

"Yes, actually," said a beast-kin who had to be a priest here. A dog-kin was my guess as to his exact species. "Don't worry; it's carefully curated to only spawn harmless animals."

"Huh, good to know," I said. I hadn't known that "curating" spawn points was possible. Was that a Druid thing, or another application of Theurgy? "I, ah . . . need to speak with whoever's in charge, or the most important person who will speak to someone off the street."

"I see," he said. "Why don't you take a wander through the garden and I'll see if the High Priestess will see you."

I thanked him and he wandered off. He hadn't asked me my name, and I hadn't volunteered it. I was wearing a false face, after all. It seemed this church was a little relaxed about these things.

I went for a wander. I wasn't alone in here; there were quite a few beast-kin of various sorts sitting around in various nooks. Most of them were dressed in Kingdom clothing rather than the leathers and skins

I'd seen some beast-folk wearing. That would indicate that they weren't Tribals, but long-term travellers or even citizens. I caught a few suspicious glances—tensions must be a little high for them with the Tribes being thought to be behind this latest outbreak. No one said anything, though, and after a few minutes, I was found by the priest and escorted to meet the High Priestess.

She was human, to my surprise. Blonde and blue-eyed and quite pretty with it. "What can I do for you, stranger?"

I ignored the unspoken question and went with the spoken one. "I've got a feeling that you can arrange a meeting for me with someone. Someone by the name of Kaito Washiyama."

"I see, and who is it that wants to meet her?"

"She might already know," I said consideringly. "So for now, I'd rather not say."

"Then what makes you think she'll meet with you?"

I smiled. "Just tell her, *Hanashimashou*."

MIDNIGHT MEETING

onnichiwa, Washiyama-san," I said and bowed as we did in Japanese investor meetings. Just like the investors back then, Kaito looked surprised and irrationally pleased to see a Westerner following Japanese etiquette, and she returned the bow. It was too bad I wasn't selling securities, as I'm pretty sure this would have pumped up my commission fee by twenty percent.

It was night, and we were in the forest. Getting out of the town hadn't been hard; for all that Talnier was besieged, most of the attack was coming from only two directions. The monsters didn't understand tactics beyond "head straight for the tasty humans," so at least half of the wall was free of attackers.

Kaito was, as Isidre had said, a cat-girl. She still looked kind of Japanese, in that her skin was tanned and her hair and furry bits were black. I wouldn't have picked it up without already knowing, though. Her eyes were much rounder than the Japanese stereotype and softly glowing purple to boot. Her ears . . . well, they derailed any comparison to Earth ethnicity that I could imagine. Cute, though.

She was wearing leather, like me, but with much less coverage. It looked as if it was designed for freedom of moment rather than protection, but Mana Sense told me it was enchanted, so it might actually be better than my own suit.

I was alone—using the Disguise spell instead of puppeteering an illusion. Beast-kin were supposed to have good senses, and they might pick up my imperfect lip sync. Kaito was backed up by a bevy of varied beast-folk, all of whom were female. They were giving us some space but were staying close enough to join in the conversation if necessary.

"You have the advantage of me," Kaito said, also in Japanese. "How should I address you?"

"I had thought you would have gotten my name from your patron," I said. Charm kept a sudden frown off my face. There was something about her speech that seemed a little off.

"Orino, could you repeat the goddess's words about our meeting?" she called over her shoulder in what must have been the beast-kin common tongue. *That* sounded all right.

A smaller beast-kin with rounded fluffy ears stepped forward. "She said that as long as the Chosen wasn't going to take an active stand against us, she would respect their cover."

Huh, a friendly gesture and a not-so-hidden warning at the same time. Pretty classy, Naldyna.

[Thank you for the compliment.]

Something must have shown on my face, because Kaito suddenly looked concerned.

"Are you okay?" she asked.

"I just . . . there was . . ." I stammered. *What the fuck was that?* "I think . . . did Naldyna just speak directly to me?"

"Perhaps?" she said, looking closely at me. "She is more communicative than the other gods, I'm told. And you have to assume that both our patrons are watching this meeting closely."

"Figures that some other god would deign to talk to me before my own patron does," I said sourly. *Did she do that so that I would lose my shit right before I start dealing with her Champion?* There was no answer this time. I got the feeling that someone was laughing at me, but it was probably my imagination.

"Just how communicative is she?" I asked.

Kaito cocked her head consideringly. "She mostly talks to her priests—the Druids," she said. "But she has spoken to me more than a few times. And I think that she spoke to everyone here before we came to be companions."

As Kaito spoke more, the feeling that she was somehow speaking wrongly continued, but I still couldn't pick up what was wrong. It wasn't an accent; I could understand them as easily as any other language or dialect.

"Right then, I'm—" I paused. I was going to give an alias, but then I suddenly recalled I'd given my real name to Isidre, which might make things difficult later. *Oh well.* "—Kandis Hammond," I said. "Call me Kandis; us Aussies are an informal bunch."

"Very well, Miss Kandis." I blinked until I realized that we were still speaking Japanese and she'd thrown a "-san" on the end of my name. "Then you must call me Kaito."

I bowed again and resolved to either add a "Miss" when I went to say her name or make sure there was a "-san" on the outgoing speech. Hopefully, Charm would be up for navigating the various levels of Japanese polite speech for myself. I knew they existed, but that was the limit of what I—*Wait. That was it.*

"Your speech is wrong . . ." I said, reviewing what she'd said so far. It was difficult since I didn't know Japanese, but when I remembered what she'd said in English and tried to translate it into Japanese in my head, it came out different from what she'd said. "You're . . ." and Charm finally came through with what was going on. "You're speaking as a man . . . did you change your gender as well as your race?"

"Ah!" she exclaimed in surprise. "You're right! I suppose that since I haven't been speaking Japanese all this time, I never got into the habit of speaking to match my new form."

"Ah, I see," I said awkwardly. "Were you trans, back home?" *Hopefully, that translates right.*

"No . . . at least I don't think so," she *(he? Let's stick with she)* said. "I never thought much about such things before. But back then it was cat-*girls* I was obsessed with, not cat-*boys*, so it seemed the obvious choice."

"Obsessed with . . . oh, I think I read a story about guys in Japan . . ."

"Otaku," she said, the word coming through untranslated. "Yes, here I am, an otaku in an isekai. It's very stereotypical."

"Otaku and isekai—those words didn't get translated," I said.

"Oh? I had heard that anime was more popular in the West now—perhaps they've entered the English lexicon?"

"Maybe?" I thought back to my uni days, Memorize cutting through at least some of the alcohol fog. There had been a movie night or two, and someone whose name I never got, explaining things . . .

"Shit, you're right, this is an isekai. Hang on . . ." I glanced back at his companions. "Aren't a lot of isekais *harem* stories?"

"Uh, yes . . ." Kaito said, looking embarrassed.

"Is there . . ." I checked. Yes, there was. "Did you take the Harem option?"

"Yes," she admitted. "I didn't really know what was going on, and it seemed such a great option . . ."

I brought up the System entry.

> **Harem: Acquire a number of companions equal to your [Charisma]. Companions will be selected to be of appropriate age, gender, and attractiveness (5 points).**

Typical System notes, leaving out all the details. "How did you 'acquire' them?" I asked. "Are they being mind-controlled?"

"I don't know how it works," Kaito said, anxiously. "I met Ettalle before I took it, and it didn't seem like it changed her at all. She was already very . . . friendly."

"They're all girls, obviously, because you're a guy . . . are they all into girls, then?" I was trying to work through the implications of this. Did the System find five gay girls at short notice, or did it *make* them?

"I didn't—we haven't—done any of that stuff!" Kaito protested, blushing. "Just some hugging."

"How old are—no," I said, interrupting myself. "I'm not going to lie; I'm a bit disturbed by . . . all of this, but it's not my business, and I couldn't do anything about it if it was. I came here with something else in mind."

"They seem happy?" Kaito offered. "And it's not like they do everything I say or anything."

"Fine. Not my problem. My problem is the griffins that are supposed to be attacking soon. Can you stop them?"

Kaito shook her head. "We don't control them; we're only predicting their behavior. The griffins will come here because they know that's where the humans who took . . . the grifflet live. If they don't find him here . . . we don't know what they'll do. They might head further into the Kingdom, even though that would doom many of them."

"They couldn't take the low mana levels," I guessed.

"Exactly."

I groaned. "I really don't want to take a side in this thing that your two gods have got going."

Kaito shrugged. "To a certain extent, doing nothing is choosing a side, is it not? We're not doing anything because we can't think of a course of action that wouldn't make things worse, but it sounds like you have more avenues than we do?"

"Maybe," I said sourly. "But speaking of making things worse, you are responsible for the double outbreak going on right now, aren't you?"

"That wasn't my decision," Kaito said, grimacing. "The Tribal Council doesn't have good relations with the Kingdom, and they felt slighted by Miss Tamayo ignoring our warning."

"Are you taking orders from them?" Not that I could judge, I'd accepted orders from Kingdom authorities already.

"Not personally, but . . ." He shrugged and looked back at the girls. "As I said, they don't do everything I tell them."

"I see." Weirdly, that made me feel a little better about the harem things. If political allegiances trumped whatever the harem bond was, it couldn't be too strong a mind control, could it? Mind you, Kaito wouldn't have done more than ask politely, I was sure. "Why don't you call them over for the rest of this conversation."

He did so and introductions were made. I got them to identify their species as well, so I didn't have to guess based on their ear shape. Okay, Fassi the rabbit was easy to guess. Wolf-kin would have been my third guess for Zichy, and I didn't really have any idea about Orino and Nori: mouse-kin and otter-kin respectively.

"Okay," I said, switching back to Latorran and relishing the fact that for once I could say the untranslated word. "Let's say I want to take Manchas away from Isidre. Not because I'm taking sides, but because I want to stop a slaughter. Isidre is bonded to the griffin, right? So is there a way to stop him from just breaking free and heading back to Isidre?"

The girls conferred. I think they switched back to their native tongue, but it made no difference to me, of course. However, it was still pretty much all gibberish to me, since they were talking about skills and magic that I didn't have much knowledge of.

Orino was the one who relayed the results. "There's a kind of spore dust, from the hatiem puffball, that induces deep sleep. So deep that it will suppress the bond between a Tamer and their Beast."

"Suppress, but not break," I said carefully.

"Yes. If you use it on either one of them, they will fall into a deep sleep and will be unable to awaken for at least an hour. After that, if they are not disturbed, they will sleep for up to eight hours. When they do wake, the bond will be gone, but it can be instantly established again if they see each other. If they're kept separate, the bond will eventually fade, but I don't know how long that will take."

"What about those magical control collars?" I asked.

The group conferred again. "That might stop the animal from obeying commands through the link, but the link would still be there. She would know where the beast was, and even see through its eyes if she's learned that ability."

"So . . ." I asked, already knowing the answer. "Do you have any of this dust?"

"Sorry, no," Orino said apologetically. "We *might* be able to find some in time, but I wouldn't count on it. Your best chance is in town. It will be known to most Alchemists and Herbalists, but . . ."

"It's a controlled substance, isn't it," I said.

"Banned," she agreed. "But Priestess Tonet might be able to find some for you. She will know if there are any beast-kin Herbalists that don't follow Kingdom law."

"And she'll go against the law herself?" I asked in surprise. "Isn't she supposed to be a law-abiding citizen of the Kingdom?"

"It's for Naldyna," Orino said simply.

As simple as that, was it? "Well, I'm not going to promise anything, but I'll look into it. I may have to send him to you for repatriation."

"We'll help however we can," Kaito assured me. I sighed, knowing that I was going to regret this.

"There *is* something else you can do for me. Do any of you know of an Enchanter living in the mountains?"

They all looked at each other. "I do," Nori said. "Mander or something, right?"

"Mandel," I said. "You don't seem to have a problem moving through the forest. Can I ask you to escort his daughter to him?"

"Now?" Nori asked.

"No, once I've sprung her from prison," I said. "She's a hostage right now."

"So the Baron might be coming after her?" Kaito asked. He looked back at the group and seemed to sense some sort of consensus. "We can keep her safe, and get her to her father."

"Thanks," I said. "Can I pass messages through the Priestess? I'll get back to you when I have an actual plan."

"Please hurry," Kaito said. "We don't know when the griffins will arrive, and they will make everything more difficult."

PIECES

S o now, maybe, I had all the pieces of a plan. I just had to put it together. I spoke to Priestess Tonet first thing in the morning, before I did a stint on the wall. I tried to impress on her the urgency of this. I kind of wanted to do this at night, and anything later than tonight was risking the griffins arriving.

Felicia didn't like my chances.

"I know Naldyna is all about living things, but I don't think they'd be crazy enough to grow prohibited species," she said. "Master Oliver told me about that stuff, but I've never seen it."

"Are there a lot of prohibited substances?" I asked idly.

"Not that many," she replied. "It's illegal to poison somebody, of course, but most poisons aren't illegal to own. Only the 'on contact' ones like this, and the ones that bypass your Stamina—like this one."

"Wait, what?"

"Most poisons drain your HP, Stamina, or mana until you die or fall unconscious. But this one just renders you unconscious until the duration is done. So it doesn't matter what your level is, it just works."

"I can see why those in charge don't like it," I said.

"I know I'd be wasting my breath if I told you about the dangers you face if you're caught with this, but at least I can give you the antidote."

"There's an antidote?"

Felicia sighed with exasperation. "We're talking about a cloud of airborne dust that renders you unconscious if it touches you. How did you think you were going to use it if you didn't have an antidote?"

"I thought the supplier would tell me how?" I said. "But if there's an antidote, I can't really rely on the one-hour unconsciousness period, can I?"

"I suppose not," Felicia said thoughtfully. "Of course, it would take a while to identify the poison and fetch the antidote. If you don't incapacitate everyone in the area, you might have as little as ten minutes, if they have a medicine cabinet in the building."

"Well, that's not great."

"Actually . . . now that I think about it, standard healing won't work on this, but I think Life Priests get a spell that will work on it."

I groaned. "I'm going up on the wall now; feel free to think about ways the plan won't work while I'm gone."

It only took two hours on the wall to use up 200 mana, which was only a fifth of my mana but would take me eight hours to recover. Like most of the mages, I was limiting my mana spend to a sustainable amount. I'd do another shift in the evening and get the mana back overnight.

Most of the mages were here for even less time. Fire, Storm, and Ice mages had damaging area effect attacks, but they did chew up the mana. It meant that they tended to have short but very impactful shifts up on the wall. They'd sit around waiting for a good opportunity, and then blast away. Most of them had more mana than me, but after three big shots, they were done.

I went back to the Temple after lunch. Priestess Tonet was waiting for me.

"I have what you need," she said. Leading me into an alcove walled off and lined with greenery, she showed me three small bags.

"It's not the only way to use the powder, but my . . . source recommends this way. If you release the first seal,"—she pointed at the wire holding the bag shut—"the second seal will hold the bag closed, but not firmly. It will break if you throw it, or hit it with an attack. That will release enough powder to knock out a target, maybe up to three if you're lucky and they're close together."

"Not the only way?" I asked, examining the bag carefully.

"There's enough powder in each bag for much more than three people if it's distributed properly. You could sprinkle a little on pillows, or use Air Magic to spread the powder . . . as long as it touches the skin."

"Scary stuff."

"And expensive," she said wryly. "The temple supports your mission as much as we can, but we don't have the funds to purchase this. My source has trusted me as a go-between, but . . ."

"Say no more, how much is the damage?"

"200 gold," she said, looking at the ground.

I winced, but I'd been told to expect something like that. I counted out the money and she accepted it with a bow.

"My goddess tells me that you are careful by nature and are unlikely to get caught using this, but *do* be careful. And try to avoid telling anyone where you got it from."

"Yeah, I'll do my best," I said, doing my best imitation of someone confident, and left.

I was really doing this, then? I guess I was. I headed back home to discuss things with Felicia. Kyle and Cloridan were still on the wall. With skills based on Stamina, they were good for hours yet.

"I still can't believe they could get it for you," Felicia said. The bags were on the table, and she clearly wanted to poke them but didn't. "I've never seen . . ."

"Well, if you want to take one apart . . ." I suggested.

"No, I can't do it safely in the time you've got," she said. "Better to keep it locked up."

"Speaking of safety," I said, reminded of something. "Is using these going to cause a whole lot of these puffballs to sprout the next day or something?"

"They only grow in specific conditions," Felicia explained. "Though . . . that might come up. I know you're not planning on killing anyone, but if the spores lie for long enough on a dead body with open wounds, they might sprout."

"That would be disturbing. Okay, don't kill anyone under the spores."

"So are you just going to wait for night, then? Do you need us for anything?"

"I think I'll take Cloridan for his general sneakiness and techniques with locks," I said. "I'm going to try to avoid fighting altogether."

Felicia nodded. "Then—" she started to say, but at that moment bells began ringing all over the city. Not for the hour, but some kind of alarm.

I poked my head out the door, to see people running for the homes. I called out to them and got "Griffins sighted! Get under cover!" in return.

Shit, they couldn't wait one more day? I turned to Felicia. "Do you need to get to the Healers' station?" She nodded. "Take Cutter with you; he won't be safe here on his own."

"Shouldn't you take him? You're going now, aren't you? Won't you need someone for the locks?"

I wanted to object, but being invisible with me was far safer than being on his own during an attack. Even if taking him on an infiltration was a terrible idea.

"Cutter!" I called, and he came in from the kitchen.

"Yes'm?"

"Get your weapons, armor, and lock picks; you're coming with me."

"Yes!" He punched the air excitedly and rushed off to get his things.

"I'm going to regret this," I said. Felicia was also getting ready.

"I'll see you tonight," she said. "After you've freed the hostage and sent the griffins home."

I rolled my eyes. "I've got to do *everything* around here."

There weren't any monsters on the streets when we headed out. It made sense that they would have spotted flying griffins from a fair way out. I explained the plan to Cutter on the way and then found a secluded spot to turn us both invisible.

Holding hands, we ran towards the citadel. It was a decision that might cost lives in the town, but this really was an opportunity that wouldn't come again. Cutter kept up with me easily enough. He had shorter legs, but a higher Run skill.

Before reaching the tower, we ducked instinctively at the sound of wings, but it was the town's griffins taking flight. From the uniforms of the riders, it was a mix of the King's men and Isidre's. I grabbed Cutter again and was about to drag him off when we both froze. The incoming griffins had come into view.

There are so many . . . I thought. They easily outnumbered our defending airforce by about . . . three to one? Honestly, it was hard to tell from this distance. We still had time, though, so I started running.

They'd closed the main doors to the tower when we got there, but a smaller door was still open. Too many people milling about to close it, and it was probably too small for a griffin to fit through anyway.

From the looks of it, they were looking to defend the tower on the ground. They'd found the pikes they hadn't been using on the wall and there were half a dozen nervous guards carrying them, looking at the sky. Not at us, though, so we slipped easily through their cordon and made our way into the building behind a messenger.

Cutter got us past one locked door before we got to our first magical alarm field. As I'd suspected, with no guards to spare, they'd locked the hostages up and turned the alarm on. Given a few more minutes, they might not even respond to the alarm, but I didn't want to take that chance.

"Wait until the other alarm sounds, and start on those locks," I said with Unseen Sound. Cutter nodded and I left him to it.

I headed to the vault. If the alarm went off *here*, it would have a much higher priority. Of course, being in the vault while guards and maybe the Baron himself combed the place looking for me was not part of my plans. I had something better in mind.

You see, detection fields tended towards the spherical. You could tweak them, according to Mandel, but it wasn't easy. Rooms, on the other hand, tended towards cubes. That did mean that there tended to be coverage gaps in the corners, but that wasn't what concerned me here. Rather, it was the fact that to minimize those gaps, Enchanters tended to extend the field through the walls.

I'd noticed it before. It was only the barest sliver of field, just a centimeter out from the wall and easily covered by my hand. But it was an alarm, and it wasn't in the vault. I put my finger on the spot.

I was a few corners and a door away from the vault entrance, so I didn't get to see the reaction. But a minute after it started, the alarm was silenced. I could hear Cutter's alarm going off now as well, so I snuck around to the entrance to see what was going on.

I couldn't get to the entrance, because Inquisitor Dunnar was standing in front of it, and I didn't want to get anywhere near him. Inside, I could hear swearing that sounded like it was coming from the Baron.

"I swear she's in here somewhere!" he shouted. Dunnar reacted with amusement.

"You're letting that girl get to you, Amaury. Wasn't she proved innocent?"

"Never trust anything when an Illusionist is involved! You know that as well as I do."

"Perhaps," Dunnar acknowledged idly. "I would have thought, though, that you'd have more concern for your town than I'm seeing."

"Bah! The soldiers can handle this well enough. And if they fail, the monsters will descend on the Rider's Academy, where the beast is. They might cause some damage looking, but it's not like they're hunting for food."

"You're happy for the King's latest project to take it all on herself?" It struck me that there was just a bit of a dangerous tone to that question. The Baron must have heard it, too, because he came closer to the door and spoke in a more normal tone.

"I'm not going to interfere with His Majesty's latest pet. But she brought this on herself, and on us. It's only right that she bears the brunt, and she'll tell you that herself."

"Mm," Dunnar grunted, apparently satisfied. "Well, in the interests of reducing your paranoia, what do you say I take the girl off your hands once all this is sorted?"

"You'll arrest her?" the Baron said hopefully.

"Oh, I doubt that will be necessary. I'll tell her the King is interested in meeting her, dazzle her with a bit of pomp and ceremony. Get her hooked on life in the capital and then step in once she falls into debt."

"Rather you than me," Marseau muttered. "I'll bet she can slip out of any simple debtors' prison."

Dunnar shrugged. "Then she'll be hunted across the Kingdom, I doubt she wants that, even if she can find a new face. I'm sure I can provide a more . . . palatable option. She *is* very beautiful."

Eww. I slipped away. I'd heard enough to know that those two would be staying at the vault for now. That was the most important fact for now. The rest I'd have to deal with later.

FİNAL WAVE

Outbreak Defense Wave 3 Completed
Accumulated Experience: 2,035,420
Contribution: 1.92%
Awarded Experience: 39,080
Enter Wave 4? [Y]/[N]
You have opted into Wave 4.
You have gained a Level!
You have been awarded 250 Ability Points.
You have been awarded 5 Development Points.
You have been awarded 2 Skill Points.

So, good news and bad news. The next wave starting must mean either that the griffins had landed on the outer walls, or that our air force had engaged. The lack of screaming suggested the latter. I still had a bit of time.

The new level was good news, but I noted with some irritation that my contribution had dropped down to less than two percent. I'd been busy with other things, I suppose.

Getting back to Cutter, I saw that he'd picked the lock and the main door was open. It was time for Jürgen to make a reappearance.

I cast Phantasmal Entity, and Cutter jumped in surprise. "That's you, Miss, right?" he asked nervously.

"Of course. Good job here," Jürgen said with a grin and went through the door. Beyond was a short corridor with six doors leading off it. Jürgen tried the first one. Somewhat surprisingly, it wasn't locked—I guess these were the low-security cells. The room was actually quite nicely furnished, and decorated with personal items. Its occupant—one of the teenagers from the feast—wasn't enjoying the luxury. Instead, he was pacing back and forth as Jürgen opened the door. He quickly whirled to face us.

"What is it? Are we—" he paused and looked at Jürgen's tabard. "You're—"

"I'm looking for Edele," I interrupted. "Where is she?"

He looked as if he was trying to say three things at once. He looked at Jürgen's armor and sword (they were decorations, really) and gulped. He'd clearly heard about someone who'd matched this description.

"Second door on the other side of the corridor."

Jürgen nodded, gave a little salute, and shut the door on the way out. The reason I was using Jürgen was that the Baron was already mad at him, so no loss if he got madder. And from the conversation earlier, I'd managed to establish at least a *little* plausible deniability that he was me. If there had been an invisible person opening the door and taking a look inside, that would have pointed a big fat finger in my direction.

As it was, the Baron was probably still going to blame me, but whatever. I opened the indicated door, and sure enough, Edele was there. She looked dressed and ready to go, which was lucky. The other guy had been the same. I guess being held in a cell while a town alarm was ringing had motivated them to be ready in case the tower was attacked.

"Edele?" Jürgen said. "I've come to take you to your father."

She didn't react immediately, staring at Jürgen with surprise until he gestured for her to come over. "Grab anything you want to keep; we won't be coming back."

She moved over to a desk and picked up a small bag. "Wait, the griffins are—"

"It will be dangerous, but you should be all right," Jürgen reassured her. "You'll see."

With that, she came over to the door, and we led her out. I was leaving the door unlocked, which might have been an opportunity for the others . . . or not. It was pretty dangerous out there, I could imagine they wouldn't want to take their chances.

Out here, the alarm was still blaring, but no one had come to see. I led my party to a room that would hopefully be out of anyone's way so that I could brief Edele and make her invisible.

"This is Cutter," Jürgen said, moving her hand to clasp his. "He's going to lead you to our safe house."

I explained how to get there by herself, in case they got separated, while she got used to the idea of holding a hand she couldn't see.

"But the griffins?" she asked.

"You'll be invisible, too, so as long as you're careful, you should be fine. Neither of you will be able to see each other, though, so keep hold. Now drink this, just in case."

Jürgen handed her one of the antidotes that Felicia had given me. Cutter had already taken his on the way. She gave Jürgen a doubtful look but downed the small bottle.

I cast Greater Invisibility and she faded from everyone's view by mine. "Wait here," I had Jürgen say, and moved on ahead.

As I'd expected, they hadn't left the exit unguarded. The door was still open, but it was blocked by three guards with spears, facing outwards. Jürgen stepped forward, carrying his payload.

I was surprised he made it up to them, but I shouldn't have been. Screams were coming from the griffins outside now, and all three were pretty focused on the outside. I imagine if they noticed him at all, they thought him to be reinforcements.

Jürgen reached out with the bag of hatiem powder and squeezed it right next to the first soldier's head. The bag was designed to be thrown, which meant a lot of the payload was expected to be wasted. Delivered personally like that, I could make the bag last longer.

The soldier sneezed, attracting the other guard's attention, just as Jürgen moved forward and around to dust them as well. They shouted and tried to turn their spears towards him, but he was too close, and the spears weren't great for suddenly turning around in a doorway. And the spores worked fast, too. They only had time for a few confused shouts before falling to the ground, unconscious.

I took a look outside, leaving Jürgen out of sight for the moment. We had attracted some attention, but there wasn't a huge crowd. The soldiers in the square had been clustered into three tight groups of six. They didn't seem to be trying to hold a line, spreading out instead in small monster-hunting squads.

That worked out well for me. The closest squad was heading over to see what was going on, but slowly, keeping their eyes on the sky. There would be plenty of time.

"Get out here," Jürgen called back, stepping away from the doorway and resealing his bag of sleeping powder. The kids came forward and he waved them through. "Go! Get home; don't stop for anyone."

I collected my bag and cancelled Phantasmal Entity. Then I staggered as the world went dim for just a second. Even with the antidote, touching that stuff was a bad idea. I placed the little ball of doom carefully in my pocket, allowing it to become invisible again, and tried to brush the stuff off my hands. Then I remembered I had to get out before the guards arrived and blocked the doorway while gaping at unconscious bodies.

I only needed five steps before I could lean against the wall out of the way and let them rush by, but it was as if I were drunk. I stayed there for a few moments, letting the shouts of the soldiers wash over me while the magical drug was flushed out of my system.

All right, time for phase two.

I had actually planned on using the puffball on this part of the operation. Aside from meaning I didn't have to kill any innocent guards, it would link the two crimes, and I was pretty sure that they would blame the second crime on either Kaito's crew or the Tribal Council in general. Which would link Jürgen to them, and hopefully away from me. But to do that, I had to get moving and actually commit my second crime.

I wanted to take a quick break to spend my points, but I really couldn't spare the attention. Invisible or not, I still needed to keep an eye out for swooping griffins, just in case one tried to land where I was. They were descending on the city now, in small numbers. The majority of them were wheeling around above the city, presumably fighting the Riders. It was hard to tell the sides apart from below, but I'd seen the relative numbers as they came in, so I wasn't hopeful of the Riders winning that fight.

The ones that landed were more of a concern. To me, and to the troops on the ground. Some troops—and civilians, it looked like—were set up on the rooftops, trying to deny the monsters a perch. What I mainly had to avoid were the monster squads running through the streets to attack any griffins that decided to open a house for the snacks inside.

Though . . . food didn't seem to be what the griffins were after. Like Kaito had suggested, they did seem to be looking for something. The ones that landed on the street would move purposefully along it, rather than smash in windows or doors.

It made it harder for me to avoid them. I had to divert a couple of times to avoid trouble, but I eventually made it to the Rider Academy and got to see why the griffins hadn't ended this already.

There were three squads guarding the compound, but none of them were at the gate. Wandering in, I saw a squad on the roofs of two different buildings, and one in the courtyard. My target, the stables, had its own kind of protection.

Bemused, I looked at the smoke drifting up in the air, from a dozen braziers arranged around the building.

What the hell?

I moved closer, wondering if the smoke was supposed to be poisonous, but none of the soldiers were wearing masks. Then the smell hit me. It wasn't that unpleasant, but it was *strong*. I almost gagged, and I wasn't actually *in* the smoke.

That was their plan, then. Block the beasts' sense of smell and then turn them away. Would it work?

Probably not. They could hope that they could keep the smoke going until the griffins gave up on using scent. But the griffins hadn't followed a scent here. They'd *known* the baby griffin was here, and they weren't going to leave just because they couldn't smell him. If they couldn't smell him, they'd start ripping apart buildings . . .

So the operation was still on. I just had to get inside without anyone seeing me—or anything that would be recognized as an illusion.

I held my nose and walked up to the big doors, where they moved the griffins in and out. They were boarded up quite securely. Moving over to the nearest brazier, I gave it a quick shove towards the building. It toppled, and the burning bucket part landed near the door.

That should be close enough, I thought and moved over to the people door further along the side. The fire bucket probably wasn't close enough to set the building on fire, but the smoke was now close enough for some of it to rise up under the eaves and find its way into the building.

The noise of the brazier falling over attracted some attention, but none of the soldiers moved to do anything about it. That was lucky. It might have been different if the building was going to catch alight, but this wasn't their problem.

It wasn't long before I heard muffled curses from inside before someone opened the door. He was wearing the uniform of one of Isidre's people, and he had a scarf tied around his face. He looked up and around, but the smoke was doing a pretty good job of keeping the monsters away. He cursed again and headed over to fix the brazier.

Ah, my nemesis, an ordinary locked door. Once more I have defeated you, I thought to myself as I slipped inside. It really was crazy just how much harder things were with a door in the picture. If I got a "teleport one meter" spell, I'd be unstoppable.

This part of the building was empty, but I could hear raised voices from the other half. Objecting to the smoke? I moved forward carefully to see who was there, mindful that the lottery loser behind me would be coming back shortly.

I hadn't really appreciated how *big* this building was. Griffins needed a lot of room, I suppose. Four rows of pens extended for the full length of the room, which was lit with glowing crystals. Just as well, since all that straw would make it a fire trap. With almost all the griffins aloft, the place looked empty, but it was easy to see the remaining exceptions. For whatever reason, the pens didn't have high walls, so I could easily see that there were two full-grown griffins and eight younger ones. Six, no seven, humans were here guarding them, including the one behind me. All of them were in a tight group, probably feeling a little tense.

Shouldn't there be more of them? I wondered. I knew that Isidre had more men to deploy. Maybe they were protecting the town? Certainly, if the plan worked, then anyone left here wasn't going to contribute to the main fight. If that was true, though, then Isidre had retired from that battle, too, as she and her baby griffin were right here.

Number seven came back and reported that he'd fixed the brazier. Complaints were made that they could still smell the smoke, but he ignored them. I carefully moved closer and got a closer look at Manchas.

I could see why everyone thought he was special. Pure white, and with an air of . . . alertness that the other griffins didn't have. He was just a baby, though, about as big as a Saint Bernard. Some of the other fledglings here were like ponies.

Okay, I thought. I took in the room, the positions of the men and griffins. *Let's get this party started.*

SLUMBER PARTY

I started by re-casting Greater Invisibility. It was a waste of thirty mana, but the bag in my pocket was only invisible because it was hidden in my pocket. If I wanted to pull it out without being seen, I needed to re-include it in the spell. Then it was just a matter of stepping behind Isidre and giving it a little squeeze near her head. There was a small visible cloud of the spores, but I think it was too faint to be seen if you weren't right next to her. It wasn't *that* well lit in here.

> **You have defeated Isidre Tamayo in non-lethal combat!**
> **You are awarded 25 XP.**

She collapsed to the ground. Or, more accurately, she slumped over the fence to Manchas's pen. I took a hit myself, but the antidote did its work. The rest of the soldiers rushed over to their leader.

Yes, that's right, I thought, stepping back to let them gather in one place. One of them decided to be a bit annoying, though. She must have been second-in-command.

"Lukas! Maik! Go fetch a Healer," she ordered, even as she bent over Isidre.

Well, fuck. I was forced to chase after the pair as they quickly ran for the exit. My stomach protested at my sudden movements when I was still a little dizzy, but I caught up to them at the door. The heavy bar that kept it shut slowed them for long enough that I was able to throw the bag at the door. It exploded into a cloud of dust that enveloped them both.

> **You have defeated Lukas Foerster in non-lethal combat!**
> **You have defeated Maik Peters in non-lethal combat!**
> **You are awarded 32 XP.**

XP for non-lethal is rubbish. That didn't mean I was tempted to kill them, though. Fortunately, since the exit was in a different room from the main stables, the remainder of the group didn't know that help wasn't coming. I took a moment to catch my breath, then another to let the dizziness dissipate.

Heading back, I saw that there had been developments. One of the group had also fallen unconscious, and the others had backed away from the pair.

"Hatiem?" one of them was saying. "Where the fuck did hatiem powder come from?"

"Could it be in the smoke?"

"Must be the Tribals getting revenge!"

That wasn't a bad idea. I snuck up behind them and cast Static Image up in the roof beams. If I'd used Phantasmal Entity, it would have been a physical figure lit by the lights below. Instead, I went for an unmoving shadow—with rabbit ears. Since they didn't notice it at first, I added an Unseen Sound of a cough.

"There! What's that?"

Too easy. From behind, the two remaining bags spread out a cloud that got everyone. They fell to the ground before they had a chance to turn around.

> **You have defeated Dominik Wurfel in non-lethal combat!**
> **You have defeated Birgit Bar in non-lethal combat!**
> **You have defeated Ulrich Krüger in non-lethal combat!**
> **You have defeated Didier Faure in non-lethal combat!**
> **You have defeated Fortun Hébert in non-lethal combat!**
> **You have defeated Kieran Hobbs in non-lethal combat!**
> **You are awarded 105 XP.**

I went to take a deep breath and then thought better of it, moving a few paces away. *Whew!*

To my relief, the griffins hadn't reacted to all of this. Aside from Isidre, I didn't know which griffins were bonded to which people, but I had assumed that most of the soldiers left behind were here because they'd bonded to an immature griffin. I kept an eye out in case any of this . . . flock started acting as though they were getting orders from a human, but they mostly just stood or sat where they were.

I looked over my target. I'd noticed before that he was one of the smaller specimens, presumably because he was young, rather than a runt. No one would go for all this trouble over a runt. Still. I didn't know how long it took griffins to mature, but I guessed it would take at least a year for this guy to be ready to ride. What had Isidre been thinking? She could have been riding a full-grown griffin right now.

Or . . . was I just being shortsighted? I'd sort of been living moment to moment since I'd gotten here. I still had the thought at the back of my mind that I'd get back to Sydney and my family at some stage. But from what I could tell, none of the previous abductees had managed to get back. Maybe I should start planning that I was going to be living the rest of my life here.

Well, maybe. Right now, I was still in the moment, and making sure my life extended past today was my main priority. I approached Manchas with the collar.

I'm sure, as a wild—or semi-wild—animal, he would have resisted the collar. But he didn't see it coming. As it had been on me when I cast invisibility, it only became visible when I let go of it, and by that time it had worked its magic.

[Follow me out of the pen], I ordered, and he complied.

[Tame] Skill unlocked.

The collar was intuitive to use, just as Kyle had said. I had doubted that mind control would be so easy, but like a skill, it seemed to know what I wanted to do and just went and did it for me. This world was dangerous and underdeveloped in so many ways, but I had to admit that bits of it were so very *convenient*.

The experience was not how a bond had been described to me. I didn't get any feedback at all from Manchas, except a sense of how in control he was. Perhaps because he was a baby, he didn't seem able to resist effectively.

Moving back to the main door, I sprayed the area with a disperse Water Stream to try and clear the spores. Then I dragged the bodies out of the way and gave Manchas his orders.

[Go out this door and fly to ~location~].

I was able to give him both an image of where he was to land and a rough direction from here.

[Avoid any griffins].

[Don't resist anyone who tries to remove your collar].

More images, this time of Kaito's crew. They had said they'd stay near the location, both for this, and to meet me when I brought Edele out.

That should do it. I'd rather it was Kaito removing the collar, but if Manchas got caught by his family, they were probably capable of removing it by force. That left the possibility that Manchas would lead a flock of angry griffins *and* the Griffin Riders right to Kaito, but I was sure that they could handle that eventuality.

I opened the door and sent Manchas out. He flinched from the smell, but the magic overrode his natural instincts. He took three steps forward and took flight before the guards could intercept him. I got out of there as well, putting as much distance between me and that stinking smoke, and left the scene to the guards.

I still didn't have time to go over my level, as I needed to get home and make sure Edele and Cutter made it back safe. *Soon*, I told myself. *Maybe while having a hot bath.*

Halfway home, I saw my first ogreling on the street.

That's not good. My bath was going to be delayed.

I hadn't fought them before, but I didn't think they were much of a threat to me. My damage was so small, though, that even backstabbing it was going to take a few rounds to kill one. Still, I couldn't let it keep trying to break down that door. It would eventually succeed.

You have inflicted 166 damage!
You have inflicted 172 damage!
You have inflicted 168 damage!
Contribution to Wave 4 noted.

Not as bad as I thought. But I wasn't close to done. More of them were coming down the street. Too many for me to stop, but I could pick off some of the stragglers.

Griffins don't swoop silently—not even a little bit; they screech as they come in—so I was able to dive to the side when one came in and picked up the ogreling I was lining up a shot on.

What the hell?

Looking up, I saw that the griffin was being ridden, so his target was probably the ogreling and he just didn't see me. Further observation revealed that the sky was almost clear of griffins, and the ones I could see were all being ridden. They were doing the same as my own accidental near-murderer—swooping down and coming up with monsters in their claws.

Does that mean it worked? The griffins went home? I resolved to get back more quickly—it was too dangerous to fight invisibly on the street now.

Once I stopped detouring for monsters, I made my way through the streets quite quickly, only slightly slowed by the need to keep an eye out on both the streets and the skies. The door to our house was barred, which was a good sign—it meant someone was inside.

I cancelled Greater Invisibility and started hammering on the door. "Cutter! Are you in there?"

There was a muffled shout and the door was opened. By Cutter.

"Cutter! You're all right!"

"'Course I am, Miss!" he said brightly. "It was dangerous and all, but I was more than ready for it."

"And Edele?"

"Her ladyship is in the kitchen," he said somewhat dismissively. "I got her some food—I've been taking care of her like you said."

"Her ladyship?" I asked, heading over to the kitchen.

He shrugged. "Well, she's a right proper toff, isn't she?"

What the . . . was my translation broken? I gave him a hard look, which he probably didn't deserve. There must be some equivalent slang which the System decided to translate that way.

"She talks like a noble?" I asked over my shoulder, but I was already in the kitchen so I could see for myself.

Edele had risen at my entrance and curtsied as I came into the room.

"My lady," she said. "Are you the one I have to thank for my rescue?"

"I am," I said. "But now I'm wondering if I got the wrong girl. Why is an adventurer's daughter talking like a noble?"

I was taking Cutter's word on this. While I had to admit that her word choices sounded more educated than Cutter's, I was pretty sure he was talking about her accent, which I couldn't hear. The System translated so effortlessly for me that it took an effort to hear the difference between languages. Distinguishing between dialects or accents was completely off the table.

The lady in question smiled nervously. "The Baron insisted on etiquette and elocution lessons for myself and the other girl. I don't know why. You mentioned my father; is he here?"

"No, he's still where you left him," I said. "Come nightfall, I'll get you out of the city and meet with a group that can take you to him."

"I see," she said. "May I ask why you didn't free my fellow hostages?"

I grimaced. "I came for you because of an arrangement with your father. I've got somewhere to take *you*. I don't know the others' stories; I don't know where they need to go, if they even have a place. I can't afford to keep hiding them in the long term; they'd just get me caught."

In theory, I could have dropped them off with her; they'd probably be just as safe, assuming Mandel allowed it. I wasn't sure if his trust issues extended to his daughter's friends and fellow hostages. But they probably did have places to go, and a mountaintop in the wilderness was the worst place for them to start that journey. She seemed to understand, just nodding sadly.

"Then, is there anything else for me to do before sunset?" she asked.

"Keep Cutter occupied," I said with a grin, "Maybe teach him how to talk proper."

It was—finally—time to attend to my level. I thought about running a bath, but . . . there was still too much going on to get out of my armor. I sat down and brought up the Ability point screen.

Ability	Actual	Base	Cost
[Strength]	3	2	37
[Agility]	3	2	37
[Finesse]	4	3	58
[Soul]	3	2	37
[Intelligence]	5	4	79
[Charisma]	10	8	163
Unspent Ability Points	255		

Let's see. I resisted the temptation to put Charisma up again. It was surely high enough. I needed to address some of my weaknesses. Intelligence to six seemed a good idea. That would increase my magic points, and be useful for other kinds of magic if I could get them. If I couldn't, it would qualify me to take a different mage profession. That would mean giving up that plus three to Illusion Magic, so only in an emergency.

That would bring the costs of all my lowest scores to 39, but I could still afford to take each of them to three. Did I want to increase Soul, though? It hadn't been doing much for me lately. It seemed safe to leave it at two. That meant I could increase Finesse, which would help my dagger work.

A few quick thoughts and my stats were increased. I turned my attention to Development points . . . when everything suddenly went white.

What!

I looked down at myself, but I was still there. It was just . . . everything else that was gone. A voice sounded from behind me.

"You would probably have wasted a lot of time looking at Development points, but all the good ones are eight points, so you're better off waiting until your next level."

I slowly turned to look at the man standing behind me. He was a complete stranger.

"Hi, I think it's time we had a talk," he said.

LITTLE CHAT

Like me, the man was standing on nothing but empty whiteness. Something about him made me think he was Asian, though tanned skin and black hair could come from just about anywhere. I couldn't see his eyes through the bizarre colored glasses he was wearing, so maybe it was his lack of facial hair. His hair was black and came down to his shoulders. Some of it was braided—thin, tight braids that ran through the rest of his hair and were finished off with brightly colored beads on the ends.

He was wearing a loose tie-dyed shirt and designer jeans. Fancy branded sneakers adorned his feet and he wore some kind of braided bracelets. His glasses . . . each lens was an oval, but they were of different size and proportions. One was filled with yellow glass and the other with green, and their long axes were tilted at different odd angles.

He looked like a mess, in other words.

"You're a god, aren't you," I said flatly. On the off chance, I silently cast Dispel Image. Nothing happened. Not "the spell didn't work," but it was as if I didn't have the spell anymore.

He nodded. "Now that I've got your attention, why don't we go someplace more comfortable."

As he said the word, I found myself in an office much like—no, it *was*—my old boss's office. Complete with its *fantastic* view of Sydney.

"You know about my world, then," I said cautiously, looking around. He'd placed me behind my boss's obsidian desk, leaving himself right next to the chairs the clients sat in. *Interesting.* I sat down behind the desk, feeling a little thrill despite myself. He waited for me to be seated and then sat down himself. I wanted to say that his designer hippie look was out of place, but some of our richer clients had been really eccentric.

"I know everything," he said, with just a trace of smugness. "Well, perhaps not *everything*, but I do know everything that you know about your world. You and all the others. Every pop-culture reference, every fashion detail, every meal you ever ate. Even the details you've forgotten."

Wow, that's not creepy at all, I said to myself. Though it seemed that the inside of my skull wasn't as private as I'd thought. The man just continued smiling, his face unreadable. If he was reading my mind, he wasn't going to tell me.

"So this is an illusion, then?" I asked. "Taken from my memories?"

"Not exactly," he replied. "This whole conversation is a memory. Instead of having a conversation, I've inserted the memory of it into your mind."

My jaw dropped. "How? *Why?* You—"

"Let's start with why," he interrupted me. "Mainly, doing it this way takes no time, so we can't be interrupted."

"If our minds are just so much Play-Doh to you, what's to stop another god from just changing—or erasing—this?"

"Ethics, for some," he said. "Others . . . because it would be directly interfering with me—in a way that interrupting wouldn't be."

My eyes narrowed. "Is that some rule of the game you're playing with us Earthers?"

"Actually, this rule goes back much further. And before you ask about the ethics of me changing your memory, I'm not doing this with deceptive intent. You've been informed about the nature of the conversation."

I glared at him, but it wasn't as if I could do anything about it. From what he said, this conversation had already happened and there was nothing I could do to stop it. Which sort of brought me back to . . ."

"How?" I asked. "How can this be a conversation if it's already happened?"

"The short answer is, I'm a god," he said idly. "An existence beyond what you can comprehend. More specifically . . . you'd best understand it as an ability to predict your future actions, for a little way into the future at least."

"So you predict what I would say . . . and then make me remember saying it?"

I glared at him, but couldn't find anything else to say. Someone who could do that—who could credibly claim to be doing that—was going to have answers to any obvious objections.

"Exactly correct!" he said brightly, answering either my thoughts or my words. "So let's move on to my apology."

"What?" I exclaimed, thrown off balance by the sudden shift.

"You were brought here without your consent, forced to take part in our . . . tournament. You've suffered privations and indignities, and I am sorry for that. I wouldn't have done it if I didn't have a greater need."

"Fuck off," I growled. "You'd do it again in a heartbeat."

"In considerably less time than that," he agreed. "But I would regret the necessity. I don't expect you to understand. Does the farmer explain his reasons to his sickle? To the wheat? To the insects he sprays against?"

He said that without changing his expression of polite friendliness, but my blood ran cold all the same.

"You know, for someone who wants me to be your agent, you're doing a terrible job of getting me on your side."

"Oh, I'm not your patron," he said, smirking. He'd clearly been waiting to drop that revelation.

"But you said you were the one—"

"That brought you here. Yes. It will make more sense when I explain some of the rules."

I sank back into my comfortable chair. "Go on." I was a captive audience anyway.

He smiled broadly and steepled his fingers. "Long ago, my colleagues and I resolved to not directly interfere in this world. Even Ashmor agreed, once it was made clear that united, the rest of us could eliminate natural death and decay even against his opposition."

He paused, seeming to know that I needed time to process that. Mortal lifespan was a bargaining chip for these people?

"The agreement was necessary, but no one liked it. Every god wanted more control over the world, so we came up with a new agreement. It's often referred to as our Game, but the stakes are too high to warrant that title."

"The stakes? You mean people's lives."

"Exactly," he said with satisfaction. "The Game is not played for status or some kind of god-currency. Each god has their own vision of *how things should be*, and each round of the Game has the chance to get them a little closer to that goal. But not every god joined in the Game."

"Fyskel and Ashmor," I said. "The book said that there had never been a Champion for either of those gods."

"Ashmor never joined the agreement. He spoils things whenever he can, which isn't often against our combined opposition."

"And Fyskel?"

"Myself? I have a different role to play. I'm the umpire."

I rolled my eyes. "The one god that everyone says can't be trusted, and you're the umpire?"

He laughed. "Humans, so shortsighted. You always have to fit things into sides. Whenever I help a nation, they get this idea that I'm on their side, when . . . well. The other gods have a more enlightened understanding."

"Right. Not that you have helped me, but if you do, I should get ready for the inevitable betrayal. Got it."

"Very wise," he said, still amused. "Now, as the umpire, I was the one who brought you over, to locations specified by your patrons." He waved his hand airily. "There are a lot of complicated rules, but what it comes down to is that the players can't do anything to you until you're in play. Now, there's a dichotomy when it comes to managing Champions, a line between two positions that most gods stand on."

"Is this to do with why I haven't heard from my . . . handler?" I asked sourly.

"Actually, it's quite common not to bother until they reach level five or so, just to make sure they've got what it takes to go further . . . but yes. One position is to just tell your champion what you want them to do and do what you can to aid them."

"That would be Kaito," I said. "Naldyna talks to her all the time."

"Mmn," he agreed. "The problem with that is that every other god knows what you're planning on doing and can act to thwart it. We're not omniscient, but you'd better believe we keep track of companions."

I felt a little sick at the thought that all nine gods were rummaging through my head whenever they felt like it, but it wasn't going to do any good complaining to *this* guy. Seeing, or I guess *knowing* I wasn't going to say anything, Fyskel continued.

"The other extreme is to tell them nothing. If you select your candidate right, you can choose one who will naturally act to change the thing you want changed, with only the occasional nudge from you."

"Wait, would that even work? If all the gods can read our minds, can't they work out what we're likely to do?"

"It's more complicated than that," Fyskel agreed. "Let's just say the art of it is in the nudges. You can set up a lot of contradictory nudges over a period of time, and then ensure that only the ones you select get to the target. It becomes a game of subtlety and misdirection, something the gods do *not* have equal amounts of."

"So being dumped in Oakway and being left in the dark is all part of some super subtle strategy, sure. Why are *you* talking to me?"

"I'm cheating," he said, grinning. "This Game . . . it definitely suits my purpose to have the gods working together, but the drawback is that I don't get to play."

I took a deep breath. "You just said that the other gods are reading my mind—how are you going to keep the fact that you talked to me from them?"

"Oh, I'm not. This isn't against the rules . . . you're not my Champion, and I can't make you do anything. But if I give you a little help, a little *nudge* . . . it could be that you'll do the thing that I want of your own accord."

He'd as much as told me that he wasn't going to tell me what that thing was, so there was no point in asking. Still . . .

"Why *now*, then?" I asked.

"Why, indeed?" he replied. "You've done a few significant things . . . achieved level five, ended the griffin attack . . . taken a stand between Naldyna and Duit. You're making the transition from pawn to player."

"Still your pawn, apparently," I said bitterly. He shrugged again.

"We're gods, Kandis Hammond. You need to stop thinking of us as merely powerful humans."

"Well if I can't get any agency or independence, didn't you say something about some help?"

"Did I? Did you need help with something?"

"Fuck off, Mister Almost Omniscient. I need help with *everything*."

"Hmmm . . ." he said, pretending to consider the question. "You seem to have your current tasks well in hand. You have some political battles ahead of you . . . but you've already noticed I'm not great at befriending humans."

"I thought you were beyond human experience."

"Well, I suppose if it was necessary . . . but it isn't. You have all the skills you need in that area. You still have numerous texts to consult, about magic and dungeon mastery, but they are all . . . around." He waved a hand aimlessly.

"What's the deal with dungeons, anyway?"

He raised an eyebrow at me, but I wasn't going to pretend that he didn't know exactly what I meant.

"The common legends have it the wrong way around," he said. "We— all of the gods save Ashmor—made the first dungeon and tied it into the

System, allowing them to be created . . . I suppose naturally is the best way to put it. Sometime later, we discovered that Ashmor had corrupted our design."

"The *good* gods created them?" Good gods was a bit of a stretch. Few people had good words to say about the God of Storms, the God of Death, or Fyskel here. Better them than the God of Destruction, though. "Why would you do such a thing?"

"Think it through. Dungeons are a self-sustaining construct that can take care of their own expansion, create food and resources, and dispose of waste all under their own power. Does that remind you of anything?"

Those attributes weren't what I thought about when I thought of dungeons, but I had to admit they were there. Which sounded like . . .

"An *arcology*?" I exclaimed. "They were for living in?"

"Until they were corrupted, yes." Fyskel had lost his amused look. "We had more than four billion sentients living in them when the . . . flaw became apparent."

"That would be the monsters?"

"Not exactly. Every dungeon is tainted with an urge, a compulsion to kill. It was so small we didn't notice it, and an ordinary sentient who'd taken the role of Dungeon Controller could resist it for years. But not forever."

"So they just started slaughtering the inhabitants?" I asked with fascinated horror.

"The first one did, at which point we had to evacuate the others. The controllers were pretty far gone by that point, but we managed to avoid another massacre. We lost even more, though, once all those people had to try surviving outside."

"And you couldn't fix them? The dungeons, I mean."

"The template was in the System by then. You can add to the System, but even we can't remove something once it's in there. We could make a new dungeon template, but we never figured out how Ashmor corrupted the first one. It was a clear win for him."

Fyskel paused. His mood seemed to have changed from smug to contemplative. "We'll talk more later," he said.

AFTERMATH

I wasn't the only one leaving the town that night, but I might have been the only one planning on coming back. I'd chosen a particularly empty part of the wall to go over. Not that it mattered to two invisible people, but every little bit helped. I'd expected to have to help Edele over the wall, but it turned out she had climbing and jumping skills higher than mine. A bonus from a well spent childhood, I suppose.

I noticed the first group of beast-kin approaching while we were on top of the wall. They were relying on stealth, which wasn't the best way to hide from someone on top of the wall you were approaching. None of the town's buildings was allowed within five meters of the wall, so there was a nicely cleared area to expose anyone trying to leave.

Unless there were no guards, which seemed to be the case. *Bribed?* I wondered as I watched the small group make their way up the wall. Edele was just as curious as I was, and I had to pull her out of the way, as they silently made their way up and over. It looked like a family, with two teen-agers and a smaller child bundled up on the mother's back. As they started down, another group appeared, and I had to get us moving before we got caught in a crowd.

Once we got away from the wall, I called up a small Light spell, both to avoid stumbling around and to keep us together while keeping Greater Invisibility up.

Kaito and her friends were right where they said they would be, and were easy to find as they'd lit the clearing with torches. A number of beast-kin had found their way here already and had gathered in a group at the far edge of the clearing. Kaito and two of her companions were standing out in the middle of the clearing. They saw the light as we approached, and once we'd entered the clearing, I dropped Greater Invisibility.

"Good evening, Miss Kandis," Kaito said as we approached. She was speaking in Japanese. I would have preferred to indulge her, but we had company, so I just inclined my head in Edele's direction. She blushed and switched to Latorran.

"Ah, my apologies—I just wanted to practice—" She cut herself off with a grimace and bowed to us both. "Lady Edele, I presume?"

"Edele, this is Kaito Washiyama. She's going to take you to your father. Or her . . . people will?" I asked.

Kaito nodded. "This is Orino. She'll be able to Wood Walk with you to the tree line of your father's mountain, and it should be a short walk from there."

"Hi!" the little mouse-kin said brightly. "We're going to be travelling together for a little bit, so let's get along!"

"Hello," Edele said timidly. "I'm very pleased to make your acquaintance." She clearly felt out of her depth, but Orino just giggled. She was, I only now noticed, awfully *busty* for someone so short.

"C'mon, we should get started right away!" She dragged the poor girl over to the main group calling out for Nori, one of Kaito's other girls.

"Nori and Orino *are* very skilled," Kaito reassured me, with an embarrassed grin. "I'm sure they'll be safe."

"Good," I said, watching Orino drag Edele and Nori over to the nearest tree. Holding both of them, she touched the tree with her bare foot, and all three of them disappeared. I blinked. "Huh. That's Wood Walk?"

"Yes, it's a useful travel skill, though only within a contiguous forest."

"Neat. What are all the others doing here, anyway?" I asked.

"Ah, well, when we mentioned to Lady Tonet that we were escorting your friend, she asked that we help a number of other refugees."

"Refugees?"

"Lady Tonet believes that life in Talnier will soon be very difficult for beast-kin in the days going forward. It's likely there will be some kind of war."

"I may have made that more likely," I admitted. "In order to divert suspicion from myself, I left a few clues to point to the Tribes."

She nodded. "Just the use of the hatiem would have done that," she said. "And the blame is not unwarranted—we did ask you to do this."

"Still . . ." I said awkwardly. "I wanted to stop the griffins, not start a war."

She nodded sympathetically. "I don't think you have. If a conflict starts, the dungeon breaks will surely have been the greater provocation. And . . ." she trailed off and paused. "I've not been told about the history here, but there is a lot of anger in the Tribes towards the Kingdom. This conflict will be welcomed by some."

I looked over at the refugees. "They wouldn't have been in Talnier if that was a universal feeling," I said.

"True," she agreed morosely. "I make a poor isekai hero. I should have stopped the others from releasing the monsters. If I'd insisted, perhaps . . ."

"Hey don't be like that," I said. "Your people have got the griffin back, *and* sent a message, right? They're not going to be looking for more trouble. And the Baron . . . he's got troubles of his own. He might not be around for much longer. A successor might be more willing to negotiate."

"Do you truly think so?"

I shrugged. "You never know—let's do what we can to help that outcome along, hey?"

She thought about that for a minute and then bowed to me. "Yes. It will take us three days to get back here after we complete this escort, but I would be honored to work with you to bring about a peaceful resolution."

I bowed back, trying to get the angle right. "The honor is mine," I said.

We sort of stood awkwardly after that for about a minute. That would have been a nice place for me to take my leave, but I had to wait for Orino to get back and let me know she'd succeeded. Not that I had any doubts . . .

Eventually, Kaito excused herself, saying she had to talk with her companions. I could have struck up a conversation with some of the refugees, but I needed a moment to think about my *earlier* conversation.

What was Fyskel thinking? My first impression was that he'd just popped in for a chat, and then left when he got depressed . . . but that wasn't possible, was it? He'd constructed that memory from scratch, so the conversation had ended exactly where he'd wanted it to end from the start. If he hadn't liked the way it had gone, he could have said different things and made it go another way.

So what had he wanted? He'd told me *some* of the rules, told me he *wasn't* my patron. Oh, and he'd apologized, for what little *that* was worth. A "sorry not sorry" kind of apology. Was that just an excuse to talk to me? A pretty transparent one, if so.

He'd told me he was going to be manipulating me, which is something you . . . don't . . . tell the person you're going to manipulate. He didn't mention anything about my current situation, just that story about the dungeons.

Was that the point? It was the last thing he said . . . and *maybe* relevant to me. It suggested I wasn't going to wean Rhis off killing—and that Marie Monteminer was a time bomb waiting to go off and kill her family. But why tell me that way? Why risk that I wouldn't catch it, or wouldn't believe it, given all the other stuff he said? He'd as much as stated that Sydney could have just been a false memory he planted.

Perhaps . . . that had all been a show put on for the other gods? But if I'd thought of that, surely they would. Especially since they could apparently read my mind. Were some of the gods idiots? Idiotic enough and proud enough to read my mind thinking this was fake and decide that they knew better?

In the end, I decided that I wasn't going to puzzle this out. I could just take what I could and see where it got me. Though, while I was speculating on the gods . . . was Duit going to out me? Presumably, he knew that I was the one who'd stolen Manchas, so all he had to do was let Isidre know, and I would no longer be welcome in Talnier. But then, he could have let her know I was coming, and I'd have been just as fucked.

It seemed unlikely that a god would let themself lose an encounter just because they didn't want to chat. So there must be some sort of rule that let Naldyna tell Kaito *some* things about me, while Duit couldn't say anything to Isidre. I was going to be leaning pretty heavily on whatever that rule was if I was going up against other Champions. I really needed to know how it worked.

My thoughts ran in circles like this for about two hours, before Orino finally returned.

"Everything's fine!" she called, as soon as she stepped out of a nearby tree. "The family is all reunited; everyone is happy!"

"Great," I said, keeping my thoughts to myself. I'd have to have a talk with Mandel about a possible future psychotic wife problem. "That's a load off my mind. I guess I'll see you again in a few days?" I added to Kaito. She nodded, so I bowed and took my leave.

Getting back in was easy enough, with one small surprise.

[Jump] Level 3 acquired through use.
For gaining a skill level, you have been awarded 1 XP.

That . . . made my jumping pretty ridiculous. I still couldn't match what I'd seen Reynard and his crew manage back in Oakway, but my long jump was somewhere around twenty meters now. Practicing on the way back, I could see why adventurers jumped around when things got serious, and why they didn't do it all the time. It felt pretty ridiculous, and it ate up Stamina, but it was *fast*. It felt as if it didn't take any longer to jump my full distance than it had back when my limit was two meters (if I was generous).

Still, it was ridiculous. If I hadn't been invisible, I wouldn't have tried it. It made avoiding patrols easier, though. The streets were still a little dangerous, but it seemed to me that they'd gotten rid of the majority of the breakthrough monsters.

The gang was all waiting for me when I got back, so I filled them in, and got to find out what they'd been doing. Kyle had fought a Threat twenty griffin, which was a pretty big deal. It had had sufficient Attack to hit him but couldn't get through his armor. He was pretty much in the same boat, doing some damage but not enough to kill it before the retreat.

Cloridan had come off the wall once his Greater Invisibility had run out and had actually been sleeping until I came back. He was going to be keeping watch for the rest of tonight since I still wasn't sure what the Baron's—or Isidre's—next move was going to be. If it was midnight arrests, I wanted us to have some warning.

So we went to bed. I thought I'd be too keyed up to sleep, but I was exhausted. I was out as soon as my head hit the pillow, and then it was morning.

Morning came with a notification.

Outbreak Defense Wave 4 Completed **Accumulated Experience: 103,458** **Contribution: 19.45%** **Awarded Experience: 20,122**

ÏNTERLVDE 2

King Alexandros, Protector of Latora, Slayer of Tyranny, and Admiral of the Eastern Seas was in a mood. Exactly what kind of mood, he wasn't sure, but he was finding the normal review of issues of the Kingdom much more of a trial than usual.

"What's this petition from Lady Rankin?" he asked Agenor, his Chancellor, while waving a parchment with far too much writing on it. He'd be damned if he was going read the thing.

"She's asking for access to be restored to her dungeon," Agenor said calmly.

"*Her* dungeon?"

"My apologies, sire, the dungeon located in her county seat, which her family has managed since the Founding."

"Ah, that dungeon. Why did I take it off her again?"

"She . . . overreached, and got exposed in the Oakway affair." Agenor said with a sneer. Despite having his own fingers in as many pies as possible, Agenor was always the first to decry anyone who was so gauche as to get caught.

"Oakway . . . she suborned a Guild official, and we lost the dungeon due to her meddling, didn't we."

"Actual fault for the loss of the dungeon was never determined," Agenor corrected him judiciously. "But bribing an official is a serious enough offense on its own."

"I said that she'd lose it until the Oakway Dungeon reformed, did I not? Has that happened?"

"Reports are that a core has formed, but it has not yet finished its first level. And . . . the concerns she expressed about her own . . . that is, her *local* dungeon, are not borne out in the Guild reports."

Alexandros glanced at the parchment again. No doubt it was filled with complaints that the Guild was incapable of managing the very special needs of her very special dungeon.

"I have full confidence in my adventurers," he declared, smirking. "Lady Rankin can wait a little longer."

"Yes, sire." Agenor paused for the shortest interval and then continued. "If I may, sire, the Oakway Dungeon . . ."

"Yes?"

"We could really use that mana in the capital."

Alexandros snorted. "It's always more mana with you," he said.

"With respect, sire, there's always demand for more mana in Dorsay. As the one responsible for allocating it, I need to chase after anything that makes my job easier."

"Would it? The more mana you have, the more the greedy fools ask for. No, my grandfather owed his throne to the Oakway clans, and I'll not begrudge them the pittance it costs to keep that dungeon running. Besides, it's turned out a number of fine starting adventurers."

"As you say, sire," Agenor said with just a hint of resignation. "The next item is the upcoming confirmation of Count Duvost."

The King grimaced. "That nasty business. Do we know yet who was responsible?"

"Count Duvost blames Duke Arryen. I'm not sure yet what evidence he has, but there's a decent chance he'll publicly accuse him as soon as he's confirmed."

Alexandros made an irritated sound. "Make sure Finley isn't in Dorsay when the confirmation is scheduled. He's too competent for me to lose. Did he do it?"

The Chancellor shrugged. "It seems likely, but we haven't seen any evidence yet. This is suggestive, though." He pulled out one of the waiting petitions. "This is from the Duke for you to deny confirmation to Aubert, and crown a cousin, Guillaume, instead."

"On what grounds?" Alexandros asked, surprised. Interfering with another duchy's successions was ambitious, to say the least.

"On the grounds of the 'false accusations' being made by the Count," Agenor said wryly. "Blatant falsehoods that render him unfit for office."

Alexandros laughed. "Well, he doesn't lack for confidence." He paused to consider. "Hold on to that," he said, pointing to the petition. "And get the Count's story before we move on the confirmation. Let's see if he's got any evidence before we proceed."

"My lord, are you going to discipline Duke Arryen?"

"We'll see," the King mused. "It was one thing when he was cleaning house in his own duchy, but if he's started expanding his influence, it might mean that he's starting to move on me."

"I understand, sire. I'll look into it closely."

"Good—but don't provide too much protection to Aubert. I've no use for young hotheads who charge straight at their enemy. Let's give the young Count his head and see if he's a worthy successor to his father—or just another victim."

"It shall be as you say, sire. The next matter is Talnier."

"Oh? Is Reece back already?"

"No, but he *has* sent back his first report."

"And?"

"He's confirmed that the assassin was from the same group that went after the Duvosts."

"So if Finley was behind one, he's probably behind the other."

"Yes. He *has* found some evidence pointing to Duvost, but he's kept this from Baron Marseau."

Alexandros nodded thoughtfully. "That's wise," he said. "Finley is probably trying to sow mistrust between the Count and his Barons. Odd that he didn't arrange for Marseau to find it."

"Yes. Perhaps his plans were foiled accidentally by the general chaos that seems to be going on there."

"Oh? What else is going on?"

"For one thing, Baron Marseau is significantly more corrupt than we thought."

"Hmmm . . . the Guild *was* complaining about his activities."

"It goes beyond simply waylaying adventurers. He's taken over one of the major gangs and controls about a third of all the crime in the town."

Alexandros frowned. "He's showing admirable ambition, but controlling the law *and* the crime inevitably leads to conflicts of interest."

"That may have already occurred, sire. Half the town's current problems have been caused or exacerbated by his criminal connections and the need to maintain them."

"And what problems were they?" Alexandros knew that Agenor wouldn't refer to simple corruption, even as extensive as this, as a problem. He saw it as a noble's natural right.

"To start with, someone started taking exception to the Baron's criminal empire, and started killing them."

"A public minded citizen doesn't seem too problematic."

"He made a point of wearing red and gold," Agenor explained wryly.

"Bold. Is he actually claiming to be one of mine?"

"It's hard to say. The descriptions of his clothing don't match any of our uniforms, and he's not very talkative."

"Well, either way, Reece should be able to take care of that. Assuming Marseau doesn't find him first."

"Quite. So, the Baron had his men combing the forest looking for the man when they were surprised by a nearby dungeon break."

The King groaned. "Casualties?"

"Thirteen dead, five with injuries that couldn't be healed."

Alexandros cursed. "We got that wall built, and we haven't had a serious monster incident since. Now Marseau gets caught outside?"

"He was compromised by his criminal connections as you predicted, sire," Agenor said, bowing.

"What else," Alexandros said, ignoring the flattery.

"That wasn't the only break; the other dungeon broke only a few hours later."

"So it was deliberate then. Are the Tribes pissed at us again?"

"They may have been provoked by the Champion of Duit."

"I thought we'd diverted her into supporting the northern expansion."

"Yes, but we agreed to help her acquire a griffin."

"What a stupid request that was," Alexandros complained. "It's all forests on the northern border; a griffin would be more of a hindrance than help."

"Well, you said at the time, that if we give her the shiny thing she wants, she'll think well of us and help us more . . ."

"Yes, yes," Alexandros acknowledged. "So how has this come back to bite us?"

"It may not have, not yet," Agenor reassured him. "She came back reporting that she'd met with the Champion of Naldyna, who told her that she had provoked the griffins."

"So the griffins are coming after her, and she's in the town," Alexandros mused. "When this is over, make some inquiries about who her guide was. We've had dozens of expeditions without provoking a response. Make sure he's held responsible for any bad advice he gave her. Otherwise . . ."

He paused and stared at nothing for a moment, considering. "Otherwise, this probably works out well for us. If she feels guilty about causing us trouble . . ."

"She'll be eager to make it up with helping us in the north," Agenor agreed. "There is one other thing. She met with an Ebon Order envoy in Talnier."

"What? What's Dark Winter's interest in this?"

"Unknown at this stage, my lord. The important point is that he was there before she arrived."

"He wouldn't have known in advance . . . is it just a coincidence, then?"

"Perhaps . . ." Agenor swallowed nervously. "But we can't overlook another possibility. If he's meeting with Champions, and he was already in town . . ."

"Then there was already a Champion in the town," said Alexandros, finishing the thought.

"And with another Champion just over the border . . . my lord, we could be looking at a Convergence within our borders."

Tonet heard the rat-kin's approach as soon as he entered the temple, thanks to Wild Vigilance. She'd had the spell up for days now, and the constant clamor of the town was putting her Pray skill to the test. She sighed and whispered instructions. The rat-kin Alchemist was escorted and guided to where she was seated in the bed of flowers she'd been meditating in. A breeze rose around the glade, rustling the leaves of the trees and filling the grove with white noise that cut out the sounds of the outside town, and reduced the chance of anyone illicitly overhearing them.

The man entered the glade and bowed, before kneeling in front of her. He waited for her to start, but she let herself enjoy the silence for a little while. Eventually, she nodded for him to start.

"Priestess, the griffins have left. Does that mean it was successful?"

She nodded and gestured for one of the Acolytes to hand over the gold and platinum. It was a heavy bag, considerably more than the 200 gold she had asked Kandis Hammond for, but considerably less than hatiem powder would normally sell for.

"It went well," she agreed. "How long before you can supply more?"

The man grimaced apologetically. "You asked for all my available stock, Priestess. To grow more, I would need access to human corpses. There are some fresh ones in town, but . . ."

"I understand," she said. "We'll see what we can do, but it does seem unlikely." It might be possible, she mused. Difficult, but stealing the bodies of guardsmen would make for an excellent provocation, if one was still needed.

"I do have the other items you asked for," the rat-kin said eagerly. "They're nowhere near as effective, of course, but they're just as . . . characteristic as the hatiem."

"Good," she said, nodding in dismissal. "Leave it with Ienge," she said, gesturing at the Acolyte. The rat-kin handed a small case over before bowing again and taking his leave.

"Lady Tonet," Ienge said nervously, looking at the opened case and the poisons inside. "With all the refugees we've helped escape, I had thought that our interests lay in reducing tensions, not escalating them."

"That would be true normally," Tonet explained. "But war is coming, and Naldyna favors the Tribes, just as Duit favors the Kingdom. We need to make sure when war comes, the Tribes have the advantage."

Ienge nodded, understanding. The Tribes could raid into Latora, bypassing Talnier, but to hold territory, they needed to take or sack the town. The light, mobile troops the Tribes fielded tended to dash themselves against the town walls, much like the monsters did. Conversely, Kingdom troops in the forest were easy meat for the Rangers and Druids of the Tribes. Whoever attacked first was at a disadvantage, which was why things had been stable for some time. But that was going to change.

"Everything changes when the Champions are called, Ienge," Tonet said. "All we can do is try to adapt to what the gods have decided to bring."

"You have failed me."

The words were harsh, but the tone was feminine and warm. Isidre felt both chastised and comforted, which was a very odd feeling. She couldn't tell if the words were in her head or aloud, but they rang through her as if she'd been sitting on a subwoofer.

"Speak. You will be more comfortable if you say the words."

Isidre wasn't sure what that meant, exactly, but she did speak up. "Ah! Yes, I'm sorry." Duit had chosen to contact her when she was alone in her room, so she didn't have to worry about others overhearing.

"Do not be concerned. This was only the opening round. Learn from it, and do better next time."

"I—I don't know what I should be learning. I don't know what happened—did Kaito sneak in and disable me?"

"It is against the rules for gods to pass on any details about the other Champions without their patron's permission."

"Wait, then the things that Kaito knew about me, you gave your permission for Naldyna to tell her that?"

"Yes. I knew that you would not be dissuaded by his arguments. And if she had approached not knowing you were a Champion, she would likely have been convinced to use lethal force against you."

"I see . . . so what should I do now?"

"You stand or fall on your own merits, but you are not alone. You have guides and companions that can be relied on. Go forth and make the world a better place."

"Should I go and help the King with his border expansion?" Isidre waited, but there was no reply. The voice was gone. Though there was no one to see it, Isidre's face hardened. She would not fail again.

interview

Cleaning up was a bitch. Outside of a dungeon, monsters didn't fade away but left all their bits to rot. The Guild had the adventurers harvest the corpses since all this food sitting outside of the walls made the area even more dangerous than normal.

At least some of it was valuable. There was a hefty tax on anything we converted to gold, but otherwise, we got to keep what we harvested. Bonfires had been set up to take care of the waste, what little there was. Just about every part of a monster was worth *something*, and there were a few experts around to point out money that was being left on the table. Or thrown into the bonfire.

It was dirty, bloody, hard work. Dangerous, too. The monsters that were attracted were naturally spawned, so they didn't suffer from the unnatural aggression that dungeon monsters did. That meant they wouldn't attack such a large group, but they hung around the edges looking for stragglers to pick off. Every now and then, we had to break off from harvesting to join a patrol to beat the edges of the forest and scare them off.

"It's great isn't it?" Felicia said enthusiastically. "All of the harvest with hardly any of the risk!" I looked at her, and then at the others. Stamina being the boon that it was, we weren't exhausted but we were mentally tired, and dirty beyond belief. The very ground that we'd been walking on all day was soaked with blood, and we'd been dissecting creatures without a break. The others were handling it better than I was, but they still looked incredulous at Felicia's statement.

"I'm glad someone is enjoying this," I managed. "Is it easier for you with the Hunt skill?"

"I guess?" Felicia mused, while effortlessly removing the flesh from the bones of some wolf-like creature with too many legs. She'd flensed it so thoroughly that even Identify couldn't tell me what it had been. In the Before, I'm sure I would have vomited at the sight, but right now, I could laugh and move on to my own animal.

It was not going to be anything like expertly butchered. At times like these, I contemplated getting the skill, but . . . no. Save the Skill points for the Magic skills. Eventually, I'd get practiced enough to qualify for the skill for free, but that did not appear to be anywhere close to happening.

Around me, most of the town's adventurers were doing a much better job of harvesting materials. After the tension of the last few days, the atmosphere was more festive. There was a lot of talk about the fourth wave, but no one seemed to have picked up that someone had walked away with twenty percent of the contribution. Math skills weren't that common among adventurers. Someone must have noticed, but they were staying quiet.

The Baron was high on my list of people who would have noticed. He would have seen his share drop by a significant amount, I was sure. The Guild officials should also have noticed, as they were keeping at least a loose track of who was fighting. It made me a little nervous about my upcoming appointment.

We kept at it until we couldn't. Quitting was more about getting overwhelmed by the gore than actual tiredness, but that was a factor, at least for me. Felicia was still good to go, but she followed the rest of us back without complaint.

"There's nothing to be nervous about," Nadine reassured us as we were ushered into Guild Master Koenig's office. "This is a routine interview for adventurers that reach level five. We'd just postponed it for most of you until your entire party had all reached that level."

"How did you know I'd reached it?" I asked, surprised. I had told my team, but there hadn't really been time to chat about it with anyone else.

"Well, I just assumed," Nadine said with a laugh. "I knew you were close, and there was a decent amount of XP this break."

"Right," I said, blushing slightly. It was obvious.

"So," Koenig said after we sat down in front of him. "You're young; you've hit level five. Welcome to the middle grade. The question is, where do you go from here?"

He looked the four of us over, making sure to make eye contact. "A lot of people quit after level five. Or at least . . . slow down. They start delving purely for the money, looking to build up a nest egg, or just drink it away. They start going for the easy fights, so as to make the most money with the least wear on their gear.

"But that's not the only way. Level six seems a long way off, but if you guys push like you've been doing, you can make it in a year, maybe less. After that, though, it gets harder."

Yeah, no shit, I thought. If we managed level six in a year, it would take ten more to make level seven. Assuming the same rate of XP gain, but the problem there was . . .

"The problem is that by that time, you'll have bottomed out both the dungeons here. You won't be able to find tougher fights, so your XP gain will stagnate," Koenig continued.

In fact, it would actually decrease, since fighting the same monster with a higher level meant significantly less XP.

"We'd . . ." I said, looking over at the others for confirmation. "We'd planned on moving to the capital when that started being a problem."

Koenig nodded. "Good to see you've planned that far ahead. I had the feeling that you weren't going to be content with mid-grades. But do any of you know anything about Dorsay?"

"Some of my relatives have been there," Kyle said hesitantly. "I've heard a little. I know it's expensive."

"Like you wouldn't believe," Koenig agreed. "And the dungeons there aren't like anything we have here. Ten, twenty levels deep, with Threat levels starting at fifteen and going up by *five.*"

My eyes widened. That would put the bottom level monsters at 65 to *115.* Killing one on my own (not that that would be possible) would net me over 125,000 XP.

"That's pretty amazing," Cloridan admitted, "But I hear there's a catch."

"Oh yes," Koenig said. "There's nothing free in this world, and there's no free access to dungeons in Dorsay."

"Isn't one of them run by the Guild?" Kyle asked.

"Yes, but don't think that means a free ride for adventurers," Koenig said sternly. His deep voice made it seem like a growl. "The Guild reserves *that* level of support for members who have truly committed to it."

Reynard had said something about this. "So we have to become Guild officials to delve there?"

"That's one option," Koenig agreed, "But there are others. The Guild serves the King, and he finds the right kind of adventurers very useful. You can read, can't you?"

At my and Felicia's nods, he pulled out and handed over a sheaf of papers. "These are examples of past contracts—I'm not offering any to you yet, but it will give you an idea of what's expected."

I cast a quick eye over the contracts. One was for a Guild official, the other two were more . . . vague. About some things, at least; for others, they were very specific.

"These seem very restrictive," I said. "Are the other dungeons completely unavailable?"

Koenig shrugged. "There are six dungeons close enough to Dorsay to make use of the mana collection. Of them, two are controlled by the King, one by the Guild. The other three are each controlled by one of the three Dukes."

"The Duvosts allow paid access to their dungeon." I pointed out. "Is that not true for the Dukes?"

"Oh, I'm sure if you paid enough money, a Duke would let you in," Koenig said. "But it would be more money than you could possibly earn in there. You'd be better off earning favors from one of them."

I grimaced. I hadn't had the best record collecting favors from nobles so far.

"It's the same for the King's Dungeons," Koenig continued. "He keeps them for levelling his people—and the treasure. If you find a way to impress him—which is possible if you're *in* Dorsay—then you can get a position at court and some access to the Royal Dungeons."

Koenig glanced over us again. Felicia was reading one of the contracts closely with a frown on her face; the other two were looking concerned. "Well," he said. "You don't need to make any decisions today, or on any schedule. If you're interested in offers, let me know, and I'll start an evaluation. Or you can inquire at any Guild branch if you've moved on from here."

"Thank you for the information," I said. "You've given us a lot to think about." I glanced at the others and we made our way out of there. Once we were out, Kyle looked as though he wanted to say something, but I shook my head to indicate it should wait until we were back home.

We had the meeting in the workshop instead of the kitchen, as Felicia was eager to start practicing with her Alchemy. It was unlocked for Healers, but she'd only recently bought some of the equipment required. Now she was tending her new furnace while the rest of us discussed Koenig's information.

The furnace, I might add, was powered with my Fire Gem, which had finally found a use that everyone else approved of. I was fine using it for hot water and cooking, but Felicia had been scandalized just as Elodie had been. Now it was installed in her cupellation furnace and she was working on combining the smaller mana crystals we'd found into higher grade crystals.

This wasn't something Healers generally did, I was given to understand, and doing it for profit would cross professional boundaries with Alchemists. Neither profession had a guild, at least in Talnier, but there were professional courtesies that Felicia maintained were important. Still, it was a fairly simple use of the Alchemy skill, regardless of your profession, so she was quite capable of combining mana crystals for personal use.

There were some aspects to combining that I wasn't sure about—I wasn't clear on the difference between the grades, but Felicia said she'd explain it once she had a few examples.

I read the contracts out aloud for the others, going over the details that I'd skimmed over in Koenig's office. They were restrictive, all right.

"The main thing that gets me about them is you can't quit," I said. "Not legally, at least, anyway. I suppose you could always skip town and change your name."

"There was a retirement clause," Felicia called out.

"Yeah, but like most of this, it requires permission from the Guild. This must have been what Reynard was complaining about. He pissed them off so they shunted him off to the lowest-ranked dungeon and wouldn't let him quit."

"I'm not really familiar with contracts," Felicia mused. "But my apprenticeship was a lot like that. Master Oliver was good about it, but you hear things—masters that basically treat their apprentices like slaves."

"I notice you still call him Master," I said.

"He still is!" Felicia exclaimed, surprised I didn't know. "I've his permission to go out and level to improve my skills, but he'll be my master until I go back and have him acknowledge me."

That struck me as a little unfair, but I supposed that if I imagined she was still in school and on a field trip . . . I shook my head and went back to the topic at hand.

"My contract with the Ironworkers guild was *not* like this," I said. "So I think it's more to do with the relative power of the parties."

I saw that I was losing my audience, so I explained. "Felicia—and all the other apprentices—needed their apprenticeship, so the standard is pretty close to slavery. *My* contract was more equitable because the Guild Master and I both had something the other wanted.

"So how desperate are we for access to the Guild dungeons?" Kyle wondered.

"That's the question, isn't it? The Guild seems to think we are—that there isn't any other way of getting higher levels. But we know there is. That Arcanist, Aghen Shadth, didn't come up through the Guild, I'll wager."

"The stories don't say where he came from," Cloridan said, considering. "And the Guild doesn't have a contract out on him like they would for a broken contract."

Assassination as contract enforcement . . . make sure to remember that. I stared at Cloridan for a second, then went on with my point.

"I think it's to do with having your own dungeon. That's why the King bans taking them."

"That could make sense," Felicia agreed. "But how?"

"We've got some time yet," I said. "We'll figure it out."

SMALL PIECES

This is a mana crystal," Felicia said, holding one out. I already knew what it was, without her telling me, so Identify didn't trigger. She was holding a small, cloudy, bluish-white crystal, about a centimeter in diameter. One of the odd things about this world was that the crystal—normally found in animals—was faceted like a cut stone. If someone had fashioned one into an icosahedron, that is. Thanks, Memorize, for that tidbit from high school geometry.

"And this is a grade two mana crystal," Felicia continued, holding out a slightly different stone. It was a little bit smaller and more clear. Less cloudy white, more clear blue.

"Okay," I said and triggered Identify on both of them.

[Identification]: Mana Crystal – Charge: 0/9 – Grade: 2
[Identification]: Mana Crystal – Charge: 0/9 – Grade: 1

"They both have the same charge, but the higher grade is smaller," I noted.

"Yes. I made the second one out of two six-point stones."

"Six plus six equals nine?" I asked.

"Yes, there's always some loss when you do it, depending on your skill level."

I ran the numbers in my head. "So this takes crystals worth 24 gold and turns them into a crystal worth 18 gold. Oh, and if an Alchemist was doing this, we'd get charged an extra gold. How much did it cost for you?"

"Not much," Felicia shrugged. "With the Fire Gem for heat, there's maybe a silver's worth of flux used up."

"So why are we doing this? Seems like it's just losing us money."

"Well, I *do* need to practice," Felicia pointed out. "As I get better, it will lose *less* money."

"That's good?" I said. "I mean, smaller crystals aren't good for much besides grinding into enchanting powder . . . but there has to be a reason people do this, right?"

"Well, that's why you don't see higher grade crystals out here. It's a different story in the capital, but I don't know why. The Alchemist that I bought the forge off of said that a grade two stone goes for twice the price of a similar size grade one. But he didn't know why."

"Something to do with the mana levels? Dorsay gets most of the mana for the entire Kingdom, doesn't it?"

"Maybe we can ask the Guild Master," I mused. I picked up the higher grade stone and tried charging it. Then I frowned and tried charging the other one.

"It's faster," I said. "To charge, I mean." I pulled the mana out again before my pool could refresh and tried both of them at the same time. "About twice as fast, I think?" I gave them to Felicia to try. Healing didn't use mana, but she had Mana Sense, which was enough to pull mana out of a mana crystal.

"That doesn't seem like it would be worth twice as much," she said. "Even with the smaller size."

"Well, you're right about needing to practice anyway, so let's try and find out why we'd want these."

"Well, if you want me to go into competition with you, just say so."

I smiled sweetly and waited for Arber to stop scowling. The look on his face was one that I'd become familiar with from seeing it on a number of experienced merchants in town. Now that I was level five, my Bargain skill total eclipsed that of everyone in town that I was interacting with.

I also had a better idea of the strengths and weaknesses of the skill. It did boost my persuasiveness, but it didn't let me strike deals that were actually unfair. If I wanted someone to give me stuff for free, I'd be better off using Charm.

The main thing Bargain did was let me know exactly how far I could go before the deal *became* unfair. I wasn't sure if I was cold reading the person I was negotiating with, or estimating costs through some supernatural means. I just *knew*, and that made the deal forgone conclusion.

So I knew Arber was going to cave; he was just being stubborn.

"This shop sells Master Monteminer's goods," he repeated stubbornly.

"It doesn't *just* sell his goods; you've got all sorts of dungeon-made and adventurer traded items here," I pointed out. "Master Monteminer told me that he didn't have any objection to you selling my goods."

He shifted his eyes away awkwardly. "I haven't had a chance to hear from him, what with the town as it is."

He was referring to the fact that the Griffin Corps were not currently available for private jaunts into the mountains. With the injuries from the wave and the current tensions with the Tribes, the Griffin Riders were operating on extra duties with fewer personnel.

"It's your shop, not his. You don't actually need his permission. Or is it someone else's permission you think you need?"

He glowered at me some more. "I don't know what you're talking about, lady."

"I know all about the deal where the Baron gets the lion's share of all the profit from Mandel's enchantments." My use of Mandel's first name should have given him a clue of *where* I learned that from. "That won't be the case for my goods; you can finally start making a profit."

He got shifty again. "If you know that, then you know the Baron takes Master Monteminer's share, which don't affect my profits none. And it's not like the master needs money."

"I mean, you'll have goods that you won't have to sell at a discount to reduce the Baron's take," I said. This was where Bargain really shone. A glance at his prices earlier had told me that he was offering Mandel's stuff at a substantial discount, and it didn't take much thought to figure out why. Ironically, if Mandel had cared about money, he'd probably have noticed the same and would have been much less doubtful about Arber's loyalty.

Arber froze at my revelation. "That—that's just crazy talk. If you go to the Baron with lies like that—"

"I'm no fan of the Baron," I interrupted. "I'm not going to him with anything."

I let him stammer for a bit, then continued. "You should still be able to run the scam. My work *is* of lesser quality than Master Monteminer's, but I doubt the Baron will know the difference. You can still offer the discount without there being an obvious price differential."

It was kind of cute that some of the fight went out of him as soon as I admitted that Mandel was the better enchanter. He really was a loyal friend. But he still wasn't sold, so I kept going. "And the fact that you won't have to fly out to the mountains to get custom work commissioned should be a major selling point."

He glared some more, but his heart wasn't in it. "I guess it would, at that. Fine, I'll stock your items. Don't think the Baron will take kindly to this, though."

"Let me worry about the Baron," I said, Charm projecting confidence I didn't feel. "Let's talk details."

There weren't any beast-kin on the streets. There had never been many, but now there were none. I knew there were still beast-kin in the town, but none dared show their faces, and from what I heard, I didn't blame them.

So racism is a thing in fantasy land as well, I thought to myself as I made my way around the central square. It definitely wasn't universal; I could hear more beast-kin defenders than there were people bad-mouthing the Tribes, but the atmosphere definitely wasn't friendly. The trouble was, even the defenders had to admit that the Tribes had probably launched the last attack. They just didn't think that we should blame the ones in the town for it.

From what I knew, most of the beast-kin still in town were staying in rooms at the Adventurers Guild. They were adventurers, of course, so they felt confident in protecting themselves, and the Guild had announced it would act to protect any Guild member who hadn't broken the King's Law. So they were probably safe but still chose not to provoke anyone, hoping that this would all blow over.

My destination was the best inn in town, the one the rich merchants stayed in. Downstairs was a common room that served expensive food during the day and expensive drinks at night. I walked up to the front desk.

"Is Master Black free?" I asked. The man looked at me and then slowly nodded, indicating a direction leading towards the back of the building.

While most inns would stick a bunch of tables in a room and call it a day, Golden Goose did things differently. Whoever owned it had heard of open plans, and didn't like them one bit. Instead, there was a small maze of differently sized tables, all separated by either low partitions or full-fledged walls. Weaving my way through, I eventually came to the table I wanted.

"I can't claim to be an expert in the subject," I said, taking a seat. "But is this really how you arrange for a clandestine meeting?"

Mr. Parkes, whom I definitely wouldn't be calling Tom, looked up from his documents and smiled.

"The Ebon Order *does* have covert agents, Ms. Hammond, but they don't go around wearing black and holding meetings with town leaders and luminaries." He gestured to the walls around us. "This is just to prevent eavesdropping and reduce the amount of gossip about my visitors."

Ms. Hammond. He'd asked about my preferred address, and I had to admit I preferred it to Master, Mistress, or even Miss. It wasn't a surprise; after all, he *was* explicitly sucking up to me, but it still felt nice that he'd remembered. Somehow, it helped me ignore the rustic setting and feel that we were professionals having a normal business meeting. Well, a bit. I couldn't ignore that ridiculous doublet. I started imagining how he'd look in a sharp Armani suit but stopped when I realized I was getting distracted.

Okay, one point to you.

Smiling as if he could see what was going through my head, Mr. Parkes offered me tea from a pot on the table. "So, to what do I owe this pleasure?"

I took the cup, which was excellent, as I expected. For all the talk of being a slave to his master, he certainly lived well.

"I'm looking for information," I said cautiously. "About this impending conflict."

"Ah." He swirled the tea in his cup. "That's certainly something I can help with. Were you looking for a handout, or did you wish to *trade*?"

My eyes narrowed, but he held up a hand to interrupt me. "I *am* to help you where I can, it's true. If I aided you without recompense, though, you would feel indebted to my master, yes?"

"I thought that was the whole idea?" I asked sourly.

"In part, yes. But recall, I was asked to gain your *trust*. Providing aid with the intention of holding it over the recipient—that engenders the opposite. As a craft guild member, you should be familiar with the notion that trust is best formed from the repetition of fair business deals."

"I'm not unfamiliar with the notion," I admitted. Brush it up with a bit more jargon, and it could come from corporate messaging. "So how much did you want?"

"I—and my master—have little use for money, but I think you're rich in the kind of currency I trade in."

Riddles? Oh—okay, obvious ones. I rolled my eyes. "Fine. I've made an agreement with the Champion of Naldyna to try and stop any war from starting here."

His eyebrows raised in surprise. Honestly, he'd probably get half of this information from our conversation, so I might as well get credit for it.

"So Naldyna's Champion is here after all? Lady Tamayo was uncertain if she'd left the mountains. And Naldyna is *against* the war?"

I shrugged. "She's not here right now, but she'll be back soon. And I don't know what Naldyna's position is."

"I would owe you a considerable favor if you could arrange a meeting for me with Kaito Washiyama."

"I'll keep that in mind," I said. "But in the meantime, can we discuss what that buys me?"

"Of course," he said. "If stopping conflict is your goal, you'll want to know about the forces that are driving the conflict."

"That sounds about right."

"First, though, I should explain what's *stopping* it. There's been something of a stalemate for the last fifteen years."

"I assumed the forest was just a natural dividing line."

"Forests don't stay in one place. They either expand through growth, or they get cut down," he explained. "In this case, the Kingdom cuts down any growth on their side of the line, while the Tribes make sure that the Kingdom doesn't touch the trees deeper in."

"How?"

"With monsters, somehow. The Tribe manage the nastier monsters, keeping them away from their settlements and concentrated on the border."

"That's not really the case around Talnier, though?"

"Talnier's on a trade route; it's one of the ways in and out of the Tribal areas. If you know the route, you can walk from here to the nearest beast-kin settlement without encountering a single monster."

"Neat. And on the Kingdom side, they can keep them back by cutting down trees?"

"Mana control. Draining the mana out of the area makes it inhospitable to monsters. And Tribal troops are no match for Kingdom numbers, heavier weapons, and coordination when the fight's on open ground."

I thought about it for a bit. "So neither side can attack the other. Hence the stalemate. So why am I worried about a war starting?"

"When it comes to war, someone always finds a way," Tom said somewhat cynically. "For the last five years, the best plan both sides have come up with is to provoke the other side into attacking."

"Which . . . would be suicide. War is even stupider than I thought."

LOOSELY JOINED

om laughed. "So let's discuss the forces that are pushing for war. At least on the Kingdom side. I can't really speak to Tribal politics."

"Sure," I said.

"To start with, Baron Marseau is heavily in favor. He rose to prominence through his prowess in battle, so he's looking for a similar chance to rise further."

"Can you increase your status if you lose the war?" I asked doubtfully. "As a soldier, shouldn't he recognize a losing battle when he sees it?"

"It's possible but certainly more challenging. Marseau would definitely *prefer* to be attacked, but I think he could be provoked into attacking. His first campaign was further west of here, on open ground, against a more traditional opponent."

"Plus he's easily provoked," I said.

"That, too," Tom agreed. "His main advisers are split. Captain Guertin is for attacking, while Captain Boivin knows his griffins will be almost useless in the forest."

"So can Baron Marseau start a war on his own?"

"No, he doesn't have the men. He'd need reinforcements from nobles higher up the chain. So Duvost, Duke Bargougne, or the King."

"Are they all in the capital at the moment?" I asked. I knew Aubert was there, so it seemed likely his boss would be present for his investiture.

"Probably," Tom said. "Though the King does have his representative present. He can get reports and send orders fairly quickly."

"So am I worried over nothing? If the Baron can't start a war . . ."

"A war is not going to start in the next few days," Tom agreed. "However, there are tensions here that can be inflamed or eased in the coming days. For example . . ."

He started talking about the various merchant factions, who were split on the idea of war. The basic summary seemed to be that the richer consortiums based in the capital were in favor of capturing new resources, while the ones actually based here would prefer a continuation of current trade. He went into details, but I glazed over them and relied on Memorize to take care of the details.

"What about the religions?" I asked eventually.

"Split as well," he said. "Duit is known to favor the Kingdom while Naldyna supports the Tribes."

"Is that tolerated?" I asked. "I mean there's a big temple to Naldyna in the middle of town. I wouldn't have thought the nobles would stand for a religion that's openly against them."

There was also the matter of the Temple aiding operations in the town that went against the ruling authorities. I'd thought at the time that they wouldn't have been suspected of that, but it appeared their opposition was generally known.

"Ah, well . . . Churches are given a certain amount of leeway on such matters. Especially right now."

"What? Why?" I asked. My eyes narrowed. "And why *now*?"

"It hasn't happened in many years, but it *is* possible to provoke a god into smiting you. Or your city."

"Oh," I said. I guess it was different when gods were real. "But then, why don't the churches just take over?"

He frowned in confusion. "They're not really political organizations?"

It took a bit of conversation before we worked out we were talking past each other. I'd had the wrong idea about churches. Direct control of territory or people by the gods was just not *done*. Though there were exceptions. Naldyna seemed to consider the northern wilderness to belong to her, and the Tribes lived in it with her permission. They revered her, but they weren't ruled by her.

I'd thought that the gods would muster their followers like troops in a war, but that wasn't what they were about. Rather than recruiting, they tried to promote that god's beliefs of how mortals should live their life. Organization—beyond that of individual temples—was unknown.

I supposed that, should they deem it necessary, a god could speak to each of their High Priests simultaneously, and manage the organization directly.

"So Church and State just . . . ignore each other," I said, bemused.

"Well normally," Tom said. "But, well . . . you lot are here."

"That changes things?" I asked, but of course it would.

"Champions often get involved in politics," he said. "And they generally get the backing of the Church. And . . ." he broke off again.

"What?" I asked.

He sighed. "And the gods have spent the last hundred years or so setting up things for you to fight over, situations calculated to generate conflict or cooperation. Knowing that Champions are within their borders is the sort of thing that makes rulers nervous. It just guarantees that *something* is going to blow up."

"That's why your master was so keen on getting a read on me?"

"That, and he wants a favor from a god," Tom said, matter-of-factly.

"He thinks I can get him that?"

"Not directly . . ." Tom shrugged. "It's difficult to negotiate with gods. All you can do, apparently, is make yourself available near a situation with Champions in the hope that a god will find you useful, and give you what you want in return."

"Seems dicey," I muttered.

"Perhaps. But there are some things only a god can do. And they do grant the occasional one of these wishes. Presumably to encourage the behavior."

That did sound like them. I would have thought that granting wishes went against their rules . . . but there was so much I didn't understand about that.

"Getting back on track," I sighed, putting the gods aside for now. "The Church of Naldyna was smuggling beast-kin out of the town. That seems pretty political to me."

"More than that," Tom said, frowning. "I'd heard they were taking them in, but getting them *out*—they're trying to raise tensions."

"How so?"

"Those scared refugees go back to the Tribes with a tale of how they barely escaped from the murderous humans. Hotheads in the Tribes start agitating for a mission to rescue the ones left behind."

"That would be what the Baron wants, though? An attack?" I wondered. "Could he provoke one by threatening civilians?"

"If the Baron was *actually* committing atrocities . . ." Tom mused. "It wouldn't look good with the other nations. He might find himself handed over to Tribes as part of a peace treaty—he definitely wouldn't be covering himself with the glory he needs for a promotion."

"So there are *some* restrictions on the Nobles," I said.

"Especially with the Inquisitor in town," Tom agreed. "He seems inclined to ignore most of the Baron's violations, but there's only so much he can turn a blind eye to."

I sat there for a moment. *Maybe that can work*, I thought, as a few scattered ideas came together. Tom stayed silent, just watching me across the table.

"Thank you," I said. "You've been very helpful"

There weren't too many people on the streets. The guards still patrolled, and the town was still locked down. But *few* wasn't *none*. I spotted my target, the wife of a well regarded merchant, probably getting her grocery shopping done. I'd found the trick to Phantom World—despite the name— was to keep the changes small. It was less to keep track of, and easier to make sure that the target didn't see or do anything that broke the illusion.

In this case, I kept the change far away. Two blocks down the street, a cat-kin burst out of the alleyway. It would have been too far for me to cast a regular illusion, but this was only in Jolie's head.

The cat-kin only got a few steps out into the street before he was pulled back by a pair of guards. Jolie couldn't see much at this distance, but the guard uniforms were distinctive. She stopped in shock. None of the other people on the street seemed to have noticed anything, and she didn't know what to do. The guards quickly dragged their victim back out of sight, and I dismissed the illusion. By the time Jolie found the courage to approach the alleyway, there was nothing to be seen.

Shaken, casting glances at the other people on the street—most of whom were guards—she continued on her way. It was just a drop of doubt. There was no proof that anything had occurred—and if pressed, she would have to admit that just seeing a cat-kin was pretty unlikely during this time. But enough drops would form a river.

I was surprised when the knock on the door came, and the guards came to search my home. For one thing, I'd expected it a day or two earlier. For another, it came during business hours instead of at two in the morning. Baron Marseau still had a lot to learn about authoritarian methods, I guess.

We had nothing to hide, of course, and the idea of unreasonable search and seizure hadn't been invented in this universe, so I let them in with a smile.

"Are we special?" I asked the sergeant, who was glumly watching his men tramping about, finding nothing. "Or is the whole town being searched?"

I was pretty sure he wasn't supposed to tell me anything, but Persuasion made short work of orders he wasn't inclined to keep anyway.

"Ah, it's everyone, but you were supposed to be one of the first," he said, blushing under my attention.

"Well, I hope you're entirely satisfied that we have nothing hidden here," I said.

"Aye, ma'am," he said. He hadn't asked to look in our safe, but it was too small to hide a person. They hadn't said, but even if I hadn't known they were looking for Edele, it was obvious from what they were checking.

"Well, I hope you have a good day searching," I said. I doubted the rest of the town would be as accommodating.

All it took was a little gossiping in the marketplace to find out that a meeting was going to be held. It was a little harder to get an invitation.

There wasn't an operational Ironworkers Guild in Talnier, but the two blacksmiths they had were quite respectful of my Anchorbury qualifications. The meeting was being held under the auspices of the Merchant Guild, and I'd managed to win a good reputation with most of the local merchants. They did tend to respect someone who could out-bargain them, which I found odd, but I'd take it.

The Merchant Guild was one of the few guilds that operated independently of a particular town. Many of its members travelled, after all. They had a much more complicated system of rank and seniority than the Ironworkers Guild had, and a tradition that the most senior Guild members in town at a particular time was in charge of Guild affairs.

This wasn't a Guild meeting, though. A number of townsfolk would be coming, and not all Guild members were invited. Representatives of some of the Dorsay-based families had made their positions on the war clear, and so word was very carefully kept from them.

I was a local, but only barely. It took a lot of commiserating with merchants over the recent loss of trade, and some bemoaning of the short-sightedness of military types before someone decided to suggest that there was a meeting I might like to come to.

It was all based on word of mouth and personal trust. I allowed that I'd like to attend, and a merchant assured me that my name had been passed on to allow me entry. When I showed up at the Guild Hall, I was a little intimidated by all the guards that were scattered around the place. It seemed that every merchant in town had contributed their guards to make sure we wouldn't be interrupted or overheard. I fell in with a few acquaintances and we moved as a group through the crowd. It was a bit chaotic—there wasn't anything as organized as a man with a list at the door. Instead, introductions were made and small talk was exchanged until eventually someone was found who agreed that yes, we were to be allowed in.

It wasn't very promising, but every insurrection had to start somewhere. I resolved to wait until the meeting started before judging if these townsfolk had what it took.

HOMEOWNERS ASSOCIATION

Without someone to run it, the meeting had devolved into chaos. Quiet, polite chaos of course—these were merchants, not adventurers. People had split up into small groups with quiet, urgent conversations, probably passing on the rumors they'd heard.

Fortunately, one of the more senior merchants decided that this wasn't going anywhere and climbed up onto the raised platform at the end of the room. I didn't know much about him beyond his name, Nicholas Winston, and that he traded in furs.

"Gentlefolk, please!" he called out. "This meeting is to help us work together, not repeat the gossip of the marketplace!"

With everyone's attention attracted, the crowd started gathering at that end of the room. People broke off their conversations and started looking at him expectantly. He gestured at a few of the others, trying to get them to join him up on the stage, but they refused. He was on his own.

I didn't blame them. I didn't want to be up there. I think everyone in the room realized that while nothing illegal had happened yet, the discussion could turn treasonous at any moment. No one wanted to be the ringleader, least of all the one standing on the stage right now. The scowl on his face suggested he wasn't unaware of the danger he was facing.

"Fine," he said sourly. "We all came here for a reason. Let's start with putting together what's going on with these abductions. Could everyone that has witnessed something come forward and tell your tale, please."

One by one, people started telling their stories. A few of the shorter or more quietly spoken ones were encouraged to stand on the stage, but most just spoke from within the crowd.

I didn't pay too much attention to what they said—I'd been the seed for most of the stories, after all. I focused on the crowd instead. Intrigue was starting to stir. I started to tease out the group dynamics, singling out the ones who were listening with anger and outrage at what they heard.

At this stage, there didn't seem to be any deliberate plants that I could tell. No one was planning on running to the Baron to sell us out. There were a few waverers, though, that would need keeping an eye on.

> **[Intrigue] Level 3 acquired through use.**
> **For gaining a skill level, you have been awarded 1 XP.**

The stories finished, and the crowd devolved again into babel. Frustration was evident on the faces near me, and was mirrored in the brave Master Winston who'd chosen to chair the meeting. The problem was that there really wasn't a lot there. The pattern of attacks on beast-kin by guards was plain to see, but no one had much in the way of evidence. No one knew of a beast-kin who was missing. No one had gotten a good look at the perpetrators.

So there was outrage, but a keen sense that this wasn't enough evidence. "What can we do?" was a common question, but no one had an answer.

I had one.

"I know *one* thing we *must* do," I said, finally speaking up when the frustration reached its peak. I paused to let what I'd said sink in, and give time for the crowd to reorient on me.

"And what is that?" Winston asked me warily.

"We have to keep these rumors from the beast-kin remaining in the town, and make sure that the Tribal Council doesn't hear of them."

Confused and angry murmurs greeted my statement. One person called out: "You mean cover this up?"

"We have to!" I called out, projecting as much as I could without shouting. "If the Council finds out about this, it could lead to a war!" That quieted the muttering, and I was able to continue at a lower volume. "The only way to end this is for the Inquisitor to bring justice to the man responsible."

"What if he's in on it?" someone called, made brave by anonymity.

"Then this goes all the way to the King," I stated. "And if that's the case, then war is inevitable."

That caused a hush to fall over my audience. "But I don't think that's the case," I said, backtracking. "If the King was aware, there would be no need for the care they've taken to keep it quiet."

"Do you really think the Inquisitor can help us?" Winston asked from the stage.

"I do, but we'll need to bring him more evidence," I said. "And we'll need time to gather it. That's why this needs to be kept secret."

> **[Persuasion] Level 4 acquired through use.**
> **For gaining a skill level, you have been awarded 1 XP.**

Oh, nice. No notification of a Social Contest, but I guess these guys wanted to be persuaded. I wondered if I got extra experience because there were so many people here?

Getting a skill up suggested that I'd made my points, so I bowed out of leading the crowd and let the others have a say. I'd planted the seeds, so with luck, they'd keep working their way around the same two ideas.

The real reason I wanted it kept secret—well, it wasn't too distant from the reason given—was twofold. First, I did want to keep agitators from using the rumors to inflame tensions. I didn't want to actually start a war, but I thought that this was an acceptable risk. When it came down to it, there wouldn't be any evidence to point to, so I should be able to benefit from the rumors while they lasted without causing any permanent harm.

The second reason was that the beast-kin in town were in an excellent position to debunk the rumors. No beast-kin had *been* lost, after all, and they were much more likely to notice that very salient fact.

Searching for evidence would keep them busy, and help them come together as a group, while I worked on the next stage.

I was surprised how much it made a difference, in the Market the next morning. Just knowing that there were others with the same views gave people the courage to push back against the bigoted sneers of the few. They only managed the mildest of rebukes, but that was often enough. Unsure of their audience, the racists kept quiet. I suppose it wasn't real change, but it felt a lot better.

Nice as it was, that wasn't a particularly useful result. Talnier wasn't a democracy, so I wasn't going to change things through popular opinion. It did make me hopeful, though, that the people I was working with weren't as socially backward as their development level suggested.

* * *

"I'm telling you, Sarge, they straight-up murdered him just off the street!" The guardsman looked nervous as he made his report to the skeptical Sargent.

"Why didn't you stop them, then?" the older man asked.

"Well . . . I'm off duty, and there was just the one of me and three of them," the younger man said defensively. "I came out of a tavern and saw it, and came looking for you."

"Drinking down at the docks?"

"You know they're the only places open after dark with the curfew."

I *tsked* to myself at this clear dereliction of duty. I guessed that even an off-duty guardsman could count on his buddies letting him go by during a curfew. No one heard me, of course, as I was invisible.

"So you're drunk, and I'm supposed to believe you saw a murder."

"I did," the young man insisted. "It was those fuckers we're supposed to leave alone."

"Recognized them, did you?"

"Made sure I would, after I got in trouble bringing one into the guard-house," the young man said sulkily. "And they weren't trying to hide; I saw them clear as day."

"S'pose it's worth taking a look," the Sargent reluctantly admitted. He whistled and his patrol stopped poking about the street and gathered around him. "Let's go," he said to his squad.

The off-duty guard led them to outside a pub near the docks. "There," he said, pointing at an alleyway. The Sargent shrugged and the squad headed over there. It took them about a minute to turn the place over; they weren't exactly forensic about it.

"There's nothing here, Pensy," he said in disgust. "No body, no blood."

"Stones are wet," one of the others pointed out. "Could have been cleaned."

"Smells like cheap beer," the Sargent sneered. "Could be someone spilled a tankard."

More like a firkin, I said to myself. I wasn't sure where that translation had come from. I certainly hadn't known the different names for small barrels before coming to this world. It *had* been cheap, though; I probably did someone a favor by ensuring it wouldn't be drunk.

"I know what I saw!" Pensy protested.

"You were drinking, you fool, you probably imagined the whole thing," the Sargent said.

"I couldn't have imagined that," Pensy denied, shuddering. "I never saw no one cut off ears before."

Finally, he mentions the ears! I had started to think he hadn't noticed. This was just going to be one of many attempts, but it would be nice if it worked.

The Sargent frowned at the detail. "Ears?" he asked.

"Yeah, it was easy to tell, on account of how he was a beast-man," Pensy babbled. "But he was already dead, so I dunno why."

The man who'd noticed the beer—currently my favorite—came up to the Sargent, his face screwed up in thought. "I've heard that adventurers sometimes get tasked with collecting ears to show they've killed a monster."

"Aye, but I've never heard of the practice for *people.*"

Well, now I felt bad. It seemed that Earth had a few things to teach this world about atrocities. I'd seen the bounty postings in the Guild and assumed that the practice would carry over.

"You don't think the Guild is putting a bounty on beast-folk?" another guard asked.

"Nah . . . no way." The Sargent shook his head. "Wouldn't be Fangs collecting on them if so. No, if there's a bounty on beast-kin, it would be coming from . . ."

His voice trailed off, but at least half the squad seemed to pick up his meaning. The alleyway got awfully quiet.

"Nah, there's no way." The Sargent shook himself and said the words with something approaching confidence. "There's no sign anything happened here, Pensy is just drunk and talking bollocks."

Pensy tried to protest again, but the Sargent glared him down.

"Still," he continued. "Keeping our hands off those bastards is one thing, but if we do see a murder, then that rule can go hang, just like the bastard responsible."

I nodded to myself and slipped away. Not much of an effect, but I knew it would take time. Brick by brick, I was stealing parts of Marseau's wall, and adding them to my own.

The rest of the week was more of the same stuff. I had to move carefully, in case someone suspected I was pulling a fast one. I started rumors disguised as someone else, I carefully staged incriminating scenes, all to build up the narrative of a Baron out of control

The merchants blamed the Guards, the Guards blamed the Fangs. It was more complicated to keep the two tracks separate, but there was a reason for it. Eventually, the two tracks came together.

"I'm here, Gaspar, because of the disturbing things we've been hearing about *your* Guards."

Gaspar Clavette was the second-in-command for the Baron's Guards. The merchants had decided to brace him, rather than his boss, Captain Guertin. This was both because he wasn't as close to the Baron and because they knew him better. There was a strong feeling among the group that Gaspar couldn't possibly be involved in this. Which was accurate.

Winston was doing the talking, but he had brought me and another merchant along for moral support.

"What are you talking about?" Gaspar growled. I was pretty sure he felt he didn't have time for this, what with his subordinates starting to act up against the Fangs. He kind of had his hands full.

"I'm talking about murder! Of beast-kin in the streets!"

"Are you mad? There's no way the Guard would be involved in something like that!"

"They would if the Baron ordered it." Winston said the words quietly, but with urgency. In our discussions to date, the merchants had danced around the idea that the most likely cause of these crimes was the Baron.

"That's—" Gaspar said, and then caught himself. It made him look guilty, but I knew the pause was that he'd just made the connection. *They* were worried about the Baron being behind crimes against beast-kin. "Do you have any proof?"

"No," Winston said sourly. "Just sightings from a distance. If we had more than that, we'd go to the Inquisitor. Instead, I'm coming to you. Tell me that he hasn't ordered this."

"He hasn't, I swear," Gaspar said. "And if he did, there's not a man under my command that would do such a thing. But . . ." he paused in thought. "My men are reporting that the Fangs are collecting bounties on beast-kin."

"That's . . ."

"Obscene, I know. We don't have any proof, either, just tales from a few drunks and vagabonds. But we did find one thing."

"What?" Winston asked curiously.

"We followed a rumor and raided a place," Gaspar said slowly. "We didn't find much, but we did find stolen Guard uniforms."

"Then you think . . ."

"I do. Tell me more about what you've found."

I kept the sigh of relief from my lips. The two independent groups had found each other now, and should shore up each other's commitment. If someone from one group thought they might have been fooled, surely the other group was operating with better information?

The storehouse where the uniforms were kept had been fairly easy to break into with the skills of an invisible Rogue. The abandoned Fang safehouse had been even easier. It wasn't much, but my groups now had some tangible evidence to point to, which should help me going forward.

Yes, things were going pretty nicely.

LOYALTIES

I'm going to kill her." Isidre scowled . . . well, not at me, I was just in the way. Sort of. All of my running around starting rumors must have been good training for Illusion Magic, because it had increased to level five. That meant more spells, and I was trying one out today.

"You don't mean that," I said. "She beat you, but she didn't hurt you."

"She stole Manchas!"

I sighed. Well, my Phantasmal Emissary did. I was invisible on the roof. This new spell did pretty much what my previous combo did, but it was *much* easier, and I didn't have to be in the same room. The range was pretty limited, I did have to follow the puppet about, but I could kick back on the roof and see through its eyes. And talk with its mouth, which was about ten times easier than casting Unseen Sound all the time.

"Look, she saved countless people in town, people that *you* endangered. You should be thanking her," I said. It was *barely* a lie. Every word but one was the truth. Still, I doubted that Isidre would react well to the truth, and Kaito *was* willing to take the blame.

"You're on her side!" she accused.

"There's no need to take sides; this whole thing is over," I claimed. Hopefully, it was. "You just can't admit you made a mistake in the first place. Why'd you even take the damn thing?"

"It just . . . seemed right," she said. "Like I was going to be a holy warrior, so I needed a special mount. That's why I went for the griffins in the first place, but when I saw him . . . I knew he was special."

"Did you get in trouble with the Baron for putting the town in danger?" I asked.

She shrugged. "At first he didn't believe it would happen, and afterwards, he was more concerned about some prisoner that escaped."

Oh, that boded well. As far as I was aware, Marseau hadn't had a chance to check up on his pet dungeon, but that couldn't last.

"The King's guy, the Inquisitor, has been on my case about it, though. He wants me to go northeast, join in on some big plan the King has got going."

"Are you going to?" I asked, carefully keeping the eagerness out of my tone. It would be nice if she left. Having someone from Earth to chat with was nice, but we didn't have that many shared experiences to talk about. Guatemala may have had McDonald's, but it was a completely different country from Australia.

I was beginning to sympathize with what Tom had told me about the ruling class's attitude towards Champions. As long as Isidre was hanging around, it meant that Duit had an agenda here. It might help or hinder me, but I was stuck waiting to find out what it was.

"Maybe," she said, but the look on her face said no. I was tempted to try Persuading her, but I held off. Back when I was a lower level, I'd noticed that I was more resistant to Social skills than the numbers would have suggested. After subtly Persuading the Merchants Association, I had the distinct impression that if I'd tried that on me, it wouldn't go as well as it had.

Maybe Count Duvost had just been heavy-handed, but I'd been able to tell that I was being managed, and could resist it to some extent. The merchants didn't seem to know what was happening. Maybe it was because my skill was higher, or because they were inclined to go along with me anyway . . . but I didn't want to risk that there was a special Champion resistance.

I'd just have to work around her until she decided to be useful.

Marseau lifted the restrictions on the town after a delegation from the merchants protested against the damage being done to their businesses. My anti-war faction was prominent in getting that delegation together, but it wasn't as if anybody was in *favor* of restrictions on trade.

We couldn't really take credit for making Marseau back down—it was obvious to everyone that the whole thing was a farce. The search of the town had been completed without anyone finding anything; the assassin had clearly left long ago.

I found the fact that the Inquisitor hadn't left, or made a pronouncement about the killing, somewhat ominous.

It seemed to me that the Baron's next order of business would be checking on Mandel in his dungeon. He hadn't found Edele here; that was the next obvious place—although he must be wondering how she would have made it there.

I'd convinced my merchants' faction that we needed to keep an eye on the Baron's activities in order to uncover his crimes. It wasn't much of an information network, just a few guards reporting what they noticed to their friends and relatives. But it was enough, because they passed it all to me.

"A whole flight of griffins is being prepared for two days' time," Noah told me. "They're taking passengers, but they haven't been told who they are."

"Interesting. Do they know where they're going?" I asked. The other merchants had been grateful that I'd volunteered to be the point of contact for all the information coming in. We weren't meeting that often, so if I'd had to wait until the next meeting for this news, the Baron would be gone already.

The merchant shook his head. "Based on the loadout, my cousin thinks it's no more than a day trip."

I smiled. "Make sure your cousin knows what the Fangs look like. I'll wager that the Baron is getting them in position for some sort of staged attack on the Tribes."

That was bullshit, of course, but the man nodded and went on his way. We didn't have much in the way of eyes on the Fangs—honest merchants and guards stood out in that part of town. But if they were taking griffins somewhere, I knew where they were likely to be going. It looked like Tom would get his meeting with Kaito after all.

"If I said I was going to overthrow the King, would you feel like you had to stop me?" I asked the group.

Felicia raised her eyebrows. "*Are* you going to overthrow the King? Tonight?"

"No," I said unconvincingly. "But some of the things I am planning to do, the King might not like very much."

"Like stealing a Dungeon core?" Kyle asked with a smile.

"Or lying to the Adventurers Guild?" Felicia tried. "Seeing that Lord Duvost gets what's coming to him?"

"Something like that," I admitted. "I don't think it's treason for me, since I was never a part of your country, but I don't think that will stop them if they start coming for me—and you, by extension."

Cloridan shrugged. "Treason is something that nobles have to worry about. Us lowly commoners are expected to keep our mouths shut and follow whoever is in charge this week."

"Is loyalty to the nation not a thing here then?" I asked.

"Loyalty is earned," Cloridan stated firmly. "How can a nation earn loyalty? No, it's the King that due any loyalty, and this one . . ." He trailed off looking at the others.

"He's all right, I guess," Kyle said. "Kept faith with the adventurers, pretty much. The nobles, though . . ."

"Yeah, no one seems to like the nobles," I admitted.

"I've heard that there *are* good ones," Cloridan replied, "But never where they're to be found."

Felicia giggled at that. "Remember, Kandis, the last set of Champions overthrew the *Empire*. We've been expecting something like this from the start."

"Okay, I guess this plan is a go then," I said. "Let me fill you in."

"So, how did that refugee escort go for you?" I asked brightly. I sat down on the forest floor, the other girls surrounding me. They exchanged glances and then sat down in front of me.

"It went fine," Orino said coolly. "Why do you ask?" The harem had been friendly enough to start, but they'd gotten suspicious of me when I'd suggested that Kaito have a private talk with Tom, while the rest of us indulged in a little girl talk.

It had amused me no end that Kaito didn't pick up on the fact that *she* was a girl and shouldn't be excluded from the girl's group. Since we were speaking in Japanese, none of the others had a chance to make that objection either.

"Just making conversation," I said. "I wanted to have a talk with you girls because . . ." I paused, not sure if I was making a faux pas. "You know that she spent Development points on Harem, right?"

Ettalle giggled, while Fassi blushed and looked away. Orino, though, kept her gaze on me. "Of course," she said.

"Well," I said awkwardly. "We don't have anything like that back home, you know? So when I heard about it, I was worried that some sort of coercion was involved."

"It doesn't work like that," Orino said. Her expression had softened slightly, which I took as a good sign.

"How does it work, then?" I asked. "I bought some coins with Development points, and they just appeared in my hand! Is that how it worked for you girls?"

Ettalle laughed out loud. "Ha! Can you imagine a couple of naked girls just appearing in her arms? She'd have freaked out!"

"No, it doesn't work that way," Orino repeated. "It was all very . . . natural."

"There was a big feast," Fassi, the rabbit-kin, spoke up shyly. "To select the companions for the Chosen. She met a lot of people, but for us . . . it just felt right. On both sides."

"That doesn't exactly reassure me that there wasn't any coercion. If not from Kaito, then from the System."

Orino shrugged. "It's not like anyone can resist their Status," she said. "I don't feel bound to Kaito, I just want to be with her."

"And you are still all your own selves? I had heard he didn't like you breaching the dungeons; that was your own will?"

"That was the will of the Tribal Council," Zichy said, the wolf-kin speaking up for the first time.

"They sought to start a war?" I asked.

"No, the dungeons were a message, expressing their anger."

"It's a shame no one's invented email already," I said, to their incomprehension. I looked over at Kaito, still talking animatedly with Tom. "She's looking for peace."

"She has been lobbying the Council," Orino agreed. "It is . . . commendable. And they do listen to Naldyna's Champion. But your King seeks to expand, and he has men like your Baron to push that expansion."

"Not my King, not my Baron," I said mildly.

"Ah . . . sorry. You look so much like one of them that I forgot." She did look embarrassed, which I had to admit was an adorable look on the little mouse-kin.

"Understandable," I said, waving a hand magnanimously. "Don't worry about it. But speaking of the Baron . . ."

I glanced over to make sure Kaito was still talking.

"What would your people do if they had advance notice that Baron Marseau was going to be in the forest—well, the mountains, anyway—in a few days?"

Orino's eyes narrowed, but it was Zichy that spoke.

"You know this?"

In for a penny . . . "I do," I said. "He'll be coming to attack the dungeon under Mandel's place, so he won't be alone. But he will be vulnerable."

"Mandel? The Enchanter? Where we took that girl?" Nori asked. I nodded. "The Enchanter lives in a dungeon?" she said wonderingly.

"He's coming after the girl," I explained. "At first, he'll send his thugs and cutthroats, but I think Mandel can handle them this time. After that fails, he'll come in force, and I'm almost certain he'll be leading his troops."

"He can't take his troops through the forest," Nori said. "He might be able to punch through on his own, but he'd lose too many men to be worth taking them."

"He'll bring them on griffins," I said. "So he's going to be limited to what he can bring . . . unless he camps outside and makes multiple trips." I was surprised at their assessment of his capacity, but he *was* a level six.

Zichy looked uncertainly at Orino. "We have to tell the Council," she said. "Even if they don't trust—" She broke off, with an embarrassed glance my way.

"You've got some options, tactically," I said. "You can confirm with Mandel that he's expecting a visit and that he's preparing to fight them off. I don't know if he can take the Baron's full force attack, but if your force was to attack from behind . . ."

"Or," I said as the silence extended, "you might just want to drive off or capture their griffins, leaving them trapped on the mountain. One thing, though, that you might want to plan for."

I looked at each of them in turn and then pointed to Kaito. "She'll be upset if this starts a war, so make sure that no one finds out who killed the Baron."

GRANTED

Can you see it? I mean, um, sense it?"

I didn't ask the question aloud. My experiment would have looked odd enough to someone who had snuck in to spy on me, but at least I wasn't talking to myself. I'd decided to do some research while I waited for my gambit to bear fruit. It was going to be a few days before Marseau left the city. I had no idea if the Tribal Council could get an ambushing force in place in time. They did seem able to move quickly, but could they put together sufficient forces? There was no way to know.

I would be sad if they waited until he finished with Mandel's dungeon. Well, for all I knew, Mandel would be able to beat Marseau. It was the fight he wanted, after all, but I couldn't help but think it was the Baron who held the advantage there.

Waiting to find out the outcome was killing me, but interfering struck me as a spectacularly bad idea. Instead, I would be spending my time shoring up support amongst the local community and distracting myself with experiments. In a few days, we'd be able to start delving again, but with the backlog of adventurers, the Guild had started a lottery for delving slots so we weren't all fighting over slim pickings.

We had not been lucky in the draw. So for now, there was this.

In one hand, I held my Dungeon core. In the other, I held an enchanted disc that must have seemed like an expensive mistake. Attached to the center was our largest mana crystal to date. Grade three—the highest grade that Felicia could currently make, with 56 mana capacity. It was about two centimeters across.

The reason someone might think that I had wasted this expensive crystal on a failed or unfinished mistake was the tendril of mana that had been whipping around randomly but had now been directed into the Dungeon core.

I'd learned that when a spell or magical enchantment needed to be *controlled* by the user, there needed to be a mana connection from the controller to the spell or item. For a spell, this connector was simply part of the spell. For an item, you generally just needed to be holding the item. Even mundanes with no magical skills could project a zero-length magical connection. (Perhaps *project* was the wrong word there.) Rune circuits seemed able to take direction from a mana input that came into it from anywhere on the circuit or the magical metal substrate.

If you wanted to control an item remotely, you needed to get creative. There was a rune pair that let two rune circuits connect to each other, but you didn't actually need it. You could just add a little offshoot line at the right spot. Left on its own, it would just slowly spew out mana, but if you used Theurgy to connect it to a mana pipe, it started acting like a USB port, able to transmit both power and data. Hopefully, power in one direction and data in the other.

Of course, doing anything with Theurgy was much harder than any other way, but in this case, I didn't have an option. I couldn't carve runes onto the Dungeon core, so all I could do was wave a mana conduit through the damn thing and hope it caught somewhere.

"Ah!" Rhis said. "I think I caught something there?"

I carefully moved the conduit back to where it had been. Something tugged on it.

"Yes . . . I can feel a mana connection," Rhis said. The connection seemed stable, so I carefully released my mental grip. Everything stayed in place, and a quick Identify showed that the mana crystal was discharging.

"Speak up if you feel your power diminishing," I said to Rhis, while keeping an eye on the mana crystal. If there was any doubt that my Intelligence score was raising my mental capacity, then maintaining two separate sensoriums would have put that to rest. Slowly and carefully, I stopped feeding mana to the Dungeon core.

"Everything seems to be fine?" Rhis said. "Is that what you wanted to test?"

"Not quite everything," I replied. "Can you . . . project yourself down the connection?" That was the best description I had for using that particular spell.

"I'll try," Rhis said, but even as he did, I knew that it had worked. A five-foot-tall image of a fox-like humanoid sprung into existence as Phantasmal Emissary was triggered by the item.

"Welcome to the real world," I said, sitting back and taking a good look at the new Rhis. He looked just like his image back in the core mental space, which made sense. He was looking around confusedly, but slowly a big grin spread across his fox face.

"Are you kidding me? You made me a new body?" he asked delightedly.

"It's an illusion," I said, waving dismissively. "It will disappear when the mana runs out. Speaking of which . . ." I glanced again at the crystal in my hand. It was over half depleted from casting the spell and would run out in about an hour at this rate. Still, that wasn't a problem. I recharged the crystal with my mana and handed the enchantment to him.

"I can hold things? Real things?" he asked. He examined the enchanted plate closely, turning it around and looking at it from all angles. I winced, my experience with cables making me expect disaster, but the mana conduit simply adjusted, untangling itself as fast as he could tangle it.

"Yep, it looks like it takes fifteen mana an hour to maintain your Core and a bit more than that to run the illusion. So that crystal should last about three hours before you'll need recharging. You can't go too far from the core, though."

"This is amazing." He started prowling around the room, touching surfaces with his free hand.

"It's the least I could do," I said, amused by the way he was touching everything. "For now, I think it would be best if you stayed in here, but how about we introduce you to the rest of the people who live here?"

I left him in my workshop while I gathered everyone in the kitchen.

"Everyone, this is Rhis," I said, leading him in. "Rhis, this is—"

"Oh, I know some of these people," he said, grinning at my friends who were staring in shock. "You're Kyle; you killed a lot of lizards. And you're Felicia; you always knew the way to go in the jungle."

"You're really . . . the dungeon?" Felicia asked. "You were watching us?"

"Of course! It's not like I had anything else to do when people were inside." He looked at the others and cocked his head. "I don't recognize you two. How many lizards have you killed?"

Cloridan stared for another second, then shook himself. "Not many," he admitted and stepped forward with his hand extended. "Cloridan's the name; pleased to meet you."

Rhis stared at the hand for a moment. He must have seen adventurers greet each other in the dungeon because he took the offered hand and pumped it up and down with enthusiasm.

"This is fun! Do I get to shake hands with all of you?"

Cloridan laughed. "I don't see why not. This is Cutter, by the way," he said, indicating our final member.

"Oh! You're so much smaller than the others!" Rhis said, moving over to shake Cutter's hand. At the last moment, he remembered to let go of Cloridan's, saving himself from an embarrassing tumble.

"Uh, yeah," Cutter said, clearly not sure what to make of the situation. "Do you want to see my knives?"

"*Do* I? Of course I do!" Rhis said enthusiastically. After looking at me for permission, Cutter led him away, presumably to his room.

"Just make sure you stay in the house!" I called after them.

"Soooo . . ." Felicia said, trailing off. "Um, why?"

"Well . . . he's a sentient being," I said. "I just couldn't stand leaving him trapped in that core, unable to experience anything. And I'm nowhere near ready to set up a dungeon."

"But he's . . . a monster, isn't he?" she asked uncertainly.

"Not like any monster I've heard of," Kyle said. "There are plenty that can talk, but I've never heard of friendly ones."

"He's not a monster, he's a monster *controller*," I said. "Which . . . makes it even weirder that he is friendly."

"Didn't you say that it was the dungeon controllers that were forced into becoming homicidal by the God of Destruction?" Felicia asked.

"I did," I admitted. "That's what makes it weird. I think that it might be because as the Master of the Dungeon, I'm stopping the corruption. Or it could be because the core isn't fully powered."

"But isn't he dangerous?"

There was a shout from the other room, and Rhis came in at a run. Brandishing a long knife.

"Ha! I know this one!" he said, as Kyle moved to cover him. "I'm *not* supposed to kill people."

I sighed and covered my eyes. "Maybe don't wave a knife around when you're trying to reassure people, Rhis."

"Okay?" He looked at me, and then at the knife, which he was now holding quite still above his head.

"Just put the knife down," I said. "And anyway, he should be incapable of hurting anyone with that body."

"What?" Rhis exclaimed. "Oh, wait, that's a good thing."

Baby steps, I told myself.

"He's holding a knife," Felicia pointed out. I pretended not to notice how Rhis brightened at that.

"Yes, but he shouldn't be able to put enough pressure on it to hurt anyone," I explained. "Phantasms *can* hurt people, but only if that's the only option to preserve the illusion of solidity. Try stabbing the table, Rhis."

He moved against the table with enthusiasm, only to find that his knife stopped dead against the wooden surface.

"It's too tough," he complained.

"No, it's the way the rules work," I said. "It's easier to preserve the illusion if you just stop pushing, so that's what happens. If you don't give it a choice . . ."

I conjured a thin needle. Placing it upright on the table, I pushed it with the flat of my palm. At first, nothing happened, then the needle sank into my palm.

"Ouch," I said. I cancelled the needle and let Felicia send a little Healing my way. "With that setup, the needle could go into me, or the table. Cancelling my momentum did nothing because my hand was a constant force."

"It could have snapped," Kyle pointed out.

"Yeah, but it was too tough for that. Oh, and when it's *forced* to do damage, it takes an equal amount, so it stops existing when the damage equals the spell total. Which is . . . a decent amount now, admittedly."

"So I could do it if I pushed slowly?" Rhis asked.

"Maybe, but I think since you—the Phantasm—are the one supplying the force, it just stops you from applying the force."

He tried it nonetheless, but it seemed to be true. No matter how hard he pushed the dagger, it failed to go into the table.

"So what now?" Felicia asked, somewhat mollified.

"Well, we can't let him out on the street, but there's plenty inside the house for him to learn about."

"That's right!" Rhis exclaimed. "I still haven't learned the names of all of Cutter's knives!" He rushed back out of the room, almost stumbling over Cutter coming in. "Come on, let's go back to the knives!"

"He's certainly enthusiastic," Felicia said.

"Long term . . . we'll see if we can take him on expeditions. At the very least, his hearing is excellent."

"That's true . . . you don't seem the type, though."

"What type?"

Felicia grinned wickedly. "The mothering type. This is the second stray you've taken in, after all."

PETITION

Thank you *so* much for seeing me this quickly." I entered the room at a brisk pace and then curtsied to Inquisitor Dunnar as best I could with one hand occupied by my leather satchel. He looked at me speculatively and then indicated that I should sit.

He'd elected to have this meeting in his host's dining hall, which meant we were going to be seated across from one another on a long, thin table. We were sitting on the long ends, though, so we wouldn't have to shout. After I was seated, he took the long trek around the table to take his own seat.

"I find myself with time at the moment, Mistress Hammond," he said as he took his seat. "Though I'm surprised to find that you are representing a consortium of local merchants. I thought you were an adventurer."

"I'm still a member of good standing with the Anchorbury Ironworkers Guild," I reminded him. "And I've started my own small commercial enterprise here."

"I see." He smiled, but it didn't reach his eyes, giving him quite the predatory look. No doubt he was thinking of how to turn this into a way to whisk me away to the capital. "I should say, though, if you're expecting me to be in charge because Baron Marseau is on an expedition, you are in for a disappointment."

"Is he away? Will he be back soon?" I asked innocently, my own smile as bright and cheery as Charm could manage. I had the impression that Inquisitors could detect lies, so I kept to questions, instead of any statement to the effect of I didn't know he was gone.

"He should be back tonight, or tomorrow at the latest. If you have something that can't wait, you can talk to his wife."

"The Baroness? Do you know, she hasn't been seen about town in the last few days. Is she well?"

Politically, the Baroness was a nonentity. As far as I could tell, she'd been selected by the Baron to be the pretty and compliant mother of his soon-to-be heirs, and while she didn't seem unintelligent, she knew enough to keep her mouth shut about her own opinions in front of him or in public. Probably a bit of a waste, but she could have done worse.

"She's fine," Dunnar said, his eyes narrowing. "Though she was complaining about the 'atmosphere' in the marketplace. That's probably why she's not been down there. Should I fetch her?"

"Oh, what a shame," I said, mentally upgrading my estimate of her intelligence. "But no, I'm actually here to see you."

I reached into my satchel and pulled out a massive document. Back home, it would probably have been eight pages of double-spaced neatly printed text. This was handwritten, though, so it came to more than forty big, heavy pages. The last two pages were entirely taken up with signatures and seals, and it came with its own rudimentary leather cover. I let it fall to the table with a solid thump and then passed it over to the Inquisitor.

"In your capacity as the King's representative, I'm presenting you with this petition."

"What is this?" he asked, even as he looked at the first page. Despite the fact that the answer was right there in front of him, I answered nonetheless.

"That is a petition to remove the Baron from his position, based on his demonstrated incapacity and numerous crimes, as listed."

"This is . . ." he gave a little laugh as he went through the pages. "Is this a joke?"

"In addition," I said, ignoring him, "it requests that Talnier be incorporated as a Free City, holding charter directly from the King." This was the same arrangement that Oakway had. This was one of the demands that helped get the merchants on my side. They liked free cities, because they had less tax.

As for the King, he should actually like the proposal. Anything that took power away from a noble increased his own. Of course, that meant . . .

"The nobility will never stand for two dungeons falling out of their control."

I coughed. "Actually, sir, those two dungeons are outside our borders and are not controlled by anybody." This was actually true. Most noble-controlled dungeons were taxed as much as the delvers could bear, and the taxes were collected at the dungeon entrance. Here in Talnier, they just taxed the merchants receiving the goods, and at a much lower level. If they taxed higher, adventurers might find it worth their while to trek out to the Tribal lands to sell the goods there.

He looked up at me. "You're actually serious. You think this is going to work?"

"Humble commoners like ourselves can only trust in the King's wisdom. Once he reads the proposal in detail, I'm sure he'll be in favor of it. Unless you are authorized to make the decision?"

He frowned. "Is this the part where you offer me a bribe?"

"Your lordship's reputation as incorruptible precedes you," I said evenly. "I brought no bribe."

There was a flash of irritation on his face at that. Did he really think I'd bribe him for this? Such a significant change would never escape the King's notice. Did he want to take my money and not deliver? *No*, I realized. *He wants to be able to arrest me for attempted bribery. Well, too bad, that's not on the agenda for today.*

"No," he said sourly. "I don't have the authority to decide on a petition of such far-reaching consequence. I do, however, have the authority to see that this nonsense never bothers His Majesty."

"I'm sure that once you've had a chance to go over the document carefully, you'll want to pass it along," I said confidently. "The seals alone should convince you that this is a serious petition to address an issue that cannot go unresolved." Those seals included one from the Adventures Guild. Once he saw that, he would know that he couldn't just disappear the petition. The Guild had their own channel to ask what had happened to the petition.

"And you think that will be the end of it?" he asked incredulously. "What do you think the Baron is going to think of this? You're just asking for retaliation."

"Anything he does against any of us will only aid the case against him," I said serenely. Actually, that *had* been a major concern of most of the signatories. That was why I was here presenting the petition—if the Baron retaliated, they were hoping he'd be satisfied with me. For myself, I was fairly sure he wasn't going to be in a position to respond, but if he *did* manage to make it back from the dungeon, I'd have to start looking into some fight or flight options.

"Fine," he snapped. "If you're so eager to see what a noble's displeasure looks like—if you're still alive and free three days after Marseau gets back, I'll pass this on to His Majesty."

I got up from my chair and curtsied again. "Thank you for your consideration, my lord. Was there anything else?"

"No. You're dismissed."

The notification came slightly after that.

You have killed Amaury Marseau in an Intrigue. You have earned 2,070 XP.

I felt a surge of both relief and guilt. I'd gotten a man—actually a whole bunch of men—killed, just by giving the right information to the right people. On the other hand, the plan was still on track.

It had been a risk, delivering the petition that early. It would all have gone south if he'd made it back, but if I'd left it until it was clear that he was dead, it would have looked opportunistic. I had another scheduled meeting with Kaito later tonight, so hopefully, I'd be able to get a report from her girls about how the operation had gone.

"I'm so sorry!" Kaito said, her voice somewhat muffled by the position she'd put herself in.

I looked down at her, disconcerted. She'd knelt down and put her forehead on the ground, like some slave before an emperor.

"Um, what? No. Get up!" Her harem members didn't seem pleased by her behavior, either, with expressions ranging from shocked to disapproving. They didn't come forward as I brought Kaito up to her feet again.

"Just tell me what's wrong," I said.

"I'm sorry," Kaito said again, her eyes downcast. "Even though I agreed to work with you towards peace, I've committed an act that may cause a war."

"I'm sure it isn't that bad," I said. I glanced over at the girls, who had now assumed carefully expressionless faces. *Really?* I guess this went some way towards reassuring me that they weren't puppets. At least not *Kaito's* puppets.

"What did you do?" I asked, projecting calm and warmth into my voice.

"Ah, it was your—I mean the Baron of Talnier," Kaito got out. "I learned that he had found out where we took that girl we saved."

"Edele," I supplied.

"Yes. He was travelling there, with a significant force to kill her parents and capture her again. I had to protect her!"

"Of course you did," I reassured her. Something seemed off about that description. Some spin by the girls, perhaps. "I take it you fought him in the dungeon, then?"

She frowned at the memory. "He was letting his men fight the monsters, while he stayed back like a coward. We only had to take a few guards out before getting to him."

"He's supposed to be level six; it can't have been an easy fight."

"No, it was the hardest fight I've been in. This was the first time . . . it wasn't a monster." She flinched when she said that, but she continued.

"He was strong, but I was faster so it was hard for him to hit me. Even so, there were a few moments I had to really focus my resolve . . ."

"Save it for the anime," I said, repressing a snicker. "But I think we're okay." I glanced over to Orino for confirmation, and she nodded.

"None escaped," she confirmed.

"You see, Kaito, from what I've been learning, the Baron was the foremost warmonger in town. With him gone, there will be much less pressure for war."

"But they'll blame the Tribes for the killing!" she protested.

"No. They knew he was going to fight a dungeon. He just got overconfident and got into a fight he couldn't win."

"Then, I haven't started a war?"

"Nah, it'll be fine." I patted her on her head, which the girls seemed to take offense at. It was the first time I'd seen a beast-kin actually bristle, with their ears and tails poking straight up. "Fine," I said, raising my hands in the air. "She's your girlfriend, you comfort her."

"Where is he!"

I wasn't surprised when Inquisitor Dunnar burst into my office. Not because it was all part of my master plan, but because I'd been hearing him shout and bluster and smash his way past more than a few doors and protesting officials.

I'd started spending more time here over the last few days, as my duties for the Peace Faction had increased. I needed a place to handle correspondence and maintain records, and this room had been found for me in the Merchant Guild Hall. It would have been quite spacious, but the filing cabinets took up a lot of it.

Still, there was room enough for me to rise and curtsy courteously towards my noble guest.

"Where is who, my lord?" I asked innocently.

"The Baron, of course!"

"How would I know?" I asked, careful not to say I didn't know. "Didn't you tell me that he was going on an expedition three days ago?"

"You already knew!" he accused. "How else would you know to deliver that damned petition on the day he left!"

I sighed and threw my full efforts into Persuasion. Back when I was level four, we'd been evenly matched. Now at level five, I had a distinct advantage. You could do something like Intimidation's aura of fear with Persuasion, but instead of fear, it projected calmness and quiet.

"Sir, do you think a document like that can be thrown together quickly? We were working on it for days before delivering it!"

He fought against it, trying to rage and bluster, but I kept up the pressure. *What would any number of retail workers have given for this skill?* I thought.

"Do you think, after all that work, we could have delayed addressing such an urgent matter?" I asked with expertly feigned indignation. "Crimes were committed!"

"You knew," he insisted. "You knew he wasn't coming back."

"If that were true," I sneered, "we wouldn't have had to write the first half of that document. Do you think we would have petitioned the King if we could just assassinate rulers like that?"

Just for a second, doubt flickered in his eyes. It was enough.

You have defeated Reece Dunnar in a Tier 3 Social Contest! You have earned 45 XP.

"We can talk again, once you've had a chance to calm down and think it over," I said, carefully keeping the gloating out of my voice. "If you truly believe that the Baron isn't coming back, then you should contact the King to discuss succession plans. With tensions as they are with the beast-folk, we can't afford to be fighting among ourselves."

"You think a pack of merchants can defend against the Tribes?" he asked incredulously, but politely.

I smiled. "If you'd read our suggested charter, you'd know we recommended defense be provided by the King's troops, garrisoned at the town's expense. The town guard would be tasked with law enforcement duties exclusively."

"An answer for everything," he said sourly.

"Once you've had a chance to read and fully understand it, I'm sure you'll have no problem recommending to the King that he accept it," I said sweetly. "It really is in everybody's best interest."

I paused for a moment, savoring this 24-hour victory. "You're dismissed."

COUP

I think you should start arresting Fang members now," I said to Gaspar. He opened his mouth, and then shut it again.

This was a meeting of the Peace Faction, but it was much more organized than our first one. For one, there were far fewer people attending. The three merchants and I had agreed to be contact points for people's concerns, and Gaspar was here representing the town guards.

It wasn't an executive council, because there wasn't anything that we could really do. We just discussed the concerns of the other members and passed on any suggestions to relevant parties. Like this.

Gaspar's first objection was going to be that the Baron would never allow it. People were still coming to terms with the idea that he wouldn't be coming back.

"Won't it be a risk, if he does come back?" Noah, one of the merchants, asked. They were always a bit timid, but I knew Gaspar was made of sterner stuff.

"If we can get it done quickly, then even if he does come back, it will be . . . already accomplished," I said. I stumbled a bit, worrying at the last second that "fait accompli" wouldn't be translated. "We've been talking about it for a while, but getting that gang off the streets would be something we could actually do about improving the safety of beast-kin inside Talnier."

By now it was pretty much an article of faith in our group that the Fangs were kidnapping beast-folk.

Gaspar's brow was furrowed with thought. "We'd want to take as many of them as we can at once . . ." he mused. "I'm not sure that we have the men to do it."

"You could get help from the Adventurers Guild," I suggested. "I know they don't usually do that sort of work, but in this case, I think you'll find them very motivated."

There were nods all around the table. Everyone knew the Guild hated the Fangs. Promises of getting rid of them were what got the Guild to sign on to our petition. Solving the problem before the petition was even accepted would make us look like reliable partners going forward.

"What about the trials?" Gaspar asked. "Without the Baron, who will judge?"

"The Baroness?" Winston suggested.

Gaspar made a pained grimace. "The Baroness has . . . left. Probably back to her own family."

"Then, who is in charge? The Mayor?"

"No one is," I explained. "Captain Guertin is in charge of the Guard, Captain Boivin is in charge of what is left of the griffins, and the Mayor . . . will continue to do as little to draw attention to himself as possible."

The Mayor basically existed to pass on the Baron's dictates to the rest of the town. Hopefully, that would change soon, and we'd get to see if the Mayor was up to his new role.

"It's a mess," I admitted, "but Inquisitor Dunnar is still in town. He normally deals with greater crimes, but I'm sure he's able to judge lesser ones."

"Will he?" Gaspar asked.

"I think so . . . normally he'd want to do a favor for the Baron, but he can't get favors from someone who isn't here. Especially with the Guild around to report everything he does to the capital."

Heads all around the table started nodding and we moved on to other things. *Now if I could just get Isidre to start being useful . . .*

Standing in the town square with a crowd of people, I couldn't help but feel surprised. Even though I'd planned for this, I couldn't believe it was happening.

I'd been fairly confident that the King would go for making Talnier a Free City. It was nothing but benefits for him, after all, and with the Baron missing and the Count yet to be confirmed, there was less than the normal resistance from the nobility. Marseau was *missing*, not dead, and the town needed leadership now, not after a prolonged waiting period.

". . . five Town Councillors elected from the residents of the town, who shall . . ." Dunnar droned on, reading out the entire document. I guessed that was one way to disseminate information when you didn't have a photocopier.

What surprised me, as Inquisitor Dunnar read out the King's Decree, was that the Charter was exactly the same as I'd outlined. *I guess the King isn't a details guy?* While the Charter was based on the Charters from other Free Cities, there were a number of details that I'd added in. I'd fully expected them to be removed or altered before the document came back. It seemed as if the King wasn't in the habit of reading contracts before signing them.

The only wrinkle was that the whole thing was up for review in two months. That was barely enough time to get things up and running before we'd have to send a delegation to Dorsay and justify everything we'd done. Reading between the lines, that would be when the nobility tried to get us fired or cancelled or whatever the term was.

As soon as Dunnar finished reading the Charter, he called for citizens to stand for election to the Town Council. I smirked a little at his technical error, but I didn't bring it up as I stepped forward. With the entire town's population gathered to hear the speech, voting would start straight after nominations were recorded.

"Councillor Hammond has a nice ring to it, doesn't it?" Felicia asked with amusement. We were talking in the sitting room while Rhis and Cutter were playing with a rubber kid's ball that I'd conjured.

"Better than Senior Mistress, that's for sure," I agreed. "And it's very gratifying that so many people picked me out for the job."

"And this is only the beginning, right? What's the next step?"

"The next step," I said thoughtfully, "Is another secret meeting with Kaito."

After the usual greetings were exchanged, we sat down on the grass in the middle of the clearing.

"We should bring some furniture, we meet here so often," Ettalle giggled.

"Actually, I'm hoping we can arrange some . . . less clandestine arrangements in the near future." I looked at Kaito. "I'm guessing you girls aren't official negotiators for the Tribal Council. Can you bring someone important enough to make a deal?"

"I suppose so . . ." Kaito said, confused.

"What kind of deal?" Orino asked suspiciously.

"Let me bring you up to date on the latest changes in Talnier." I explained to them how it was that the town had changed status to a Free City, with an elected government, and that I had been elected Councillor.

"Ah! That's good news!" Kaito exclaimed. "With you on the Council, it will be much harder for the warmongers to take control."

"That's part of it," I agreed. "But remember that under the new rules, the garrison here will answer directly to the King, and he's at least war-curious."

"That's true," Orino said slowly. "He's always trying to expand at the expense of others—mostly the forest."

"Right. I need to manage expectations here—I can't control the King. But there's one thing he likes just as much as more land. Money."

"The Council isn't going to give you money," Orino told me.

"Well, it just might—indirectly. I'm hoping that if the City of Talnier can extend diplomatic recognition to the Tribes, they might be willing to establish a trade route."

"With the city, not the country?" Kaito asked. "How would that work?"

"Carefully, like any new international agreement," I said. "I'm hoping that once we get it in place, and the benefits become obvious, the King will see the wisdom and get behind the idea. Maybe even to the extent of actually recognizing the Tribes."

"What's in it for us, though?" Zichy asked. While Kaito seemed somewhat taken with the idea, her harem was more suspicious.

"Trade benefits both sides or it doesn't happen," I told them. "I don't know exactly how yet, because I don't know what you guys are willing to sell or what you want. That's why I need someone with knowledge and authority to hash out an actual deal."

"You must have a general idea of how to proceed, though," Orino interjected.

I nodded. "I figure the first thing is for you guys to create a safe path through the forest to your nearest population center. That's assuming there isn't one already, of course."

"So, creating a literal trade route," Orino replied.

"Yeah. If it were the Kingdom, we'd want to build a road, but that takes time, and don't think you guys like them very much." Varied noises of disgust told me that I was right. "Now, what the merchants would like is for their caravans to be given guides and safe passage through the forest, so they can go and trade their goods directly with your villagers."

"That is . . . unlikely," Orino told me. "The Elders won't want Kingdom caravans in the inner forest."

"Right. So what we do is we establish a trading post, either in the city or outside the walls. That can be where the goods are exchanged, and your folk can be responsible for transporting them to your villages."

The girls all looked at each other, but they didn't seem to see anything objectionable in that proposal. "What goods, though?" Orino asked.

"Well . . . that's going to take a meeting between my merchants and your Elders to hash out," I said. "But for starters . . . I know you've abandoned the two dungeons near here. We're pulling out a wide variety of alchemical ingredients from the chimera one, it's likely that some of them are of use to you."

"Perhaps," Orino said doubtfully.

"C'mon, Orino, we have to try! It could lead to peace!" Kaito urged her.

"Will it? She sounds like she's more interested in wealth than peace!" she snapped back.

"Peace and prosperity go hand in hand," I said. "You can't have one without the other."

"Fine! We'll bring it to the Council, and see what they say," she said.

"That's all I ask. Thank you."

The elections had been a simple affair. The Charter just stated that the Councillors were to be elected, but in the future, I hoped to introduce the idea of electorates and campaign periods. We didn't even have set terms—but that was more to do with the fact that the whole arrangement was a probationary one.

The five Councillors were me, the ex-mayor, Noah from the Peace Faction, another merchant who hadn't been in the Peace Faction, and a senior Carpenter. Inquisitor Dunnar was filling in for the yet to be appointed Alderman, who would be overseeing the application of the King's law. He looked *so* happy to be here.

I was the only woman, which seemed par for the course, but I wasn't sure. I'd had a difficult time getting a handle on sexism in Latora. There didn't seem to be a general belief that women were inferior, but nevertheless, men and women separated themselves into separate roles, apparently of their own accord. No merchant treated me as lesser because I was a woman, but women merchants were vanishingly rare.

Back in the chamber, the first order of business was whether there should be any positions or responsibilities aside from the general Councillor.

"I think we need three, at least," I said. "Mayor, Treasurer, Secretary. The Treasurer needs to have Calculate and Scribe, while the Secretary just needs to have Scribe."

There was some discussion around the table about what duties those roles performed. I shared my own understanding, which caused a few raised eyebrows.

"Wait, everything we discuss should be written down? And made public?" That was Delmar Balend, the other merchant.

"Of course," I said, like it was obvious. "We do this job at the behest of the people of Talnier; they should be able to see the quality of the work that we do. We'll also need something to show the King in two months."

They didn't like that, but no one wanted to argue it. It was difficult to argue for keeping secrets from the King in front of his Inquisitor. Everyone agreed with the need for a Treasurer, and Andre, the ex-Mayor, was obviously eager to have his job back.

I let the two merchants argue over who should be Treasurer. I'd vote for Noah when the time came, but I didn't really care. Secretary was the job I wanted. Officially, the Mayor ran the meeting, but the Secretary wrote the agenda and produced the official record of what happened.

Figuring that I'd network a bit while the merchants argued, I turned to the Carpenter Chaney. He was an old man, and from what I'd heard he'd had a hand building most of the buildings in Talnier.

"Ah, who gives a shit," he said in response to my question. "Gotta be one of them, and I can't tell the difference, to be honest."

I chuckled. "Why'd you take this job?"

"Workers said we needed someone to keep the rich folk honest. I'm mostly retired from working now, so I've got time." He looked at me closely. "You're not just a pretty face, are you? That idea of the meeting notes . . . you've done this before."

"Not exactly," I denied. "I've just heard about the best way to do this sort of thing."

He nodded slowly. "Well, at least one of us knows what they're doing, at least."

When we voted for Treasurer, Cheney voted with me, and when we voted for Secretary, the vote was unanimous for me.

> **You have defeated Aubert Duvost in an Intrigue. You have earned 125 XP.**
> **You have defeated Victor de Bargougne in an Intrigue. You have earned 245 XP.**
> **You have taken control of a Territory: City of Talnier. Claim? [Y]/[N]**

. . . What?

EXPLANATIONS

I stared at the notification in confusion. It must have been a full ten seconds before I noticed that no one else was saying anything. When I looked away from the blue box, I saw that everyone else was frozen.

"Don't worry, it's not a time-stop effect from the Territory notification," a familiar voice said. I turned my head to see Fyskel, sitting in a chair that hadn't been there before, *at a space on the table* that hadn't been there before.

"You," I said.

"Me, indeed." He gave me a little grin. "You're a lot calmer now. I think we'll be able to have a much more productive discussion than last time."

"Will we."

"Oh, yes." He leaned forward conspiratorially. "You have questions, after all."

"Are you going to answer them?"

"Eh." He waved a hand noncommittally. "Let's not get into spoilers."

"Fine." I looked at the box, still hanging there, but I had more pressing concerns than that. "Let's talk about me getting home."

"You can't." Fyskel shrugged. "That's beyond the power of any of the gods."

"You brought me here, though," I said. "Why can't you send me back?"

Fyskel sighed. "That knowledge can't help you," he said. "It will only confuse you and hurt your feelings. Can't we just leave it at 'can't'?"

"You said you're predicting my dialogue," I said evenly. "Aren't you able to predict what my answer is going to be?"

"Yes," he said sadly. "If I *don't* tell you, the question will eat away at you and continue to distract you from your missions. This way, you're more effective. And by warning you,"—he gave me a sly smile—"I get seen as a more empathic figure, helping us work more effectively together."

"Or it would have, if you hadn't been a smart-ass about it."

Fyskel sighed theatrically. "I'm sure you noticed that the body you came here with isn't the same one that you had before."

"Yeah . . ." I said warily. I had noticed a few things. Like being drop-dead gorgeous all of a sudden.

"No need to thank me," Fyskel said, smirking. "The System handled all that."

"Wasn't planning to."

"So there are two reasons for that," he explained. "One is that if you enter this world with a physical body, the System detects and treats you as a demon, and you don't get anywhere near as nice a treatment as you did."

"What's the other one?" I asked, my unease spiking. I'd noticed the change, but I'd assumed that my body had changed, not that . . . it was missing.

"The other one is that we only brought your . . . well, call it your soul across, so we needed the System to provide a body to put it in."

"My body is back on Earth? I'm dead?" My voice hardened as another thought flashed through my mind. "Did you fucks snatch my soul out of my body?"

"That's a lot of outrage for someone who didn't really believe in souls about four seconds ago. Unfortunately, the answers to all those questions are some flavor of I don't know."

"How is that possible!" I yelled. "You stole my soul and you don't know where you snatched it from?"

"You have to understand that other worlds are outside our area of influence," Fyskel calmly explained. "We can't extend most of our powers or senses out there, so we're limited to examining and affecting the more ethereal side of things. We didn't have any way of *perceiving* your body at the time, so we have no idea if you were in it when we brought you here. But we don't think so."

"*Why not?*" I said, glaring. *This is just a memory*, I told myself. *Even if you could punch him, there'd be no point.*

"There's a lot we don't understand about other dimensions," Fyskel admitted. "We don't know why Earth is the only one with people available to us. And we don't know why your memories all stop at the same point in time."

"What do you mean?"

"You don't remember dying, do you?" he asked. "Nor do you remember the incredible pain of your body being severed from your essential essence. No. Your memories of Earth stop exactly where they did when we first found you. It took us forty-three minutes to make our decisions of who to take, but no memories were added in that time. To any of you."

"Well, maybe I was asleep?"

"Seven billion of you?" Fyskel laughed. "Even if that were possible, you do lay down memories during sleep. Even before you start dreaming, the traces of unconsciousness are unmistakable. And absent."

"But, what does that even mean?"

"We speculate, but ultimately we don't know. What matters is that we can't send your current body back, and we don't know if there is a body remaining to receive your soul. You have memories of Earth, and they *are* valuable. But you are a creature of Ryvue now, and won't ever be anything else."

I stared at him in horror. Everything I knew was gone forever?

He sighed. "I can tell that you need some time to absorb all this. I *did* warn you. You might prefer if we left it here, but then you'll be stunned in the middle of an important meeting with an unknown dialogue box in your face."

I stared at him for a bit, before realizing what he was talking about. *Shit! The meeting! The Territory!*

I took a deep breath.

"Okay, what can you tell me about Territory management?"

"Absolutely nothing. I can't just give information out to a Champion; it would be showing favoritism."

I slowly counted to ten, getting to four before I yelled. "Then what are we having this conversation for?"

"Calm down there," he said, grinning like the ass he was. "You should be able to work most of this out by yourself. To start with, I don't imagine you have any questions about the notification itself?"

I looked at the box again. "I got notified because I got elected and I won the first vote? Am I going to lose the territory every time I lose a vote?"

"Power in a democracy *can* rest on a knife edge, but it's not *that* volatile. The System has determined that you are the most likely leader to determine future policy going forward, so it's offered the city to you. Losing a vote won't lose you the city, unless it's a crucial one."

"It used to belong to Aubert," I said thoughtfully. "So that's why I got the Intrigue notification from him. Is Victor the Duke?"

"Yes, so you also stole it from him," Fyskel agreed. "The King isn't on there as you still maintain at least nominal fealty to him, and Marseau isn't on there because he's dead. You might want to think about answering the question."

[Y], I thought, making the box disappear. "Wait, if this is a memory . . ."

"Yes, you'll have to accept the offer again. Don't worry, I know what happens next."

What happened next was nothing.

"Shouldn't something be happening?" I asked.

"Why should it?" he replied innocently. "Have you requested any information?"

"Right. Status." The familiar blue sheet came up, but there was nothing different about it.

"If it makes you feel any better," Fyskel said airily, "Most territory owners never find their way onto the page. They still manage to affect things, but only unconsciously. For the most part, that means that things continue to operate as they always have."

Territory. The System had used that word too, it sounded like a clue. *[Territory Status].*

[Territory Name]: Talnier **[Territory Type]: Free City** **Population: 1,436** **[Territory Points]: 0** **[Roles]** **[Customization]**	**Liege: Kingdom of Latora** **Vassals: None** **Threats: Tribal Confederacy, Barony of Seren, Duchy of Arryen, Duchy of Bargougne**

"That's a lot of threats," I mused, my eyes going to that section immediately. "Wait, I thought you said this was hard!"

Fyskel chuckled. "You still haven't noticed it," he said. "Try saying it aloud."

"Territory Status. Territory Status." Each time, the screen came up as before. I wasn't hearing anything unusual . . . wait.

"Status. Professions. Log. What the hell?"

"*Most* of the System interface is translated into the native language of the user," Fyskel explained, still chuckling. "That includes the commands—*except* for a few."

"Status and Territory Status are in English!" That was why, I realized, people here called the System the Status. They didn't know what the word meant and thought it was the name.

"Strange, isn't it?" Fyskel chortled. "English was unknown in this world until we contacted your universe. Imagine our surprise when we realized it was somehow embedded in our deepest mystery."

"So why do people know Status but not Territory Status?"

"Only a few people in a country are authorized to use the latter, and they have a tendency to not pass it on if they *do* know. Now that we're not hand-holding, the knowledge tends to die out over a few generations."

"Even with the Priests of Knowledge about?"

"Toriao is pretty much constantly pissed with rulers who try to restrict knowledge of magic. She's instructed her priests to never reveal that word."

"Charming."

"Eh, it works out," Fyskel said. "It's not like there's anything necessary in there, after all."

What is in there? I wondered. I would have asked, but I knew that would just be an invitation for Fyskel to be difficult. Instead, I started going through the highlighted options on the screen. Territory Name and Territory Type just seemed to be an option to change either one. Territory Points just got a help file.

> **Territory Points are used to purchase all options in [Roles] and [Customization]. Gain Territory Points by improving your Territory!**

"Since you're wondering, I didn't write the help files," Fyskel said. "Though I have been inspired by them from time to time."

I snorted with derision and continued on. Roles gave me a very complicated screen. After studying it for a while, I ventured a guess.

"I can . . . create professions?"

"That's right," he said. "Some professions are universally available, while others can only be taken from within a particular territory. You're inheriting a bunch from Latora—those were created by the current King's grandfather."

Huh. That did sound useful. It looked like some kind of point system kept professions from being too good, but I could think of a few ways to use this—once I got some points.

Moving on to Customizations, I saw . . . a lot of options. It looked as though I could control all sorts of tiny little civilization details. I could have women addressed as "Ms.," for example, or set the standard greeting to "Whassup?" Clothing fashions, cultural norms . . .

"Is this mind control?" I asked, horrified and fascinated at the same time.

"Not exactly," Fyskel replied. "Most of that gets pushed through Charm, with a few bits going through other skills."

"So this is where Charm gets its information from? I curtsy because eighty years ago, some guy decided I should?"

"You don't *have* to curtsy, though," Fyskel pointed out. "You just know that that's the best action to take at those times."

"So if I changed curtsying to bowing . . ."

"Most people with Charm would just switch without thinking about it. They'll probably *notice*, but you know how easy it is to just go with Charm's flow. People without the skill would take longer to start doing it, but they'll soon pick it up."

"Still feels creepy," I muttered.

"Well, you don't have to use it. Of course, you're inheriting the settings from Grandpappy Nestor, so there will be an effect even if you don't change things."

"Even so . . ." It did creep me out, but ideas were already coming to me about how to use it. Developing a healthy corporate culture was such an important part of running a corporation, and a town wasn't any different, really. If I could install a culture of professionalism and honesty, it would go a long way towards reducing crime and corruption.

I could feel that I was talking myself into it, so I put it aside for now. It wasn't like I could do anything without Territory Points.

"Well, I think this conversation went much better than the last one," Fyskel said. "It's been fun; are you ready to go back to your meeting?"

Right, the actual meeting. "Sure," I said, casting my mind back to where it had been before Fyskel showed up. "Lay it on me."

He snapped his fingers, and everything started moving again. The box appeared, and I selected *[Y]* again.

Whew, I thought. *Time for a nice, exciting budget meeting.*

MONIES

I really wanted to focus on everything that had happened in that time-stop. I wasn't sure if I wanted to yell, vent, or think about the consequences. What I did know was that I didn't have time to do any of those things, as I was in the middle of an important meeting. How important? Well, the first item on the agenda had awarded me a city.

"The second order of business is the monies found in the, er . . . previous Lord's treasury," Mayor Andre said, reading off the paper in front of him.

"How much did Lady Valerie take with her?" I asked.

"Actually . . . very little. It seems that recent events had increased Lord Marseu's . . . concerns for security, and he'd locked up the majority of the treasury while he was gone. With him holding the only key . . ."

Everybody stared at the Mayor, who wilted under the attention. "So the Barony was operating for the last week without funds?" I eventually asked.

"Some funds were left available to officials, but essentially yes." The Mayor glanced nervously at the Inquisitor. "That fact lent a certain *urgency* to the need for some sort of succession plan. I wouldn't want to presume, but I think that might have helped prompt His Highness's granting the Charter."

Somehow, I kept the smile off my face. That paranoid idiot had really helped me out.

"So under the supervision of Lord Dunnar, workers broke open the vault and we've been taking inventory of the contents."

"Does the money belong to the city, or to Lady Valerie?" I asked.

"The case could be made either way," the Mayor said, looking again at Inquisitor Dunnar. "Her Ladyship has not yet pressed a claim, and given what we've discovered, she may not want to."

"What have you found?" Noah asked.

"There is a considerable amount of gold—almost a third of the total—that isn't listed on the books."

"More money than we thought doesn't sound bad," Councillor Balend put in.

"The implication, though, is that this money was acquired by illegal means," I pointed out. "And the tax hasn't been paid, either."

"Exactly. If Lady Valerie *was* to claim the monies, she would be admitting her complicity in the very crimes that your petition accused him of."

Inquisitor Dunnar spoke up. "His Majesty has stated that he will make no final decision until he's heard from the Lady. In the meantime, consider the funds to have been awarded to the city."

I winced, but only on the inside. Money that might get taken away later was almost a liability. Still, it might not.

"I presume the King's tax has been taken from the additional proceeds?" I asked. Faces winced around almost all the table. Nobody likes paying taxes. The two merchants had faces that were particularly pained.

"Ah . . . I suppose that would be the best course of action," the Mayor managed to get out, carefully not looking at Dunnar.

"A wise decision," the Inquisitor intoned, giving me a glance of annoyance. Had that been a test? A pretty weak one, if so. Unlike the others, I was actually ecstatic about the idea of sending off a massive tax payment.

I had expected the treasury to be empty. We'd collect taxes, of course, but in two months we'd be showing up to the King with empty hands and budget promises. Now, we'd be showing up with a big, fat cash payment in the bank.

55,000 gold added to Treasury.
1 Territory Point has been awarded!

I blinked, and then blinked the message away. *Okay* . . . I glanced at the documents on the table. That amount was the sum that the Baron had *legally* acquired. There was still the untaxed 30,000 gold—that would presumably be added to the Treasury once the tax was assessed and the remainder awarded to us.

After talking about the money, we moved on to where to keep it. The tower was the traditional center of power in the town, so it seemed a natural idea for us to move in and take it over, but I had another idea.

"The King will be sending troops soon," I said. "We don't want to mix them up with the Guard, and it seems to me that the tower is perfectly placed to be the command center for defending the wall."

Dunnar looked at me curiously. He was naturally suspicious of me, and any gifts that I might come bearing.

"Are you saying we should build a new Council House?" Cheney asked, perking up for the first time now his profession had become involved.

"Yes. Something built for the purpose off the main square," I said. Setting up shop in the tower wouldn't be *bad* (I remembered the working plumbing), but it would be isolating and intimidating. If I wanted to get participatory democracy going, people would have to be *invited*.

We didn't come to a decision on that one, but Cheney agreed to come up with some construction proposals.

"Now," I said. "I'd like to discuss some trade possibilities." The merchants leaned forward, always eager to hear about a new opportunity. The others just looked confused.

"We should be getting a delegation from the Tribes in the very near future," I explained. "They're interested in setting up a trade route with their nearest village."

The merchant's eyes gleamed, but they deferred to Dunnar as the Inquisitor spoke up.

"Treating with foreigners is beyond this Council's authority," he said with just a touch of condescension. "Only the King can decide if negotiations are to be held."

I smiled. "Actually, if you check our Charter, it specifically authorizes us to conduct mercantile and other agreements with nearby settlements."

He stopped, suddenly unsure of himself. *Yeah, he hasn't read the contract.*

"Did you want me to show you the relevant section?" I asked politely.

He narrowed his eyes. "I do remember something of that sort," he admitted. "But that cannot infringe on the King's prerogatives regarding foreign nations!"

"The Tribes aren't a nation, though, are they?" I countered. "Not in the King's eyes, at least. I understand the lack of acknowledgement is quite the sore point with them."

"Yes, but . . ."

"So the nearest Tribal settlement is just that, a nearby settlement. The Charter is quite clear." I paused to let that sink in. "The wording was authorized by His Majesty . . . are you saying he made a mistake?"

> **You have defeated Reece Dunnar in a Tier 3 Social Contest! You have earned 25 XP.**
> **Social penalties have been waived.**

I let him off the hook for losing as we had a long meeting ahead of us, and he'd be fuming if he couldn't speak against me. He took the gift with ill grace, but the conversation now moved on to the actual deal. I admitted I had no real idea of what they would have on offer, or what they would need.

"Spoken Wood," Cheney said. "That's what we need from them."

"What's that?" I asked. The merchants were both nodding thoughtfully at the idea, so I knew it was a good one.

"The Tribals don't cut down the trees—don't like us doing it much, either," Cheney explained. "But trees get old, need to be thinned out, and wood's too useful to do without. So they've got a profession, called Tree Speakers or some such, that can talk to the trees, get them to shed branches, or even pull themselves out of the ground."

"Sounds nice," I said. "But does that make the wood better?"

"You bet. They talk out all the knots, get the grain moved how they like it, even shape it into tools before it falls off. Planks, if they want to trade. It's mighty fine wood. Never saw Spoken Wood that was less than Perfect grade."

"It's rare to see it in the Market," Councillor Balend put in. "Since there's no official trade, you mainly see it as completed tools coming in from the north."

"Great. And what are we going to offer them?" I asked.

"I don't think they have many metalworkers," Noah mused. "I wouldn't be surprised if they were limited to dungeon-produced works, and what they trade from other nations. Steel and silversteel goods should be welcomed."

"That's great," I said. "Councillor Balend, since Noah is going to be working on the budget, can you sound out the Merchant Guild and get some proposed prices and available numbers of goods for when the negotiations start?"

"Of course," he said. "And, please, call me Delmar. We're all equals around this table, are we not?" He glanced at Noah, clearly trying to convey something without words.

"Sure thing," I said. "And remember to contact all the merchants. We can't let this historic trade deal get caught up in accusations of special dealing and corruption."

"Of course," he replied, with slightly less enthusiasm this time.

I made some notes for the minutes, and then we moved on to other business.

"Damn!" I said, sinking back into our comfortable chair. "Thank the System for Endurance!"

Felicia looked over at me, amused, from where she was sorting the fruits of her Alchemical labors.

"You don't have Endurance back home? How did you do anything?"

"We just had regular endurance, and it wasn't as good," I admitted. "We got tired a lot. Oh, and we had coffee. That helped."

"Sounds terrible. Did things go well?"

"Yeah, actually. Dunnar complained a lot; I had to win three Social Contests against him."

"Three? How was he able to go up against you three times?"

"Oh, I waived the penalties each time," I said dismissively. "If I'd kept them up, he would have waited out the 24 hours and then gone complaining to the King."

"Won't he do that anyway?"

"Perhaps, but it looks a lot better for me if I didn't take advantage. And the King will be getting a big fat payment, so I think he'll be feeling positively about me."

"Don't count on the gratitude of nobles," Felicia said seriously.

"Is that a saying here? It sounds like it should be."

"It is back in Oakway; I haven't heard it anywhere else," she replied. "But I think it's good advice, especially after Anchorbury."

"Yeah, well, I'm not counting on his gratitude, I'm counting on his greed. I want him to think I can get him more money if he lets me get on with it." I looked over at her. "How are the preparations going, by the way?"

"Slowly, but we've got plenty of time, don't we?" she said. "I still need to get my Alchemy skill up to make the higher grades, but these will make a nice base to work from."

"Our slot is coming up tomorrow," I said with some satisfaction. "We should make some progress in resource collection then."

"No politicking?"

"Not tomorrow, not unless the trade delegation shows up." Felicia gave me a look and started to say something. "And I'm supposed to get a warning before they do," I interrupted.

"Good—we've all been looking forward to completing the thing."

I nodded and then laughed. "It feels weird to actually look forward to combat and traps, but I really do after sitting in a room talking for six hours."

"You must be getting used to life here, then," Felicia snarked.

"I guess I must be," I said thoughtfully. "That reminds me, I didn't tell you about my *other* meeting."

I had to hand it to Fyskel—judging by results, there wasn't a better way to get me to stop worrying about earth-shattering revelations than to force me to manage five egos through starting up a new city. I'd actually forgotten about the whole thing—not literally; thanks to Memorize, I could repeat every word—but the conversation had slipped my mind until now.

Retelling the experience to Felicia, I was struck by fear. Just what had they done to me—or should I be worried about what had happened to me before they found me? Assuming, of course, that any of it had been true.

Felicia was much more interested in the Territory stuff, especially once I used illusions to show her the screens.

"I never knew that nobles had this available!" she exclaimed. "What are you going to do with it?"

"I think I'll wait until I have more points, and a better understanding of all the options," I said. "Did you know that different countries have different professions?"

She nodded. "Travellers from other countries often have professions that don't show up in the Status. They don't stop working outside the country, but you can only take them if you're in the country."

"Well, at some stage I'll take a look and see what's available for officials . . . but right now, I'm more concerned with whether I'm dead or not."

"Of course you're not dead, silly! Didn't you get a good idea in Anchorbury about what the living dead look like?"

I laughed. It was true, I had seen a variety of undead back there. "You know what I mean. If my soul was just lying around for the gods to take . . . I had family back home; were they all dead as well?"

"But you already knew you weren't ever going back," Felicia pointed out. "You just didn't want to acknowledge it."

"What do you mean?" I asked.

"You read the book about all the other Champions—well not *all*, but a bunch. None of them ever went home; they all made new lives here."

"That's . . ." I protested, but it was true. I'd thought that they must have all just given up, or found life better here . . . but *all* of them? Some of them must have tried harder than I had.

For the first time, I started thinking seriously about living the rest of my life here.

DEEPEST

The marketplace was different now. It wasn't the greetings—Talnier was small enough, and I was personable enough that I'd already met most of the people that shopped here regularly. It was a sense of deference. Before, I'd been one of them but now I was set apart, a noble in fact, if not in name.

People still came up to me, but now it was as supplicants—or future supplicants in most cases. No one really knew what they wanted out of the new regime, or what I could do for them, but they knew I was *important*. So they gave me little gifts, or discounts at the stalls I shopped at, hoping to curry favor.

It was nice . . . better than nice, if I'm being honest, but I needed to stop it. It made me feel like a mafia boss wandering through his territory, and I felt that if I let it continue, that's what I would become. Rewarding my followers with power and maintaining a power base through patronage and bribery.

I wasn't sure of the best way to handle it, so I just politely refused the gifts and tried to . . . connect with the people who came up to me. I tried to reestablish the relationships I had with these people three days ago.

It certainly gave Charm a workout, but I got almost as much use out of Memorize. Remembering their names, their family members, the topics of conversation from the last time we'd talked . . . hopefully it made a difference.

Is this what politicians do? I wondered. I was a politician now, after all, so despite my distaste for the role, I'd better lean into it. Better a politician than a mafioso, after all.

With all that going on, my simple morning food run turned into an hour and a half of schmoozing. Which led to breakfast being late, and our first dungeon trip for a while getting delayed.

"If you knew that was going to happen, you should have sent me shopping," Felicia pointed out as we moved through the forest.

"It was my turn, and besides I didn't *know*," I replied. "I thought there might be something different and I wanted to see what it would be like."

"Then you should have sent me shopping and focused on politicking."

"Then *I* wouldn't have gotten any breakfast," I groused. "If I hadn't had that excuse to leave, I might still be down there."

"Is this going to be a full-time thing?" Cloridan asked. "Are you going to give up on delving?"

"I don't think I can afford to," I answered. "I still want to level, after all, and the XP from Social Contests is terrible."

"True," Felicia agreed. "But we won't be able to take up Guild Master Koenig's offer if you're stuck here in Talnier."

"Aaah, you're right. I'd been thinking that we could check out Dorsay's dungeons when we reported to the King, but we'd need a contract to get in, won't we?"

"The Guild's dungeons, yes," Cloridan said. "You could try your luck getting in the King's Dungeon."

"Or a noble's," Felicia put in.

I sighed. Just one more thing to worry about.

"Well, for now, we've got this delve; let's focus on that and worry about the future tomorrow."

The delve was . . . okay, I guess. Maybe Rhis's rants were getting to me, but I was starting to see his point about just rolling the dice for your dungeon design. We hadn't taken Rhis with us. Not only would he have complained incessantly about the dungeon, but we weren't sure what would happen if we took a Dungeon core into another dungeon.

By "not sure," I mean we had a bunch of likely scenarios, all of them horrible. From another dungeon break to the two cores trying to eat each other. None of my group had ever heard of such a thing, and the consensus was that if it had been tried, it hadn't ended well.

I'd made a note to revisit it after we'd had a chance to visit the Monteminers and talk with Marie. As a dungeon herself, she might be self-aware enough to say what would happen. Unfortunately, that was on hold due to the soldier shortage. Private use of griffins was suspended until the King's troops arrived, which wouldn't be for a little while yet.

I really wanted to visit and find out what had happened, and how they all were. You'd think that my new position might free up just one quick flight, but no. The Griffin Riders answered to the military commander, and as he had not arrived, they weren't listening to anyone.

Getting back to the dungeon, or the Forbidden Laboratory (as no one called it), it continued downwards for just one more level further than we'd already gone. Just like the others, it consisted of rooms linked together in a maze. It kept using chimeras, but naturally, they were bigger and tougher.

A couple of traps spiced things up, but the monsters were the real threat. Random combinations each time meant you couldn't really predict what was going to come next.

"I think I want to call roachquid as the new worst," Kyle said as we finished up. He'd been right in the thick of the fighting, so he was covered in goo and . . . ichor? I wasn't sure what you called insect blood.

"No way, the centipig was way worse," I said with a shudder. That had been an arena fight, so there'd been room for the fifteen-meter-long abomination. Centipig had been the System's designation; it didn't seem to care that it had only consisted of about thirty double-sized pig halves.

"Are you really going to complain about all that free bacon?" Kyle asked incredulously.

"It was creepy as fuck," I said, "and we couldn't carry nearly enough to make it worth it." Pigs weren't an alchemical ingredient, as far as anyone knew, so the meat had been just ordinary pork.

"Well, that won't be a problem if we get the right reward, right?" Felicia put in, bringing us back on track.

The chimera dungeon mostly dropped monster parts as the rewards—there were potions for the floor levels but little in the way of items. The exception was the final level, which we'd just reached.

"Hoping for the bag?" I asked. It would dramatically increase our earnings from this dungeon. All the known rewards from this level used some form of spatial magic, but the bag was easily the most generally useful.

"I'll be really annoyed if we get something like the shelter," she agreed.

"Well do you want to do the honors?" I asked, pointing at the chest behind the giant roachquid. Getting to it would mean wading through a few inches of what was covering Kyle, but I hadn't noticed Felicia being particularly squeamish.

She gave me a look, but just said, "Fine," and lifted up her skirt to her knees to trudge through the muck. When she got to the chest, she took a deep breath and opened it.

"Huh," she said. *Not the bag, then*, I thought. She pulled out a ring.

"Oh, that one's not bad," Cloridan said. "We'll find a use for it, but it will sell for a good price if we don't."

"Yeah, you want it, Cloridan?"

"I think our gallant and gorgeous leader should have it," he said, managing a bow in my direction. He was pretty clean—he'd been on top of the roachquid and had gotten good at avoiding the blood spray from his strikes.

"Don't tell me you don't want it—think of all the knives you could hide," I said. "Or Kyle could use it for his armor."

The ring didn't hold as much as the bag—maybe only half a cubic meter, from what I'd heard. But unlike the bag, you could add and remove items just by thinking about them. With a bit of practice, Kyle could store his armor and equip himself directly from the ring.

"That'd be neat," Kyle admitted. "But you don't need to don armor quickly when you're delving. You always go in prepared."

"You're the one that is getting into situations where you need to hide evidence or bring in tools without people seeing," Cloridan explained. "It's nice for any of us, but vital for you."

"Well, I don't want to say no, but . . . don't people check for spatial rings?" I asked.

"Hmmm, if only there was something an Illusionist could do about that," Cloridan said wryly.

"Okay, point," I admitted. "Give me the ring."

Felicia handed it over and I put it on. It gave me a strange feeling of . . . slots. Empty spaces that weren't really spaces. I thought about putting my daggers in them, and the daggers disappeared, leaving me with an equally odd sensation of two of the spaces being filled.

"This is a very weird feeling," I said, bringing a dagger back into my hand. "Is the core around here somewhere?"

"You're not going to take this one as well?" Kyle asked, alarmed.

"I just want to look at it," I assured him. It took a little searching, but we eventually found a hidden door that opened to reveal the glowing blue orb.

"This dungeon doesn't have a master, does it?" I asked while studying the intricate mana flows.

[Mana Sense] Level 4 acquired through use.
For gaining a skill level, you have been awarded 1 XP.

Well, this was the most complicated mana construct I'd studied. Even my own Dungeon core was simpler, probably because it wasn't operational.

"I don't think so," Cloridan said.

"Why not? Mandel seems pretty happy with his dungeon."

"Well . . ." Kyle said. "No one really knows how it works. Maybe Master Monteminer got some instruction from somewhere, but what most people know is that if you touch the core, either you take it and kill the dungeon, or you disappear."

I blinked. "I'm glad I didn't know *that* in Oakway." I thought about it for a bit. "So that must be what happened to Rhis? And Marie? They became dungeon controllers and got . . . sucked in."

"So if there's already a controller, you're safe and can become a master?" Felicia speculated.

"Not quite. Rhis was worried about me displacing him, so that's clearly something that can happen."

We all stared at the orb for a bit.

"So . . ." Felicia eventually asked. "Is there a controller in there?"

"Rhis was complaining that this Dungeon was very unimaginative," I said. "Could be there's no actual intelligence behind it."

"So you're not going to try mastering it, then?" Cloridan asked.

"Not today. I'll talk to Mandel about it, see what he knows." I said.

"I guess we're putting in for another slot next week?" Felicia asked. "Keep going until we get a bag?"

"Sure," I sighed, "More random monstrosities for a while."

"I wouldn't have thought that you'd be so eager to move on to the Ogre Temple," she said. "Or have you gotten over killing humanoid monsters?"

"I got over it back in Oakway," I said. "I'm not happy about sentient creatures being turned into killing machines, but I've accepted I can't do anything about it."

"Really? Acceptance? That's not like you."

"Well. After having conversations with a god . . . either they would *like* to undo Ashmor's work and *can't*, or they want this situation to continue. Either way, I'd have to be more powerful than a god to do something about it."

"Oh, that would be ambitious," Felicia said smiling. "You'd have to subvert the Status to your will, bring down the gods, and change the laws of the universe."

"Why does it sound like you're making me a to-do list?" I protested. "I just accepted that it was impossible!"

Everyone laughed, the traitors. Grouping up, we triggered the return teleport and returned to the surface.

DELEGATION

Business meetings were so much easier than diplomatic ones. Companies—most of them, at least—don't have pride to worry about. They're there to make money, so who cares about details like where the meeting is held or what shape the table is?

Of course, there were always a few egos that showed up now and then. Business owners or investors that needed others to admit just how important they were. At the firm, the word for these people was *marks*. Honestly, if your decision about a multimillion-dollar investment is predicated on the other side providing you with the right coffee, or calling you sir, or holding the meeting in a strip club, then whatever. The firm would bend over backwards to stroke your ego, and then shave an extra percentage point off your profits. Thanks for your business.

It was different for nations. They all had their pride. Sometimes, they also had very real concerns about getting killed during the meeting. So before we could start negotiating with the Tribal delegation, we needed to hash out every detail of how the talks would be held, allay their security concerns, and continually convince them that this would all be worth their time.

This couldn't happen with the actual delegates, who would only show up once they were ready to talk, so there were numerous messengers going back and forth before the big day.

For our part, we didn't have any pride to worry about—at least I didn't—so we saved a little time by just agreeing to whatever they wanted. Hold the meeting outside the walls? Sure, should we provide a tent? The nights were getting cooler, after all.

No guards for us? Sure, all we required was me, the King's representative, and a scribe.

It was all very tedious, but we got through it. Eventually, I found myself in a hastily raised pavilion, standing across from two distinguished representatives.

Painstakingly detailed protocols dictated that I should speak first, to introduce my delegation. I started off by breaking them.

"Before we start, I'd like to acknowledge the traditional custodians of this land on which we stand. I wish to acknowledge and show my respect for their Elders for their service and their wisdom."

I bowed. "I present myself, Councillor Kandis Hammond, and Inquisitor Reece Dunnar as your delegates for these negotiations."

I didn't look at Reece, but I was pretty sure he was attempting to glare at me through the side of his head while maintaining a professional smile at our guests. We had hashed out how this was going to go beforehand— this was a negotiation between the City of Talnier and the Tribes, and the King's man wasn't a part of it. He was there only to make sure I didn't overstep my limits and wasn't to say anything unless he needed to speak for the King.

He had needed to actually reread the contract before he would admit that this trade deal was within our specified rights. I'd made the offer to take him along, just so he could make sure that I didn't promise anything from the King. The fact was (I pointed out) that I didn't have to—but I was happy to have him along just to showcase my loyalty to His Majesty.

I'm sure it burned, but what was he going to do? Not go? Go but spoil the talks? He was smart enough to know that if he did that, then he'd get blamed for the loss of tax revenue.

My attention was on the delegates who looked more than a little surprised. They looked at each other, and it was the elder of the two who spoke. Another protocol violation.

"Fine words, Councillor," he said. He was an owl-kin, with a lined face and snow-white feathers. His companion was a wolf-kin, with black ears and hair. I wasn't actually getting better at identifying beast-kin species, but these two had been identified as part of the preparation. We all knew who we were; introductions were just part of the protocol.

"I only wish they were worth more, as I can speak only for the city behind me," I replied. "Inquisitor Dunnar speaks for the King, should his word be needed."

It was interesting. Now that I knew what was going on, I could feel the different options that Charm had made available. I could be diplomatic using Latorran ways, or I could speak as a Tribesman would. I had elected to go for Latorran diplomacy, with a small smattering of Tribal respect towards the Elder, which he seemed to appreciate.

It wasn't just Charm, either. When I focused on other language options, my Gift of Tongues told me that not only did the two in front of me have their own Tribal common tongue, but they each spoke their own Tribe's private language. I made a note to myself to keep track of what language they were speaking and not reveal that I understood it. Even if they knew I was a Worldwalker—and I wasn't sure if they did—I didn't want Dunnar to know.

The two of them looked at Dunnar, who didn't say anything—which made him the only one in the tent who was following the script. They looked back at each other, and then the owl-kin nodded. The wolf-kin turned back to me and bowed.

"I present myself, Anas of the Black Moon Clan and this is Elder Tinidan of the Smoke-Ghost Tribe," he said. *And we're back on the script.*

I acknowledged the introductions and then the negotiations began.

The trade route was a nonstarter, as I'd known it would be. I brought it up, as I'd promised my backers that I would, but even before I spoke, Bargain informed me that Tinidan would never allow a road through their forest.

I still pushed for it, though, for a variety of reasons. Firstly, it prompted them to detail their own ways of moving goods, which they viewed as superior. Secondly, it gave them an opportunity to vent about their grievances with the Kingdom. I offered my condolences, of course, and regret that I couldn't do anything about them. That helped, but I think what really mollified them was seeing Dunnar's face go red as he was unable to answer back while his Kingdom was bad-mouthed.

All of that helped clear the air, while we ostensibly discussed the already dead topic of the road. Relations were much more cordial when I moved on to my actual proposal.

"A permanent trade post?" Anas asked.

"There are a number of ways we could set it up, but the general idea is a common marketplace where your merchants can trade with ours," I said.

"Inside the city?"

"There are enough beast-kin living here for me to know that they don't have any problem adjusting to living behind walls," I said wryly. "However, there might be some advantages to extending the city beyond the walls and having the trading post there."

I gave the pair of beast-kin a knowing look. "Previously, it's been too dangerous for civilians to venture outside the walls, but with your people living here, I've got a feeling it will be much safer."

"Possibly," the Elder said, keeping his poker face. When I'd learned that the Tribes managed the migration patterns of monsters, it seemed obvious that they'd directed one of them straight at Talnier. If I asked about it, they'd deny it, but it must be one of the worst kept secrets. Acknowledging it without accusing anyone should get the path adjusted without anyone having to say sorry.

The two of them shared a look and then the wolf-kin continued. "Exiles and adventurers are one thing, but we cannot have our people living under foreign rule."

"Actually," I said. "Talnier is largely self-governing, with a Council selected from and voted on by residents." I paused to savor the moment. "Which your people would qualify for."

Elder Tinidan raised his eyebrows "You would permit our people to sit on your ruling council?"

"You can't!" Dunnar interjected. "They're not citizens!"

I glanced at both of them. "I thought this might come up, so I borrowed the Charter so we could check the wording," I said calmly. An effort of will brought the Charter out of my spatial ring and onto the table. Obviously, we didn't just lend the document out to anybody, but as a Council member, this was a perk I was able to grant myself.

Dunnar slumped. No doubt he was remembering how his previous objections went, but I continued on. "As you can see here for both voters and qualifying for office, residency is the only requirement. Which is defined here, as living within the city bounds for one month, while not having been incarcerated for more than a week during your time of residence. Talnier has always been open to non-citizens living there, and this remains the case."

Elder Tinidan took in Dunnar's demeanor. "This does not seem like a popular measure with your higher government officials," he stated. "Is there not a possibility that this document will be withdrawn or changed?"

"His Majesty considered this document very carefully before awarding it to us," I said blandly. "There is a review in a few months, but I'm confident of getting it confirmed. We can always make our agreement here contingent on this document remaining unchanged."

"I see," Elder Tinidan said, his eyes twinkling. Making a valuable trade deal contingent on the Charter remaining unchanged would make my position much stronger with the King, and he clearly saw that. "I do believe that would reassure us of your intentions."

I gave a kind of half-bow from my seat. "I'm happy to hear that. Shall we move on to details? Or would you like to peruse the Charter first?"

"I believe we would like to go over this document," Elder Tinidan said. "It will be important to understand the rules by which this agreement will be governed."

"Quite," I said, refraining from glancing at Dunnar. *Always read the contract.*

So we did read the contract, before moving on to the details. Taxes, everybody's favorite subject, weren't actually negotiable on my part, but thanks to the Charter eliminating the noble middlemen, they were quite reasonable. I'd asked around among the merchants, and they compared quite favorably to other nations that traded with them, like Odiera, without having to worry about expensive shipping costs.

When it came to goods, they were quite interested in our manufactured goods and cereal crops. They *were* willing to sell Spoken Wood—at a price. Given that they weren't clear-cutting and were only selling surplus trees, I'd been worried that they wouldn't be able to meet demand . . . but at that price, it would remain a premium product. Instead of taking as much as they could get, our merchants would have to live with as much as they could afford.

When it came to dungeon-produced goods, there was an interesting diversion.

"We would prefer," Anas said, glancing at his Elder for support, "that our people delve directly and bring goods home to us."

"Is that different from the beast-kin currently delving as Guild members?" I asked.

"It is," Anas stated firmly. "They are all people who have left their Tribe—voluntarily or otherwise. They could not join your Guild otherwise."

I frowned. "What happened, then, to all those who returned home during the last trouble? Were they all exiles?"

"Exiles are rare," Anas reassured me. "Most of the refugees were still on good terms with their families and either petitioned to rejoin their Tribe or stayed as guests until the trouble died down. A few . . . there are Tribes that accept applicants from all species."

"That's good to know," I said. "As regards to delving, I already checked with the Guild, and they don't feel they can restrict the dungeon to Guild members, as it isn't on the King's land. Was there a particular reason your people didn't delve there before?"

"It wasn't considered wise to fight too close to the human border," Elder Tinidan said blandly. "Parties that were worn down from delving could be easily ambushed."

I nodded. We'd had that problem before. "Will there be large numbers of Tribal delvers?"

Elder Tinidan nodded. "Perhaps as many as ten parties," he said.

I winced. "With that kind of increase, the Guild is going to want to keep the current slot system in place."

"Slot system?"

"A schedule for delvers, to minimize conflicts over the resource. Instead of fighting over who was first to get there, each registered party gets assigned a delving time by the Guild."

"It sounds like a fair system," Elder Tinidan commented.

"Sure, but for it to work with your people, they'd have to register with the Guild—and there would need to be some way of resolving disputes between parties. Right now, that's done by the Guild as all the adventurers have to bow to their authority. If your parties aren't going to accept that . . ."

"Ah. Yes, there is a problem there. Perhaps a Tribunal with representatives from both sides?"

"If it's evenly split, what happens when there's a dispute between different races, and each Tribunal member sides with their race?"

"That would be a rare occurrence, I would hope?"

"Hope for the best, plan for the worst."

"Hmm. We'd need a neutral party to be a deciding vote . . . and I can't think of any that are available."

We hashed around it for a while, but we ended up making it the Town Council's problem. There was the hope, after all, that there would be Tribal members on it in the future.

The rest of the talks went quite well. By the time we had finished, I thought we had the makings of a very profitable trade agreement. We agreed to take it to our respective Councils and planned a signing ceremony for next week.

BANKING

It may have been autumn, but the sky was clear, and standing out in the open was pretty uncomfortable and boring. I tried to take my mind off it by thinking about banks.

The fact that Fantasyland didn't have banks was an itch at the back of my mind that I couldn't scratch. They didn't even have the concept. Felicia and Kyle had just looked blankly at me when I brought up the idea. They knew about *loans*, sure, but loans here were done on a personal basis. Either you got a loan from a rich friend, with the understanding that you'd pay it back when you could—possibly with interest, depending on how good a friend they were—or they weren't a friend, they were just rich. Much like when the mafia loaned you money, they now owned you until the loan was repaid. That was mostly a game for nobles, and it was part of their poor reputation. There was some middle-ground—guilds would occasionally loan startup funds to a member who was just starting—but those cases were practically family already.

The people here didn't think they were missing out, but I was sure that there were a lot of growth opportunities that were being lost. I wasn't sure *why* they didn't have banks, but I had a suspicion that it might be because of dungeons.

History wasn't my subject, but the firm loved playing up its connection to the past. There had been a display of the history of banks in our lobby for twelve weeks, so I'd picked up a few things. Banks had developed out of the medieval profession of money changing.

You have to understand that by modern standards—and perhaps even by their own standards—monetary systems in medieval times were just insane. Never mind the fact that every kingdom, principality, or independent city felt the need to issue its own currency. We have that issue today. In those days, though, there were no standards—for any country— about the size, purity, or denomination of its coins over time. If you were lucky, they might stay the same for the reign of a single king. But that was very much the exception. Most kings varied the currency according to their finances and the current value of precious metals—which varied hugely as different mines were discovered or tapped out.

Given how long coins lasted, even if you were just dealing with a single country's currency, there could easily be fifty or a hundred different coins that you needed to know the value of if you wanted to trade. It took a professional to handle that sort of complexity.

So money changing became a niche occupation that was difficult, but insanely profitable. After all, if you're the person who knows the value of both sides of the trade, and the other guy doesn't . . . well, it becomes what my old boss used to call a moderately favorable trading environment.

Now, if you're trading money, you need to store a lot of it, which means you need a lot of security to keep people from stealing it. Pretty soon, the money changers were the best protected places in town, and they set up a side business in storing other people's money. At first, they charged for the service, but then they realized that they could *lend the money out*, started *paying* interest, and there you have your banks.

So why didn't it happen here? Well, first of all, no money changers. Nobody minted coins in this world—they all came from dungeons. And while rulers could customize the name and design of the coins through the Territory Status interface, they all had the same weights and purity.

Second of all, while this world did build vaults for security, the great majority of fortunes were kept in people's pockets. Or at least in their spatial bags attached to their belt. Spatial bags weren't *cheap*, but once you hit the point where you were carrying hundreds of platinum coins around, it made sense to just get a bag and keep them all in there.

Vaults were seen in this society as something for organizations that needed to control access to their fortune but didn't want to restrict it to just one person. I suppose we should have counted ourselves lucky that Baron Marseau had just locked his fortune up and not taken it with him.

Which left me in a bit of a quandary, as I wanted to encourage development in Talnier, but that took money. So much money. More money than the Town Council had available. We did have taxes, but that was all going on other things . . . like what was happening today.

"Talnier welcomes the brave and gallant Royal forces sent from the King himself to protect us . . ."

The Mayor was making a pretty speech, while the rest of us stood on the dais and tried to look happy at the bunch of extra mouths to feed. Well, it wasn't like they'd be doing nothing.

> **Additional Defense detected – 1 Territory Point awarded.**
> **New Threat detected – Hector Rodakis.**

Well, shit. I'd expected the troops to be a mixed bag, but this suggested that the Captain was going to be actively trying to take control of the city from me. Despite my trade agreement efforts, the Tribal Council hadn't disappeared from my list of threats. At least we had some more defenses, and I had some more Territory points. I hadn't gotten any more when we'd added the illicit funds to the treasury, leading me to guess that I got one point for each 50,000 gold added. Hopefully, I didn't lose them when we spent the money.

I eyed the new threat to my rule as he joined us on the dais to get introduced to the people and ourselves. Wait, I didn't like the sound of that. The threat to our fledgling democracy—that sounded better.

He was a big guy, blond and blue-eyed and with a face that was . . . rugged, I guess. Strong chin, clean-shaven. He looked every inch what a military hero was supposed to look like. Considering that his men had marched up here in just a day or two, he had the stats to back it up.

We exchanged names, bowed or curtsied as required, and then the Mayor started explaining where they would be quartered. We'd be providing the upkeep, which meant housing, feeding, and clothing them. They had their own uniforms at the moment, of course, but we'd be washing them, fixing them, and providing new ones as required. They'd be taking care of their own armaments, but they might well be monopolizing our existing weaponsmith.

We needed to expand our weapon production, which got me back to thinking about encouraging development—and banks. I let the procession leave me behind as they headed up to the new barracks, while I thought about it.

Making it a function of the Council was the wrong idea, I thought. Not just because I wasn't a Communist, but because when I thought about the idea of setting up a bank, I started to smell the possibility of money. A bank without competition would be fantastically profitable, and I wanted those profits to belong to me.

But I didn't have enough money. Given the novelty of the idea (and the lack of support from the Crown), I wouldn't be able to loan more than I had. In fact, I'd probably have to keep a massively inefficient stockpile until people got used to the idea. And that was assuming I could get people to keep their money with me.

I needed investors. *The solution to, and cause of, most of a firm's financial difficulties.* Nobles were out, of course. There weren't any here and I couldn't trust them besides. Adventurers, though . . . they certainly earned money quickly, but they tended to spend it just as quickly. They'd probably appreciate the idea of a steady cash flow, if I presented it right.

"What do you mean you're going to solve your literacy problems?" Felicia asked. "You don't have a problem with literacy?"

"There aren't enough people with Scribe, is my problem," I explained.

"Oh right, you were going to set up a school or something?" she said, casting her mind back to my plans in Anchorbury.

"That was the old plan," I said excitedly. "Now, I can create a new profession that unlocks Scribe and Calculate—and doesn't have any prerequisites!"

"Can you do that?" she asked skeptically. "Wouldn't someone already have tried?"

"I think there's a general consensus that too many wizards are bad for a kingdom," I said. "And the best way to keep people from being wizards is to keep them from reading."

"Are they bad for the country?"

I shrugged. "When I say consensus, I'm talking about between the King and his predecessors—oh, and I guess some nobles might have access to this interface as well."

"So you figure that they're wrong."

"I feel sure that isn't an unpopular opinion. Now, hang on a sec while I go through the interface and see if it is possible. I want to run through it with you before I commit to it."

I opened up Territory Status and went into the Professions tab, and selected New.

> **Profession Name:** [ ]
> **Profession Description:** [ ]
> **Prerequisites:** [Level 2] [Stat-based] [Skill Based] [Special]
> **Skill Unlocks:** [ ] [ ] [ ] [+] [-]
> **Skill Bonus:** [ ] [ ] [ ] [+] [-]
> **Special:** [+]
> **Territory Point Cost:** 3
> **Development Point Cost:** 5

I played around with the options for a bit. There seemed to be a template for each value of level prerequisite, changing the number of skills and, as it went higher, changing the Development point cost. Prerequisites lowered the Territory point cost, but I didn't want too many of those. Soon I had something like a profession.

> **Profession Name:** [Talnier Official]
> **Profession Description:** [Bringing civilization to the world, one ledger at a time]
> **Prerequisites:** [Level 2] [Intelligence 4] [None] [None]
> **Skill Unlocks:** [Scribe] [Calculate] [ ] [+] [-]
> **Skill Bonus:** [Bargain] [Persuade] [ ] [+] [-]
> **Special:** [+]
> **Territory Point Cost:** 2
> **Development Point Cost:** 5

Four was the minimum requirement for stats and saved me one point. Now I had to decide on another two skills, or get rid of them and have a minimalist profession. I tried it out and saw some odd stuff. When I removed the Skill Unlock, the Territory point cost went down by one, but when I removed the Skill Bonus, the Territory point cost went up to four, while the Development cost went down to zero.

A profession that was free to take did appeal, but I didn't have four Territory points at the moment, so I added the skills back in again and went looking at the skill list. It wasn't long before I found the perfect skill.

> **Profession Name:** [Talnier Official]
> **Profession Description:** [Bringing civilization to the world, one ledger at a time]

Prerequisites: [Level 2] [Intelligence 4] [None] [None]
Skill Unlocks: [Scribe] [Calculate] [Bureaucracy] [+] [-]
Skill Bonus: [Bargain] [Persuade] [Bureaucracy] [+] [-]
Special: [+]
Territory Point Cost: 1
Development Point Cost: 5

Putting the same skill in both slots reduced the cost as well, I saw.

"What do you think?" I asked Felicia. I made an illusion of what I was seeing.

"What does the Bureaucracy skill do?" she asked. I could tell she was looking at the skill description as she asked.

[Bureaucracy]: Skill for managing and navigating professional organizations

"How do you navigate an organization?" she asked incredulously.

"Eh, it's about knowing what forms to fill out and who to talk to, to get things done," I said. "Probably things like filing and developing procedures to get things done as well."

"I see . . . did you want to add in a language?"

"There isn't a language skill; I checked."

"No, languages are bought with Development points. Some professions have a bonus that would normally be bought with Development points. I've never seen a profession with a language, but it should be possible, and you want to promote ties with the Tribes, right?"

"Right," I said. That was what the Special section was for. I went into it and found that I could, indeed, add a language. I could even . . .

Profession Name: [Talnier Official]
Profession Description: [Bringing civilization to the world, one ledger at a time]
Prerequisites: [Level 2] [Intelligence 4] [None] [None]
Skill Unlocks: [Scribe] [Calculate] [Bureaucracy] [+] [-]
Skill Bonus: [Bargain] [Persuade] [Bureaucracy] [+] [-]
Special: Language: Latorran/Tribal Common [+]
Territory Point Cost: 2
Development Point Cost: 5

If they didn't know Latorran, they'd get it, while if they did, they'd get Tribal Common.

"So you take the profession, and all of a sudden you speak Tribal?" I said.

"That's how languages work," Felicia said. Just like it was common sense.

CAPTAIN

I wanted coffee. I didn't *need* it. Endurance was overkill when it came to powering through desk work, but I *wanted* it. Sitting at a desk going over papers had reawakened old habits, causing the craving. I made do with tea.

In lieu of coffee, Huette brought over a small folder. "The report on the attack on the barracks last night," she said, handing it over. ". . . and Captain Rodakis is here to complain about it," she added.

I frowned. "Which one of those got delayed to get them turned into the same agenda item?" I asked.

"I rushed the report because the adventurers said that he found out about it at the time, and wasn't pleased," she explained. "The Captain has been waiting for about half an hour?"

I sighed. "That's fine. Send him in, please."

I skimmed the report as I waited for the man. This would be our first actual meeting, not counting our brief introduction during his arrival. Back then, I hadn't really grasped how big he was. He didn't have to stoop in the doorway or turn sideways to get in, but it was close enough that he had to be a bit nervous.

"Madame Councillor," he said, giving me a brief bow.

"Captain Rodakis, how nice to see you," I lied. "Please take a seat." There wasn't room in my office for me to join him on his side of my desk, but I gave the little seated bow that Charm told me was an appropriate greeting from a superior. I was, technically, his superior here. So very technically.

"I prefer to stand, ma'am," he said, stiffly.

"Well, I prefer you to sit," I said evenly. "Otherwise, I'd think that you're trying to intimidate me, looming over me the way you are."

"Of course, ma'am," He gingerly lowered himself into the one chair that would fit in my office. He needn't have worried; it had been supplied by a craftsman with a high skill, so it was much tougher than it looked.

Okay. Dominance established. I've got my desk—such as it is—in front of me to establish a zone of authority. *It would have worked better if I had a bigger desk, but then I'd have needed a bigger office.*

"So what can I do for you, Captain?" I said, smiling warmly. I was pleased to see it had an effect. *Thank you, Charm.*

"I—well—it's about the attack last night?" he said, suddenly less certain.

"Ah, of course. I was just reading the report now," I said. "Would you like to read it yourself?"

"A report? I'm not used to getting reports from adventurers."

"I insisted on it as part of the hiring conditions," I explained, smiling wryly.

"So you did hire them . . . to protect the barracks." He frowned. "May I ask why you thought my unit incapable?"

"I don't think of them as incapable at all," I said easily, leaning back as much as I could on my uncomfortable chair. "I'd wager that their capability would be at its low ebb last night—just moved in, recovering from a long march—but that wasn't why I tasked adventurers to guard the barracks."

"Why then?" Rodakis asked, eyes narrowed.

"I assume you've been briefed on the recent . . . tensions between the townsfolk and the Tribals," I said. I was sure that he had. Exactly what that briefing had consisted of . . . I had my suspicions.

"Of course," he said, giving away nothing.

"My understanding is that there are elements of the tribes trying to disrupt the trade treaty and provoke an attack from the Kingdom." Given my audience, I chose not to mention the *other* group. "I thought it likely that they would try to attack your men when they were at their most vulnerable."

I tapped the report. "It was only a small group, but if they had made it past the sentries, they could have done quite a bit of damage amongst your sleeping men."

He shook his head. "My men would not have been caught napping!"

"That wasn't my main concern," I said.

"It wasn't?"

"An attack—successful or not—would have been a provocation, would it not? You would have felt the need to respond. Successfully dealing with it would have left us with five dead beast-kin bodies—which the Tribes would have taken as a provocation in turn."

"You think they were sent there to die?" he asked, taken aback.

"I think that however it ended, a confrontation would have served the ends of whoever sent them."

"So you hired adventurers."

"*Beast-kin* adventurers," I said, stressing the word. "The attackers might have been willing to die, but they weren't willing to murder their fellow beast-kin."

"But . . ." he trailed off. "Your people let the miscreants go!"

"Two reasons," I calmly explained. "One, there was no attack, so there was no reason to stop them. They committed no crime. Two, they were concerned that if they went after the attackers, they'd circle around and have another try at you. It's all in this report."

I passed the sheaf of paper across the desk.

"Of course, it's a shame we weren't able to arrest them, but the conspirators know that we're on to them now, so I'd expect them to think twice before trying anything else."

And that goes for anyone else that might be thinking of starting trouble.

Rodakis looked down at the report and then back at me, warily. "I can keep this?"

"Of course; you are responsible for the defense of the city, after all. Since you're here, I wonder if we should discuss protocols for all the potential traders arriving once this treaty is signed. We wouldn't want our golden geese to be harassed at the gate, would we?"

"No. The King wouldn't like it if this new source of income was impaired."

He looked at me and sighed. I smiled back with not a trace of sincerity and braced myself for a long discussion. *Thank goodness for Endurance.*

"Huette, could you bring us some tea please?"

Having arrived back home, I sank back into my comfiest chair and let out a sigh of relief.

"Cloridan, did you forget that I can always see through my own illusions?" I asked the empty air in the corner.

Cloridan appeared with a frown. "I thought it might be different if it was an item casting the spell," he admitted.

"Fortunately, no." That had been a serious concern, but I guess Cloridan had been out when we were testing it. "I was already leery of making that thing. If I couldn't see through the invisibility, I'd have had nightmares about someone using it against me."

"Fair enough," Cloridan said, shrugging.

"So did it work?" I asked.

"Perfectly," he replied smugly. "Neither side knew I was there."

"And you could follow them back?"

He nodded. "They eventually regrouped at the Temple of Naldyna."

"Ugh." This wasn't exactly an "oh shit" moment. I'd known that the Temple was willing to act against the Kingdom authorities—this just showed that they were still at it.

"Did you actually see who they talked to in there?"

"No, I stayed well clear. Spies and thieves entering their temples . . . well, it's not a guaranteed smiting, but there's a good chance Naldyna would have identified me to her priests, at least."

"You don't think she identified you?"

"Well, it's a given that she *saw* me, Greater Invisibility or no. Generally, they don't do anything about it as long as you don't challenge them directly. I'm not sure how the rule changes when I'm working for a different god's Champion."

"Yeah, me either." I paused to think about what this meant. "I guess my next move is to see if Kaito can put some pressure on her to cut it out," I mused.

"You think that will work?"

"I have no idea about how it works when a Priestess is at odds with the Champion," I admitted. "I guess we'll see."

"Thank you for the warning, but I don't think it applies to us," Mandel said, sipping at an excellently brewed cup of tea. The new troops in place meant that the Griffin Riders were free to take transportation jobs, so I could take a much-delayed trip to see him and his family.

"Why not?" I asked, sipping at my own cup of tea. Edele had been with us earlier, thanking me for getting her out of the Baron's clutches, but she had "study" to do. "Study," when I'd asked, had turned out to be killing dungeon monsters under her mother's supervision, which felt all kinds of weird, but I was trying not to judge.

Marie was also here with us—splitting her attention that way was apparently something a dungeon could do. As an apparition, though, she didn't have any tea.

"I've felt the compulsion you describe," she said, "And while it *is* there, I've never felt in danger of it overcoming me."

"Has it grown over time?" I asked. "I got the impression that it took a while before anyone noticed it in the original dungeons."

"Not noticeably," she said thoughtfully. "I may have reduced the compulsion by all the recent killing."

"Right . . . on another subject, do you think that it would be safe to bring Rhis into this dungeon?" I asked.

"I don't think so," Mandel said. "Kari told me that if you bring a second core into a dungeon, it tries to take over the mana. It only ends when one of them loses and becomes a secondary core."

"I've never heard of that," I admitted.

"I hadn't either. Kari told me that having one provides a few benefits, but nothing overwhelming. For one, it can link two mana pools into being the same dungeon."

I thought about it. "You're right, it doesn't sound overwhelmingly good. I can't really think of an advantage over having two dungeons over one."

"It might provide benefits for the master of that dungeon," Mandel said. "They don't want to leave the dungeon, so having it in two places gives them more options."

"Can you be a master of two dungeons?" I asked.

"I . . . don't know." Mandel paused in thought. "I don't *think* so, but that's just speculation."

I nodded. "Any idea why Marie can talk to us? I asked around, and I haven't heard of another dungeon that does that. Rhis doesn't know how she's doing it, either."

"It's a feat," Marie said. "You get them based on your level . . . not the levels of the dungeon, but your own level. I actually kept my level from when I was alive, so I qualified for a few feats right from the start."

"As the master, I was able to communicate with her from the start as well. It takes away from combat potential, so I doubt many masters allow it."

"It also mentioned a requirement that I understand a mortal tongue," Marie added. "Rhis was probably—maybe still is—getting a translation when he speaks to you."

"How many dungeons have masters, do you think?"

"No idea," Mandel replied, but then reconsidered. "All of the big Mage names are probably masters. After a little while spent terrorizing everyone, they end up settling down in a tower and hardly ever leaving. That says master to me."

I nodded. "The noble dungeons?"

"Maybe . . . they have social obligations, so they can't just stay in their lair. Maybe the real power stays in the dungeon, and the heir actually deals with the politics?"

"That didn't seem to be the case in Anchorbury," I said. "But . . . do you need for there to be a controller before there can be a master?"

"Yes, absolutely." Mandel nodded with certainty. "Kari told me that was the case."

"How did she find out so much about this?" I wondered. "It's not common knowledge among adventurers."

"She didn't say . . . but I know she visited a Sage somewhere in Saarwald several times."

Saarwald was the duchy to the south, I knew, but not much more than that.

"I'll have to find out where, and take a trip," I said. "What else did I have to ask about? Oh yeah, mana crystals."

"What about them?"

"Any idea why they're the currency in the capital?"

"Mana is the real currency in the capital," he corrected me. "Crystals are just how you store it."

"So . . . higher grade crystals are more valued because you can transfer the mana quicker?" I guessed.

"Partly. Also, they hold more. That's not really a concern with spatial storage . . . but making a noble wait for their payment to complete can be a big deal."

"What do they use all that mana for?" I asked. "Is there a noble skill that uses mana?"

"Not as far as I know. They partly use it for taxes—the King uses an immense amount of it."

"And what does he use it for?"

"The defense of the realm? His own comfort? I can't really say for sure." Mandel shrugged. "But eventually you'll go to Dorsay and see for yourself. They use mana for everything there."

CONSOLIDATION

Would have thought you'd be too important to bother with the likes of me," Marlon said, shifting uncomfortably on his bench.

I wasn't the cause of his discomfort. Well, I was ultimately, but the reason he looked so nervous was sitting beside me. I didn't need a guide to visit the information broker this time, and I could probably take care of myself. That didn't mean I wanted to be bothered by the rough crowd that hung out in this tavern, so I'd brought along an escort.

"Is my companion making you nervous, Marlon?" I asked. He looked at me sourly.

"Last time, Cloridan brought you here. He's a local—I know where I'm at with him. This time you're bringing in this slab of Arryen muscle, so who knows what to think."

Kyle just smiled. He wasn't wearing his full armor or carrying his shield, but at level five, he was just starting to project that aura that I'd first noticed on his grandfather. An aura of power, of danger. I supposed that I had that too, but it was difficult to tell. I was pretty sure that no one in this room was over level four. Maybe if they'd spent time on the wall, but they didn't look the type.

"Don't expect anything, Marlon, and you won't be disappointed. We're here for the same reason as before."

"The Fangs aren't around anymore, but I'd have thought that you knew that already," he said shiftily.

"Something wrong with that?" I asked. "They sounded like they were everyone's problem."

"More like . . ." he dropped his voice and looked around. "I had a thought that you had something to do with that."

I kept my face expressionless. "Where did you hear that?"

He grimaced. "Don't need to hear anything. Someone goes down, someone goes up, doesn't take a genius to figure out the connection."

"You want to be careful who you pass that speculation on to," I said coolly. "Someone could get the wrong idea."

"Oh, I'm careful," he said bitterly. "Not like anyone smart enough to pay for that can't figure it out on their own."

"Why even bring it up, then?" I asked.

He glared at me sourly. "You're paying for smart, so it does me no good to play dumb."

"I suppose." I looked him over carefully. Something seemed off about his demeanor, but Intrigue wasn't giving me any warnings about deception. He was just upset about something? I decided to continue.

"You're aware of the upcoming trade deal," I said, not making it a question. He nodded impatiently. "There are two parties trying to sabotage it," I continued. "I want to know what they're up to, who they're talking to."

"Who are we talking about?" he asked.

"Tonet of Naldyna and Captain Hector Rodakis."

"Toriao's secrets!" he swore. "Are you trying to get me killed?"

I frowned. "I'm not asking you to go up against them."

"You might as well be—starting with a Priestess. You think I want a god on my case?"

"I have some reason to believe that she's not acting in Naldyna's interests on this," I said.

"You think that a Priestess is going against her goddess?" he asked incredulously. "I can tell you she ain't, on account of the temple not being on fire."

"Not against, just that Naldyna doesn't hold an opinion on this matter," I explained.

"Got your own in with the goddess, then?"

"In a way. I've talked with her Champion about this, and she's in favor of the deal."

"No way is the Chosen of Naldyna in this town."

"Not *in*, correct. I spoke with her outside. She's in the area, I think because of Isidre's presence."

"Whom you are *also* on a first-name basis with," he noted sourly. "You're acquainted with some very dangerous people there."

"If you say so," I said with some amusement.

"Your funeral," he muttered under his breath. "So what you're saying is that Naldyna isn't going to rat me out to her Priestess if I start a watch on her."

"I think so," I said. "Obviously, don't try infiltrating the temple . . ."

"Like I was going to do *that*."

"Then you should be all right. If I've figured out the rules of this game they're playing, then they don't reveal stuff that affects the actual play. If you focus on what she's doing to sabotage us, then you should be fine."

"Easy for you to say. Feels weird for a church to be interfering with things, though. I guess with Chosen wandering round, there's going to be all kinds of strangeness."

"Quite. You don't have any problems with the other name?"

He scowled. "He's even more dangerous if he finds out. Until he settles in, though, he's got no way to do that."

I nodded. "He'll probably be trying to set up some kind of network. I want to know who's in it, and what they're telling him."

"So this is going to be more of a steady retainer than a one-off payment," Marlon said. I couldn't see the gold coins in his eyes, but Bargain could hear them in his voice.

"Indeed." I dropped a small stack of coins on the table. "Each week, but I expect results."

Marlon's eyes glinted, but he didn't take the coins. "You know, the good Captain is from the capital. Likely he's got more gold than you do."

"You won't be taking his gold," I said confidently. I put an extra coin on the stack, though, awarding him the point.

"Why not?"

"If Hector scuppers the deal, and throws us into a war with the Tribes, your income—not to mention your life expectancy—is going to drop precipitously."

"There are ways to profit from war."

"Please, it doesn't even compare. Plus, I'll wager that Hector is doing this with an eye to getting the nobility re-established here."

He scowled some more, but like most commoners, he had no love for the nobility.

"Are you really that different, though?" he asked.

I shrugged. "Judge for yourself when I'm done. I'm not going to set myself up in the tower. The profits from the trade deal will get spread around. Among the merchants, mostly, but you know that their gold gets spread around."

He looked unconvinced, so I kept going. "Taxes taken by the Council will be spent on improving the city. Where do nobles' taxes go?"

He sighed, defeated for the moment. "Their pockets."

I was surprised that I didn't get a notification for a Social Contest, but that must all have been in the context of a Bargain. I left the money on the table and stood.

"I'll see you next week, then."

He looked up. "I may have some . . . expenses."

I shrugged. "Clear them with me first, if you don't want to risk them coming out of your pocket."

He nodded slowly, and I left.

Kyle wasn't exactly our espionage expert, but he knew enough to make sure we were well clear before he spoke.

"He didn't say anything about it."

I sighed pensively. "He wouldn't have if he had noticed, probably. We'll just have to wait and see what Cloridan finds out."

I'd left Cloridan there, invisible, to see what Marlon did after speaking to us. My own bit of due diligence. Cloridan said the man could be relied on, but I'd feel better if we had eyes on him, at least some of the time.

Sometimes, I thought I might have my fingers in too many pies. The rest of the time I knew it to be true. Adventurer, Enchanter, Trader, Politician . . . part of me wanted to just pick one and stick to it. Some of it, though, was necessary.

While it felt like adventuring was a hobby that was distracting me from my other pursuits, nothing could be further from the truth. Adventuring was my real job. It paid in experience and gold, and I needed both, badly. In this world, that wasn't so unusual. Most nobles had some sort of access to a dungeon, and they made sure to get the most out of it. Resources and levels, the key to power here.

So that was why I found myself again at the bottom of the Forbidden Laboratory before a week had gone past. I'd managed to finagle an earlier slot, since I'd be busy next week with the new traders arriving.

This time we'd gotten lucky, and Felicia was gloating over her new spatial bag. It had been a good run . . . but we weren't finished yet. This part wasn't *strictly* necessary for anything, but I really wanted to know.

We stood around the core, with everyone maintaining a careful distance. I conjured a Phantasmal cage around the sphere. Open at the top, and with a solid floor, it looked awkwardly placed but it was firmly wedged in and would last long enough.

I came forward with the other cage that I'd carried all the way down here. It carried a rabbit that we'd found topside. Well, hunted. It had taken all the skills of an invisible Cloridan to sneak up on it and grab it unharmed.

The rabbit was a natural spawn, not part of any dungeon. I'd been a bit nervous bringing it in, but everyone reassured me that it wouldn't cause a break—and even if it did, the dungeon was at a low ebb at the moment, getting run to completion every day.

The rabbit's cage was a Phantasm as well, of course, so once I placed it over the other one, I could dismiss it, dropping the rabbit neatly in the cage with the core. I could have dropped it right on top, but that felt . . . wrong somehow. There wasn't much room in there, though, so we didn't have to watch the rabbit hop around for very long before it touched the sphere.

And disappeared. We all blinked in surprise for a bit.

"All right, then." I dismissed the cage, and we all watched the core for a bit longer. It didn't do anything. With Sense Mana, it was clear that there was a lot going on, but I'd be hard-pressed to judge if it was *different* something.

"Are you going to try and become the master of it?" Felicia asked.

". . . No? No. Make one change at a time and see what the effects are, that's the rule."

"Effects?"

"Well, we were speculating that this dungeon was pretty boring because there was no real intelligence behind it, right?"

Felicia shrugged. "Well, that's what Rhis insisted was the case. I don't know, though. Of all the dungeons we've seen, it's been the most varied."

"Yeah, but when you know it's just mashing on the random monster button the whole time . . . he's got a point."

We'd all learned by now that arguing with Rhis about this was pointless, and a good way to waste half an hour in a seemingly endless rant. He wasn't here, though.

"So, we need to see if having a rabbit as a dungeon controller causes changes. Is a dungeon better, or worse for having a controller?"

Cloridan frowned. "It changed already, though, remember? The first time we went through, it changed up all the traps."

"I'm starting to think that wasn't a coincidence," I told him. "I reckon a god might have put their finger on the scales to make things harder for us."

Everyone got a little nervous at that thought. "Why not worse—or why not try again, if someone was trying to kill us?" Kyle asked.

"One thing I've noticed about the gods is that they're really keen to counter each other. From what Fyskel said, it's *possible* for one of them to sneak something by the others, but the bigger the change, the more likely one of them will notice and stomp on it."

"Which means doing it *twice* is out of the question," Kyle mused.

"Doesn't mean they won't try something else. But if they're limited in what they can get through, we should be able to take care of it like any other random danger."

"I wonder," Felicia said, "if there is such a thing as a random danger for us."

"Maybe not," I acknowledged. "But if we can't tell the difference, we just have to take things as they come."

BUSTED

Yes, it's about the notice you posted," Nadine said, escorting me into the Guild Master's office. "We had some questions."

I swallowed. It hadn't been an hour since I'd posted an ongoing job request for anyone delving into the Forbidden Laboratory asking them to note the exact date and time of their delve and any changes they'd noticed. Now I was getting called into the Master's office, and from the look on his face, he wasn't happy. The desk he was sitting behind wasn't small—I was jealous—but he made it look like it.

"Questions?" I asked, doing my best impression of someone innocent.

"Yes!" Koenig growled loudly. "Mainly—why do you think there'll be changes!" Despite the wording, it was more of an accusation than a question.

"Oh . . . well, we may have . . . seen a small animal touch the core of that dungeon, and we were curious about what effects it might have, and over what time period they occurred."

Technically true, but I didn't think it would fool them. It was more like a fighting retreat while I worked out how concerned they were.

"You're not supposed to touch the cores! It's dangerous!" Koenig yelled. One of my Social skills was telling me his anger was at least partly feigned, but I thought it wise to show some fear anyway. Not that it was hard—the man was pretty scary when he tried to be.

"We didn't—like I said, a rabbit did." I backed away a step, but he gestured for me to sit in the chair in front of his desk. I obeyed.

"Did it disappear?" he asked, more calmly.

"Yes." I looked at him appraisingly. Apparently, some people here knew how dungeons worked. "Do you know what happened to it?"

He scowled at me. "Information on such matters is restricted to higher-level guild members. You still haven't said if you're interested in signing up."

"Not any time soon," I said carefully. "I've found myself with a few too many responsibilities to give myself over to the Guild."

"So I've noticed, *Councillor*. Just remember that your office doesn't get to direct the Adventurers Guild."

"I never said it did," I assured him. "And I thought our negotiations about managing access to the *Tribal* dungeons went very well with all parties satisfied with the results. Was I wrong?"

"That was all fine," he said, waving a hand dismissively. "What I mean is, don't think your new rank allows you access to Guild secrets."

"Are they really secret if they can be learned by some simple observation?" I asked lightly.

"The King's Law states that you are not supposed to touch the cores!"

"And I didn't." His phrasing was a little different from what I'd heard, though. I might have to look it up. The law as I'd originally heard it stated was that you couldn't *take* cores. That sounded far more sensible, as forbidding people to touch cores was unenforceable.

I kept my thoughts to myself as Koenig blustered for a while longer about the dangers.

"And now everything is going to change!" he cried, exasperated. My skills perked up. This was the actual reason for his anger.

"You know what keeps delving safe!" he continued. "It's knowing the dungeon, knowing the threats. Things are going to get more dangerous for your fellow delvers from here on."

"I think most of the groups here are wary enough," I countered. "It's not like that dungeon never changes—there was that change my first day here."

He frowned. "That doesn't sound like a coincidence now. Did you have something to do with that?"

I shrugged. "Not as far as I know."

"You're trouble, Councillor Hammond. I should ban you from the dungeon."

"That seems a little unfair when I haven't broken any Guild rules."

"None of the written ones," he muttered darkly.

I raised an eyebrow. "I imagine if it came out that there are secret rules that everyone is supposed to follow, you might get—at the least—a lot of queries about what they are."

"Bah! Just . . . stay away from the cores. No more experiments!"

"Of course," I lied. "I'll do as you say."

It was only after I left that I realized that there hadn't been a Social Contest notification. Why was that?

One reason, I supposed, was that I hadn't really wanted anything from the confrontation. But Koenig had, or so it seemed . . .

Checking my Log, I saw that he had attempted both an Intimidate and Persuasion, but both had been unsuccessful. Social skills, I gathered, were not the Guild Master's forte. But if he'd tried to get me to stop . . . he should have gotten a notification for losing, and I should have gotten one from winning? Unless he hadn't really wanted to stop me.

It had seemed, for quite a lot of that conversation, that Koenig was spouting something that he was legally required to, but didn't actually care about. The bit about endangering adventurers was real, if overblown—in my opinion, anyway.

If he had tried and not gotten a notification, he must have known that he hadn't convinced me, but he let me leave all the same. Could he stop me? The business about banning me from the Dungeon wasn't a serious threat. Without a fortification and guards at the entrance, there was no way he could stop me from entering, and he knew that.

And he let me keep the notice up. Arguably, any damage I'd caused had been done. Recording the changes didn't hurt, and might help—although I was sure that the Guild would be collating their own list of changes to add to the guide.

All in all, it seemed as if he didn't actually care, but he was required to at least discourage me.

I sighed as one last thought struck me. If he hadn't actually cared about convincing me, had he actually used his full skills on me? I supposed that I shouldn't write off his Social skills so quickly after all.

A free feast was a lot less appealing when you were the one paying for it. Not that *I* was, but it was my budget that it was coming out of. Among the many innovations that needed to be added to this world was a tax write-off for entertainment expenses. I added it to the list.

The expense was necessary, though, as we were celebrating the opening of the North Market. It wasn't much more than a few tents so far, but there were goods and there was trade.

Many of the participants from the town were slightly on edge. They weren't used to being outside of the walls, but the unconcerned presence of the Tribals set most of them at ease. The alcohol probably helped, too.

I was seated at a table close to the center of it all, with the luminaries of the town, and the leaders of the delegation. We had an actual feast, with courses and dishes and such, while the hoi polloi of the common townsfolk made do with free meat, bread, and ale. Oddly, at least to my mind, it was the meat that was the cheapest of those three. Monster meat was still oversupplied thanks to the breaks, while wheat and ale had to be imported.

We'd lured the townsfolk out here with free beer, but we didn't really have any purpose for them, aside from getting them used to the area. They had responded well, mixing with the newcomers and generally appearing to have a good time. In the same vein, this was the first time I was interacting with most of the people at this table without some kind of deal to be hashed out, so I was at a bit of a loss.

Charm took up the slack, making small talk and making it seem as if I was having a good time, but my mind couldn't leave off thinking about the many things that I had to be concerned about.

Two of them were at the feast. Priestess Tonet wasn't seated at the main table, but she was in my line of sight, laughing and having fun just like everyone else. Kaito had assured me that she would no longer be plotting against us, but I was not entirely convinced. The fact that she was in attendance reassured me more—she was unlikely to stage an attack on herself.

My other problem was actually sitting two seats down from me. Captain Rodakis was also unlikely to stage an attack on himself—his guards were responsible for the security of the town, after all. From what I could learn about him, he was still feeling out the situation he found himself in. Maybe for tonight, at least, I could relax and not worry about disaster.

Yeah, right. I smiled and nodded, and chatted amiably with my fellow townsfolk. Maybe everything would go right, for once. There were guards on the wall, and around the perimeter of the celebration. For that matter, no one in their right mind would attack a crowd with so many adventurers. Some were wearing less armor than normal, but they were all still armed and dangerous.

As people finished their meals, they got up and started to mingle. The amateur musicians that had been playing accompaniment music moved on to something more danceable. I kept a grimace off my face. Not only did we not have any Bards out here, but Latorran music was somewhat backward for my taste. I had really wanted to supply my own tunes, but exposing my companions to my musical taste had convinced me that Latora was barely ready for classical music, and wasn't at all ready for rock.

Actually, there were some professional, or at least specialized, musicians that would be playing tonight. The delegation had brought a small troupe, but it had been agreed that since they didn't know any Latorran tunes, they'd put on a show after the dancing was done. I'd smiled and agreed with the rest, but I was expecting folk music.

For now, there was time to kill, and networking to be done. I maneuvered myself out of my chair—the dress made it a more complex operation than it had to be—and lightly stepped over to where Rodakis was sitting.

"Would you like to dance, Captain?" I asked, with a smile as sharp as a knife. I turned Charm on full boil, and let him have the full impact. He never stood a chance.

> **You have defeated Hector Rodakis in a Tier 3 Social Contest! You have earned 45 XP.**
> **Do you wish to waive the Penalty? [Y] / [N]**

"I'd be honored, my lady," he managed to get out. He stood and offered me his arm.

"Interesting," I said in a low voice. "Did you really object to dancing that much?"

"I . . . I thought it would be best as the leader to remain aloof from activities my men are participating in." It wasn't a lie—I don't think he could tell a lie under the circumstances. But it wasn't the entire truth either, or so my skills were telling me. I quite liked this feeling of power, of having control over the much larger and stronger man. Was this what it was like when a guy beat someone up? Something about that thought soured it for me.

> **Penalty has been waived.**

I saw the moment Rodakis felt the penalty lifted. He perked up and looked at me questioningly.

"We're going to be working together to protect this town, Captain. It wouldn't do for me to be holding a threat like that over your head."

Except, of course, the threat had already been made. Saying I wouldn't do something was just a polite way of saying I *could* do something. But if I made a point of dominating him every time we had a meeting, he'd just avoid me at all costs, and do his negotiation with arrows.

That didn't mean I turned Charm off, though. For one thing, I needed it to get through the moves of the dance we now gracefully joined. And for another . . . well, the primary use of Charm was to get people to like you. Throwing Seduction into the mix should turn up the heat a little. With just the bonus, not the actual skill, I doubted it would add more than a certain flavor to my Charm offensive. Given his level, I wasn't going to cause him to embarrass himself on the dance floor. But it should get him thinking along the right lines at least.

After all, as the old saying went, *Keep your friends close, and your enemies even closer.*

OTOME

The expectations around sexual availability and the customs around how relationships are negotiated have got to be the trickiest things to master in any society. I was lucky to have Charm, but even that only provided a guideline of how to act in the moment. It really didn't help in gaining an understanding of what was going on, of exactly what the things I said meant.

No one ever talks about it. Children just grow up learning by example, absorbing it from the air. I hadn't had that kind of time, so I'd locked myself in a room with Felicia with some alcohol and a whole lot of pointed questions.

I'd asked for her permission to do that, of course. She'd laughed, but her amusement hadn't lasted past the third question. At the end of the session, an agreement to never speak of it again had been gratefully accepted by both parties.

It turns out that women in Latora *were* expected to behave as modestly and chastely as you might suspect if you'd ever watched a movie set in medieval times. It wasn't as bad as some places I'd heard about from my history—no one was regulating button fanciness, for example. Despite legal equality (which had come as a surprise to me), women were expected to sit back, shut up, and let the men do the talking and the wooing.

There was a double standard, though, and it wasn't the usual male-dominated one. Well, they had that as well, so I guess it was a triple standard.

The exception to all the rules was adventurers. They could do whatever they liked—within the law, of course. They—we—didn't get to commit crimes with impunity. But all the scandals that get whispered about, all the "just not done" things, just did not apply to adventurers. It was a hole that you could drive a truck through because *anyone* could be an adventurer. Technically, it was regulated by the Guild, but it wasn't like anyone else had asked to see my card. Anyone could pick up a sword or a knife and start swinging at monsters, and they would be an adventurer.

This freedom came with costs, of course. Adventurers weren't seen as reliable fellow citizens. I'd noticed that there was a divide between towns-folk and adventurers, but I hadn't really grasped its significance because it didn't seem to apply to me. I had moved back and forth between the groups without any resistance.

Part of that was my high Charisma, but another part was the unac-knowledged foolishness of the system itself. Because becoming townsfolk was just as easy as becoming an adventurer—you just had to say that you were. So when I wore my leather armor, people saw me as an adventurer, and when I wore a fancy dress people saw me as a respectable member of society. They *knew* both were true, but they buried that knowledge and reacted just to what they saw in front of them.

Which wasn't as crazy as it sounds, because while adventurers weren't seen as respectable, they were one of the few pathways to *becoming* respectable. If you couldn't inherit a profession from your parents, adven-turing was one of the few ways of getting the money to start up your own business. Almost every merchant, smith, or farmer either started off as an adventurer or had an ancestor who was one.

Just another reason to bring banks into this world.

So where did this leave me, having just dragged the good Captain Rodakis out onto the dance floor? Well, if I had read the situation cor-rectly, he was currently in a state of cognitive dissonance. I *should* have been a meek and modest woman and let him do the manly thing and ask me. Since I was an adventurer, though, my forwardness was only to be expected.

Normally, he would never allow himself to be snared by a lowly adven-turer. However, I was *actually* Councillor Hammond, the most beautiful and eligible woman in the city, if I do say so myself. If anything, I out-ranked him. He should have asked me—and perhaps he had planned to. But . . . and then we were back to the start.

"Confused" perhaps covers it. As we moved in time to the music, I could see him try to clarify both his thinking and my intentions. You can talk during a dance, but it doesn't lend itself well to conversations where you have to think very hard before each exchange.

It was fine for me, as I just had to smile and avoid any firm commitment while exuding a friendly (perhaps more than *just* friendly) air. He was second- or triple-guessing himself every time he tried to say something, which didn't leave him with much time for actually talking. I think he might have been more confused when the dance ended than at the start.

Of course, then it got complicated.

When the dance ended, I took a step back to deliver a curtsy and a final line, but to my surprise, Tom was suddenly standing between us.

"May I have this dance?" he said. I was startled and froze for a brief moment. Before I could recover, he took hold of my arms and whisked me away.

He didn't drag me; he actually lifted me just a bit off the ground so that he could get more distance before I unfroze. Carrying me in that awkward way wouldn't have been possible without the super-strength I'd always assumed that he had but had never seen him use before. It also depended on *my* strength. My surprise was holding me rigid for that brief moment. Without my enhanced strength, the sudden acceleration would have flopped me out of his grip like a wet noodle.

It was less than a second, and only a few steps, but it felt as if Rodakis had just disappeared from in front of me. The next thing I knew, we were on the dance floor waiting for the next song.

"What are you doing?" Tom asked. His voice was low and intense. "Don't you know he's here to kill you?"

"Here at the party?" I replied, still a little bit behind from the sudden changes. The music started up again, and I let Charm move me the way I should go. He led, of course.

"Here in Talnier," he said impatiently. "There's no way that the nobles haven't approached him with an offer to give him a title if he can get rid of your upstart Council."

"That's the Council though, not just me. I'm just one replaceable member."

He swung me around gracefully and we moved into the next set of steps. "Only if he hasn't realized you're the motivating force *behind* the Council. It's only a matter of time before he comes after you."

"Well, he's not going to do anything in front of all these witnesses," I reasoned. "I should be safe for tonight, at least."

"That doesn't mean that you should be letting him get close to you! He's—"

"Are your motives any more pure?" I asked, looking up at him closely. His speech didn't stutter, but he did blush, which was interesting. I let myself "accidentally" move a little closer than the proper distance.

"That's not relevant to this discussion." He was trying for a cold tone, to shut this conversational direction down, but his expression—and his intensifying blush—gave the game away.

"Your intentions seem very relevant to me," I asserted, as we swayed back and forth. Our bodies were apart again. More than a moment would have attracted attention. "I have to say, I had thought you a more . . . worldly man. Have you not mingled much with adventurers?"

"Nobles, for the most part," he said stiffly. "While I've delved, that was training to serve my master, not adventuring."

I giggled. There was that attitude again. It seemed that Envoys were grouped in with the proper people. I glanced around until I found Rodakis again. He was on the edge of the dance floor, looking at us intently. I gave him a grin.

Was this . . . helping me? It was true that a great way to make someone want something was to tell them they couldn't have it. Having two boys fight over me wasn't something I really wanted (childish thrills aside), but I might be able to make it serve my purposes.

"Look," I said. "I want to be on friendly terms with Captain Rodakis. If that gets in the way of your mission, then too bad."

"It's not the mission," Tom said. For the first time since I'd met him, he seemed lost for words. "I don't often have permission to get . . . close to people. I don't want you to die and waste all of my master's efforts."

Is he serious? I thought, shocked. Or was this Seduction at work? I guessed I would have to take it seriously either way.

"I've been aware of the Captain's intentions since he arrived," I said. "And the intentions of the nobles from Bargougne and Arryen. Why the other duchy hasn't taken an interest, I don't know."

He looked at me with surprise, and I gave him a little smile. "I have sources of information other than you."

"I see," he said, looking a little relieved. "Then can I assume that you actually know what you're doing?"

"Tom. I've been jumping from one half-baked plan to another since I got here. That hasn't changed, I've just gotten a little better at it."

He snorted, and went to say something more, but the music ended, heralding the arrival of Rodakis.

"Captain," Tom said, not bowing. The two of them sized each other up, and I thought for sure that they were going to bash their chests against each other.

"Ah, Captain Rodakis, I don't know if you've met Envoy Parkes."

"Envoy?" Rodakis said, startled. He glanced at Tom's all-black outfit. "From the Ebon Order?" he asked. There was a hint of a sneer in his voice, but I could tell he was somewhat put off.

"Indeed, Captain. I would have made myself known to you, but my remit is limited to contact with persons of *political* importance."

"The Baron would have barely qualified as such before his death," Rodakis replied. His eyes flicked towards me as he asked, "Do commoner Council members rank with nobility now?"

"Perhaps, perhaps not," Tom said. "I can hardly go into details about my business here. The presence of a Chosen in Talnier is enough to justify my presence." He wasn't so gauche as to glance at me when he said that, but I could tell from his wry smile that he was enjoying the double meaning.

"I suppose." Rodakis glared at Tom, just a little. I could only assume that they were both trying Intimidate and finding themselves evenly matched. "In any case, you've had your turn—"

"Actually, good sirs," a familiar voice interrupted. "I'm sure the lady won't refuse a dance from her oldest and dearest companion."

I turned to see Cloridan grinning like the rogue he was. "May I have this dance?" he said.

"Of course," I replied, and we left the two to their standoff.

"Ah, at last, a chance to dance with the fair lady," Cloridan said, grinning.

"Aren't you seeing someone right now?" I asked.

"I've already danced with Noemi," he answered. "Then I told her I needed to rescue you from your admirers."

"A selfless sacrifice for the team," I snarked. "Without hope of reward."

"Actually, hope springs eternal, or so I've found in my case. Things are going pretty great with Noemi, but as long as I'm hoping, I might as well hope for a—"

"Yeah, bury that hope." As we continued to dance, I saw someone who had been keeping to themself for the last few days.

"Cloridan, I'm going to have to cut this dance short."

He sighed dramatically. "I've reached too high, and now I have to be shot down, is that it? Alas."

"Shut up, you horndog." I indicated a direction, and he glanced over at Isidre. She was standing on the edge of the crowd, looking at the dancers.

"Ah, more business? I'll leave you to it then."

We disengaged from the dance, and I walked over. "Isidre. It's Kandis."

Isidre looked at me, confused. "Kandis? I'd heard that you were on the Council now, but you look different?"

"Yeah," I said. "I guess we need to talk."

CHAMPIONS

I gestured to Isidre that we should move somewhere more private.

"I told you that was a disguise, didn't I?"

"And this is another one, is it?" she asked. "You seem . . . different, beyond the obvious changes."

That would be due to the fact that she could feel my Charisma now. It was a pain not being able to use Social skills through my puppets, but at least I was immune to the reverse.

I shrugged. "I'm not great at the whole 'different faces' yet," I admitted. "I should have used different names, but it's a pain to keep track of."

"And this face . . . has taken over the town?"

I detected a hint of accusation in her voice.

"I am bringing democracy to this town," I firmly corrected her. "And prosperity. You would not believe just how primitive their financial institutions are—"

"They had the Baron to lead them . . . he died and—did you kill him?"

"No." I looked her in the eye. "The Baron was a criminal. When he didn't come back from wherever he went to, he wasn't able to keep his crimes out of sight anymore."

"That can't be right," she said, shaking her head. "The Baron, he was fighting the Tribes, he wanted me to—"

"The Tribes aren't the enemy!" I exclaimed. "Look around you! They're just people with cute ears. Trading with them is going to make us all rich."

"You were the one who brought them in," she said wonderingly. "You were working with Kaito since the start."

"For peace! We've both been working to de-escalate both sides, calm them down—"

"And the Baron was in the way of that, wasn't he . . . and so was I. You probably brought the assassins in . . ."

"Hey! The walls are a joke as far as stopping any high-level person goes," I said. "It didn't take Illusion magic for that guy to sneak in and kill people. I had nothing to do with it."

That halted her for a bit. "Perhaps that's true," she said. "But you *were* working against me during the griffin attack, weren't you?"

"I was fighting on the walls," I said, my voice hard. "I must have missed seeing you there. That's part of why I'm a part of this community and you're not."

"No wonder I lost," she said bitterly. "I was up against two Champions at the same time."

"Isidre . . ."

"No, I get it now. I'll get out of your way."

"Don't be like that," I pleaded. "You can do a lot of good in this town." *If you can get your head out of your ass,* I added mentally.

"I'll go east," she stated. "That's where the King has been asking me to go."

"That's the other contested area," I said. "Isidre, if you start a war there . . . the lives and well-being of everyone around you right now will be thrown into the fire."

"I'm not going to start a war," she said flatly. "But if one starts, I'll win it."

She turned to leave, but was struck by a sudden thought, and turned back. "Will you be one of the representatives that sees the King?"

"Probably," I said warily. I mean, it wasn't a sure thing. It was still a long way off. I could die, or we could rebel by then.

She nodded. "I shall look for you in the capital at that time, then. We shall see which of us has been more useful to the Kingdom."

She turned to leave again, not waiting to see my shrug. *Is that what we're competing in? Doesn't seem like something I should care about.*

I let her go and moved on to my next order of business. Neither of my erstwhile suitors were visible, which left me free to do some networking. There were a lot of adventurers in this crowd, and they weren't drunk yet. This was the perfect time to try and round up some investors.

Kaito sighed. "I'm sorry," she said. "I'm glad that you didn't kill her when you had the chance, but this is going to cause a lot of trouble for everyone."

"Yeah," I said morosely. "I didn't even think of it at the time, but I'm starting to regret it." We were meeting outside the city again, her girls keeping a close eye on me to make sure I didn't get too close.

"Don't. I don't believe that the Champions are meant to kill each other," Kaito said.

"Well, sometimes they work together, but there are definitely times when they haven't," I said, recalling the histories I'd read.

"Yes, but deaths are rare—at least from other Champions' hands. I think that is what separates us from people from this world. They find killing to be far too easy a solution."

"That's . . ." I looked at her in disbelief. "That's a *very* rosy picture of our world."

"I don't mean to call *us* saints." She waved my objection away. "Only to say that here, they are worse. Killing is encouraged here—by the world itself. In our world, killing is properly seen as a last resort. I think that might be why we were Chosen."

"To teach these guys nonviolence?"

"Think about what we know about our small group so far. All ordinary people, yes? No mercenaries or soldiers, or hardened criminals."

"All from different cultures . . ." I added.

"Yes! Pitted against each other to fulfill the gods' tasks . . . the only thing that binds us together is our shared circumstances." She seemed excited by the idea, as if she was on the edge of a revelation.

"And yet, when we clash, we tend not to kill . . ." I said, trying to follow where she was going.

"We talk, we compromise, we remove ourselves from the equation," Kaito continued. "Even your argument with Miss Isidre fits the pattern."

"Okay, but why is this important?"

"The gods, of course, Miss Kandis. These things we are describing, the gods are very bad at them, yes?"

"I suppose. Wait, you think they brought us here to teach *them* how to negotiate?"

Kaito laughed. "Well, perhaps. I'm sure they have many reasons. As many reasons as there are gods."

"Probably more," I agreed. "Fyskel seems like the type of guy to have at least three reasons for anything he does."

"That's probably true. Anyway, I just think amongst those reasons, serving as an example for them is one of them. Or it should be."

"Maybe. Seems like hubris to be teaching a god anything, though."

"Perhaps. I haven't been struck down yet, though." She rose from her cross-legged position on the ground with an ease that I was envious of. I suppose that my empowered body could actually manage that now, but I'd wimped out and conjured a low chair for our chat.

"I will head east as well, and see what I can do to defuse tensions over there," she continued. "I may not be able to reconcile with Isidre, but I should be able to prevent any provocations from becoming incidents."

"I'd go with you, but . . ."

"You are needed here," she told me firmly. "The accord is still fragile. I've spoken to Tonet, and she has agreed to cease her activities, but in the absence of both of us, I fear she may resume."

"Do you know why she was trying to start a war?" I asked. "It might help future negotiations if I know what her goals are."

"She was unwilling to be specific . . . I suspect it may be actual hatred on her part," Kaito mused. "Though she is not a beast-kin, she is close to many families that have been wronged by the Kingdom. The degree of your independence from the Kingdom was of great interest to her."

"Maybe if I was open to discussing reparations," I speculated. "Though the King, and probably most of the townsfolk, would have conniptions at the idea."

"That would probably be well received on her end," she agreed. "But I'll leave that discussion to you."

I stood up as well, and she bowed. "For now, I must take my leave, Miss Kandis. May we work together again."

I returned the bow. "Let's hope. Good luck on your journey, Miss Kaito," I said, hoping that the honorific would get translated through.

It had taken a lot of schmoozing. My Bargain skill had gone up a level, and I thought Persuasion might be close to one. In some ways, though, it had gone a lot faster than I thought it would. At this scale—a single town, with not very large amounts—money moved a lot faster than I was used to. Bank transfers were incredibly convenient, but they weren't as fast as a bag of platinum coins handed over the table.

You might think that counting the coins would slow things down, but Identify sped things up immensely. I could glance at the bag, see how much was in there, confirm it with the investor, and write out the receipt.

Storage was an issue. For now, I was using my ring. It meant that I had to carry my daggers again, but we should have something more convenient soon enough. At the moment, we had a building—that was being strengthened, and I was consulting with Mandel on an enchantment design for a secure vault. The Bank of Talnier was in business!

Now, my first employee (Huette was paid by the Council) was putting the final touches on the contract for my first customer. Since we were starting small, Mr. Vaillancourt was only borrowing 10,000 gold to set himself up as a Stonemason. I had a feeling that masonry was due for a resurgence.

Part of my feeling was all the new construction, but we were also going to be reopening the nearby quarry. It hadn't been used since they'd built the town wall, and even then it had been too much trouble to work. Most of the stone used on the wall had come from Anchorbury. Shipping costs had been outweighed by the need for the heavy guard that the workers had needed.

It must have been quite an impressive undertaking, only slightly diminished in my mind by visions of stoneworkers tossing the heavy stone blocks like bricks. Now, though, after talks with our new friends, we could expect the monster spawns to be greatly reduced. All we needed to do was clear out the existing spawn points, and we should be good for a minimal guard.

New resources, new business. It felt like usury to be charging fifteen percent per annum for these loans, but the looks of relief and gratitude from prospective clients eased my fears. From the looks of it, at these rates, we'd have more applicants than we could afford once the economy picked up. Rates might have to go as high as thirty percent just to reduce demand . . . unless I could start getting paper money accepted.

"That all seems to be in order, Mister Vaillancourt. If you understand your obligations, please sign here and you can have your money."

Delmar, my new employee, was one of the first new Talnier Officials. He wasn't much older than Cutter, really, but he hadn't wanted to spend the rest of his life as a butcher like his father. He'd jumped at the chance for a profession with merchant skills and applied to work for the Council. I'd poached him with a higher-paid job, and now he was my new banking clerk.

He'd almost quit in the first week, as I'd started training his Scribe skill up by making dozens of exact copies of the forms to fill out for applicants. Next was training in procedures, but that did have to wait for clients to practice on. For now, I was shadowing him through each part of the process, but he'd soon be ready to do a lot of it on his own. Naturally, I was making sure I was the one to personally authorize all the loans.

Smiling a customer service smile, I moved over to Delmar and retrieved the prepared bag of coins. The leather bag thumped down on the desk. Its weight was considerable, about five or six kilos. *Yay for super strength.*

[Identification]: **Bag of Platinum Stars (1,000)**

"One thousand platinum; please confirm and sign here," I said. Vaillancourt glanced at the bag and signed the receipt. Delmar made a note in the book.

"Congratulations on being our first customer," I said. "Good luck with your business."

We shook hands, he thanked me, and we did all the social niceties involved in saying goodbye to someone you'd just given a lot of money to. We were finally a going concern.

SCİΠCE!

The Forbidden Laboratory had changed and it was all my fault. At least that was what the accusing glares of the Guild officials said each time someone came in with a new story. No one had actually died from the changes, so mildly annoyed glares were all I had to put up with.

Now, finally, I would get to see the changes for myself. It wasn't easy making time for a delve, but like a morning exercise routine, you just had to do it. Delving every week wasn't ideal for grinding, but with all the new delvers from the Tribes, once a week was all we could get.

Constantly working as a group had improved our teamwork and now our group was a finely tuned monster-killing machine. Standard procedure now was for Kyle to be the only visible combatant. It was Felicia's job to stay three paces behind him, while my position was behind and to the right of her.

Cloridan, of course, was right out in front, behind the monsters. Arranged like that, the invisible combatants could stay out of one another's way. Kyle didn't have to worry about where any of us was and just concentrated on holding his line.

As the one who could see us all, I was responsible for directing the battle. Doing so with Unseen Sound was a little awkward, but the simple formation didn't need much in the way of direction, just warnings when things went wrong. Since I was also the one in charge of contingencies—blinding opponents, casting temporary shields, doing . . . miscellaneous things with water . . . it worked out well.

Integrating Cutter into the formation was proving more challenging. He just didn't have the stats to go against a lot of the monsters down here, so he couldn't back Kyle up. Invisibility would help him, but then he'd either be getting in the way of Kyle or Cloridan. For now, he was back with me, visible and charged with attacking anything that got past Kyle. That only tended to happen with groups of smaller monsters, so it was generally safe. Not that safety was a huge priority for Cutter.

"Oh, come on! I can get in there!" he protested to the empty air beside him. I tightened my grip. Ostensibly, I was holding onto him so he knew where I was. I didn't need my hands to cast spells, and I still had one hand for my dagger if I needed it. The *other* reason was that even if I wanted to waste five mana repeating myself, he wasn't in a mood to listen.

"Just stay back, I've got this," Kyle called back. Cutter danced with frustration, not in a mood to enjoy his free XP.

He had made great strides in the last few weeks, though. Through dint of much effort, Cloridan had finally convinced him that a more martial profession would suit him than Rogue. It was the lure of bigger weapons mostly, but the fact was that we didn't need *two* Rogues. I had been sure he'd go for Fencer, but right now he was leaning towards Ranger due to his recent wilderness experience. He wouldn't meet the requisites for either until he got some more Ability points at his next level, though. Or he aged a bit, which was apparently not an option.

In preparation for his new profession, we had upgraded his equipment. His old partial plate and dagger were gone, replaced by silversteel chainmail, dagger, and a longsword (enchanted by me, of course).

"Cutter, if you can't delve safely, you'll have to stay overground and hunt in the forest," I projected. He scowled, but stayed put. Hunting had gotten scarce around the town since the Tribes had redirected the monsters.

In front of us, the felibull slumped to the ground, Cloridan's daggers in his back.

> **Your party has killed a Felibull – your experience share is 234 XP.**

At the notification, Felicia skipped forward, circling around her boyfriend, and descended on the fresh corpses. Now that we had a spatial bag, we were harvesting a lot more of our killed monsters, and felibull was at least partially beef, so it should be in demand. Kyle and Cloridan moved to the two exits, making sure they were still closed and listening for the rats.

Cutter and I got to work searching for the key. They were one of the things that had changed. To progress to the next level, you needed three keys, which were to be found in three of the twelve rooms on this level. To date, no patterns had been found in *where* the keys were placed. It appeared to be random for each group, but the Guild was recording details of where each team found their keys, hoping to find a pattern.

Instead of three straight routes, this level now arranged its rooms in a four-by-three grid with four straight passages running along the length of the arrangement. Each room had a door to the passage on each side of it, so there were multiple ways to progress. If you knew which rooms you needed, you could get through with just three fights. Without that knowledge, it averaged about ten.

Cloridan waved to attract my attention, so I lowered the output from my Light spell. Everyone looked over at Kyle. When they saw him looking around as well, they reoriented on Cloridan's door. They couldn't see him, but the light was a sign that the rats were passing by.

The rats were another random factor, so I noted the room we were in, and which corridor the rats had wandered down. The rats—a whole swarm of double-sized nasty critters—wandered the corridors at random intervals. If they heard anything, they'd come into a room and either attack the party or join in an existing fight.

Swarms were actually a weakness for our party—I missed having Janie's Firestorms to clear a corridor of weak enemies—so we stayed quiet and careful. A few moments later, Cloridan waved the all-clear, and I returned the light to its normal level.

Having signals and procedures for this sort of thing meant that I could keep up my spells instead of recasting them for each fight. It killed the banter that we'd normally have indulged in, but it was *much* more mana efficient.

"I found it!" Cutter called excitedly. He managed to keep his voice low as he brandished our second key.

"Good job," Kyle said. He was the only other one who could talk without a spell. "Go help Felicia with the harvesting."

I abandoned rummaging through the broken glassware and joined them, waiting until Cutter had picked a corpse to work on before picking my own. It must have made a disturbing sight for the others. I, at least, could see an outline of Felicia and myself, but the others would see two corpses apparently dismembering themselves.

There wasn't another rat patrol while we'd finished harvesting, so we waited until they came again. Once they'd gone, we moved on.

* * *

The second floor was also changed, but not as drastically. The twisting tunnels that made up the maze had gotten narrower and even more twisting. The chambers where monsters had been found were now more . . . habitable. If you were a rat, that is. Filled with straw, rags, and food waste, they made perfect dens for the graxis rats that filled this level. They lived in the chambers, but they weren't limited to them. The dog-sized creatures crawled through the tunnels looking for intruders.

They were attracted to light, so I extinguished my spell, and we broke out the darkvision potions. If we'd wanted to kill the maximum number of rats, we could have barricaded a chamber and fought them as they came, but we had other plans. For one thing, previous reports had suggested that there was no limit to the number of rats, or at least not a reasonable one.

Tunnels had been found, too small for a human, but large enough for a rat. The theory at the Guild was that part of the dungeon wasn't meant to be delved, but was set aside for rat breeding. Having your monsters breed more of themselves saved on mana costs. Rhis had talked about this. At length.

There hadn't been enough reports to be sure, but it seemed that the maze shifted with each visitor. However, there was a way through with minimal killing. Six of the chambers were unoccupied, and if you passed through them, you'd get to the final boss without any encounters, bar the first room.

Of course, you had to find those rooms. Most people had to choose a tunnel and see if it led to a fight. If it did, then backtrack and try again. It got a little trickier if you were following another party and the chambers hadn't been repopulated, but we were the first for today.

We also had an invisible scout to find the way without getting into any fights, so we passed through this level without difficulty. The rest of the dungeon was unchanged, as of yet.

"So what do we think?" I asked the group. We'd reached the bottom and had collected our random treasure again. This time it was one of the less appreciated spatial boxes—a masonry workshop. A box the size of a brick, it could be opened and unfolded a ridiculous number of times into a small room set up for a mason to use. It wasn't great.

I mean, sure, if you wanted to trek into the wilderness and set yourself up as a Mason, it was pretty great. But who did that? Generally, you wanted to set yourself up surrounded by civilization, where workshops and tools were easily found. Aside from the contents, the only thing the box would store was stone—and not a lot of it. There had been some speculation about using such boxes for the upcoming quarry opening, but no one had been very enthusiastic.

"Well, it's just as we'd heard, wasn't it? Nothing new since yesterday," Felicia said.

"The second-level boss was new," I pointed out. "It was a chimera before. I'd say the fact that a greater graxis has been swapped in means that it's finished the second floor and is going to start on the third floor."

"I get that rats are more efficient than chimeras," Kyle said, "but just about anything is, so why rats? Should it be mutant rabbits?"

"Maybe the new controller finds rats more threatening than rabbits," I mused. "Or . . . it's weird, but rats are associated heavily with laboratories where I'm from."

"They are? Wait—you know what a laboratory is?" Felicia asked.

"You don't?" I asked, surprised.

"Well, I know the *word*," Felicia emphasized. "In stories, it's a room where the evil Master Arcanist fights the hero sometimes. It's got something to do with magic? But I thought your world didn't have magic?"

"In my world, it's a room, or a building of rooms, that are set up to study something," I explained. "You have different laboratories for different fields of study. I had thought that the name of this place was supposed to suggest that this dungeon was a place where somebody had been studying the way to make chimeras . . . did none of you get that?"

There were shrugs all around.

"No one really pays attention to dungeon names," Kyle said sheepishly. "I never gave it much thought."

"Okay . . ." I said slowly. "So, I was also thinking that the new levels—at least the first one—were a lot more like how labs are set up in my world. The interiors of the room as well, at least if it wasn't so wrecked."

"That *is* odd," Felicia agreed, "but where do the rats fit in?"

"Well, labs are often set up to study living things," I explained. "For a lot of experiments, one living thing is as good as another, and rats are really cheap, so they get used a lot."

"So . . ." Felicia trailed off, trying to make sense of it. "Do you think the dungeon got that from you? Or was there some previous civilization that had a similar arrangement?"

"I don't know." I paused to think about it. "Actually, where do dungeons get their names from? The two out here are named something appropriate for what they are, but Oakway was named after the town . . . or was the town named after the dungeon?"

Kyle and Felicia shrugged. "I don't know," Kyle said. "Both of them were there when my family arrived."

I made a note to remind myself that Rhis must be *much* older than he seemed to be. "The latter would make more sense," I speculated. "I don't think Rhis, or whatever is behind dungeons, would know or care about the town."

Rhis wasn't there to ask, of course. He was back in town, or at least his core was. Rather than being left on boring guard duty, he'd asked to be unpowered for the duration of our expedition. Despite my misgivings, he assured me that he experienced no time when he wasn't powered, and hence no discomfort.

"Anyway," I said, putting all the speculation aside. "We came here to do our own experiment." I removed another cage from my backpack, and we did the Phantasmal cage again. This time it was a squirrel that we dumped in the pen.

"Any reason it's a squirrel this time?" Felicia asked.

"Not really," I replied. "I did want a different animal, in case it needs to be different to replace the existing controller."

We all watched as the squirrel explored its new pen. It looked nervously at us, and then dashed around, looking for a way to escape. It wasn't long before it touched the orb.

"Nothing happened," Cloridan said.

"Yeah," I said slowly. "Just what we predicted. So it should be safe for one of us to touch it."

PARANOIA

Are you sure this is a good idea?" Felicia asked. "I mean, I know that this is what we discussed, but now it's time to do it . . ."

"I'm pretty sure I'll be okay," I said. "I've picked one of these up before."

There were some uncertain looks around the group, but no one wanted to object.

"All right, then," I said, and placed my hand on the core.

> **Do you wish to assume control of the Dungeon? Corporeal form will be abandoned. [Y] / [N]**

[N], I thought, and the message went away.

"Okay, so this is pretty much what happened last time," I said cautiously. "I removed it at this point, but—wait, I can feel something."

There was no notification, and the mana machinery that the core was composed of whirled as enigmatically as ever. But I *felt* something. Something . . .

"Urggh . . ." I groaned as it hit me. Something strong, controlling, and above all, malevolent. It was trying to take control of me, via something more basic than skills.

And it was stronger than me, I could tell. It was still gathering its power, uncertain of its strength, but I could feel that it wouldn't be long before—

I felt a blow to my arm, and then my body hit the stone floor. *Ouch.*

"Are you all right?" Felicia said. Not waiting for a reply, she sent some of her healing power my way.

"No," I admitted. "Gonna recommend *not* doing that again. That was . . . unpleasant. And dangerous."

"What happened?" Cloridan asked.

"I think . . . the dungeon tried to take control of *me*," I said slowly. "Probably would have managed it, if you hadn't broken the connection." I looked over at Kyle. Based on his new position, he'd been the one to rush over and hit my arm with his shield. "Thanks," I said.

He nodded. "Happy to help," he said.

"So . . ." Cloridan asked. "Why didn't that happen with Rhis?"

"Good question," I said. Despite being healed, the floor felt surprisingly comfortable. Couldn't stay here forever, though. With an unladylike grunt, I pushed myself off the ground. "I guess . . . because he got disconnected from the dungeon? Or the external mana construct, as the boxes called it."

"Because you pulled the core immediately," he mused.

"Yeah, so when I contacted him, he didn't have mana to power himself. Whereas this one . . ." I shuddered.

"So does that mean you won the fight without noticing, or just that he elected not to fight?" Cloridan wondered aloud. "And if it's the second . . . will Rhis try to dominate you if you put him in a dungeon again?"

"I—" I stopped, unsure of what to say. "I don't know. What I felt—you know I thought that Rhis's bloodthirst was from him being a carnivore, but that mind—it wasn't what I'd expect out of a rabbit."

"Do you think that was the corruption from Ashmor, that Fyskel mentioned?"

"I guess so. It was about as malevolent as I'd expect from the god who wants to destroy everything. The thing is . . ."

"What?" Felicia asked as I paused for more thought.

"The thing is, why did no one mention it before?" I wondered. "Not Mandel, not the Guild."

"Maybe Master Mandel did the same thing as you?" Kyle suggested. "And the Guild hasn't told us *anything*."

"Yeah, but it seems like there would be a difference between 'here is the secret to taming dungeons' and 'don't touch the core or it will mind-control you.' Don't you think?"

"If they thought we wouldn't believe them . . ." Felicia suggested.

"They'd still try it," I countered. "Even if we just went ahead with it, we'd be better prepared for it . . . more likely to succeed? Is that what they're trying to prevent?"

Cloridan grimaced. "Letting the dungeons eliminate their competition? That'd be pretty cold."

"Surely not," Kyle interjected. "The Guild has always tried to protect adventurers . . . going back generations."

"Maybe it's just a small clique within the guild that's keeping the secret," I said. "Or maybe . . . maybe I'm just being paranoid, but . . ."

"But?" Cloridan asked.

"Well, to paraphrase an old saying . . . the first rule of being mind-controlled by a malevolent entity, is that you don't *talk* about being mind-controlled by a malevolent entity."

Everyone looked at me, but nobody said anything.

"So you think . . ." Felicia eventually said. "That Master Mandel, and certain key Guild leaders, are being controlled by dungeons and are lying to us about it?"

"I don't think it," I said hastily. "I just think it's a possibility that needs to be considered."

"But that's . . ." Felicia said, appalled.

"If anything, we should suspect *you* of being controlled," Cloridan pointed out. "We know you've been in contact with two cores, and you cart one around with you most places."

Felicia managed to look even more shocked at this idea. Kyle remained his stoic self, while Cutter . . . it looked as if most of this conversation was going over his head. He was scraping his sword against the dungeon wall, waiting for the grown-ups to finish.

"I suppose that's true," I said glumly. "I might have brought the whole thing up as some sort of double bluff so you wouldn't suspect me. How does one prove they're not mind-controlled anyway?"

Everybody looked at each other, but no one said anything. Then Kyle spoke up.

"Mind-mage," he said.

"No one trusts mind-mages, though," Cloridan said scornfully.

Kyle shrugged. "True, but what else is there?"

"This is ridiculous!" Felicia exclaimed. "We're not going to suspect Kandis of being controlled, and it's just as nonsensical to suggest that the Guild is."

"What *protects* against mind magic?" I asked.

"Soul," Cloridan told me. "I don't think there's a skill for it."

I groaned. "Great, everybody's dump stat."

"Hey! I've got six Soul," Felicia said, annoyed.

"Sorry," I said. "I guess you're the one person that we can hope isn't already controlled then."

"Nobody is being mind-controlled," she said firmly. "It's a silly idea."

There was another awkward silence. It didn't look as if the boys thought it was silly. I could rule out me being controlled, at least. The other Guild people, though . . .

"Look, let's get back and ask Rhis about this," I said. "He does have a tendency to not bring up things you don't ask about."

"Of course it works that way," Rhis said, confused. "Why wouldn't the connection work both ways?"

"So every time someone tries to take over a dungeon, they risk being controlled? What happens to them?"

"I don't know, really; no one ever tried to control me until you came along."

"So we already had a contest?"

"You don't remember?" Rhis asked. "Well, that's a bit embarrassing." He flicked his ears. "Yeah, right after you picked me up, there was a contest. I've got to admit that I wasn't at my best, having just had my dungeon snatched away, and with all of my mana draining out of me. I tried to take control of you, get you to stick the core back in, but I didn't get very far."

"I . . . didn't even notice," I admitted.

"I'm not really surprised," he admitted. "I got . . . perhaps 'smashed' is the right word, by a strong desire for me to shut up and not bother you."

"That probably describes my thoughts at the time," I said. "I was really busy getting out of there."

"In any case, I didn't last long before shutting down. I don't remember you actually getting out of the dungeon, so I couldn't have lasted for more than a minute?"

"So . . . no hard feelings?"

"For what?"

"For destroying your dungeon? For enslaving you? Actually, have I enslaved you?" I was grasping at straws here, but I really didn't feel that I was controlling Rhis.

"Try just willing me to do something, without saying what it is," he suggested.

I blinked and thought about him spinning around. He did so without hesitation.

"Yeah . . ." I said to the others watching. "That was what I thought of him doing."

"I thought it would be like that," Rhis said. "You haven't been doing a lot of ordering me around, except for the no killing. And I don't have a way to kill people, so it's a moot point."

"Do you resent it? The enslaved part, I mean."

"Huh. Yeah, a human would resent it, right?" He looked at the others for confirmation. "But no . . . I don't really feel bad about it at all. I think that I'm made to either kill or serve. Either one."

He shrugged. "After all, I tried to do the same to you, right?"

"That doesn't make it all right," I told him.

"Shouldn't I be telling you that?" he asked, amused. "Are you going to stop doing it? Set me free?"

"I—can I do that?" *Is there a command, or do I just will it?* I frowned in thought, concentrating.

"Wait!" Felicia interrupted. "Isn't your command the only thing stopping him from killing people?"

"Well, not the *only* thing," Rhis replied. "With an illusory body like this, I can't even hurt a fly."

"But you can move your core around, right? You could take it somewhere with high enough mana and start a new dungeon, couldn't you?"

"Actually, what's stopping you from doing that now?" I asked. "I haven't been specifically forbidding that."

Rhis thought for a moment and then shook his head. "I can't right now," he said. "As my owner, only you can instantiate a dungeon."

"So if I *did* free you, there'd be nothing to stop you."

"Well, a few things," Cloridan said. "He'd probably make a run for the forest, but he'd have to get past the wall before his mana ran out. Chances are, someone would stop him and get their hands on his core before he got there. Then *they'd* be his new owner."

"Or I'd be theirs," Rhis said, with some glee. "Honestly, I'm not sure what I would do—I think that if you freed me, my mind would change a fair bit from what it is now."

"Then . . . let's put emancipation to one side for now," I said, sighing. "And talk about the other problem. Rhis, do you think if you took control of someone, you'd be able to maintain control if they weren't touching the core?"

"I should think so, as long as they were within my influence," Rhis said thoughtfully.

"Not outside the dungeon?" I asked hopefully.

"No . . . although—there was an item available in the store that let you keep control of monsters when they were outside. That might work."

"The store?" I asked.

"That's where you buy stuff when you're a dungeon," Rhis said, condescendingly. "I never bought that item, though; I never had monsters leave."

"What the . . . no, that's not important right now. If you had a human, what would you do with them?" I asked.

"Killing! No, wait, that seems like a waste." Rhis paused, thinking. "People are good at killing other people, but I wouldn't be able to spawn more of them so . . . maybe talking to other people? Find out what's happening outside of me, maybe getting others to do things?"

We all looked uneasily at each other. "Like maybe form an organization that encourages people to raid you, but leaves your core alone?" I suggested.

"Yeah! that'd be great. Sounds pretty hard, though." He looked around at our grim expressions. "Why all the glum looks?"

"I still don't think it's possible," Felicia said. "It's just not . . ."

"It *is* a thing, for people with their own dungeon to not leave them," Cloridan pointed out. "Mandel, for one."

"But most of the big names do leave," Kyle said. "At least early on. They tend to become recluses as they get old, not suddenly. Shadthe definitely had his Tower of Black Ice while he was running around laying waste to Odiera."

"We could drive ourselves crazy speculating," I said. "But really, we don't have any evidence either way. But I'm thinking this means we don't want to take the Guild deal."

"We could probably figure it out about Mandel," Cloridan objected. "Didn't you hear about the circumstances of him getting his dungeon?"

"If we could trust him . . . everything I know is from him. But he said that his party leader put Marie in the core when she got injured in the dungeon. Then she brought it to him."

"So that sounds like how you got Rhis. The party leader—"

"Kari," I supplied.

"—might have been controlled, but if she removed the core right away, she probably would have won the contest."

"Then he took over the core before . . . planting it? Is that the right term?"

Everyone looked at Rhis, who shrugged.

"I've never done it," he protested. "Why should I know?"

"Sure. So the core would still have been weak, so he probably won his contest."

"Maybe she didn't try?" Felicia suggested. "She was his wife, after all."

"Maybe . . ." Rhis said. "But what she was like outside isn't necessarily the same as what she is like in the core. I wasn't much like a fox when I was a dungeon, and I'm even less so now."

"And that was a decidedly unrabbitlike presence I felt before," I agreed. "There's definitely *something* of Marie in there, maybe all of it, but we can't take that for granted. Still, either way, it sounds like Mandel is free."

"Which just leaves the Guild," Cloridan said.

"And the nobles, and the powerful wizards," I replied. "But I can't think of anything we'd have to do differently in those cases."

"The King's got his own dungeons," Cloridan pointed out. "Aren't you going to see him in a few weeks?"

BİRŦHDAY

My birthday arrived. I knew that it did, because there was a System notification.

> **Your Age has increased to 25.**
> **You have been awarded 5 Ability Points.**
> **You have been awarded 2 Development Points.**

It was . . . a bit of a nonevent, really, just a reminder that I wasn't done improving my stats. Not that five points were going to go far, but I did have more points coming down the line from my later levels.

It was also mildly interesting that it seemed to work off my actual age. I'd lost track, but some calculations suggested that this was my actual birthday, or pretty close to it, if I counted the number of days from when I'd left to my Earth birthdate.

Latora had a different calendar, which didn't seem to correspond at all to ours. Twelve months, each of thirty days, which divided easily into the 360 days of the year. It sounded like one of the calendars we'd used before we worked out how long the year was, but apparently, the year really was 360 days. There was no seasonal drift.

It seemed too perfect to be true, but on reflection, the gods could have adjusted either the rotation of Ryvue or its distance from the Sun. It wasn't like I had a timepiece from Earth that could tell me how long a local hour was. It felt about the same, but I wasn't an atomic clock.

It turned out that birthdays weren't as celebrated as they were back home. Maybe the fact that the System kept track of them meant there wasn't the same need to recognize them. Or maybe it was just a less consumer oriented society. I got some mild congratulations, a bit of teasing about being old now—which Cloridan joined in on, very hypocritically—but nothing else. We all had far too many other things to worry about.

"So what brings you *all* to my sitting room?" Mandel asked curiously. Normally it was just me coming to see him, but under the circumstances, I wasn't willing to be here without the full group.

"Well . . ." I said cautiously, "I don't suppose I'd be able to persuade you to step out of your dungeon for a bit?"

He raised his eyebrows. "I'm sure I don't need to tell you that that is a very suspicious request. Why?"

"We—I wanted to check if you were wearing a magic item that linked you to your dungeon," I admitted. Since he was probably not controlled, we had decided to go with an open approach. This dungeon wasn't *so* advanced that we couldn't escape if Marie took issue with our questions.

"I am actually wearing such a device, as it happens." He raised his eyebrows again, as everyone on our side of the table tensed. "I constructed it when we started our little plan. If I had been separated from Marie by the Baron, I didn't think she'd have been able to pretend that she was impaired."

He grasped his left upper arm with his other hand, and something was released from under his clothes, slipping out of his sleeve. He set it down on the table. It was a silvery band, which looked like—

> **[Identification]: Silversteel Control Link – Quality: Great – Properties: Enchantment (Link), Enchantment (Shape Metal)**

—*that.* Oh, great. It's not a dungeon item, though?

"The Shape Metal rune is so that it can fit snugly on my arm," he explained offhandedly. "And the link goes to a small disk attached to her core. Is there a problem?" he continued, looking at our tense expressions.

"Well, the thing is," I said awkwardly. "From what I can tell, that link can go either way . . . and we recently learned that Dungeon cores can control people who touch them."

"Ah." He looked concerned for a moment and then became relaxed, even amused. "I assume you learned this the hard way. Should I worry about *you* being controlled by a dungeon?"

"Only Kandis touched the core," Felicia said insistently. "And she's not controlled! We'd be able to tell."

"Just what I'd expect a thrall to say," he pointed out with a smile.

"Thrall?" I asked.

"I believe that's the correct term. It shows up in a few places in the dungeon management notes. I wasn't sure exactly what it referred to until now."

He paused for a moment, looking thoughtful, while we tried to come up with something to say. "I suppose that means I can offer you some peace of mind—if you trust me, that is."

"How so?" I asked, leaving the matter of trust aside for now.

"Well, thralls and monsters are treated much the same—most of where I see the word is in phrases like 'affecting thralls and monsters.' So I know that a thrall entering a dungeon will trigger a dungeon break, just like a monster would."

"I see . . ." I said thoughtfully. He would know if we were thralls, so that was why he was mainly amused by our predicament. "Can you suppress a dungeon break?"

"Possibly. I've never had to try. But I would definitely know. And if it helps, I'm almost positive that my dungeon has no motivation to cover up for another dungeon's actions."

"So it comes back to whether we can trust you or not," I sighed.

"You've obviously decided to grant me some trust, just from the fact that you've brought this to me," Mandel pointed out gently.

"True," I admitted. "It's just very easy to get caught up in paranoia over this."

"I imagine so. For my own part, I feel far removed from the possible machinations of foreign dungeons. Having to deal with them must make for a less sanguine perspective. I have some questions, though."

"Oh?"

"What were the circumstances of the control? I never experienced any serious effort from Marie to take over my mind."

"Well, if your first contact was like you described, she wouldn't have been operating on full power. The core I touched was connected to its dungeon."

"Ah, yes, that would make a difference. The 'mana construct' as the Status calls it may spring from the core, but it is orders of magnitude more powerful. I already keep Edele away from our core, but I shall install additional precautions."

"Good idea," I said, and then hesitated. "Do you intend for Edele to succeed you?"

"I do, though that should still be some time away. I don't want Marie to be left alone, so if Edele isn't willing, I will have to see about . . . ending the dungeon at some point."

"If she removes the core, the dungeon will start to break down, but there might be time for her to take control and put it back," I informed him. "If not, she'll have to start again and build a dungeon from scratch."

He waved a hand dismissively. "I will make sure to tell her at some point. For now, I'm more concerned with her finding a nice boy and getting us some grandchildren."

"A dungeon dynasty," I said, smiling at the idea.

"My original plan was for Marie and me to live out the rest of my life in isolation. But contact with the beast-kin has changed my thinking."

"Are they delving regularly, then?"

He nodded. "Apparently, dungeons are rare in their territory, except at the edges. Something to do with how they channel their mana."

"So you're no longer a recluse . . ."

"I haven't exactly become sociable. But the visitors are good for Edele—she needs to interact with people."

"Beast-kin aren't going to give you grandchildren, though," Cloridan put in.

Mandel shrugged. "There are humans among the Tribes. Not many, but I've asked some of the party leaders to see if they can direct any eligible bachelors our way."

I cleared my throat, as this conversation was making me uncomfortable. "We were hoping to ask you some questions as well," I said. "There's supposed to be a dungeon item that you can buy, that allows you to control monsters outside of the dungeon."

"Really? Let me see . . ." his eyes went unfocused as he looked at the air. "Ah, yes, I see. It's called a controller extension. Yes, it works on thralls. Expensive."

"What does it look like?" I asked.

"By default, it's a collar," he said thoughtfully. "But this sort of thing requires a certain amount of customization when bought . . . different neck sizes and such. Yes, it can look like almost anything that encircles a neck or limb. So necklace, bracer, ring. It needs to touch the skin, though."

"That's a fairly wide variety," I said, dismayed.

"I wouldn't let it concern you. You should be able to discern one through Mana Sense. A connection with such a long range should make quite a distinctive mana conduit."

Oh, of course. I felt pretty stupid. I needed to get in the habit of using Mana Sense to spot magic items and spells. Although from what I knew about *concealing* such things . . .

"Can dungeon items conceal their mana use?" I asked.

"Well, there are runes for it . . . it's not normally done, but it's certainly possible," he agreed. "You have Dispel Illusion, don't you?"

"Dispel Image, yeah."

"That should work against most attempts to conceal via runes," he said. "Dungeon enchantment is unsurpassed in complexity and technique, but it's not normally all that *strong* in terms of effect totals. You should be able to overpower any concealing enchantments."

"Huh. What's the etiquette on casting that on someone without their permission?" I asked, looking around to add my team to that question.

"Well, if they can detect it, then it's a little like slapping a guy to see if he's a werewolf," Cloridan said. "Maybe you could explain you were just checking to see if they were being controlled by a murderous inhuman intelligence—but they might not take it well."

I nodded as if he were making sense, but internally, I had questions. *What? They have werewolves here? I thought there was a strict separation between monster and human?* I couldn't ask those questions in front of Mandel, though, so I held them in and made a note to ask them later.

"If you don't have an illusion on you, is it detectable?" Felicia asked.

"You know when an illusion has been dispelled," I told her. "But if you're not the one who cast it . . ." I thought back to the raiders back in Anchorbury. They hadn't reacted at all to losing their disguises. "No. You don't feel anything."

"Then it sounds like you have a working countermeasure," Mandel suggested.

"What about Enchantment?" Kyle asked. "Are there runes that stop mind control?"

"There is a rune that wards against it, and I even have it," Mandel said proudly. "I should mention that I've only heard of it working on the more normal mental magic . . . but mind control is mind control, probably."

"Yeah, I think I need to make that a higher priority," I agreed. "But right now, we have more mundane security concerns.

"Ah yes, this vault of yours. Perhaps, if this goes well, I should become a client. It might make transactions easier."

"We're always happy to have new customers at the Bank of Talnier," I said with my best smile.

"I'm sure. Now . . ." We started discussing security arrangements. I was going to be crafting some of the lesser wards, to save on costs, but we couldn't afford to skimp on protection for the main vault. While it would be alarmed, of course, we'd be using a combination of high craftsmanship totals and magical reinforcement to try and ensure the vault was as impenetrable as possible.

Nothing was truly invulnerable, as the Baron's vault had shown. What we could mainly hope for was to make it difficult enough that it couldn't be broken into without a significant investment of time—or power.

It was expensive, but this was what some of the investor money was earmarked for. We'd have to get Mandel in to actually engrave the walls, so we scheduled a time for that.

Then we headed back, somewhat reassured by what he told us.

"I can't believe I didn't think about checking for mana strings," I said, once we'd landed and dismounted.

Cloridan looked as if he was going to reply, but he paused instead. He snorted with amusement and indicated with a nod that I should look behind me. "This should be interesting," he said. "Want to take my arm?"

Looking over, I saw that Captain Hector was standing in the street, obviously waiting for me.

PROPOSAL

Captain Hector was waiting for me. I hadn't actually been troubled by either of my suitors since the festival, but that wasn't to say there hadn't *been* trouble. The two of them had clashed on a few occasions in the days following. Not *fought*, just expressed a full and frank exchange of views, as the politicians liked to say.

I knew about it, not because I was there, but because their voices had been sufficiently raised for *everyone* present to make out what they were doing and who they were talking about. Gossip spread, and it made its way straight to me because everyone wanted to see my reaction to the latest spat. It was like being a YouTuber—everyone wanted to see my reaction videos.

Not that I gave them one, of course. It was mortifying enough that the whole town was gossiping about my prospective partners, I wasn't going to add to the fire. This was . . . not what I had in mind when I asked Hector to dance. At least it kept the pair of them busy. Had kept. Hector's presence suggested a new phase was about to begin.

"Captain," I said as he bowed politely. "Is there a reason you're accosting me in the street?" I cast an irritated glance at a number of gawkers. People avoided the Griffin Academy when they could, but even so, there were a few people around, and he'd already attracted their attention. After a glance at me to check, the rest of my team gave us some space.

"There is," he said sourly. "That annoying envoy . . . he's been having me watched—every time I go near your street, he shows up and sticks his nose into my business."

"So *you* had the Griffen Riders report to you when I took a trip. Have you been waiting outside since I left?"

He flushed. "I also had the watch inform me when your griffin was sighted," he admitted. "It gave me enough time to get down here."

"I guess Mister Parkes missed a trick," I said. I would have continued but I was interrupted by a notification.

You have defeated Arno Brasseur in an Intrigue. You have earned 31 XP.

Who? What's going on? I thought.

"My lady?" Hector asked, noting my confusion.

"It's nothing," I said. "I just got an unusual notification."

Arno Brasseur didn't spring immediately to mind, but a few moments of searching my memories did bring him up. An adventurer, melee fighting type. I'd talked to him briefly, looking for investors, but he hadn't been interested. Why was I Intriguing him? Or, rather, why was he Intriguing me?

"Hector," I said, returning to the matter at hand. "Tom doesn't control my social schedule. If you want a private meeting when you show up at my house—I'd prefer if you arranged a time in advance—he can't force his way in."

"He's very aggravating," Hector admitted. "He easily provokes me to a state where I'm not fit to be in your company."

"That's . . ." I paused. What was *that*? A skill? Charm used in reverse? Did fighters get a taunt ability? Or was Hector just easily manipulated? "That's a pretty poor showing for a Captain of the King's Guard."

"I'm aware, my lady," he said looking at the ground. "Social skills are not my forte, as you are well aware."

"Fine. So I'm not going to have a serious discussion in the street, so do you want to escort me home?"

Emotion flashed across his face, too quickly for me to read. "As you wish, my lady." For a moment, he looked as if he wanted to offer me his arm, but when I stepped forward at an angle to move well clear, he gracefully turned and let me walk beside him.

We set off, not saying anything further. I thought about how he'd been speaking. Charm informed me that all the "my ladies" hadn't, strictly speaking, been correct. I was no lady, and as a knight, he shouldn't have been offering me the courtesy. It *was* a courtesy, though, not an insult, so it suggested that he was trying to butter me up—and that what he wanted from me was more personal than political. Which was about what I had expected, so I turned my attention to my recent Intrigue victory.

I checked my logs as my entourage and I progressed down the street. I didn't normally think of my crew as an entourage, but something about the situation seemed to demand it. Perhaps it was the way they deferred to Hector, while Hector deferred to me.

My logs showed only a recent test against Bureaucracy, which was a surprise. I hadn't expected to actually see Intrigue tested—despite having the same name, Intrigues were all about competing through others. They normally involved a bunch of skills being tested over a period of time—or no skill tests at all. I hadn't yet seen a direct Intrigue-to-Intrigue conflict.

Bureaucracy was a surprise, though. I had picked up the skill—for free, via "demonstrated competence" when I had finished setting up the policies and procedures for the Talnier Bank. Despite it quickly going up to rank three, I hadn't actually felt it was doing me any good. I'd chalked it up to being because I was writing the procedures, rather than learning them. Seeing it there suggested that I should check at the bank for answers, but I wasn't going to do so while I had Hector with me.

Once we got home, I received Hector in my sitting room. He looked around, surprised, but I couldn't tell if his expectations had been disappointed or exceeded. It had taken a while, but I was pretty pleased with how the room had turned out. I had no idea if it met the standards of a lady's parlor, but it served well as a room for a Councillor's informal meetings. Hector was seated on a lovely couch across a small table from me on my matching couch. We smiled at each other, as I wondered if he'd wait for tea to be served before starting his pitch.

He did not, which meant Felicia got to interrupt him just as he got started.

"Ah—thank you," he said, as she passed him a cup and saucer. Startled by her sudden entrance, he didn't say anything until she'd left the room.

"Please, you were saying?" I prompted him.

He hemmed and hawed a bit, but eventually started his pitch.

"My lady, are you . . . at least it was my understanding that you would be . . . the one to present the case for continuing the current Charter."

I sipped my tea. "That's correct."

"You must be aware that there is considerable opposition to the proposition."

"From the nobility, yes," I allowed. "But unlike Talnier, it's not a matter for a vote. The King will decide."

"Of course, but he does not make decisions in a vacuum. The nobility advises, and they can bring considerable pressure to bear in pursuit of their favored option."

"Can they," I said noncommittally. I knew this, of course, but I still didn't know where he was going.

"The process would go more smoothly if the nobility's goals were in alignment with yours."

"I'm sure, but we're both aware they want a new Baron installed here."

"There is still room for compromise," he insisted. "If you were willing to bend on the necessity of the Charter, they could support a bid to raise your station."

"Could they." Was this their offer? It seemed . . . uncharacteristically generous. "You're saying that if I switch to pushing for a barony, they'd support me getting the title?"

"Well . . ." Hector hedged. "You'd also need to tie yourself to someone that they thought was . . . sound. By marriage," he added, looking embarrassed.

"This offer isn't coming from the nobles," I said as it dawned on me. "It's *your* offer."

"It doesn't have to be me," he said, backpedaling furiously. "And I can't give you assurances yet as to whether they would accept it. But I think they will."

I sipped my tea, while I tried to think about how to turn him down. He took this as permission to continue his case.

"You've attracted the attention of the King, which makes them nervous," he explained. "They'd never agree to your ascension unless you showed them that you would be subordinate to them from then on."

"Wouldn't they rather install one of their own?" That one being him, from what I could gather.

"Better to turn a potential enemy than spend resources replacing them," he said. "And . . . from what I've seen, what I've heard, you prefer compromise and deals to direct conflict. Doesn't this fall in with your own preferred method?"

True enough. But there were a few problems with this plan. For one, I had no intention of being subordinated to the nobles. For another, I didn't want to become part of their corrupt hierarchy. Hector was handsome enough, but I didn't want to get married to him.

On the other hand, if I stated that marriage was out of the question, we would probably be back to "kill or be killed," which I wanted to avoid—especially the second part of that.

"Well, that is certainly a very generous proposal," I said. "I'm sure you'll understand that I'll need some time to consider it."

His face fell, but he rallied strongly. "Of course, my lady." He hesitated. "Please don't think of this as a deadline—the offer will remain open, but . . . it would be much easier, for all concerned, if you could answer me before you leave for Dorsay."

"I'm sure that's true, but I think I'll need to go to Dorsay before I can give an answer. I need to evaluate the situation at court before I make any permanent commitments."

"That's disappointing of course." He swallowed a gulp from his own cup. "At the dance—I thought that you might be encouraging such an offer from me."

I gave him as warm a smile as I could manage. "I was certainly aiming for a more amicable relationship, but marriage was very far from my mind."

"Then, if there's nothing else, I shall await your decision, my lady." He took a last gulp of tea and set the cup carefully down on the table.

"One thing," I said. "The nobles you represent, they are a faction at court, yes? Which one?" *Who's your backer?*

He looked surprised at the question, but after a short delay, answered it. "The faction led by the Duke of Arryen. Are you familiar with the factions at court?"

"Not in any great detail," I admitted. "But it will help to know which one is a potential ally."

In the privacy of my head, I was thinking something completely different. Duke Finley was the one behind the assassination here, and was *probably* behind the old Count Duvost's death as well. As Hector took his leave, I let Charm handle the formalities while I focused on what this meant for my immediate survival prospects.

"So . . . are you going to marry him?" Cloridan asked with admirable diffidence. I noted that his act didn't extend to pretending that he hadn't been listening in from the other room.

"No," I snorted. "I've seen what the 'backing' of a noble faction looks like, and it involves one too many poison daggers in my back for my tastes."

"Wouldn't it help you, though?" Felicia asked, coming into the room with Kyle. She'd either been eavesdropping as well, or Cloridan had filled her in. "You'd be able to deal with them as an equal . . . well most of them."

"That's part of the problem," I explained. "I'd be buying into their bullshit power structure, when what I want to do is replace it."

"Sounds good to me," Kyle said. "One good noble can't make up for the damage one bad noble can do." We all looked at him, and he got embarrassed. "That's what my dad would always say."

"Well, your dad knew what he was talking about," I decided. "So no title for me—I'll just keep delaying answering Hector for as long as I can. Right now, though, I have to figure out how I beat Arno's Intrigue without even knowing that I was fighting him."

BUREAUCRACY

I strode into the bank, looking for damage, alert to danger. It was after closing time, but I did own it, after all. Contrary to my expectations, I found everything was in order.

Delmar was still here, working on the paperwork. I *might* have overdone it with my bookkeeping requirements. Lacking Excel and printers made complying with modern audit requirements much more tedious. Scribe helped—it was much faster for someone with the skill to write with the ridiculous feather pens we had to use than I could really believe possible, but it could only do so much. I'd had to make some compromises—it wasn't like PricewaterhouseCoopers was going to be going over the books anytime soon—but it still took a lot of writing to stay compliant.

Delmar looked up when I entered but quickly went back to the books.

"Delmar," I said. "Was Arno in here earlier?"

He looked at me blankly, so I elaborated further. "Big man, melee adventurer type. I want to say . . . black hair?"

"Oh," he said dismissively. "He was here, yes. He tried to get some money without going through the procedures."

"Did he . . . threaten you?" I asked curiously.

"He might have?" Delmar replied, still more focused on his work. I let the silence extend. Eventually, he raised his head and looked at me. "What about it?"

"Arno's a level five—at least," I said. "I don't know him all that well. "You're level three—are you in the habit of shrugging off Intimidation from someone like that?"

A puzzled look spread across Delmar's face. "No? Maybe he didn't have Intimidation?"

"A fighter without it? Unlikely." Intimidation was an easy unlock if you were a little bigger and stronger than someone else. Most people unlocked it when they were kids, and the ones that became fighters tended to find it an irresistible purchase. A bit of a waste, since they rarely had the Charisma to use it . . .

"Check your logs," I suggested. He got a blank look on his face for a moment.

"It says . . . an Intimidation effect was resisted by Bureaucracy . . . but that's not my skill total. Is that *yours*?" He looked at me incredulously. "Just how high *is* your Charisma?"

I raised an eyebrow. I'm not sure if the ability to do that came with higher Dexterity or greater Charisma, but I was glad to have it. "Did you expect me to answer that?" I asked.

"No, sorry, I was just surprised." Delmar flushed at his lapse.

"Have you ever heard of someone using someone else's skill totals?" I queried.

"No . . . but I don't know much about Bureaucracy," he admitted.

"Neither do I . . ." I mused. "I guess I'll need to find answers elsewhere. You're going to be locking up soon? I assume nothing came up while I was away."

"Yes—to both questions," Delmar nodded. "It was all quiet, except for Arno. There are some applications for you to look over tomorrow."

"All right, I'll see you then."

Though it was too late for business, the Guild was open until late. Adventurers weren't much for business hours, and the place also served as a bar. While the receptionist counter was closed, the bar staff could still get word to the management if you needed it.

While I waited to see if Nadine was available, I cast my eye over the patrons. Sure enough, Arno was there, drinking and laughing it up with his party and a few others.

"Arno!" I said with false familiarity and friendliness. He looked over when I called. At the sight of me, a look of guilt flashed across his face, but he hid it well and managed a fairly convincing portrayal of a guy who's just been approached by a hot girl. Unfortunately, he overshot a bit.

"Hey! You looking to party, girl?"

Now I didn't really know Arno well. But I was fairly sure he knew a bit about me, and my position in town. But . . . I was still a Guild member, still one of them. So addressing me like a common whore wasn't *entirely* beyond the pale. It was dumb enough, though, that a few of his companions glanced at him with concerned expressions. More entertaining was *his* expression. He knew he'd fucked up as soon as the words had left his mouth.

I took a moment to let that sink in for him. *Just* a moment; I didn't want to give him enough time to double down.

"I just heard that you tried to shake down my clerk for gold," I said, loudly enough for the next table over to hear over the din. The concerned looks became alarmed and one of the men next to Arno slowly started edging away from him. The next table suddenly became very interested in what I was saying and fell silent. This attracted the attention of further tables, who quieted down to try and figure out what was going on. A bubble of silence spread out from where I was. I filled it.

"Tried, and *failed*, at Intimidation," I said, with a bit of a smirk. "Against my *level three* clerk."

There was a beat, and then half the room started roaring with laughter. The tension that had been building was released, with only one embarrassed person as a casualty. Arno didn't much like being laughed at, I could tell. While I could have taken this to the Guard, the fact was that a failed Intimidation wasn't really a crime in the same way a failed assault was.

Though, now that I came to think of it, I doubt the Guard would bother arresting someone for losing a fight they started. Maybe sometimes. Regardless, while I was relying on the rule of law to protect my business, this seemed like a better option. I let the laughter die down before I spoke again, enjoying the embarrassment on Arno's face.

"Really, though, how did you expect it to end up?" I asked. "Even if it had worked—do you think Delmar wouldn't have gone to the Guard? That he wouldn't have remembered your face?"

If Arno had a plan for those contingencies, he wasn't sharing it, preferring to make himself as small and unobtrusive as possible. I kept going.

"But the dumbest part is this," I said, still talking loudly enough for the room to hear me. "Half the people in this room are investors in that bank. That means you were stealing from them, just as much as you were trying to steal from me."

The room got quiet again, as quite a few people in the room suddenly realized that they could have been affected by this. My point made, I dropped my voice, just addressing Arno.

"That's right, you just tried to steal from half the people in this room," I repeated. "The richer, more successful half. I won't tell you who, I'll let that be a surprise for you—the next time you're in a dark alley."

There was no notification, since there wasn't anything I actually wanted from Arno, but from his face I was fairly sure my Intimidation had been successful. I gave him a smile.

"Well, I'll leave you to your drinking; I see that the Deputy is ready for me now," I said, and left him to his life.

"What was that about?" Nadine asked as I approached.

"Just business matters," I said. "I realize you're off the clock, but can I ask you a few questions?"

"I suppose," she said. "We can talk in my office. It's quieter."

"Thanks," I said, following her in.

"So what did you want to talk about?" Nadine settled in behind her desk, leaving me to sit in one of the uncomfortable chairs at the front.

"Well, I had a question about Bureaucracy," I explained, "and the Guild is just about the only organization in Talnier that might have a need for it."

"True enough," she replied. "The King's Guard is big enough, and spread out enough to need it, but they prefer to keep order with force of personality."

"I just had my employee win a Social Contest with my Bureaucracy skill while I was out of town. Is that a normal thing for that skill?"

"Of course, that's what the skill is for. If someone with Bureaucracy skill sets up an organization, anyone in the organization with Bureaucracy can use the Founder's skill total as a defense to avoid violating the organization's rules." She paused, frowning in thought. "How do you have the skill without knowing this?" she asked.

"The help screens aren't very . . . helpful," I said.

"Yes, but . . . I would have assumed to get the skill, you would have been part of an organization that had it? Was that not the case?"

"It's available as a skill in the Talnier Official profession," I said, deflecting her question. She narrowed her eyes at me, and then stared at nothing for a moment.

"This . . . when did this become available?"

I shrugged. "Recently?"

She frowned. "This implies a certain degree of . . . independence from the Kingdom."

This could get messy. The Guild report directly to the King . . .

I kept my worries off my face and simply shrugged again. "We *do* have a degree of independence. It's not like the Latorran-specific professions have gone. I'm sure any noble could have done as much for his territory."

"The nobles don't—" She cut herself off. "But you do. *You* know about the Territory Status."

"That's not a state secret, is it?" I asked lightly, keeping my concerns to myself. Fyskel had said that the current King didn't know about it, so if the Guild did . . .

"I can't talk about that . . . but Koenig will want to speak with you."

I'm going to get scolded again? Do not like.

"Now?" I said, instead of protesting.

"No, he's drinking and this is important, but not urgent," Nadine said, with just a touch of embarrassment. "He won't want to be bothered."

"I didn't see him outside," I noted.

"He doesn't drink *here*," she explained. "Because he doesn't want to be disturbed when he drinks. Can I ask you to come back in the morning?"

"Is that really necessary?"

"You may be a Councillor, but you're still under the authority of the Guild." The glare she gave me was suitably authoritative, but I sensed some doubt. Perhaps she wasn't certain of her authority. Even so, I wasn't going to challenge it. A scolding would be unpleasant, but it wasn't the end of the world. If Koenig decided to take things physical, it would probably be the end of me.

"Fine, but this seems unfair. You can hardly hold what I already knew against me," I complained. "It's not like I'm stealing Guild secrets."

Although, speaking of Guild secrets. I focused on my Conceal Mana spell. I just about always had it up, but Dispel Image wasn't strictly an Illusion spell, so I wanted to make sure it was still covered. Then I activated Sense Mana and took in what I was seeing.

As always, it was a mess. Mana of one kind or another was always flowing, floating, or moving around in some other fashion. Still, a person's mana was fairly self-contained, and as I concentrated, I couldn't see mana conduits coming off of her.

[Dispel Image], I cast silently.

"So did you have any more questions about Bureaucracy?" Nadine asked.

"What? Oh . . . no. I think you actually answered everything in that one sentence." I cast my mind back to what she had said . . . and indeed, she'd covered the basics. I could maybe worry a little less about what would happen to my bank while I was away.

"Thank you for the help, and I guess I'll see you tomorrow." I got up, gave a little curtsy, and showed myself out.

As I headed back to the gang, I felt a new worry start to worm its way into my list of concerns. Exactly what was that concealed spell that I'd seen on Nadine doing?

SCOLDİΠG

Koenig glowered at me from across the desk.

"Here we are again, Councillor," he said sourly.

"I'm not sure I've done anything to deserve that attitude," I said. "Are you going to accuse me of stealing Guild secrets or something?"

"No," he sighed. "Though I would like to know where you found out that bit of information."

"Someone told it to me." I shrugged. "I'd prefer not to say who . . . but it's no one from Talnier or part of the Guild."

"Why not name them, then?" Koenig frowned, probably trying to think of someone outside that group that I might know.

"It would say a little too much about me," I hedged. I was keenly aware of both Nadine's absence and that of their truth-telling item. Without being able to see it, I couldn't illusion it, but I wasn't sure if it needed to see me to tell if I was lying. So I was playing it safe.

"Fine," he said. "Moving on. Are you any closer to deciding—you and your team—if you're going to progress further in the Guild?"

"I don't want to close off any options at this stage," I said. "But we're not greatly enthused by the offer."

"You won't find a better path to progression," he said urgently. "And our requirements can . . . be reduced."

"I need to look at the alternatives before I can give an answer," I said carefully.

"Alternatives? You mean the nobles have made an offer?"

"More like they've offered to make an offer," I said, grimacing.

"Those grasping thieves . . . listen, you can't choose them over us. You know as well as I do what they're like."

"True . . . but the only thing I know about the upper levels of the Guild is that they're keeping secrets."

"You can't . . ." His eyes were getting a little desperate, so I decided to throw him a bone.

"Don't worry, I don't plan on telling the nobles about Territory Status." I gave him a few moments of relief before I hit him with the bombshell. "You'll need to convince me not to tell the King, though."

Watching his face closely, I thought I could see the actual thoughts go through his head. First, shock that I knew they were keeping the King in the dark, then annoyance as he realized it was a guess on my part that he'd just confirmed.

I gave him a smirk, just so he'd keep thinking that. Of course, I already knew the King didn't know . . . but it would be difficult to explain just how I knew that.

"Maybe you could start with an explanation. Aren't you supposed to be loyal to him?"

Koenig considered me for a moment and then sighed. "I suppose with what you already know, there's no point in hiding the rest."

I kept my face blank. *Obviously*, he was still going to be keeping secrets—I was starting to suspect the Guild was stuffed full of them—but accusing him of it wasn't going to get me anywhere.

Actually, wasn't he being too reasonable about this? Was he still playing nice to recruit me? I'd been expecting threats by this stage, but perhaps my expectations were being misled by movies. The Guild wasn't the government, after all. While they had jurisdiction over me, they'd lose it if I just decided to quit adventuring.

"The noble families, most of them, are older than the Kingdom," Koenig started, unaware of my speculation.

"They date back to the Empire, or even before," I agreed.

He nodded. "*Some* of them were on the right side during the Fall. They saw the corruption and supported the Champions in the fight. But most of them—the survivors, at any rate—either sat out the fight entirely or switched sides when it looked like they were going to lose."

"In return for keeping their privileges, no doubt."

"*Some* of their privileges. Some of them are still complaining about their losses."

It had been eighty-odd years, but that didn't surprise me in the least.

"King Nestor knew from the start that it was going to cause trouble, but only a few of the Champions lived after the Fall, and they were split between the three successor kingdoms. He was too weak to eliminate them . . ."

"So he compromised, no one was entirely happy, and the Kingdom wasn't perfect," I finished for him.

Koenig frowned at being interrupted, but he kept going. "King Hector knew that the nobles thought long-term and that they'd work to undermine their restrictions over time. So he founded the Guild as a countervailing organization."

"So the Guild and the nobles have been . . . not fighting, I guess, but in a conflict over who's in control for the last eighty years."

"Oh, there's been fighting," Koenig corrected me. "Some of it in secret, but there have been large-scale battles."

They couldn't resolve this in the King's Court? I wondered. Kaito's theory about the people of this world relying on killing more than we did flashed through my mind. But this didn't sound that much different from historical conflicts back home. As long as one side was unable to accept the outcome, violence was always a possibility.

"So how's it been going?" I asked.

"It's gone back and forth over the years, but right now it's been swinging the nobles' way," Koenig admitted. "The current King . . . he's too close to the nobles, has been since before he ascended to the throne."

"Which brings us to Territory Status," I realized. "You kept this from him because he'd tell the nobles, and you want to keep this from them."

"Yes . . . the secret was entrusted to us by his grandfather, but we didn't feel either of his two successors could be trusted with it."

"Well . . . congratulations on keeping it a secret for this long. Must have been hard when just saying the right words can reveal it."

He gave me an unamused look. "Are you going to work with us?"

"I think we can come to a deal, now that the cards are on the table."

"A deal," he said flatly. "And what is it that you'll be wanting from such a deal?"

"Nothing much . . ." I said slowly. "In fact, nothing that you shouldn't be already doing."

I paused, considering. How far could I trust the Guild? Not very far. They were still keeping secrets about dungeons, not to mention the mana conduits coming off of the two of them. Felicia and I had done some investigation there, but while it was suggestive, we didn't have anything solid.

For one thing, there were two of them. I'd checked when I entered Koenig's office, and both of them were sporting invisible mana connections.

The other thing we'd learned was that the conduits seemed to be heading in the direction of Dorsay. It was hard to follow them for any real distance, but they definitely left the building. Nadine's conduit was back to being invisible this morning, which we thought meant one of two things.

First, the spell was cast by a human and they'd recast the Conceal Mana. The other possibility was that it was a dungeon item (or a dungeon) that automatically refreshed the spell every 24 hours.

The main difference between these possibilities was that either someone knew we were fucking around with the Talnier Guild management . . . or they didn't.

Koenig hadn't brought up the spells, and I wasn't going to, either. I couldn't see a good outcome there, and plenty of bad ones. So the best plan seemed to be to proceed without revealing too much.

"Go on," Koenig prompted cautiously.

"From what you've said, the Guild must be in favor of the Free City charter. Just by existing, it strikes at the nobles' power."

"That's true as far as it goes," he said slowly. "We have some concerns that it may . . . change into something that we'd approve of less."

"How suspicious of you." Well, I couldn't blame them, really. "Would it reassure you if I agreed to consult with you over any changes made in the Territory Status?"

"What? Consult?" he said, confused.

"I'm not giving you control over any changes I make—I suspect that would result in me losing the access. But I want input from a broad base when it comes to making decisions like these—and you already know about it, so I won't be risking details getting out."

"That would be . . . nice," Koenig said, shaking his head. "But I was asking about what *you* wanted."

"I want the Guild's support," I answered. "I suspect Talnier has some significant challenges in the near future, and I want the Guild to go beyond what it would normally do for a local authority."

"What kind of challenges?" Koenig asked warily.

"If you're aware of Territory Status, then you should know it lists active threats," I explained. "Currently, the threats are listed as Seren, Arryen, and Bargougne." Hector was listed as a separate threat, but my assumption was that he was part of the Arryen threat. I wasn't sure why the other threats were listed by the province names, and not by the noble in charge . . . another mystery of the System.

"Arryen is a surprise," he mused.

"The Duke was involved in the recent assassinations. I'm not sure exactly what he's trying to do, but he has some interest in both here and in Anchorbury."

Koenig looked surprised. "The Inquisitor did say he suspected the Duke's involvement, but you're stating it as fact? Interesting."

I shrugged. "I have my own sources of information. So given these threats, the logical time for at least one of them to make a move is while I'm at the capital."

"You think they'll bring troops in?"

I frowned. "I *didn't*. I thought Latora was more law-abiding than that until a few of the things you said. Are we not under the protection of the King?"

He snorted. "There are technical loopholes you can move an army through, but I'd worry about the troops that are already here."

"I am. I'm fairly certain that Captain Hector is at least sympathetic to Arryen's cause. I'm *hopeful* that he won't make a move until I get back."

"Hmm. You can perhaps expect Arryen to defend you from a Bargougne attack, but I wouldn't count on them not to ally against you."

"So you can see why I need allies of my own that I can count on."

He leaned back and grimaced. "Adventurers don't do well against troops, generally. They don't take well to command, and there isn't any one of us that has Leadership."

"The level difference must make up for that, at least a bit."

"Some," he agreed. "But if you're imagining us as irregular troops like the Tribes have, you're wrong. *They* have Leadership; they don't limit it to nobility as we do."

"I've made some inroads with the Tribes, but I can't ask them to fight against Kingdom troops," I admitted.

He nodded. "It would start a war, and set you back some."

"Yes. Even if adventurers can't stand up to troops in the field, having them active should act as a deterrent. The nobles won't have planned for them to be acting in an organized fashion. I'm also thinking your other branches can let us know if a noble is massing troops."

He nodded slowly but was still reluctant. "You're probably underestimating how fast a force can move," he warned me. "Leaders can boost Run if they're not expecting to be ambushed. Having to move together slows them down some, but it's still lightning fast. We won't be able to get word here much faster than the troops."

"I see . . ." That was a blow, but I kept going. "Well, there's also plenty to do inside the town. I've arranged for my investors to keep my bank protected, but we might see sabotage in the town, assassinations of key personnel . . . if Hector hasn't turned entirely, the presence of a Royal official might help remind him of where his loyalties are supposed to lie."

"All right, already." He shook his head, but he was on board. Then he got a sly look. "Adventurers do need to be paid, though . . ."

I sighed. "I don't have unlimited funds available, but I should be able to convince the Council to budget for a share. Let's discuss the details."

ABOUT THE AUTHOR

Christopher Hall, also known as Maxlex, is the author of the Phantasm series. Hall started writing his first novel while sailing the Tyrrhenian Sea one summer, the salty night air flavoring and enriching his worldbuilding. Since then, he has continued to hone his craft while holding down diverse jobs in metalworking, marketing, perfume sales, and briefly, modeling. In addition to writing, Hall's interests include illuminated lettering and artisanal brewing. He endeavors to convey a sense of l'esprit in all his creative pursuits.

DISCOVER
STORIES UNBOUND

PodiumAudio.com

Printed in the USA
CPSIA information can be obtained
at www.ICGtesting.com
CBHW030228150924
14303CB00004B/41

9 781039 426573